VICIOUS CIRCLE

C.J. BOX is the winner of the Anthony Award,
Prix Calibre 38 (France), the Macavity Award, the
Gumshoe Award, the Barry Award, and the Edgar
Award. He is also a *New York Times* bestseller. He
lives in Wyoming.

ALSO BY C. J. BOX

VICIOUS CIRCLE

C.J. BOX

HEAD of ZEUS

First published in the UK by Head of Zeus in 2017

Published by arrangement with G. P. Putnam's Sons, an imprint of
Penguin Publishing, a division of Penguin Random House LLC

9 7 5 3 1 2 4 6 8

A catalogue record for this book is available from the British Library

ISBN (HB): 9781784973131
ISBN (TPB): 9781784973148
ISBN (E): 9781784973124

Book design by Lucia Bernard

Printed and bound in Germany by CPI Books GmbH

Head of Zeus Ltd
First Floor East
5–8 Hardwick Street
London EC1R 4RG

WWW.HEADOFZEUS.COM

To the Budd family,
and to Laurie, always

vi·cious cir·cle

noun

1. a sequence of reciprocal cause and effect in which two or more elements intensify and aggravate each other, leading inexorably to a worsening of the situation.

PART ONE

There is no trap so deadly as the trap you set for yourself.

—Raymond Chandler, *The Long Goodbye*

WYOMING GAME WARDEN JOE PICKETT FLICKED HIS EYES BETWEEN the screen of the iPad mounted in front of him and the side window, as the vast dark pine forest spooled out below the Cessna Turbo 206. He tried to keep his eyes wide open so he wouldn't miss anything, but he fought against his instinctive reaction to close them tightly in anticipation of the inevitable engine failure that would result in his quick and fiery death in the Bighorn Mountains.

For the first time in his life, he understood the desire for the fidgety solace of a set of prayer beads, and he wished he had some.

It was Halloween night, and the pilot, John Wilson "Bill" Slaughter, a stout and compact man in his early sixties with an aluminum-colored crew cut, eased down the nose of the small plane. Black timber filled the windscreen. Joe tried to breathe.

"Twelve hundred feet," Slaughter said through the headset to both his copilot, Gail Herdt, and to Joe, who was looped in.

"Roger," Gail said.

Both Slaughter and Herdt were retired from the military, as well as members of the Wyoming Wing Civil Air Patrol. Herdt was an art teacher at Pinedale Middle School, and Slaughter had a small Angus cattle operation near Torrington.

"Why twelve hundred feet?" Joe asked, trying to keep the panic out of his voice.

"We normally don't drop below two thousand feet at night," Herdt said calmly. "It's not considered very safe."

"So don't tell anyone," Slaughter said.

Joe asked, "Then why are we doing it?"

She looked over her shoulder at him alone in the backseat. "To see better," she said, matter-of-fact.

Joe nodded. His mouth was dry and he felt like he would throw up at any second. He'd been gripping an overhead strap so hard with his right hand, he'd lost all feeling in his fingers. His stomach surged with every turn, drop, and climb.

"Is he okay?" Slaughter asked Herdt.

"Are you okay?" she asked Joe directly.

"Dandy," he lied.

The crowns of lodgepole pines shot by below them so quickly it was mesmerizing. The crowns of the trees rose from the inky forest and were illuminated light blue by the slice of moon and the hard white stars. The visual maelstrom of passing treetops reminded Joe of snow blowing through his headlights in a blizzard. The trees seemed to be so close he could reach out and touch them.

"We hardly ever crash," Bill Slaughter said.

Herdt laughed and told him to stop it.

Joe stared at the back of Slaughter's round head and tried to burn two holes in it with his eyes. Although he appreciated the time and effort that went into being members of the Civil Air Patrol, he didn't appreciate their black humor at the moment.

"SO WHAT'S THIS GUY LIKELY to do if he finds himself lost?" Slaughter asked Joe through the headset.

"What do you mean?"

"Is he the kind of guy who panics?"

Joe thought about it. "No. He's too dumb to panic. And he does know these mountains pretty well. He used to guide hunters up here."

Slaughter said, "The reason I asked is that we've learned over the last few years, if the lost person is young, they start climbing to try to find a cell signal on the top of a mountain. If they're older, they tend to walk down along a creek or stream."

"That makes sense," Joe said. "My guy would walk down. My guess is he'd follow a spring creek until it joined one of the forks of the Powder River. Then he'd find a ranch or another hunting camp. I could also see him breaking into a cabin or hunting trailer and going to sleep without even imagining that someone might be looking for him."

"Oh great," Herdt said.

"What doesn't make any sense, though," said Joe, "is why he'd just walk away from his elk camp in the first place."

"I hope we find out what made him leave," Herdt said. "I'm always curious to find out how people get lost."

"It adds to our experience bank," Slaughter added. "We're constantly learning, all of us. The biggest thing I've learned is, people do stupid things for not very good reasons."

"Sounds like him," Joe said.

Herdt chuckled.

"Hold it—what's that?" Joe asked when the iPad screen suddenly filled with what looked like white upright sticks or chalk marks on a blackboard—scores of them.

THEY WERE LOOKING for a missing hunter named Dave Farkus. Farkus was a former energy worker, former hunting outfitter, former fishing guide, and was currently an unemployed layabout collecting dubious disability checks. He'd been missing from his elk camp since twelve hours before. Because of a forecast of a massive fall blizzard on the way, the available window to search for him was closing.

Farkus's hunting partner, Cotton Anderson—a welder who'd recently lost his job due to the energy bust—had called in the incident to Twelve Sleep County Sheriff Mike Reed, who in turn called the Wyoming Office of Homeland Security, who called the Air Force Rescue Coordination Center, who called the Joint Operations Center, who called the Wyoming Wing

Civil Air Patrol, a part of the National Guard, to look for the missing hunter.

Sheriff Reed told Joe that, according to Anderson, he'd returned to their camp the night before to find Farkus gone. Farkus's pickup was there, a fire had been built, and steaks were thawing on top of the cooler. Farkus's hunting rifle was leaning against a tree trunk and his holster and backup handgun hung from a branch. A nest of empty Coors cans lay at the base of a camp chair and an opened can of beer was in the armrest. But no Farkus.

Joe knew no normal hunter would go out without his rifle. And Farkus would *never* leave a full beer unless he had a desperate reason to do so.

Anderson tried to reach Farkus on his cell phone but there was no signal. Then he tried to radio him on his cheap Motorola walkie-talkie and finally received a reply.

At least he *thought* it was Farkus's scratchy voice that replied, twenty minutes after the first shout-out, *"They're after me . . ."*

But Anderson couldn't swear it was his buddy's voice. And he couldn't swear that the words weren't actually "Bear with me," or "I have to pee."

Anderson had stayed up late drinking Jim Beam and fired a series of three rifle shots—the universal signal for *Come back to camp, you fool*—but Farkus never responded with three shots of his own.

When Cotton Anderson emerged bleary-eyed from his tent at midmorning and confirmed that Farkus hadn't come back during the night, he drove his pickup to the Crazy Woman Creek campground, where he received a cell phone signal and reported Dave Farkus missing to the sheriff's department.

Joe had been drafted to accompany the Civil Air Patrol because of his familiarity with the missing hunter. That Farkus had antagonized Joe for years was not apparently a consideration.

Joe was scared to fly in small planes. He preferred to conduct searches for missing hunters by horseback or ATV.

So when, during its run-up, the Cessna shivered and trembled on the concrete like his Labrador, Daisy, when she spied a pheasant, Joe silently prayed for his life and cursed Sheriff Reed for suggesting he be the one to go on the air search, and at the same time cursed Dave Farkus for getting lost.

NOT THAT JOE DIDN'T WANT to locate Dave Farkus and talk to the man. He did. He'd been trying to reach him after Farkus left a very late-night message on his cell phone two nights before. The call had come from a phone with an UNKNOWN NUMBER designation, which was strange in itself.

An obviously inebriated Farkus had slurred a long but troubling voice message that had curdled Joe's stomach.

"Joe, this is Dave. Farkus. Dave Farkus. Dave fuckin' Farkus, your pal from many an adventure.

"Anyway, I was closin' down the Stockman's Bar tonight and I heard something—overheard a conversation, I guess you'd say—that you would definitely be interested in, because it was about you and your family. At least I'm pretty sure it was . . ."

The message was long and rambling. At the end of it, in the background, at the last few seconds of the voicemail, Joe heard a female voice say, "Okay, that's enough, damn you," and the call was abruptly terminated.

The message was still on his phone, and Joe had listened to it three times with his wife, Marybeth.

TREETOPS CONTINUED to flash by below the Cessna. Joe found he started to get dizzy if he stared straight down too long, so he tried to focus more on the big picture. Although he had spent weeks and months in his district and these mountains, he was taken aback by how vast and complicated the terrain was.

The forest was checkerboarded with mountain meadows and occasional timbered squares. The folds of the black velvet contours gave way to violent gashes where small streams tumbled white over rocks. The remnants of the first snows already clung to the alpine slopes that were exposed to the north and to draws that received very little sunlight.

The only artificial lights they'd seen came from isolated hunting camps or campgrounds. Elk season had opened earlier in the week and hunters were out in force. Joe had been patrolling fourteen hours a day since the opener and had issued two citations for game violations.

Adding to his normal duties was the distressing realization that a well-organized poaching ring was operating in his five-thousand-square-mile district, as well as in the adjoining districts to the east and west. Callers to dispatch had reported seeing up to three shooters killing multiple antelope, deer, and elk in areas that were not yet open for hunting or at night.

Joe was particularly disturbed by the incidents because the

killings seemed to be indiscriminate and the shooters atypical. Cow elk, calves, doe deer, and antelope—it didn't seem to matter what species or sex were being targeted and taken. Usually, bad guys went after trophy animals, not anything and everything they came across. The evidence of illegal trophy hunting was a decapitated carcass, since the shooter was only interested in the antlers or horns.

That wasn't occurring with this poaching ring because they were apparently loading up their carcasses and hauling them away, instead of leaving the meat to rot in the field. That meant Joe couldn't do field necropsies on the dead game to find spent bullets that could be matched with specific weapons.

He'd traded notes with fellow game wardens in the adjoining districts and found out that similar reports had come in near Gillette to the east and Jackson Hole to the west. Vague descriptions of two different vehicles—an older-model red pickup and a white Chevrolet Suburban 4×4—had been described at the scenes, which matched what Joe had heard.

Joe hated poachers and he wanted to find them and arrest them. He didn't like the idea of criminals operating with impunity in his backyard. But he'd been stymied for the past two months. There had been no tips from citizens as to the identity of any members of the ring, and literally no evidence on the ground to follow up on besides gut piles. The shooters apparently picked up their shell casings from the ground after firing, because none had been found. They hadn't opened themselves up to discovery, as often happened, by posting photos or videos of their crimes on the Internet. And because the poachers were targeting non-trophy game, no taxidermists could report receiving suspicious heads and horns. Joe was vexed by the crimes and clueless in regard to the identity or motivation of the poaching ring. Even his agency director, Lisa Greene-Dempsey, had fired off several *What are you doing about this problem?* emails to him.

His best chance to catch the criminals was to increase the odds that he'd stumble upon them while they were shooting their targets, or else that a legitimate hunter would see them in the act and call it in—and Joe could get to the location in time to arrest them. That was the main reason he'd been spending so much time on patrol, forgoing both weekends and the Labor Day holiday.

The adrenaline pumping through his body, as well as the buzz of the engine, kept him from realizing how bone-tired he was.

Or how cold. He wished now he'd accepted their offer of an insulated flight suit. Instead, he wore his red WG&F uniform shirt with the pronghorn antelope patch on the sleeve and his J. PICKETT, GAME WARDEN name tag and badge. He rubbed his hands briskly on his Wranglers to offset the icy leakage from the windows and a vent on the floor. He'd long before lost feeling in his feet.

SLAUGHTER HAD ANNOUNCED that there were a number of search patterns available—grid aligned, circle, creeping line, expanding square, parallel, route, and sector—but that they were going to be using the expanding square. They'd started with the approximate coordinates of Farkus and Anderson's elk camp and were gradually flying farther from its apex, utilizing sharp left turns.

"I wish more hunters carried PLBs," Slaughter grumbled.

"Personal locator beacons," Herdt translated for Joe.

"I know what they are," he said. "We always recommend them to guys when they're in the field. But you know how it is—no one ever thinks they're going to get lost."

"Do you have one?" Slaughter asked Joe.

Joe confessed that he had one but rarely remembered to take it along with him.

"Maybe someday we'll be searching for *you*," Slaughter said.

"Maybe," Joe agreed.

THE CESSNA WAS EQUIPPED with a FLIR, which Joe had learned was an acronym for "forward looking infrared." The football-shaped device was mounted to the aircraft under the left wing, which is why Slaughter kept banking left on the expanding square. The FLIR detected the heat signatures of living creatures on the ground below and broadcasted them to the mounted iPads inside the cockpit.

Slaughter had told Joe the FLIR was sensitive enough to detect a still-warm fire ring or a lit cigarette if the surrounding temperature was cool enough—even from thousands of feet in the sky. It could even show which specific vehicles had just arrived in a parking lot full of thousands of them by the ghostly white glow of warm tires.

WHEN JOE SAW those white hash marks on the screen and asked, "What's that?" Slaughter said, "Elk."

"Elk?"

"Their coats insulate them so well they don't put out enough heat for the FLIR to pick up," Slaughter explained. "All you can see are their legs."

Joe leaned closer to the screen. Several of the chalk marks were moving. Then several of the animals broke into a run and peeled away from the herd. All he could see were disembodied white stick legs strobing through the trees.

"WE'VE GOT ABOUT ten more minutes of fuel before we need to head back," Slaughter announced over the intercom.

"Fine by me," Joe said.

"We've covered about sixty-four square miles around the elk camp," Herdt said after checking their location against a topo map on her lap. She was using a yellow highlighter pen to re-create their pattern on the map.

What didn't need to be said was that, if Farkus was actually down there, he hadn't shown up on the FLIR. Which meant he was no longer putting out any heat.

Which meant . . .

"Now what are we looking at?" Joe asked, pressing his index finger to the screen. "Another elk?"

The image was thicker, taller, and a brighter white than the elk legs had been.

Joe leaned over and looked out the side window. The timber was too thick to see anything on the ground clearly.

Herdt said, "It looks like a man."

Not a man, exactly, Joe thought, but the negative white image of a man standing deep in the timber. Then he was gone.

"What just happened?" Joe asked.

"He stepped behind a tree," Herdt said. As the plane turned left, a shoulder appeared on the screen, as well as a foot at the base of the trunk. "He's trying to stay out of view."

Joe thought, *Why?*

"He can hear us flying around him, right?"

"You bet he can."

The screen went dark. "I lost him," Joe said.

Slaughter banked sharply, and Joe felt his weight shift until he was pressed against the left door of the plane. He hoped it had a really good lock.

"There he is," Herdt said with triumph. Joe heard the sound of screen captures being made on her iPad.

But he still couldn't see anything but black on the screen.

Herdt twisted around and showed him how to use the side icons on the iPad to expand the field of vision, until he could once again see the ghostly form trying to hide behind a tree. He pressed an icon that looked like crosshairs in a rifle scope to lock in on the figure. Despite the angle of the plane and the constant vibration inside from the engine, the image was remarkably still and clear.

"Okay, I've got him again," Joe said. "Farkus, you idiot. Come on out."

"Coordinates," Slaughter said to Herdt in a stern military voice.

Herdt looked away from her iPad and called them out. Slaughter repeated them over the radio mike to the Joint Operations Center. That way, Sheriff Reed's search-and-rescue team knew where to locate Farkus on the ground. *If* it was Farkus.

"Why isn't he trying to get our attention?" Joe asked. "If that was me, I'd be jumping up and down, waving my arms. What's wrong with him?"

Herdt said, "He might be injured."

"Sometimes," Slaughter added, "lost people get so disoriented they try and hide from rescue attempts. It's bizarre, but it's happened before."

Joe shook his head, although he knew neither Slaughter nor Herdt could see him do it.

"Our work is done here," Slaughter said, and Joe felt the airplane level out and begin to gain altitude. Herdt was busy up front noting the coordinates in a spiral pad.

Joe was transfixed on the screen as the ghostly white figure got smaller.

At first, he thought there was a malfunction of some kind on the iPad when he caught a glimpse of four white smudges instead of just one.

He reached out and expanded the field of view. The figure they'd first seen—whom they assumed was Farkus—was clearly in the foreground. But beyond him were three other human images. They were advancing through the forest and converging on the lone figure.

"Look at the screen," Joe said.

"Come again?" Slaughter asked, irritation in his voice.

"Look at the screen."

Joe glanced up to see that Herdt had stopped writing and had manipulated her iPad until the four images appeared as well.

"What is going on?" Herdt asked.

"Three heat signatures are closing in on the one we found," Joe said.

They were so far away now that the white smudges were tiny and faint.

"Bill, we have to go back," Herdt said to her pilot.

"Negative," Slaughter said. "We barely have enough fuel to make it back to Saddlestring."

"Please, Bill?" she asked.

"Negative. I'm sorry. Maybe you're looking at the search-and-rescue team as they found him."

Joe didn't point out that Sheriff Reed's SAR team was still at their command post at the base of the mountain. If they'd moved out, he knew they would have heard it on the radio.

"If we could risk another pass, I would," Slaughter said. He sounded like he meant it. "We've accomplished our mission and found the guy. But we're in the danger zone of running out of fuel if we don't beat it straight back. I haven't seen any places in these mountains to try and land a plane."

"Okay," Herdt said, resigned. "Let's go home." She turned off her iPad and returned to her report.

Joe didn't want to get between them. And he couldn't wait to get back on solid ground.

That's when he saw a star-shaped flash on the screen. Then another. Then a staccato burst of flashes that were faint and distant but distinct.

Joe thought, *Flashlights?* But why would rescuers blink their beams at the man they were trying to save?

Then it hit him and he went cold. They were muzzle flashes.

"I think I just saw a murder," he said.

Herdt looked sharply around, and Joe felt the wings waver slightly when what he'd said registered with Bill Slaughter.

Joe looked up from the screen and stared at nothing. In all his years in the field, he'd never witnessed a murder. There was a lump in his throat and he felt guilty for cursing Farkus earlier. Farkus—or whoever he was—hadn't been hiding from the Cessna. He'd been hiding from the three men who were after him.

He knew there was little they could do—or have done—given the circumstances. He also knew the images he'd just seen would stay with him for a very long time.

And he doubted he'd ever see Dave Farkus alive again.

Two nights earlier

DAVE FARKUS SAT ON THE FARTHEST STOOL FROM THE DOOR IN the Stockman's Bar in Saddlestring and poured Clamato juice into a mug of draft Coors until it was coral red, and then completed it with four dashes of Tabasco.

He admired the drink for a moment—the new bartender, Wanda Stacy, was watching him out of the corner of her eye—then he tipped it back and swallowed nearly half of it in five big gulps with his eyes closed. He placed the mug back on the bar and moaned with pleasure.

Farkus was sixty-one and shaped like a fat bear. He had rheumy eyes, jowls, thick muttonchop sideburns, and a veiny, bulbous nose. His snap-button shirts, it seemed, kept getting smaller. He wore heavy lace-up outfitter boots because he wanted folks to know that he used to be one. Pink foam covered his upper lip.

"Perfect," he said. "A fucking *perfect* red beer."

"I can't see how you can drink those things," she said with her hands on her hips.

"You don't understand. Red beer is medicine. We used to drink it for breakfast every morning when I guided elk hunters. It cures hangovers, headaches, whatever. You should invite me behind the bar so I can show you how to make one."

"No, thanks," she said.

Farkus was the only customer still in the bar, except for two hipster tourists who were finishing up a game of eight ball on the pool table in the back. He always chose that particular stool for a lot of good reasons, not least of which because it was closest to an ancient diorama behind glass of dead ground squirrels in little cowboy outfits playing pool on a miniature table. The display was getting old, though, and it bothered him that the squirrel leaning across the table to make a shot had lost both of his little dried ears, which now lay on the felt table. They looked like tiny dried leaves.

The best reason to choose that stool, though, was when he found out why ex-sheriff O. R. "Bud" Barnum had always chosen it, even for his morning coffee: the acoustics.

Although the people who had constructed the Stockman's back in the 1930s—with its knotty pine, burled posts, and low ceiling—had likely not designed it any way in particular, all of the sounds inside the bar were somehow funneled to that last stool. He heard the loud click of pool balls striking, the muttering of the players, even the wet snoring of the owner in the corner near the door.

That last stool was the catbird seat for a man who liked to know the local gossip. And that man was Dave Farkus.

THE HIPSTERS HAD PLAYED nervously for the past two hours, their heads snapping up every time the front door opened. They seemed to think a redneck cowboy would walk in and pound them into jelly for no good reason, Farkus thought. When he walked past them several times on the way to the toilet, he growled at them like an angry dog, and he could tell it unsettled them.

"Did I tell you I was going elk hunting tomorrow morning?" Farkus asked Wanda.

"Only about four times," she said.

He drained his mug and held up two stubby fingers. "Another Coors and another can of Clamato, barkeep."

"Don't call me barkeep."

"My charm offensive doesn't seem to be working."

"Oh, it's offensive all right," she said. But there was a little bit of a smile there when she said it. Whether it was at him or at her own joke remained to be seen. Probably her own joke, he concluded. Wanda had been around the area for years and she wasn't known for her quick wit.

Wanda was being trained to be the head bartender by Buck Timberman, the longtime owner of the Stockman's, who was nearly ninety years old. That was Timberman slumped and sleeping in the back corner of the bar with his chin on his chest and his glasses perched precariously on the end of his nose. The old man was still lean and ropy and everyone's trusted confidant. He'd always been that way, Farkus knew, but he was even more revered now that he'd lost his hearing and simply nodded sympathetically at customers who told him about rotten ranchers, deals gone wrong, and cheating spouses.

Wanda was a big woman who had been described as voluptuous forty pounds ago. Despite that, the twice-married former rodeo queen still wore tight jeans, pointy cowboy boots with the pants tucked into the shafts, wide bejeweled belts, and scooped long-sleeved tops that showed a lot of cleavage. Farkus had been tempted to tuck a dollar bill between those breasts more than once when she delivered the makings for red beer, but if he did it she'd likely break his jaw.

"Did I ever show you my front tooth?" he asked Wanda.

She looked up from where she was plunging dirty glasses into the sink. She paused and squinted.

"What about your tooth?"

"You'll have to get closer so you can see it," he said.

He could tell she was really thinking about it. She didn't want to come down the length of the bar to satisfy him, but her curiosity had gotten the best of her.

"See what?" she asked, getting closer while she dried her hands on a bar rag.

He bared his teeth and fit the nail of his little finger into a vertical slot on his top left incisor.

"You've got a slot on your tooth," she said, disappointed.

"You know how I got it?" he asked, waggling his eyebrows.

"No, how?"

"Biting off fly line on the river."

She just stared at him, not getting it.

He said, "I'm a hell of a fly fisherman, you know, but I'm an even better instructor. I could teach you. Women are better natural fly casters than men, because you don't overpower the rod and act like you know everything when you don't. I'll have to take you sometime."

She shook her head and walked back to her dirty glasses. "Not if it means I'll get slots in my teeth."

He momentarily dropped his head at her rebuke. He would never tell her he got that slot in his tooth by sawing furiously back and forth with a thin nail file, thinking it might impress potential female fishing clients, but it had never worked and wasn't working now.

He wished Wanda wasn't as dumb as a chicken, because the later it got the better she looked to him.

THE HIPSTERS FINISHED THEIR GAME and put up their sticks. On the way out, they asked Wanda if she could recommend a good cheap motel with clean rooms, a gluten-free breakfast, and free Wi-Fi.

"You might try Denver or Seattle," she said.

Farkus got a laugh out of that—two Wanda witticisms in one night!—but after they left, she went back to scowling at him.

Nothing worked on her, it seemed. Flattering her, telling her stories, laughing at her jokes, trying to make *her* laugh—nothing.

He'd tried to tell her about his trip to Hollywood to sell his story about how he and Joe Pickett had escaped death by bullet, fire, and a dangerous whitewater river a few years back as the forest burned down around them, but she wasn't interested in the least after she'd found out he hadn't met Leonardo DiCaprio or Larry the Cable Guy out there.

He'd told her about guiding some mercenaries into the mountains in search of a couple of mountain-man brothers and barely living through *that*, and it hadn't impressed her, either.

And he'd told her about the time he was literally hit by a drift boat in the river that contained three murdered men in the bottom of it.

Nothing.

In fact, he could tell by the tilt of her head that she hadn't believed him even when he'd implored her to look it up or, better yet, ask Joe Pickett.

His problem, he decided, was that his life had been filled with too many exciting adventures for someone as dumb as Wanda to believe him.

He looked at his wristwatch. He'd been in the bar since eight and now it was midnight. He knew it was Buck's custom to close down after twelve instead of two if there weren't enough customers to make it worthwhile to stay open.

Although he'd already had ten red beers, he couldn't be expected to fund Timberman's retirement all by himself.

FARKUS STARED into the bottom of his mug at the last inch of his beer. He felt sorry for himself, which had once been a new experience for him but was now occurring with more and more frequency.

Without actually recognizing the day, month, or year that it had started, he was cognizant of the fact that he was on the downhill side of his life and that he had very little to show for it except for those odd adventures, usually involving Joe Pickett. And even with those on his résumé, and despite his retelling of them to people like Wanda or the bored Hollywood "producers" he'd met, Farkus had actually been more of a bystander than a participant. No one would remember him except as the man who always seemed to be in the wrong place at the wrong time. That wasn't much of a legacy.

His daughter had moved to Missoula to become a professional lesbian and she'd no longer talk to him, and his ex-wife called only when she was drunk and needed money. There would be no grandchildren to remember him and to listen to his tales. Even his dog had run off.

He looked up from his mope when he realized Wanda had made her way down the bar and was standing right in front of him on the other side of the counter. She leaned in toward him and he stared at the top of her freckled breasts. He'd had enough beer that there were four of them, and he had no objections to that at all.

"I'm up here," she said.

His gaze rose to her face.

"You've run us out of Clamato."

"Oh." Maybe *that* would be his legacy, he thought sourly.

She had full plump cheeks and there was a smear of lipstick on her front tooth.

"So if you want another red beer, you'll have to make do with pure tomato juice."

"I'm probably going to call it an evening," he said. "I'm going elk hunting—"

"—*in the morning*," she said, finishing his sentence. "I'll ring you up."

As she said it, the door opened and he felt a puff of cold air from outside and heard the clumps of footfalls on the wooden floor behind him.

He started to turn on his stool to see who'd come in, but he was transfixed by the look on Wanda's face as she beheld the new customers. Her eyes had narrowed and her mouth had formed into a smile both provocative and predatory that she'd apparently kept locked away in a vault until then. Farkus suddenly felt like he was now a hundred miles away from her—an afterthought in her rearview mirror.

"Hello, gentlemen," she said over his head as the new customers walked behind him toward the pool table.

"Evenin'," one of them replied.

Farkus looked up to see the square-cut face of a handsome young man in a sharply creased cowboy hat pass between the bottles on the mirrored back bar. The cowboy swiped two fingers along the edge of his wide-brimmed cowboy hat toward Wanda as he went by.

"Four draft Coors and four shots of Beam," he said. His voice was high and twangy, but not unpleasant. "We'll be sittin' at one of those booths in the back."

"I'll bring them right over," she said as she reached up and flipped her hair with the back of her hand. She was flirting with this man in a way she'd never flirted with Farkus.

"Appreciate it," the cowboy said.

Farkus didn't want to spin around and stare. He knew there were four of them—three men and a woman—and the worst thing to do late at night in a bar was to glare at newcomers who were younger and bigger than he was. He could almost hear *What are you lookin' at?* in his ears. The cowboy who had obviously charmed Wanda seemed like the alpha dog of the pack. And he seemed familiar to Farkus, although he couldn't quite place him.

"Do you realize who just walked in?" Wanda whispered to Farkus.

Before he could speculate, she was practically dancing away on the rubber bar mat to fetch the beer and pour the shots.

"I'll take another one before you close out," Farkus called to her.

She rolled her eyes with annoyance and cursed under her breath at the intrusive order. He was obviously distracting her from serving the cowboy and his friends.

FARKUS SAT RIGHT THERE on his magic eavesdropping stool with his back to them as Wanda delivered the tray of drinks to the group who'd taken over the farthest booth in the back. He looked under his armpit as she walked behind him and slammed his can of beer down on the bar (no tomato juice). He'd never seen her sway her hips like that before.

He listened as she asked them what they were in town for, which turned out to be elk hunting.

"Elk hunting?" she said. "I love elk steaks better than either moose or beef. I'd do anything to get a couple of packages for my freezer."

She'd never told Farkus that.

"Well, maybe we'll get lucky so you can get lucky," the cowboy said.

"Maybe we'll both get lucky," she laughed. On his stool, Farkus rolled his eyes.

"You never can count on those elk being where you think they'll be."

She told them about going hunting with her dad when she was a little girl and how sad she was when he'd shot an elk and hung the carcass up in a tree. She said she tried not to think of that bloody body up there when she enjoyed elk steaks. The story went on for a while.

The cowboy did the talking, and he was polite but succinct with her. Farkus thought it was obvious he didn't want to be rude to her, but he wanted her to go away.

"Well, wish us luck," the cowboy said, signaling an end to the conversation.

"Wish us both luck," Wanda said with that laugh again. "Let me know when you need another round. The first one was on the house."

When she returned to the bar, her face and neck were flushed.

Farkus said, "You've never bought me a round even once."

Instead of answering him, she said again, "Do you know who that is?"

THE CONVERSATION IN THE BOOTH was led by the cowboy, who had—deliberately, Farkus thought—lowered his voice. Still, Farkus could catch some of what was being said to the others.

"The plan is to be methodical, like we talked about," he said.

"We come at them from all angles and hit 'em on the edges—hit 'em hard. I want to make him suffer."

That got Farkus's attention, but he tried not to show it. Instead, he sipped at the can of beer with his back to them. The beer wasn't very cold. He thought Wanda had purposely given him a can that hadn't been in the refrigerator very long.

Then the cowboy said, "Hold on a minute."

The man got up, and Farkus could hear his boots clomp along the wooden floor, and he could see Wanda suck in her belly and look up in anticipation. But instead of coming all the way to the bar, the cowboy stopped and fed quarters into the jukebox.

Garth Brooks's "Friends in Low Places" filled the saloon, followed by Blake Shelton's "Came Here to Forget."

After that, Farkus could only hear certain words and phrases during the pauses in the songs or between songs. But he heard enough to keep interested.

"Squeeze him in a vise . . ."

"Keep our stories straight . . ."

"Don't do stupid shit . . ."

"Gay Mormon won't know what hit 'im . . ."

Gay Mormon? Huh? Farkus was momentarily confused by the phrase. It addled his mind and he didn't bother to excuse himself when he slid down from his stool to lumber back to the restroom again, because Wanda had forgotten he was still at the bar. Instead, she was excitedly talking to a girlfriend on her cell phone about who she'd just met.

Farkus nodded his head as he passed them. The cowboy was lean and hard and his face looked to be constructed of a series of smooth, flat white rocks—sharp cheekbones, wide jaw, heavy brow. There was a two-inch scar on his left cheek that looked like an inadvertent sneer. His neck was as wide as his jaw, and he projected raw physical power. He wore a crisp long-sleeved shirt, the kind preferred by rodeo cowboys.

He paused talking as Farkus walked by them.

Across the table from the cowboy were two other men, both with a hint of menace about them. One was big with wide shoulders, a round face, and dark distant eyes. He had black hair sprinkled with silver and a large nose that looked like it had been broken more than once. The other was leaner, with reddish hair and a five-day growth of beard. He had alabaster skin and was absolutely still except for the movement of his steel-gray eyes, which had flicked from the cowboy to Farkus.

Farkus couldn't see the woman clearly because she had a dark hoodie pulled over her head and her face was in shadow. She'd pushed up the cuffs on her sweatshirt, though, and he noticed multicolored, sleeve-length tattoos on her forearms and even on the backs of her hands.

WHEN HE RETURNED from the toilet, Farkus didn't sit back down on his stool. Instead, he waved down Wanda. She covered the mouthpiece of her cell phone and glared at him.

"I need to close out now."

"Call you back in a minute," she said to her girlfriend.

As Farkus dug cash out of his wallet and the opening guitar licks to Johnny Cash's "(Ghost) Riders in the Sky" leapt out of the jukebox, he signaled for Wanda to get closer.

"Is that Dallas Cates back there?"

"Who else do you think it is?"

"I didn't realize he was around."

"Neither did I, or I would have put on my Spanx and dressed up a little."

"Can I borrow your cell phone real quick? Mine's dead."

"Why don't you learn to plug it in?"

"I'll be real quick," he said.

Reluctantly, she handed over her phone, with a warning that her battery was just about dead as well.

Then he walked straight outside. Farkus glanced at Timberman in the corner as he passed him.

Still sleeping.

ON THE SIDEWALK in front of the Stockman's, it smelled like fall in the air, like elk-hunting season.

Although Joe Pickett's phone went straight to message, he continued. "Some guys and a gal. I didn't know any of them but Dallas Cates. I remembered what he looked like from them rodeo posters they used to have up in Welton's Western Wear. Yeah, three guys, one gal—did I say that? Anyway, they were talking low, but really saying some shit, you know?

"Hell, I didn't even know Cates was out of prison in Rawlins. Did you?

"When I heard 'gay Mormon,' I couldn't figure it out. Then

it hit me. They wasn't saying 'gay Mormon' at all. They was saying *game warden*.'

"So . . . call me. I'm going elk hunting tomorrow, but you need to know what I heard. If I don't answer, come by our camp if you want to, but be sure to knock first. Ha! Bring a horse so you can help us drag out an elk if we get one. And bring whiskey. It'll be my info for your whiskey, which sounds like a good deal for both of us.

"We're up there on the South Fork of the Powder River—way up, maybe a quarter of a mile below tree line. Me and Cotton Anderson.

"Boy, they was really talkin' shit about you. You'll want to know, believe me. In general, they was planning—"

Wanda snatched the phone out his hand.

She said, "Okay, that's enough, damn you," and terminated the call.

"I wasn't done," Farkus said.

"I don't give a rip," she said, and turned on her heel and strode toward the front door.

Which opened before she got there. The doorframe filled with Dallas Cates and the larger of the two men.

Farkus froze on the sidewalk.

Cates stepped aside to let Wanda in, but he gracefully plucked the phone out of her hand as she went by. When she turned to object, he said, "I'll bring it back to you in a minute, darling."

She went back inside, but not before the big man squeezed through and shut the door behind him.

Farkus knew he couldn't outrun them, but he thought he might be able to talk himself out of it.

Cates held the phone up and scrolled through the screen. The dim light illuminated his features and made him look diabolical, Farkus thought. The large man stepped out to Farkus's left on the sidewalk, blocking an exit that way.

"I know who you are," Cates said. "I know you were trying to overhear us talking in there. Dave fuckin' Farkus. My dad used to clean out your septic tank, and sometimes you even paid him for it."

Farkus recalled the early-morning arrivals of Eldon Cates in his C&C Sewer and Septic Tank Service truck. The predawn *beep-beep-beep* of that truck backing up outside his double-wide had awakened him from many a hangover.

"There," Cates said. "I've memorized the number you called and I'll look it up later, but I'm pretty sure I know who it was."

"I called my wife to tell her I was coming home," Farkus lied.

"When I was here last, you were single as hell and trying to score anyone you could find who'd fall for that fly-fishing scheme," Cates said with a laugh. "Nobody's dumb enough to marry a loser like you, Farkus."

"Please, I—"

The big man reached for something tucked into the back of his belt and started to move in, and Farkus raised his arms in order to ward off any blows.

That's when Cates said "Rory" with an urgent tone.

Rory stopped two feet away from Farkus, and Farkus opened his eyes slightly. Rory quickly morphed from reaching for a weapon to pretending he was pulling up his trousers.

A Twelve Sleep County Sheriff's Department SUV was cruising down Main. It slowed in front of the Stockman's Bar, and

Farkus recognized the driver as Deputy Lester Spivak. Spivak had recently been named undersheriff for the department. He'd replaced Edgar Jess Boner, he of the unfortunate name, who had taken a better-paying job in North Dakota.

Farkus had never been as thrilled to see Deputy Spivak as he was at that minute. Spivak was squinting through the passenger window at the three of them out on the sidewalk.

Cates reached over and clapped Farkus on the shoulder as if he were saying good night to an old friend.

Under his breath to Rory, Cates said, "Let's go finish our beers after walking our old buddy Farkus out of the bar."

To Farkus, he said, "Wave to the nice officer and show him everything's all right."

Farkus did as he was told.

Spivak waved back and the SUV sped up and continued down the street.

As he opened the door to go back inside, Cates said to Farkus, "We'll be in touch sooner than you think."

Farkus's hand was trembling so hard it took half a minute to slide his key into the truck ignition and pull away.

He couldn't wait to disappear into the mountains and away from Dallas Cates.

JOE WAS STILL UNSETTLED BY WHAT HE'D WITNESSED ON THE
iPad when he rolled his green Ford F-150 pickup to the front
gate of his home and shut off the motor.

The scene down below in the timber ran through his mind
in a continuous loop. Even during his briefing with Sheriff Reed
at the airport, he'd watched the white figure emerge from behind the tree and flee while starbursts flashed on the black
screen. He wasn't even sure it had been Dave Farkus down there,
he'd reported to Reed, or even that the three figures who moved
through the forest had assassinated someone. But it sure felt
like that.

Also unsettling was that the only illumination from inside
his house was from the living room and Lucy's bedroom. Now it

looked lonely. When he'd drive up the mountain road while all the girls were there, his home was lit up at night like a steamboat on a dark river.

That was when his oldest daughter, Sheridan, twenty-two, was briefly back at home after graduating from the University of Wyoming the previous spring. And when April, twenty, was still there, before she'd enrolled at Northwest community college in Powell.

Sheridan was "taking a break" after college and had landed a job as a hostess at an exclusive high-end guest ranch outside of Saratoga, Wyoming. Neither Joe nor Marybeth knew exactly what "taking a break" meant, and Joe suspected Sheridan didn't know for sure herself. Nevertheless, she seemed to enjoy the job despite the long hours and sometimes unreasonable demands from guests, who paid more than $1,500 a night to ride horses, fly-fish, and explore mountains and valleys away from civilization. Sheridan joked that she'd spent her formative years enjoying those activities and it hadn't cost her a dime.

April had surprised them both by applying for and receiving a scholarship on the college rodeo team, specializing in breakaway roping. Breakaway roping was a timed event that was a gentler hybrid of calf roping—the rider roped a calf but the animal wasn't jerked to the ground or tied up. April had saved enough money working at the local Western-wear store to buy a competent roping horse, and she was participating in college rodeos throughout Wyoming, Montana, Idaho, and the Dakotas.

Eighteen-year-old Lucy, a senior at Saddlestring High School, was seven months away from moving on as well and leaving Joe and Marybeth with an empty nest. Lucy was the most sensitive

and intuitive of the three girls, and she seemed to be almost embarrassed to be the last one still at home, as if her presence were
keeping her parents from their next stage of life. She seemed to
be in a hurry to join her sisters out in the world. Marybeth was
resigned to the future, although she wasn't excited about it.
She'd told Joe that her relationship with Lucy had gotten closer
and more full since the two older girls had left. She'd miss Lucy
terribly.

Joe opened his truck door and swung out. His Labrador,
Daisy, who was no doubt put out that he hadn't taken her along
in the airplane, was inside the living room on her hind feet,
watching him through the window and steaming up the glass.

"ROUGH NIGHT?" Marybeth asked as Joe removed his boots and
jacket in the mudroom and placed his Stetson crown-down on a
shelf.

"Yup."

She sat at the dining room table stacked high with piles of
paper and three-ring binders. She'd changed into sweats, and
her blond hair was in a ponytail. She looked remarkably youth-
ful in her smart glasses. He could tell she'd already fed the horses
because there were stray stalks of hay stuck to the fabric of her
pants.

"I bought a bucket of chicken on the way home tonight and
most of it's in the fridge," she said. "I thought you might want
some for your lunch tomorrow."

"Thank you." Joe never turned down fried chicken. "You're
working late."

She sat back and sipped at a glass of red wine. "I've got to. I spend all my day trying to do my job and dealing with all the construction guys, and the bureaucrats who want to keep the construction guys from constructing anything."

Joe nodded as he opened the cabinet and closed his hand around the neck of a bottle of bourbon. As the director of the Twelve Sleep County Library, Marybeth was running day-to-day operations and coordinating the construction of a new library building funded by a bond issue the county voters had passed the previous summer. It was the culmination of an effort to which she'd devoted years: convincing citizens that a new library was needed. After two unsuccessful tries, the bond issue had finally passed, and now she felt she owed it to the voters to do everything she could to make sure the library was finished on time and under budget.

"Let me clear some room," she said, reaching out to sweep aside some of the paperwork on the table.

"Don't worry about it," he said while pouring the bourbon over ice in a glass. He fished the bucket of chicken out of the refrigerator and took a bite out of a thigh as she watched him warily.

"*Really?*" she asked. "For dinner you're going to eat over the sink and drink bourbon? Has it come to this?"

She was kidding, but only a little.

"Takes me back to my single days," he said.

"You couldn't afford bourbon."

"True enough."

"So tell me, were you able to locate your buddy Dave Farkus?"

"I think so," he said.

"Well, that's good news."

"Not really."

AFTER JOE RECOUNTED the flight and what he'd seen via the FLIR, she shook her head sadly and got up and poured a second glass of wine. A second glass was rare, he knew. She was as troubled now as he was.

"Do you think the shooters located him because you were flying a circle around him in the plane?"

"That's what's eating at me," Joe said. "We might as well have been trailing a banner that said, 'The guy you've been hunting for is right here.'"

"Don't beat yourself up," she said. "There's no way you could have known someone was after him, right? And there's no way you can even be sure it was Dave Farkus."

"True. But it was somebody, and I just sat there and watched it happen. It kind of makes me feel . . . dirty. Like I saw something I shouldn't have seen: the last seconds of a man's life."

She shivered and took another sip of wine. Marybeth had once referred to Farkus as the Zelig of the Bighorns for his uncanny knack of turning up in the middle of dangerous situations time and again. Just like her husband.

"And we know who did it, don't we?" she asked.

"We don't know that at all," Joe said.

She leaned forward and lowered her tone, because Lucy was in her bedroom not far down the hall and she didn't want to be overheard.

"It was Dallas Cates."

"He's the number one suspect."

"Has he been arrested?"

"No. And I can't guarantee he will be."

"Take off your law enforcement hat and put on your thinking cap," she said. "We know Dallas Cates was released from the penitentiary less than a year ago. We've been waiting for him to resurface. *Dreading* is a better word.

"Then, two nights ago you get a message from Dave Farkus saying he saw Dallas here in town. Maybe Dallas saw him and figured out he might contact you. So he went after him with two of his friends to shut him up."

Joe nodded.

"We know Dallas is capable of anything and we know he's likely to come after us," she said. "You need to talk to Mike Reed about finding Dallas and his thugs and arresting them tomorrow."

"It's not as simple as that," Joe said.

"I know it isn't. You need evidence and probable cause. I haven't lived with a law enforcement officer all these years and not learned that. But we know in our hearts who did this and why, right? And we need to nip it in the bud before things get worse for all of us."

"Nip what in the bud?" Lucy asked from the hallway. "Is this about Dallas Cates being back in town?"

Joe and Marybeth exchanged looks.

NEARLY TWO YEARS BEFORE, April had been beaten and dumped along a county road outside of Saddlestring. The immediate suspect had been local rodeo champion Dallas Cates, with whom April had run off to travel the rodeo circuit. Eldon and Brenda Cates, Dallas's parents, had fought for their son's innocence with the same zeal they had mustered trying to convince the community to pay special honor to Dallas's rodeo championships and standings.

Brenda, in particular, had felt that the community had always looked down on the Cates family as white trash, and she resented that Saddlestring wouldn't erect highway signs that said, SADDLESTRING: HOME TO PRCA WORLD CHAMPION COWBOY DALLAS CATES at the entrances to town.

It had been more than a year since Joe had testified at her trial, and a few months longer since he'd seen her splayed out on her back on the floor of the root cellar where she'd fallen. Her husband, Eldon, was pinned beneath her and was already dead.

Brenda's arms were at her sides and her legs were motionless but askew from breaking her back in the fall. Her sack-like floral-print dress was hiked up over her enormous white thighs and she was physically unable to reach down and smooth it out. She had no feeling from her neck down.

Her wild and hateful eyes had pierced through the darkness and raked over Joe, and her mouth had twisted into a snarl. He'd never forget the chill that had gone through him, or the guilt he felt witnessing her complete and utter humiliation. At that moment, he thought, she probably wished that she'd died along with her husband and her oldest son, Bull. She'd probably assumed that Dallas was dead as well.

The worst scenario possible for Brenda had occurred and she was fully conscious to experience it, and Joe had not only been responsible for it—in her view—but he was also the only eyewitness to her ignominy.

It hadn't mattered to Brenda that the men in her family—and Brenda herself—had spent decades alienating their neighbors in the rest of the county. Eldon was notorious for cheating and overcharging customers for rural water and sewer work, and the only thing that had kept him in business was lack of competition. Eldon and Bull had antagonized other big-game outfitters in the area by vandalizing their hunting camps, claiming for their own clients or for themselves trophy elk that had been killed by others, and flouting territorial understandings between guides as to who hunted where.

Bull and Timber, the middle son, had grown up intimidating schoolmates and getting in trouble with the police. Timber, in fact, had preceded Dallas in the state penitentiary, for carjacking.

Dallas himself had been implicated in but not arrested for the sexual assault of a new female student at his high school. She'd been found beaten and dumped on the side of a county road—much like what had happened to April.

For more than twenty years, when bad things had happened in Twelve Sleep County, the first thought of every law enforcement officer was: *I bet a Cates boy is involved.*

Joe had been convinced Dallas was responsible for April's injuries, even though some of her belongings had been found on the property of a local miscreant and survivalist named Tilden Cudmore—who had a history of cruising the highways for prey. April hadn't been able to shed any light on the matter because she was in a drug-induced coma in the hospital.

But all the actual evidence had pointed away from Dallas—

41

who'd claimed to be recuperating from rodeo injuries at the Cates family compound at the time—and toward Cudmore. Cudmore was arrested and all but confessed to the crime in open court, but he hanged himself in his cell before he could be convicted.

Despite the evidence pointing to Cudmore, Joe had circled back around to the Cates compound. His investigation had triggered a chain reaction that resulted in the deaths of Dallas's two brothers, Bull and Timber, as well as their father, Eldon. Joe had killed Bull in self-defense, and Timber had fallen—or been thrown—from a hospital balcony in Billings. Brenda, now a quadriplegic, was serving a life sentence at the Wyoming Women's Center in Lusk for kidnapping and conspiracy to commit murder.

Dallas Cates had been severely injured by Joe and was later convicted of the only charges County Attorney Dulcie Schalk could pin on him: five counts of wanton destruction of big-game animals, specifically five elk that Cates had bulldogged to death in the snow near the family compound at the base of the Bighorn Mountains.

A wanton destruction charge, article 23-3-107 in the Wyoming Game and Fish Department provisions, was a violation that constituted a first-degree misdemeanor and often resulted in a heavy fine, forfeiture of vehicles and weapons used in the crime, and a loss of hunting privileges. But in an obvious effort to get Dallas off the streets after he'd vowed retribution on Joe, she'd argued for sending him to the state penitentiary in Rawlins. Judge Hewitt had agreed with her and sentenced Cates to two to four years.

He'd served twelve and a half months.

For the past year, Joe, Marybeth, all three girls, and the law enforcement community in Twelve Sleep County had kept their eyes out for the return of Dallas Cates.

Joe had approached every fisherman and hunting camp with extra caution in case Dallas was there. He'd purchased a Smith & Wesson Airweight .38 revolver for Marybeth to keep in her purse, and canisters of pepper spray for all three girls. Marybeth and Dulcie Schalk often rode horses together, and for the past year the two of them had also gone to the shooting range together, because Dulcie had also bought a weapon.

T. Cletus Glatt, the editor of the Saddlestring *Roundup* and a bitter man who'd lost a series of high-profile jobs at much bigger newspapers throughout the country due to downsizing and his repellent personality, had seized on the potential of Cates's return. He'd questioned the "overcharging" by the prosecutor and had even written an editorial titled "Will Dallas Cates Come Back for Revenge?"

And now perhaps he had.

Joe had set off the vicious circle with the Cates family and it had yet to close. He thought about it often and questioned some of the actions he'd taken because he'd been convinced of Dallas's guilt. Brenda *herself* had believed her son guilty, because he'd gotten away with past crimes, and she'd defended him with the single-minded ferocity of a sow grizzly protecting her cub.

That Joe could have never predicted how catastrophic the outcome would turn out to be for the surviving Cateses was something he wrestled with. It had kept him up nights for the two years since it happened.

He put himself in the cowboy boots of Dallas himself. What would he himself do, Joe thought, if someone was responsible for the slaughter of his father and brothers and the crippling of his mother, not to mention inflicting the injuries that ended his championship rodeo career?

Joe could understand why Dallas wanted to exact revenge.

That was the problem.

"WHERE DID YOU HEAR that Dallas Cates was back in town?" Marybeth asked Lucy.

"I saw it on Facebook. Somebody thought they saw him driving down a county road."

Lucy had become a beautiful young woman, no doubt about it. Joe noted with alarm the second looks and outright stares from males as she passed by, even though she seemed to ignore them. Lithe and blond, she was underestimated by most of those around her, he thought. They didn't know her depth or her empathy for others. She'd grown up in the wake of her willful older sisters and had learned to keep quiet, listen, and operate on the margins. She knew more about what was going on with every member of their family than anyone else, including Marybeth. She'd learned to survive by not standing out, he thought. That she was embarrassed having just been voted homecoming queen at her high school said a lot about her.

"We were just talking about Dallas," Marybeth said. "There isn't proof he's back, but I wouldn't doubt it."

Marybeth turned to Joe. "That's why he needs to be arrested."

"First things first," Joe said. "You know what happened last time when we all thought he was guilty and we went after him with blinders on. We overlooked the obvious bad guy."

"So what's going to happen?" Lucy asked. "I know you can't just go out and pick him up because of what he might do."

"You're right," Joe said, "but he may have already committed a crime tonight."

He briefly told her what he'd seen from the airplane.

He said, "I'm going to meet the sheriff and his guys first thing tomorrow and we're going to go into the mountains in search of the body of a man named Dave Farkus. At least we assume it will turn out to be him. Then we'll proceed from there."

"And it will lead to Dallas Cates," Marybeth said. "Then they'll arrest him and send him away for the rest of his life."

Lucy nodded, but she wasn't convinced.

"I'll text Sheridan and April," she said. "They need to know he might be around."

"Good idea," Marybeth said.

"Keep your pepper spray near you at all times," Joe said. He'd told all of his daughters that so many times, they could finish the sentence for him.

AS THEY GOT READY for bed and she was washing her face at the bathroom sink, Marybeth said to Joe, "I sometimes get the impression you almost feel sorry for him."

"Who? Dallas?"

"Who else have we been talking about?"

He was laying out his clothing for the next morning because he'd be getting up at four-thirty to meet Sheriff Reed at the command center by six. It would be cold in the mountains.

"I wish things had gone a different way, I guess."

"We can't change that now," she said. "Dallas could have made the decision just to cut his losses and drop it. He could have thought about how Brenda created the mess in the first place and put the blame on her instead of you, or he could have found Jesus in the penitentiary and learned to forgive and forget. It's not your fault that he didn't—it's his."

Joe sat down on the bed. She was right, as usual.

He said, "I can kind of see why he's the way he is. I'd probably be like that if I grew up with a mother like Brenda Cates. But if he tries to harm anyone in our family, things are going to get real Western real fast, and Dallas Cates is a dead man."

"And no one in this valley would have a problem with that," she said.

He looked away. He knew she was correct. He also knew he'd have to be careful.

Most of all, he needed to make sure he was in the *right*.

THE SNOW STARTED MIDMORNING. IT FLOATED HEAVILY THROUGH
the boughs and dispersed into drops on contact, much like a
late-spring snow, but it wasn't yet sticking to the pine-needle
floor of the forest.

Joe reined his horse, Toby, to a stop in a small meadow and
climbed off. He wanted to pull on his raincoat before his clothes
were soaked. While Joe could trust Toby not to spook when he
unfurled his jacket, he didn't know enough about the other
horses he was riding with to assume they wouldn't panic. He
knew through years of experience dealing with injured or
stranded hunters that all it took was the unfurling of a coat or
the snapping of a horse blanket to make an already jittery horse
bolt and run off. A sudden movement—or in some instances

simply a lone plastic grocery bag caught in a tree—could kick in the *I am prey—Run!* instinct of some mounts.

One by one, the other riders stopped their horses and did the same. There were six of them in the search team and seven horses. The riderless horse was being trailed by one of the deputies.

The team was made up of Undersheriff Lester Spivak and deputies Justin Woods and Ryan Steck. Steck was a new hire fresh from college and the Wyoming Law Enforcement Academy. Gary Norwood, the county evidence tech who had likely never been on horseback before, was also along. And Cotton Anderson had made the case that he should be involved as well, because he was the last person to see his hunting buddy Dave Farkus alive.

Spivak had taken the job from a similar position in eastern Pennsylvania, where he'd been chief investigator for a larger sheriff's department. He was compact and intense and his East Coast accent was tinny and distinct. Although he'd never lived in the Mountain West until recently, Joe was impressed how quickly he'd taken to it. Eastern Pennsylvania was also rural hunting country, Spivak said, so the transition wasn't as difficult as he thought it would be. He'd moved with his wife and daughter to a house outside of town, and he'd already bought two old horses. The tin in his voice was gradually smoothing out and words didn't come out of his mouth in torrents unless he was excited.

Spivak had been named by Sheriff Reed the official team leader for the search-and-rescue team, although he deferred to Joe on which route they should take into the forest and how they should proceed, since he didn't know the mountains well. Their primary goal was to ride to the location pinpointed by GPS coordinates made by the Civil Air Patrol the night before, and possibly establish a crime scene and retrieve a body.

Their secondary goal was to get out of the mountains before the first big winter storm hit.

They'd already failed at that.

SHERIFF REED HAD REMAINED at the command center in the campground. Reed had been crippled by a bullet several years before while he was running for sheriff, and he'd lost the use of his legs. Although he was more than capable of performing all of his duties and responsibilities, to the point that it was easy to forget that he did them from a wheelchair and a specially equipped van, his riding a horse through the timber was impractical and would have severely slowed them down.

Instead, Reed stayed in radio contact with Spivak and Woods and tracked their progress through the forest on a topo map spread over a picnic table. He'd also ordered the team to turn around if the storm hit early, because he didn't want them to risk their safety or their lives.

"I don't know how you people do this," Norwood moaned to Joe. "My butt hurts and it feels like the insides of my thighs are rubbed raw."

The evidence tech had climbed off his horse and was bent over next to it with his head down and his hands on his knees. He'd let the reins slip to the wet grass when he dismounted.

Joe reached over and gathered them up. "First time on a horse?"

"First and last, if I have anything to say about it."

"We still need to ride back out."

"Thanks for reminding me," Norwood grumbled.

BACK ON THE GAME TRAIL, Joe goosed Toby a little so he could ride abreast with Cotton Anderson. Anderson was in his early sixties and sported a thick white mustache that sparkled with moisture from the falling snow. He wore a wide-brimmed cowboy hat with a Gus McCrae crease and a red silk bandanna that poked out of his Carhartt jacket. Joe knew him slightly from when he'd cited him years before for fishing without a conservation stamp.

"So how did you two lose each other?" Joe asked after a short discussion about how miserable it was riding a horse in a snowstorm.

"Me'n Dave?"

"Yes. I would have thought you'd hunt together."

Cotton sighed and said, "Normally we would. Usually, we pick a big timber stand and one of us walks through it after the other one is set up on point, in case the elk run out. Or we just settle in up in the rocks, where we can glass the meadows for when the critters come out to feed."

"But not this time," Joe said. "What was different?"

Cotton looked over warily and didn't answer. Joe knew the look. It was the look a suspected violator got when Joe drove up to the house, knocked on the door, and said, "I guess you know why I'm here."

Cotton was contemplating whether to tell Joe the truth or make up a story.

Finally, he said, "We're lookin' for Fark, right? We just care about finding him right now. We're not hunting elk and you aren't on patrol, right?"

Joe stifled a smile. "I'm not on patrol, but I'm always on duty. Are you asking me if I'd write you up for a violation right now if you confessed to one?"

"Yeah, I guess so."

"It depends how bad it is."

"Didn't you arrest the governor once for fishing without a license?"

"Yup."

"So that story is true."

"It is."

Cotton thought that over. Finally, he said, "You know where our camp is, right? Back there on the bank of the South Fork?"

Joe said, "I think so. Just a clearing next to a big granite rock with a fire pit and a game pole nailed to a couple of trees?"

Joe didn't mention the empty beer cans strewn about or the broken glass tromped into the mud. He hated a dirty camp. Farkus was famous for always doing the absolute minimum required in any situation.

Cotton said, "That's it. Not much to write home about. Fark used to use it when he was a guide. But the great thing is, we could drive our vehicles within fifty yards of it, drag the tents and coolers over, and nobody ever bothered us."

Coolers in a camp attracted bears and other predators. Food

was supposed to be hung at least ten feet up in a tree that was at least a hundred yards from the camp itself. But Farkus wasn't only lazy, he was old-school. He'd rather shoot at a visiting bear than prevent it from showing up in the first place.

Joe bit his tongue and said, "Go on."

"You sure you ain't gonna write me up?"

"It depends on what you did."

"That's not real sporting, you know."

"It's as far as I'll go."

Cotton rolled his eyes and blew a disgusted breath through his nose. Joe thought Cotton and Farkus made good hunting partners. The two of them belonged together.

Cotton said, "Okay, well, when we pulled into where our camp was, I looked up, and damned if there wasn't a cow elk and calf standing right there in the trees. Right there! You know how unusual that is. I knew they'd run off if I climbed out of the truck and stood there loading my rifle, so I grabbed this"— he patted the holster of a handgun on his belt—"and shot her right there."

Joe shook his head. It was a violation to hunt elk with a Colt M1911 .45 *and* to fire it from inside a vehicle.

"I know, I know," Cotton said before Joe could speak. "I shoulda got out and used my rifle, because that cow just run off on me after I popped her. It wasn't enough gun to put her down."

Joe said nothing, which made Cotton nervous enough that he talked faster.

"I knew I had a wounded elk out there. I didn't know how far she'd go before she laid down.

"So instead of helping Fark set up the camp like I normally

would have, I grabbed my rifle and took off after that cow. There was a blood trail, not much of one, but I followed it for eight hours, and I never did find that elk."

Joe looked over and Cotton wouldn't meet his eyes.

"I hate to tell you that story," Cotton said. "Not because you might give me a ticket, but because I was so fucking stupid. I hate to wound an animal and not find it. I hated to give up on her trail that night, but I was starting to run out of light, so I headed back. When I finally got back to our camp, Fark wasn't there, just like I told the sheriff. I thought he'd show up any minute, because he left the steaks out and everything, but he never came back."

"What time did you get back to find him gone?" Joe asked.

Cotton tipped his head back and looked at the sky. "It was about an hour before it got dark. So maybe around five-thirty."

"Did you look for Farkus the next morning?" Joe asked.

Cotton shrugged. "I circled around the camp for hours, but didn't get too far away from it. Remember, I didn't know which direction he'd gone. I didn't want to get lost myself, and I didn't want to be gone from the camp if he came back. So finally I called it in."

"Did you ever locate the dead elk?"

Cotton looked down at his hands as he rode. "No."

"Did you see or hear anything that suggested there were others up here?"

"I thought I heard another truck in the late afternoon. That was about seven hours after I left to find that cow elk—so maybe around four or four-thirty. But I couldn't tell if it was coming toward the camp or driving away. I never saw it."

Joe said, "Did Farkus mention anything to you about hearing something in the bar the night before?"

Cotton said, "You gotta understand, we barely got a chance to talk to each other. He came by my place at six in the morning and we drove separate vehicles up here. We barely exchanged three words in the morning. When we got to our camp, I shot at that cow and took off after her. And I haven't seen or talked to him since.

"You know what his last words to me were?" Cotton asked.

"What?"

"Well, first he cussed at me for making him set up the camp by himself. Then he said, 'Cotton, you dumb-ass, you shot that elk in the butt. Joe Pickett will jump down your throat if he finds out.'"

Joe said, "He was right. But I'll wait until this is over."

Cotton moaned. "I should have kept my mouth shut."

"No," Joe said. "You should have killed that cow elk and not let her run away to suffer and die and leave her calf out here alone."

"Do you think I feel good about that?" Cotton said. Joe was surprised that the man's eyes were moist when he looked over. "Do you think I'm proud of the fact that I left my hunting buddy?"

Joe didn't respond.

"Fark was right," Cotton said. "You can be a real hard-ass."

"COTTON SAID he heard another vehicle up here around four or four-thirty that afternoon," Joe said to Spivak after he'd slowed

Toby so the undersheriff could catch up to him. Cotton had ridden ahead, grumbling under his breath.

"I don't think he told the sheriff that," Spivak said. "That's kind of important information for us to know, wouldn't you think?"

"Yup."

The two rode side by side, and Spivak leaned over and spoke quietly.

"Do you think Cotton had anything to do with it?"

Joe shook his head. "I think if anything, he's dumber than Farkus. Lazier, too. I think Cotton was trying to track down a wounded elk like he said he was. That, and avoiding the work of setting up the camp."

"Four-thirty," Spivak repeated. "So we can assume that's when Dallas Cates showed up to confront Farkus. We can also assume Cates parked where Farkus and Cotton left their vehicles, which would cut off any escape down the road. So maybe Cates confronted Farkus on foot at the elk camp and Farkus took off running."

"Maybe," Joe said. "Cotton said Farkus was gone when he got back around five-thirty."

"And it's dark at, what? Six-thirty?" Spivak asked.

"Yup. Six forty-one, to be exact."

When Spivak eyed him, Joe said, "I keep track, because it's illegal to shoot a big-game animal beyond thirty minutes after sundown."

Spivak said, "Ah, good. So now we have the basis of a timeline. It means that poor son of a bitch Farkus was likely being hunted that night and all the next day. They didn't find him until last night, which tells me a couple of things.

"First, Cates was determined to find Farkus, even if it took that long. That's a real commitment. Second, Cates knew these mountains well enough to stay up here and track down a man who'd hunted around here for years and knew this country well."

Joe nodded, waiting for more.

Spivak was square-jawed and clean-shaven, and his uniform, even after riding for hours, looked crisp and neat. Joe thought he would look like a cop even if he wasn't one. He'd become involved in his church and the community. The undersheriff had a twelve-year-old daughter named Caitlin who was a prodigy as a gymnast. Lester and his wife spent their weekends taking her to gymnastics competitions, where she usually won. He'd tell anyone who was around him that she had the potential to be an Olympian, if only they could find a way to send her to an elite camp—which they couldn't do on his salary. Joe, like many others in Twelve Sleep County, thought Spivak would likely succeed Sheriff Reed when the sheriff retired.

"You know, I partly blame myself for this," Spivak said.

"For what?"

"I saw Farkus outside the Stockman's Bar the night before he went hunting. I cruised by and saw him out there with two other men. I know now the one in the hat was Dallas Cates. I don't know who the other one was."

Joe was interested.

Spivak sighed and said, "You know how it is when you do this job long enough and sometimes you just get a feeling about something. When I first saw the three of them, they were standing close together on the sidewalk—which meant to me they were either really close friends or they were about to get into a fight. I was thinking fight by the way Farkus was standing. He was back on his heels like he was ready to take a punch.

"But when I drove closer, Cates and the other big guy kind of separated from Farkus, and Farkus turned and waved at me like everything was fine. Like we were big buddies. I *should* have stopped and questioned them, but they didn't give me any reason to do that, and Sheriff Reed doesn't like to hear that his guys are out rousting innocent civilians with no probable cause. But if I had, I could have positively ID'd Dallas Cates and we'd know for sure he was back in the county. It might have scared him off coming after Farkus the next day."

"You can't blame yourself for that," Joe offered.

"I know. But I had a gut feeling when I first saw them that something was going on. I should have followed up."

Joe wished Spivak had, too, but he didn't want to make him feel worse than he already did.

"I talked to Wanda Stacy this morning," Spivak said. "She's the one Buck Timberman picked to take over day-to-day operations at the Stockman's. She's the wrong choice, but that's between those two. Anyway, Wanda said she could positively identify Cates if she saw him again. She described two other guys with him in the bar that night pretty well. One was a big guy with a busted nose, and the other one she said looked like a weasel. Plus some gal they were with, but she didn't get a good look at her."

"Is that the best description she could come up with for the two males with Cates?" Joe asked. "A broken nose and a weasel?"

Spivak snorted. He said, "I don't think Wanda really paid any attention to anyone other than Dallas Cates."

"Ah," Joe said. "I've seen what kind of effect he has on some women."

"I bet you have," Spivak said.

"It sounds like Cates was the only local, or Wanda would have said otherwise. That's interesting."

"Maybe Dallas recruited some help," Spivak said. "He's always attracted people to him, even when he was in high school. He's kind of a charismatic son of a bitch."

Joe grunted.

"So we know we can place Cates and his pals in the Stockman's that night with Farkus, where Farkus overheard them plotting something, according to that message he left you. That might be motive right there."

Spivak's horse was getting ahead. Joe clucked his tongue, signaling to Toby to speed it up a little.

He asked, "When Wanda says there were two men and one woman with Dallas Cates, does that mean they all came in together or they met up inside?"

"I got the impression from her they all came in together and left together after Farkus went home, but I'll follow up with her on that."

Joe nodded but didn't say anything.

"We need to find those bastards before they hurt anyone else," Spivak said, his voice getting tense. "Dallas Cates is a cancer on the good people of this county. He comes from a white-trash family that's poisonous to anyone with whom they come in contact. I don't want my beautiful girl growing up in a place where they have to deal with scumbags like Dallas Cates running around."

Joe was surprised at Spivak's vehemence. He'd never seen him so passionate.

"Let's not get too out in front of our skis," Joe said. "Think about what happened last time."

"What happened was that the Cates family declared war and they lost. You of all people have to agree with me on that, right?"

Spivak leaned forward in his saddle and searched Joe's face for something. He said, "You've been affected more by the Cates clan than just about anybody."

"I have," Joe said.

"We all know what he said before he got sent to Rawlins. How he was going to come back here someday to settle scores. And it looks like he's only getting started."

"Let's just make sure we do this right," Joe said. "What I mean is, I don't want to get carried away going after him if the evidence doesn't support it. The reason he spent less than two years in prison and he's out now is because we bulled ahead in the wrong direction for too long. Dallas is smart. He takes after Brenda, not Eldon. He won't make it easy, and he would happily lead us down the wrong path so we screw up. I'm just saying we need to go into this with our eyes wide open to the fact that maybe, just maybe, he isn't behind everything that happens."

Spivak looked at Joe with pained surprise.

"We don't know what Dallas and Farkus talked about," Joe said. "We don't know if Dallas came up here after him, and we don't know if Dallas tracked him down and murdered him. We don't even know if it was Farkus I saw on that screen being gunned down. So I think we should figure those things out before we decide the only thing we can do is put Dallas Cates in the ground."

"What are you talking about?" Spivak was obviously offended.

"I'm just saying we need to keep an open mind," Joe said. "We're assuming it was Cates. But what if it wasn't? I've been chasing a poaching ring for two months and haven't made a lick of progress. What if Dave saw something go down and the violators realized they'd been seen and decided to go after him?"

Spivak shook his head. He said, "Joe, I'm open to any theory that makes sense if the evidence supports it. I'm not here to target one individual. I'm not a rogue cop. I'm not a vigilante."

"Good."

"I'm disappointed that you even suggested it. All I'm doing is coming up with a logical theory that factors in what we know so far."

"We don't know all that much, Lester," Joe said.

"We all need to be on the same page," Spivak said. "I can't have guys on my search-and-rescue team who're questioning everything I do."

"I understand."

"Do you, Joe?" Spivak asked.

Before Joe could respond, Spivak's radio crackled to life. It was Sheriff Reed asking for their location.

Joe used the opportunity to pull up on the reins so Spivak's horse slipped past him. Then Joe guided Toby back into the string behind Spivak.

They'd talked enough, he thought.

IT WAS SNOWING HARD when Joe saw the three ravens circling over the trees several hundred yards ahead. He knew the presence of ravens meant something was dead. That's how he'd located dozens of game carcasses over the years.

He got Spivak's attention and leaned forward in his saddle to point out the birds. Spivak did a cross check of the coordinates on his handheld GPS.

"We're here," he said to Joe and the others.

Joe felt himself tense up and he checked his weapons. His .40 Glock was beneath his coat, and he undid the bottom two buttons so he could access it if need be. His Remington 870 Wingmaster twelve-gauge shotgun was in the saddle scabbard.

THE BODY WAS FACEUP and splayed out in the snow. The metallic smell of blood and the musky odor of viscera hung low in the air. As the horsemen appeared, ravens lifted heavily off the body with strips of flesh in their crimson beaks.

Predators had disemboweled the body and ripped off most of the soft tissue including the face. Joe recognized Farkus's outfitter boots and .30-06 rifle pinned beneath him though, and Deputy Steck found a wallet with Dave Farkus's ID, EBT card, and twenty-eight dollars in cash.

"It's Fark, all right," Cotton said with a choke in his voice.

AS SPIVAK GAVE OUT ORDERS to photograph the scene and tape it off and Norwood bent down by the body to begin his preliminary examination, Joe tied off Toby and walked back into the trees in the direction from which they had come.

Snow sifted down through the pine boughs and created a hush in the forest. The voices of Spivak and the others sounded tinny and discordant. Cotton swore to the sky that he'd get the bastards who did this to his friend.

Joe bent over and threw up his breakfast. His eyes stung.

Farkus had been unique and usually a thorn in his side. But he'd also risked his own well-being by calling Joe and leaving a message about what he'd overheard. It was admirable and selfless, Joe thought, even if Farkus hadn't left enough information for him to act on.

The night before, Farkus had been hiding behind a tree until the FLIR picked up his thermal aura. Now he was nothing more than cold meat.

As he walked back to the crime scene, wiping his mouth on his sleeve, he heard Spivak communicating with Sheriff Reed on the radio.

"Yeah, we're ninety-nine percent sure it's him," Spivak said. "Norwood is doing his thing now . . .

"Yes, sir, we're doing a thorough job before we bag up the body and bring it down. The scene's taped off and photographed, but it's also deteriorating fast with this snow. It's a real cowboy crime scene at this point. There's already too much accumulation to find tracks or footprints . . ."

"Great," Spivak said before signing off.

He announced that Sheriff Reed was issuing a county-wide APB for Dallas Cates and two unknown males and an unknown female.

JOE BENT OVER to help Norwood and Deputy Steck roll the body into the body bag that Norwood had laid out on the ground. Disturbing a body was frowned upon, but when it was in the forest, it was necessary to get it out before more predation occurred or a bear or mountain lion dragged it away. Joe kept his eyes averted and did it by feel. Farkus's feet were stiff within his boots.

He heard Spivak shout from somewhere in the trees on the other side of the small clearing where the body had been found. The snow was falling too hard for Joe to see the undersheriff.

"Brass here," Spivak said, meaning shell casings. "Brass all over the place. This is where they ambushed him. Norwood, get over here. Let's get these casings bagged up before the snow covers them all."

"Sorry, guys," Norwood said as he stood up. He stripped two pairs of blue medical gloves from a box in his kit and tossed them to Joe and Steck. The body was half in and half out of the body bag. Entrails snaked from the body cavity across the snow. "Push all those guts inside the bag and zip it up."

"I'm gonna be sick," Steck said.

Joe chinned toward the woods behind him and said, "There's a place I know right back there in the trees . . ."

Spivak said to Steck, "Yeah, don't worry about the body. I've done this enough, I don't get sick anymore. Step aside and gather up that brass and any other evidence you can find."

Steck stood and left eagerly.

Spivak looked at Joe, then at the body. "I can handle this," he said.

"You sure?"

Spivak nodded. He seemed to be waiting for Joe to leave before he began the grisly work.

Joe nodded back. He was grateful.

But he thought it odd how eager Spivak seemed to be to dive in.

LATER THAT AFTERNOON, RANDALL LUTHI PRESSED HIS BACK against the southwest corner of the log house and stared straight ahead. The five-shot Savage .17 bolt-action rifle was pointed muzzle-down along his right leg.

Beyond a crude lean-to built of two-by-four framing with corrugated metal sheathing, the snow fell lightly on the treeless bench. Clumps of snow stuck to the tips of the sage, making it look remarkably like the blooming cotton fields of his youth in Hale County, Texas, and for a moment he was transported back there to Plainview, smack in the middle of the panhandle, which was smack in the middle of nowhere.

This was like the panhandle, he thought, in that it was in the middle of nowhere as well, but much farther north and much higher in elevation. And it was cold snow out there and not cotton.

Above the rolling sagebrush vista and beneath the heavy storm-cloud bank that had brought the snow was a thick blue band of mountains, their peaks obscured. The band of mountains was dark and it was damned cold up there, too, and probably snowing much harder.

If he never went back into those mountains again, it was fine with him. He'd discovered that mountains only looked good from a distance or in a painting. When a man was actually in them, it was elemental and brutal and there were animals there who could eat him.

There was a reason why all the towns up here were on the flats.

People shouldn't live in the mountains, Randall Luthi had decided.

HE INCHED CLOSER to the corner of the house and slowly, slowly peered around it.

The small herd of pronghorn antelope were less than a hundred yards away, the closest they'd been all afternoon. Seven does and one nice buck. The buck lorded over his harem and steered them with twitches of his head, as if he were herding them in slow motion to Luthi.

Luthi had been observing them, watching them graze closer, for the past two hours. It had tested his patience, and he'd thought about raising the rifle and taking a long shot, but he didn't want to miss and spook them. He'd seen antelope run and they were damned fast. He'd heard they were the second-fastest mammal on earth and he believed it.

It was the buck he wanted, but he'd make do with a doe if that was the only good shot he'd get. He didn't care that much because he was hungry and he wanted fresh meat.

He knew that the .17 rifle he'd found inside the house in the gun case was made for varmint hunting, not big game. The bullet was smaller than a .22 round, but it shot flatter, faster, and was accurate at much greater range. If he placed the shot just right—right in the head—it should bring down a pronghorn.

To his dismay, the herd had pretty much stopped moving closer. The herd seemed to sense he was there, he thought. When the buck looked over in his direction, Luthi leaned back so his profile couldn't be seen on the side of the building.

THE FIRST IMPRESSION he'd had of the abandoned Cates compound when they drove in was that it had been built in a stupid location. Back in the panhandle, small ranches were near rivers or bodies of water and surrounded by oak trees for shade against the brutal sun.

Why Dallas's father chose to put up his house and outbuildings in the center of a saddle of rolling sagebrush hills without a single tree in sight seemed ridiculous. Especially when there were sharp draws bordered by mountain juniper and caragana bushes within sight on the sloping side of the foothills that marched toward the mountains themselves.

Why build a place so isolated, so exposed, so barren when he didn't have to? There was nothing to break the wind, and the sun would pound the roof and yard without any shade.

But after observing the small herd of antelope eat their way closer for hours, he understood. There was no way to sneak up on those pronghorns, no way to drive to them or cut them off, because they could look up and see everything for ten miles in each direction. Unlike wild turkeys and feral hogs that stayed in heavy brush for concealment back in Texas, these animals did the opposite. They wanted to be in the open, where nothing could approach them without them knowing about it.

Eldon Cates apparently thought the same way.

RANDALL LUTHI WAS FIVE-FOOT-SIX and wiry, with close-cropped ginger hair and a five-day growth of beard that was coming in pinker than he wanted. He had gray eyes, a long thin nose that ended in a point, and an upswept jawline that, to some people, made him look in profile like a weasel. That's what they'd called him behind his back in the Wyoming State Penitentiary—the Weasel—but never to his face.

The stupid Mexican who'd called him Weasel in that saloon in Rock Springs had found out that it wasn't a wise idea after all when Luthi had grabbed a beer bottle by the neck, broken it, and ground the jagged edges into the man's face, even after the Mexican went down. It took four men to pull Luthi off of him, but not before a bucket of blood had been spilled and the cops had been called.

The cops had searched his car and found the weed and the

guns intended for some motorcycle guys in Sacramento and that was that. Randall Luthi's first job as a courier had turned into a miserable failure. All because he'd stopped for a beer along I-80.

Luthi didn't regret disfiguring Pedro Moreno's face—the man was an illegal roofer, after all—but he did regret stopping in Rock Springs, because that meant that the Wyoming State Penitentiary would be his new home.

Rock Springs. He'd never go to that damned town ever again, that he knew. One of the prison tattoos on his back, done by an inmate he'd trusted not to screw it up or misspell the words, read FUCK ROCK SPRINGS.

HE KNEW IF HE MISSED the pronghorn, there would be a good chance they'd be eating two-year-old Dinty Moore stew and canned green beans from the pantry again.

He craved fresh red meat and a lot of it. Back in Texas, he used to order his steak medium or well-done. But after two and a half years in the penitentiary eating processed food products that were the wrong color, he lusted for bloody meat that was barely cooked rare. He used to have dreams of eating a sixteen-ounce T-bone, throwing the bone aside, and lapping the greasy red juice from the plate.

This was his chance.

LUTHI LEFT HIS POSITION and walked behind the house. He thought if he put the house between him and the antelope and used the natural slope of the yard to remain hidden that he could get a closer shot. If he couldn't see the animals, they couldn't see *him*. He hoped the antelope couldn't hear the tinny sound of digital gunshots from the PS2 inside—probably Grand Theft Auto again—and that they couldn't see him when he bent over and duckwalked.

Would they smell him? He didn't know. He really didn't know much about pronghorn antelope because those creatures didn't exist in the panhandle. Someone—probably Dallas—had told him the meat was mild-tasting, like goat meat. Not that Luthi had ever eaten goat meat, but it sounded like something he'd like to try.

He crawled across the neglected yard with the rifle in the crooks of his arms. When he got to the far edge, he thumbed the safety off the rifle and rose up slowly.

The antelope were walking away. They were nearly two hundred yards from him.

He cursed and raised the rifle. It had a scratched-up scope mounted on it and he settled the crosshairs on the top of the buck's head right between his pronged horns. At that moment, the buck stopped and turned his head, as if sensing what might be coming. But he didn't run.

Luthi took a breath and leaned into the synthetic stock of the rifle. Moisture beaded on the plastic and fogged the lenses of the scope a little. He started to squeeze the trigger—

And Rory Cross came out of the house with a *bang* of the screen door that instantly made the antelope streak away. Apparently, he was done playing Grand Theft Auto.

Luthi fired anyway and a sharp crack rang out that was quickly swallowed by the sagebrush prairie. He had no idea where the bullet had hit.

"What in the hell are you doing?" Cross laughed. He had a big laugh, because he was a big man.

Luthi stood red-faced, and pointed to the northeast, where the white orbs of antelope hindquarters could still be seen bobbing through the distance.

"What does it look like I'm doing? I'm trying to get us some food, and you scared them off by banging that door open."

Cross looked from Luthi to the retreating herd, then back to Luthi again.

"Dallas will bring us a bag of groceries from town anytime now. He said he knew a way to get in and get out without being spotted by anyone."

"How's he gonna do that?" Luthi asked.

"I don't know, but Dallas is Dallas."

Luthi knew what he meant. Dallas was capable of accomplishing things no other man could do. The more outlandish, the easier he made it look.

"Besides," Cross boomed, "antelope tastes like shit, anyway."

"How do you know that?"

"That's what I heard. They've got big adrenaline glands from running all the time. The adrenaline taints the meat and makes it taste like shit."

"That ain't what I heard."

"You heard wrong."

"Dallas told me they taste like goat."

"Goat?" Cross asked with another laugh. "*Goat?* Who wants to eat a goddamn goat?"

"I do. At least I'd like to try. That canned stew ain't any better than prison food. I thought we were done with that."

"I told you, Dallas is bringing real food. We'll have a feast tonight."

"What if he doesn't?" Luthi asked, thinking Rory Cross was big, all right, but a well-placed .17 round between his eyes would drop him like a dry bag of Quikrete.

Cross said, "If he doesn't, we'll eat stew. Now, why don't you come on inside? You heard him. Dallas asked us not to be out walking around, in case some local rube might see us and call the cops."

Dallas had warned them: the local cops were corrupt as hell and they'd had it in for every member of the Cates family since he could remember. The cops used to pull his brothers, Bull and Timber, over anytime they felt like it, just to try to get them to overreact. Unfortunately, his brothers were prone to overreaction.

They'd harassed Eldon when he was driving from septic tank to septic tank, Dallas said, and they'd even pulled over his mother, Brenda, claiming her taillight was out. It was, but any other citizen of Twelve Sleep County would have gotten a warning. Brenda received a ticket.

The family used to say the only thing they were guilty of was DWC—Driving While Cates.

And if the cops got a tip that someone was occupying the old Cates compound, they'd make up a reason to raid it. Dallas didn't want that. No one did.

Luthi sighed and started for the house. He said to Cross, "Just quit banging that screen door every time you go in or out."

"Yes, Mother."

"Fuck you, Rory," Luthi snapped.

Cross laughed again. "Hey, I found a bottle of cheap whiskey hidden behind some cleaning crap under the sink. Ancient Age, it's called. I'm thinking the old man was hiding it from Brenda and it's been under there the whole time since they departed this place."

Luthi stopped. "Whiskey?"

"Damn right."

"Why didn't you come out and say so?"

"I just did," Cross said, turning and going inside. He let the screen door bang behind him.

Luthi felt his hand grip the Savage tighter.

SINCE THEY'D RETURNED from the mountains, Luthi had wandered down the halls and into the rooms of the old Cates place. No one had been inside for almost two years.

The old fading family photos in the hallway were a revelation. Ninety percent of the shots were of Dallas from rodeos across the nation. Dallas riding saddle broncs and bulls, Dallas winning saddles and buckles, Dallas holding up his state wrestling championship ribbon while in high school. There were a few background images of Bull and Timber, and Eldon appeared only in full-family photos standing uncomfortably next to Brenda.

Luthi stared long and hard at the few shots of Brenda. She had short iron-gray hair that was coiled close to her squared-off face. In some shots, she wore rectangular metal glasses, but no lipstick or makeup. She was unexceptional, with wide hips in floral dresses. Her legs and ankles were thick, her feet stuffed into heavy brogans. There was nothing about her to suggest that she was like what Dallas had said about her—that she was a kind of genius—except her eyes. They glared at the camera with an intensity that suggested deep levels of awareness and anger just below the surface. But if one covered her eyes with their pointer finger, as Luthi had done by raising his hand and pressing it against the cheap glass of the photos, the woman was homely, overweight, and plain.

Five days before, Dallas had unlocked the front door and led them in and showed them around before assigning Luthi to Bull's bedroom and Rory to his parents' room. Luthi hung back while Dallas, in a barely controlled rage, pointed out how the county had let the house he'd grown up in go to shit.

The plumbing was wrecked, the landline phones didn't work, no one had bothered to empty the refrigerator or freezer, and the clothes hamper in the hallway was still full of dirty clothes that had been shredded by mice. Mouse excrement dotted the kitchen and bathroom floors, and feral cats had been sleeping on the living room couch, which stank of urine.

Not only that, some locals had broken in and spray-painted words on the walls, including CATESES CAN BURN LIKE THE TRASH THEY ARE and DIE IN HELL, BRENDA, and even HELTER SKELTER.

Dallas stood there, shaking, with balled fists, and said if he ever found out who had entered the house and done that, he'd tear them apart limb by limb.

Luthi felt Dallas's embarrassed rage deep inside him and empathized, thinking that if anyone had done this to his mother and daddy's home, he'd likely feel the same way. Except that he hated his daddy and had zero respect for his doormat mother, who'd looked the other way when Daddy beat him and locked him in that closet. Still, if he'd grown up with normal people, he could imagine feeling the sense of outrage and invasion Dallas did.

ON HIS FIRST DAY IN PRISON, Luthi had been assigned to cell 27-A with Rory Cross and an effeminate Canadian hipster named Jason Pinder from Jackson. To impress Luthi, as well as intimidate him, Rory had beaten Pinder to a pulp with his fists in the hallway after lunch and left the man bruised and bleeding. When the infirmary released Pinder, Rory pounded the man's head against the cinder-block walls inside the cell until he could no longer speak.

Rory made it clear he wasn't to be messed with and that he could protect Luthi from predators because he was the biggest and most vicious predator on the block. Although he'd intimated that Luthi would acquire additional insurance against others, that Luthi *could be his bitch*, Rory had never actually followed through on his threat after Dallas was assigned to their cell on a trumped-up Game and Fish Department violation.

That's when the three of them bonded: three white guys with persecuted blue-collar backgrounds in a sea of brown, red, and black. One of the trio, though, was a rodeo star who could do fifty perfect push-ups and a couple hundred sit-ups. COs even asked him to sign rodeo stills.

It was clear by the second day who the leader would be.

What a story he had to tell, and what a proposition he had to make them.

THE THREE OF THEM had been in the minimum-security block because they were doing short time and their release dates were staggered. Rory Cross was the first one out. As he'd promised, he hung around Rawlins to wait for the other two: Dallas, then Luthi, a week apart.

While he'd waited for them, Rory told them, he'd worked minimum-wage jobs at the Tractor Supply, at Walmart, and for a short time was a check-in clerk at a budget motel.

Rory had been in for aggravated assault and battery (6-2-502 in the Wyoming state statutes) on Lander police officers during a Fourth of July parade. Luthi had listened to lots of Rory's stories and had learned to discount the details of them by half for a more accurate representation.

Nevertheless, according to Rory, he'd grown up in Torrington on the eastern side of the state and had once been a promising defensive linebacker in high school. All the college scouts (which to Luthi meant one or two) were looking at him, until he stomped on the chests of two opposing players (Luthi thought one) with his cleats and kicked the victims repeatedly in the helmets long after the play was over. The assault was captured on video by the mother of one of the victims and posted on YouTube and immediately went viral and was viewed by millions (*thousands*) of viewers. Thus, Rory was expelled (*probably true*).

After four (*two and a half*) long years on a highway construction outfit, he'd driven to Fremont County to interview for a job on an exploration survey crew. Unfortunately, he'd arrived too late Friday night to talk to the crew chief. Saturday was the Fourth and after one or two (*nine*) beers at a bar, he'd decided to go out to watch the parade. When he'd stepped outside, he was immediately hit in the eye by a piece of hard candy thrown from a flatbed trailer of Girl Scouts.

Surprised and enraged because he thought he might be blind in his right eye—his rifle and pool-shooting eye—he found the Jolly Rancher on the sidewalk and threw it like a missile toward the offending Girl Scouts. The candy bounced off the forehead of a little blond girl and she lost her balance and fell off the trailer into the street. A couple of cops walking the parade route rushed to the little girl, and an outraged titter arose from those crowding the sidewalk. The girl turned out to only be bruised—"a little drama queen fraud in the making," Rory said—but the whole troop shrieked and pointed at him as the villain who had launched the projectile.

Rory had tried to explain to the two cops what had happened, that he was only acting in self-defense, that he might be blind in his right eye, when two additional town cops (*so, two total*) showed up and one of them jabbed him in the ribs with a stun gun. The fifty thousand volts (*ten thousand volts—still a lot*) made him "go off on them," sending three of four (*one of two*) of them to the Regional Hospital and landing him in the Fremont County Jail, and later, serving three to five years (*this was correct*) at the penitentiary in Rawlins.

Where he met Randall Luthi and Dallas Cates and protected them both from the gangs and hard-timers.

LUTHI DROPPED the .17 rifle on the couch and found Rory at the kitchen table with the bottle of Ancient Age in front of him. It was nearly half gone.

"Did you already drink all that?" he asked, plucking a plastic drinking glass off a stack of them and pulling out a chair.

"Naw. Eldon must have been working on it before he was killed."

Luthi poured three fingers. "Wish we had ice," he said.

Although Dallas had managed to get the backup generator in the garage going, because the county power had long been shut off, no one had thought to fill the ice trays in the freezer compartment of the refrigerator with water.

Rory said, "Maybe Dallas'll think to bring a bag."

"Yeah, maybe."

Luthi took a small sip and let it burn his tongue. It was hard getting used to the effects of alcohol again, as it had been the other night at the Stockman's Bar, but it was well worth the effort.

"Not very fine whiskey, is it?" he said to Rory.

"Cut it with a little water or 7-Up and it ain't so bad."

"I'll try that," he said, reaching for a warm can of 7-Up on the table.

He tried it again and winced. "Better than nothing, I guess. You heard anything from him?"

Rory chinned toward the cheap prepaid cell phone on the table. "Nope."

Dallas had purchased two at a convenience store—one for him and one for them—and loaded them with twenty-five dollars of credit.

"He said not to call him unless it was an emergency," Rory said. "I don't think a bag of ice is an emergency."

Luthi sipped at his glass until it was gone. Then he poured more whiskey and soft drink into it.

"Better on the second go," he said.

"Everything is," Rory agreed.

"What's that mean?"

"I was thinking about bitches."

"Oh."

THEY WERE ON THEIR THIRD DRINK when the phone lit up with a call. The number was unknown.

Luthi and Rory exchanged a glance, and Luthi finally reached for it and punched the talk button.

"Yello," he said, deepening his voice and trying to flatten out his Texas drawl.

"It's me," Dallas said. There was an edge to his voice and Luthi sat up straight.

"Is it him?" Rory asked.

Luthi nodded that it was.

"I've got two local yokels on my ass right now," Dallas said.

"They haven't turned their lights on, but they're coming up behind me."

"Where are you?"

"I'm on the Winchester Highway with the supplies, and I've got less than two miles before I turn off on the gravel."

"Can you lose them?"

Dallas said, "I'm not even gonna try. If I do, they've got a reason to take me down."

"Gotcha."

"Okay, here they come."

Luthi could hear a siren in the background, then two.

"I'm sure I won't be back tonight," Dallas said. His voice was calm. "You guys know what to do. Call the number that's programmed into the phone and tell 'em what happened. Then get the hell out of there."

Luthi looked across the table at Rory, who'd turned white. He'd obviously overheard what had been said.

"Don't know who might be listening so I won't say more," Dallas said. "You know where to go and what to do. They'll probably be out there later tonight, is my guess."

"We know what to do," Luthi said.

The sirens were so loud now he could barely hear Dallas speak, and he couldn't be sure if he'd been heard.

"It's that asshole Spivak," Dallas shouted. "He's telling me to pull over."

"Asshole," Rory repeated.

"Keep your phone on," Luthi said to Dallas. Then: "Did you get that?"

"Got it," Dallas said.

There was a muffled sound, but the phone was still active and receiving on the other end. Luthi searched for the speaker button, found it, turned it on, and placed the burner on the table between him and Rory.

They heard Dallas say, "What can I do for you, Deputy Bonehead?"

"It's Spivak. Keep your hands on the top of the wheel and don't move them."

"Of course. Is there some reason you pulled me over? I know I was under the speed limit and carefully obeying all the traffic laws."

"You know why I pulled you over, Cates. Now reach down with your right hand and turn off the truck—slowly. Then hand the keys to me."

"Can I ask—"

"Just fucking do it, and do it now."

"Yes, sir."

Luthi pressed his index finger to his lips to remind Rory to keep quiet. He placed his other index finger on the phone itself to mute the microphone, because he didn't trust Rory to be still.

A background hum, obviously the motor, went silent. Then a jingle of keys.

"Here you go, Officer."

"Now slowly step out of the car."

"You don't need to point that gun at me. I haven't done anything wrong and I'm cooperating with everything you ask."

"Get the fuck out of the car. Now."

"Let's just be calm and cool about this, sir. I'm taking my left hand off the wheel and reaching down to grab the door handle. My right hand is staying on the wheel."

"Who are you talking to?"

"Nobody."

A third voice said urgently, "He's got something on the seat next to him. *It might be a gun.*"

"It's a phone," Luthi mouthed.

"It's a fucking phone, you assholes," Rory growled. Luthi was glad he'd covered the mike.

There was a crash of glass and the sound of blows. Dallas grunted and said, "*It's a phone, it's a goddamned cell phone.* Why did you break my window out? Why are you hitting me?"

The connection went dead.

"THOSE PIGS," Rory said. "They picked him up for nothing at all, just like he said they would."

"They'll be out here for us next," Luthi said, shaken.

"I'll fucking kill them," Rory said.

"We need to stay calm and remember the plan. We need to wipe down this place and grab our go-bags and walk right on out of here before anybody comes."

"Wipe it down with what?"

"There's Windex and Clorox under the sink, right?"

Rory nodded.

"Every surface, he said. Don't forget the doorknobs and handles."

"It ain't right," Rory said as he pushed away from the table.

"You start," Luthi said. "I'll make the call."

———

HE ACCESSED the saved-numbers screen on the phone. There was only one, area code 307. A Wyoming number. There was no name associated with it.

With Rory frantically wiping down the counters in his peripheral vision, Luthi punched the number.

It rang a dozen times and didn't go to voicemail. He didn't know how long he should wait.

Finally: "Yes?"

It was a very soft female voice. That surprised him.

"This is Randall Luthi."

"I don't know anyone by that name." He could barely hear her. He guessed she was speaking so quietly for a reason.

She said, "Do you have a message?"

"Who am I calling?"

"It doesn't work that way. Do you have a message?"

He looked up at Rory, who was in the process of dutifully spraying the surface of the refrigerator with Windex. Rory offered no help.

"Yeah," Luthi said, "I guess I have a message. The cops grabbed Dallas Cates tonight. That's all I know."

"I'll pass it on," she said, and disconnected the call.

"Well, that was fucked up," he said aloud before pocketing the phone.

THEY THREW THEIR GEAR and guns into the back of the 2012 Polaris Ranger 500 side-by-side in the shed and climbed in.

Rory had remembered to pack the Ancient Age in his go-bag. Luthi didn't mind riding shotgun because he had very little experience driving an off-road utility vehicle.

In fact, he'd never even sat in one before Dallas showed it to them and did a run-through.

"You got the map?" Rory asked as he gunned the motor and blue smoke filled the shed.

Luthi smoothed the topo map across his knees and nodded.

The Polaris roared out of the shed and straight across the sagebrush flat where the pronghorn antelope had been grazing.

Rory drove fast and the machine bucked through the high brush. Luthi hung on and tried not to be thrown from the ATV when Rory made a sharp left turn.

The snow was barely sifting through the air and it was getting colder and darker by the minute. When they reached the top of the first rise, Rory slowed the vehicle to a stop so they could consult the map Dallas had marked for them.

"We're here, I think," Luthi said, pointing to the map. "We need to keep going west."

"Yeah," Rory said with sarcasm. "That's where the mountains are."

Luthi didn't want to go back up there.

He looked over his shoulder and was surprised how far they'd come. The Cates compound was a small dark disturbance in the sea of white.

"Uh-oh," he said. "Look."

Rory turned as well.

In the distance, flashing red and blue lights coursed down

the Winchester Highway. The lights slowed for the turnoff that would lead them to the Cateses' place.

"Nick of time," Rory said. Then: "Bunch of jackwads."

"Turn the ATV lights off. We don't want them to see us up here."

"Hell with that," Rory said, reaching for the shifter. "We'll be gone before those assholes even think to look up here."

They shot over the rim and plunged down the other side.

THAT NIGHT, IN A SHABBY TWO-BEDROOM RENTAL IN POWELL three blocks from the small campus of Northwest College, April Pickett sat at her desk and finished up a bowl of leftover chicken soup. She really tried to get interested in *Candide*, a novel by a Frenchman named Voltaire that had been assigned in her freshman English class. Even after reading the first five pages seven times over, she still couldn't get it. The prof said it was supposed to be funny. She had yet to even crack a smile.

Not all of the books she was forced to read were as awful. For example, Hemingway's *The Old Man and the Sea* was okay because it was about fishing. She thought maybe her dad would like it. But *Leaves of Grass* by Walt Whitman made her almost tremble with rage that she was spending hours with it when she could be doing something worthwhile like grooming her horse, throwing a rope, or hanging out with the other members of the rodeo team. Not that the guy didn't seem to love America—he did, and that was nice—but he did it in such a softheaded and exaggerated way that it put her off.

April was not a natural reader like her older sister, Sheridan, or her mom and dad, or even Lucy. There had always been better things to do with her time and she got bored easily. Plus, doing the same thing everyone else was doing rubbed her the wrong way. But to stay on the team, she had to do what she had to do to keep her grades up.

The only line she liked and remembered from Walt Whitman was "Resist much, obey little." She'd posted that line on her Facebook profile and thought that maybe it would make for a good tattoo.

It spoke to her. The rest of Walt Whitman she could take or leave.

IT HAD BEEN JOY BANNON'S IDEA, this community college thing, and like most of Joy's ideas it had turned out to be a good one.

Joy, like April, had worked long hours as a salesperson and stocker at Welton's Western Wear in Saddlestring. April had started there her junior year in high school and Joy had come later.

For a while, it was a great job. Welton's was the unofficial center of the cowboy universe in the county and April was its princess. She was able to meet rodeo cowboys when they came through to promote clothing lines they were associated with, and she was able to buy her own stylish clothing at forty percent off retail. April was knowledgeable and friendly and knew the latest fashions—Miss Me, Aura from the Women at Wrangler, Rock & Roll Cowgirl, Cruel Girl, Cowgirl Tuff—except if customers were asses. Then she'd tear them a new one.

It was at Welton's that she first met Dallas Cates. Before that, the closest she'd ever gotten to him was the life-size cardboard display of him wearing "Dallas Cates Endorsed" shirts and jeans.

He was older, good-looking, charming, and had a hint of menace about him to which April was immediately drawn. His reputation as a hound dog aside, he'd been nothing if not charming and polite to her. He'd offered her front-row tickets to the rodeo that evening, where he won the saddle bronc buckle, and he'd invited her out afterward and didn't try anything inappropriate. Not that she would have resisted much at the time.

He'd even made a point of saying that, before they went on a *real* date—she knew what that meant—he'd like to meet her parents, which surprised her.

It was the first time she'd seen her dad take such a hard line against anyone she liked. Sure, he'd greeted several boys with his stupid "I have a shotgun, a shovel, and ten acres of land" warning he always used, but with Dallas it was serious and personal.

He'd been right. She still regretted running away with Dallas, although the first few months on the circuit with him had been wildly adventurous and thrilling. She'd stayed with him in nice hotel rooms in big cities as well as in motels he shared with other cowboys.

But being with Dallas meant sharing him with rodeo

groupies—buckle bunnies—he seemed to have stashed in every state. She was supposed to take that in stride, but she didn't, and they had screaming fights that soon became the talk of the rodeo crowd.

Then he kicked her out of his truck on the side of the road.

And everything else happened.

WHEN APRIL FINALLY RETURNED to work, Joy was still there, but the allure of working at Welton's was gone. April found out that she'd forever be known as the girl who took off with Dallas Cates, and she could hear other employees and customers whispering about her and pointing her out.

April had not really hung out with Joy at school. Unlike April, Joy was a local ranch girl who was studious and not boy crazy. She was thinner and plainer than April, and didn't turn the heads of the cowboys when she walked by, even in her super-stylish Cruel Girl jeans. Her passion was horses.

The only person April knew who was as crazy about horses as Joy was her mother. Therefore, April had never been that interested in them.

Resist much, obey little.

On a late Saturday afternoon with no customers in the store, Joy had turned to April and said, "Look at us."

"What about us?"

Joy thrust her arms out to encompass the entire store. "We've been here a long time doing the same thing. Clothes and boots come and go. If we stay here we'll still be making minimum wage a year from now and doing exactly what we're doing now."

"So?"

"So is this what you want to do for the rest of your life? Sell clothes and boots?"

April shrugged, but she thought, *Of course not.*

Joy went around the counter and pulled up a website for college breakaway roping. April was intrigued.

She said, "I can ride okay, but I don't know anything about roping."

"That's the thing," Joy said. "Nobody does. But I've got an aunt who works at Northwest College in Powell. She told me that in order for the rodeo team to get funding, the college has to include a women's event, so they came up with this. It's better than barrel racing because you don't need to spend eighty thousand dollars on a horse, and anyone can do it. They're desperate to put a team of girls together, and right now they'll take anyone who's been around horses."

"Anybody?" April asked. "Even us?"

"That's what I hear from my aunt."

April looked at the photo of the current rodeo team posing with their coaches. "I might have had my fill of rodeo cowboys."

"Really?"

"Well . . ."

Joy had horses on her ranch. Her dad was willing to lease one to April if the two girls were serious about going to community college together.

IT HAD GONE WELL, April thought. She and Joy got along, and they'd recently placed third and fourth at the Casper College rodeo the week before, which was unusually high for rookies. April had surprised herself to discover she could throw a rope, and she liked the sport because it went easy on steers.

She liked the team because it gave her a solid base of operations in a new environment and she got to travel around the region. Not to mention, half the cowboys were in love with her, even though she'd given none of them the time of day. April had been to the big leagues, even though it was under regrettable circumstances. These poor boys had no idea.

She knew that one of the reasons she enjoyed Powell, college, and the rodeo team was that no one had ever expected her to go in that direction. Contrariness was fused into her nature. In the past, she'd shot down every suggestion of college her mother had made, because if she had taken the suggestion it would have seemed like it wasn't her idea. April was hardwired that way, and she knew it.

She also knew that her parents were thrilled that she'd applied to Northwest and received a rodeo scholarship. Despite that, she wasn't ready to quit. She knew they wouldn't have been shocked if she'd run off and become a carny or something like that. But her going to college—that was a shock to them.

They were waiting for the other shoe to drop. So was she.

But for now, there was no reason to quit.

JOY WAS EASY to get along with. She rarely had boys come to the house, and she was a good cook and a reasonable roommate. She didn't make demands or talk too much or play the drama queen.

She was also practical. It had been her idea to confine all

their alcohol drinking to the unused breakfast bar so that if someone like a rodeo coach suddenly showed up, they could sweep all of the cans and bottles into the strategically located trash with one move rather than running through the house gathering them up.

Except for the fact that Joy sometimes borrowed April's clothes without asking, they got along well. April chalked up Joy's annoying habit to the two of them having so many similar clothes and outfits, because they'd both bought nearly everything they owned at the same store: Welton's. That, and the fact that Joy was the only girl in her family, and she was used to everything belonging to her. April had endured two sisters and all the battles that entailed, so she was used to guarding her possessions and fighting for her territory.

Still, though, it miffed her when she was searching for something in her closet only to find out that Joy had already taken it.

But given the traumas she'd been through in her life, April was aware that borrowed clothing didn't really rank very high, as aggravating as it could be at times.

As if to remind herself of that fact, she'd been fuming about her missing rodeo team jacket when Lucy had called to say Dallas Cates was out of prison.

It was a day April knew would come but hadn't looked forward to.

She hadn't seen him since he kicked her out of his pickup, but for better or worse—mostly worse—he still occupied a place in her heart. They'd had fun for a while, and at the time she was sure she was in love with him. That was hard to let go of completely, despite what had happened later. He'd told her he loved her as well—probably along with twenty other girls, but it still meant something, and she'd believed he meant it at that moment. An hour later, who knows?

But she'd never actually said good-bye.

Dallas had made no attempt to contact her after he'd been convicted and sent to prison. She didn't know if he had access to a computer, but there hadn't been a single email or social media post. Not even a letter.

She didn't know if Dallas blamed her for what had happened to his family and him, or if he saw past it. But she knew he'd made threats against her dad and others in law enforcement.

These were things she thought a lot about but had been able to push off to the side as long as Dallas was in the penitentiary. Now that he was out, she'd have to confront them.

Would he try to see her again? And if he did, would he want her back or try to hurt her? Dallas was fully capable of both. Did he now consider her a traitorous extension of her father, the one who'd been responsible for taking down the Cates clan?

April hoped that with his toxic family mostly gone, and after a stint in jail, he might turn into a different person, but she wasn't sure it worked like that. Dallas had been unconditionally coddled and protected by his mother all his life. With her in prison, he'd be in a new world. How much of that old world remained inside of him?

Lucy had texted to tell her in order to make sure she was armed with the pepper spray their dad had given them all.

Sheridan's pepper spray was in her backpack, but April

thought: *To hell with that*. Next to the canister of spray was a 9mm semiauto she'd borrowed from one of the rodeo team cowboys.

SHE WAS ON PAGE SIX of *Candide* when she heard a key in the front door. Joy was involved with a campus Bible study group and attended their meeting once a week.

"I'm back," Joy said after she closed the door behind her.

"Hey there," April said.

"I brought back some little sandwiches from my meeting."

"Thanks, I'm okay. I had some soup."

"Ah."

April could hear Joy rattling around the kitchen when the doorbell rang.

"Got it," Joy called out.

A moment passed. April envisioned Joy peering out the peephole in the front door.

"Some chick who thinks it's still Halloween," Joy said. Then: "Did you order pizza?"

"No."

"Hmmm."

Joy unlocked the door and opened it.

"Trick or treat," a female voice sang out.

Joy said, "Hi. We didn't order pizza."

"Trick or treat."

"Seriously? Aren't you a little late for that?"

The female voice asked, "Are you April Pickett?"

April stopped reading. She didn't recognize the voice and was not expecting a visitor.

Joy said, "Why do you ask?"

The front door banged open and Joy screamed. There was a sudden flurry of thumps and footfalls.

April felt a bolt of electricity shoot through her and she flung herself out of her chair for her gun, but recalled that she'd left her backpack in the living room. Joy's scream ended so abruptly that April felt the hair prick up on the back of her scalp.

She ran out the bedroom door, into the hallway, and around the corner.

Joy was on her back on the floor, writhing. A figure in a dark hooded sweatshirt was on her knees, straddling her roommate, bending forward in concentration, and April couldn't see her face because of the hood.

They were struggling, and that's when April saw the knife blade plunged halfway into the side of Joy's neck. The stranger was leaning forward, trying to get leverage so she could push it in farther. Joy had both of her hands gripped around the arm of the attacker, trying to stop the progress of the knife. They were at a standstill, and all Joy had accomplished was to push back the sleeve of her assailant, revealing a slender white forearm.

On the floor beside them was an open pizza box and a cheap plastic Halloween mask of Casper the Friendly Ghost that must have come off during the attack.

April's backpack was in plain view on the table, but she'd have to somehow get by Joy and the attacker to get to it.

April yelled *"Stop it!"* and the person on top of Joy froze and looked up. She was a gaunt woman with a long face and thin lips that were pulled back to reveal a top row of small yellow teeth. The edge of the hood obscured most of her face, but April locked on to one pale green eye for a second before the woman looked away. That eye, and the glimpse of solid multicolored tattoos on her exposed arm all the way to the top of her wrist, burned into April's brain.

The woman flung herself back and the knife pulled out. Joy's hands went to the wound in her neck, and bright red blood pulsed out between her fingers.

April stepped on the cushion of their old recliner and vaulted over it toward the table and her backpack, but by the time she fished out the 9mm, the woman was gone through the open front door. April could hear footfalls down the sidewalk and into the street outside.

Rather than pursue her, she tossed the gun aside and knelt down over Joy. Her friend's eyes were wide open, and April had never seen her look so terrified.

Although she couldn't speak, Joy's eyes seemed to ask the questions *Why?* and *Who was she?*

April covered Joy's hands with one of her own to try to stop the bleeding. With her other hand, she plucked her cell phone out of her pocket. It was hard to dial 911 because her entire body was trembling.

"You'll be all right," she said to Joy. "You'll be all right . . ."

As the dispatcher picked up, April looked down to see that Joy was wearing her rodeo team jacket.

The one with *April* in script over the left breast.

EARLIER, JOE HAD FOLLOWED THE PURSUIT AND APPREHENSION of Dallas Cates over the radio in his pickup via the state-assisted law enforcement communication system known as SALECS. He was patrolling the breaklands at dusk, too far away to assist, and he wasn't wanted or needed there anyway.

Both Sheriff Reed and County Attorney Dulcie Schalk had made it clear—in a professional way—that they were fully in charge of the murder investigation, and after locating Farkus's body, Joe was no longer to be involved. Dulcie made the point that, because of the personal animus and history between Joe and the Cates family, it would be cleaner all around if Joe stepped aside. She was already laying the groundwork for a trial and she didn't want any unnecessary complications.

Joe was fine with that, and after giving his statement he'd spent the rest of the afternoon talking with happy elk hunters who were thrilled that the snow had caused the herds to move down from the high timber. He'd inspected a half-dozen carcasses hung in elk camps. All the hunters' licenses and permits checked out, and he issued no warnings or citations.

The hunters he spoke with were oblivious to the events that had occurred in the mountains around them the past two days, although several asked about the lost elk hunter. They were ethical sportsmen who'd obtained meat for the winter for their families.

Joe admired them and liked being around them.

Then a call came from dispatch that a cowboy at the Thunderhead Ranch had reported that he'd seen two men emerge from a white SUV on BLM land adjacent to the property and gun down three antelope out of a large herd. The cowboy said he watched through binoculars as the shooters rumbled across the sagebrush, threw the dead animals in the back of the vehicle, and drove away "like they just stole the truck."

Joe got to the location to find three steaming gut piles and no trace of the poaching ring.

AFTER HE'D RETURNED to the breaklands frustrated again, he'd overheard back-and-forth exchanges between dispatch, a reporting party, and Reed and Spivak.

The dispatcher said, "RP is a checkout employee at Valley Foods. She is on the line and says a man fitting the description of Dallas Cates is currently filling up a cart with groceries inside the store."

"Is he alone?" Spivak asked.

"Affirmative."

Which could mean he was by himself or that his buddies were sitting in their vehicle outside the store, Joe thought.

"How did the employee know we were looking for him?" Spivak asked.

"She heard about the APB. Oh, and she's my sister."

"Ten-four. On our way."

Joe was once again reminded how quickly news spread in his small town, especially if it involved a member of the Cates family.

Within a few minutes, Spivak reported that he'd located an unfamiliar older-model four-wheel-drive Dodge in the parking lot of the grocery store. He requested a license tag check.

Joe's interest perked when the dispatcher replied that the vehicle was registered to one Eldon Oscar Cates—Dallas's father—and that the tag on the license plate was expired. Plus, a taillight was out.

It made sense. No one had been at the Cates compound to pay for annual renewals for almost two years and to place the small metallic stickers on the plates. Dallas had come into town hoping no one would connect the old pickup to him.

Spivak requested backup, and Deputy Steck arrived on the scene. They held back, though, because they didn't want to confront Cates inside the store. They assumed he was armed, and they didn't want to risk the safety of other shoppers or store employees.

They parked their cruisers in a weedy field adjacent to the grocery store parking lot and waited until Dallas emerged, laden with grocery bags. Cates was alone. He placed the groceries in the back of the Dodge, looked around but apparently didn't see them, and then rolled out of town onto the state highway in the direction of his family home.

Spivak kept the Dodge in sight, but waited for authorization from Sheriff Reed to pull the man over.

"We've got eyes on the son of a bitch," Spivak reported.

"Be careful," Reed warned. "Assume he's armed and dangerous."

"Should we take him on the highway or at his place?"

"Highway. He's alone in his truck, and it's possible his buddies are waiting for him at the home. They're likely to be armed as well. There's no hurry to get them involved. We can move on them once we've got Cates in custody."

"Ten-four."

JOE PERCHED his pickup on an overlook and glassed the breaklands below through his spotting scope. The snow had stopped and the sky had cleared. The setting sun was transforming the muted beige-and-gray-sagebrush landscape into something dramatic and electric. Herds of pronghorn antelope that had been practically invisible under the overcast skies now stood out like beacons. Campfires and Coleman lanterns from hunting camps pierced through the deep shadows.

He couldn't concentrate on what he was seeing through his lenses. Not until the SALECS band crackled and Spivak said to

Sheriff Reed, "We have Dallas Cates in custody. He's cuffed and in the back of my rig."

Joe closed his eyes and breathed a sigh of relief.

Spivak said, "That's not all. I searched his vehicle and found a .223 Smith & Wesson M&P15 rifle under the seat. I sniffed it and it smells like it was recently fired. Plus, we can match up the slugs to those found in Farkus's body."

"You're *kidding*," Reed said.

"There's dried mud and pine needles on the truck mats that look a hell of a lot like what we traipsed through in the mountains this morning," Spivak said. "I can't tell for sure, but there are what looks like smears of blood on the inside door panels. Like someone with bloody gloves got in and shut the door."

"Good work, good work," Reed said. "But don't forget: the only thing we can charge him with right now is expired tags and that taillight."

Spivak sighed audibly.

"We've got to do everything right this time," Reed said. "Step by step. Don't touch anything else inside the vehicle. Lock up that truck and tape it off and don't move it until the tow truck shows up. That truck is a crime scene and I don't want anybody getting inside until we have it secure and the evidence techs can go over it."

"Yes, sir."

"Stay right there," Reed said. "I'll call up the rest of the department and we'll meet you there. I'll stop by Judge Hewitt's house on the way out and get a warrant signed to search the compound. We should be prepared to arrest his buddies and bring them all in."

"Ten-four."

"Hold tight and keep me posted," Reed said.

Joe could imagine the sheriff wheeling himself out through the door of his office and fitting on his Stetson. He could also imagine a sullen Dallas Cates slumped in the backseat of Spivak's vehicle.

Dallas had miscalculated, Joe thought. He should have fled the county or bunkered himself in where he couldn't be found.

But he'd apparently returned to his family home, and possibly brought his friends along with him.

Most criminals weren't very smart, Joe reminded himself. That's why they were criminals.

But Dallas Cates?

JOE TURNED on his headlights and rolled his pickup down from the perch to illuminate the old two-track road. He'd waited fifteen minutes since the exchange between Spivak and Reed. He guessed it was long enough for Reed to climb into his specially equipped van, stop at Judge Hewitt's house just minutes away to get the search warrant signed, and be en route on the state highway to meet up with Spivak and Steck.

A jackrabbit ran down the two-track ahead of the pickup. It feinted to the left, then the right, but kept going straight ahead.

Reed picked up on the first ring.

"We got him, Joe."

"I heard everything over the radio. How long can you hold him on expired tags?"

"Overnight at the most. I know it's weak, but it's a start."

"So he didn't struggle?"

"Spivak said he argued a little bit, but he was cooperative. I think he knows better than to try and resist."

Joe knew exactly what that meant. The deputies were likely prepared to take out Dallas Cates once and for all if given the slightest provocation. Cates would certainly know that.

"Has he said anything?"

"I haven't questioned him. He's in the back of Spivak's unit, so he's got time to stew. We won't formally interview him until we get him back to the shop. You heard about the rifle, right?"

"Yup."

"Those were .223 casings we found at the murder scene. If we can match them and the slugs with this rifle . . ."

Joe nodded to himself. "Was that the only weapon he had with him?"

"As far as I know. We haven't done a thorough search of the pickup or the compound yet. I'm sure we've also got him on multiple parole violations," Reed added. "He's not supposed to be in possession of firearms or liquor. The clerk at the store said he bought groceries and six bottles of the hard stuff. So, bottom line: we can hold him long enough to firm up the arrest. I'll talk to Dulcie, but I'd like to overcharge him to the point that he'll have trouble making bond. I don't want him out on the street."

Joe winced at the word *overcharge*. He was grateful they were having the conversation over their cell phones and not over the radio, where a civilian might hear it on the police band.

"What's the plan with his buddies?" Joe asked.

"We're going to surround the house and ask them to come out peacefully. We'll tell them we have Dallas in custody. When they come out, we'll put them in separate units and keep them that way."

"On what grounds?" Joe asked.

"Who are you—Dulcie?" Reed asked.

"Just curious."

"We'll come up with something," Reed said.

Which meant, Joe knew, that Reed was planning a high-risk interrogation squeeze play. No doubt it had been okayed by Dulcie, or Reed wouldn't be proceeding with it. In the squeeze play, the suspects would not have the opportunity to get their stories straight with one another before they underwent isolated individual preliminary interviews.

It was almost unfair. Even if the suspects were entirely innocent, which was doubtful, it was almost impossible for three human beings to tell exactly the same story about their whereabouts over the last few days with exactly the same detail. Joe knew this from his own family. After an event where all of the girls were present, like a trip to the county fair or an argument about something, all three would present different versions of what had happened, even though they all were in the same place at the same time.

It was the same with multiple-party interrogations. There would be errors and omissions. Reed's interrogators would compare notes and go back to each suspect with a list of discrepancies they'd found and hint that others in custody were telling either completely different versions of where they'd all been the day before or hint that the others were implicating the suspect in question.

The idea was to get one of the men in custody—or maybe all of them—to cut a deal and rat out their buddies. The understanding would be that the first man to point his finger at the others would be treated with the greatest leniency, or maybe even be given immunity in exchange for his testimony.

All of this needed to be done quickly and before Dallas and his friends demanded lawyers and stopped the questioning. There weren't three public defenders in Twelve Sleep County—only Duane Patterson—and it would take time to get out-of-county counsel to get that all sorted out. Time and confusion was on the side of law enforcement, which would continue to apply pressure in the form of detaining the men in separate cells and implying—but not outright saying—that their buddies were singing to the cops like birds.

It had the makings of a slam-dunk case.

And it made Joe uneasy.

"Mike, is this coming together as smoothly as it seems to be?"

There was a beat before Reed asked, "What are you asking, Joe?"

"I'm not sure."

"This is good police work, is what it is," Reed said defensively. "We might be able to put Dallas Cates away before he does any more damage to anyone in this county. You of all people should be happy about that."

"I didn't say I wasn't happy."

"Good. Now, I've got to go. I'm meeting my team before we go out to the Cates compound."

"Be careful and please let me know what you find," Joe said, and disconnected the call.

He felt bad for casting a pall over the proceedings, especially if Dallas Cates and his friends could be put on ice.

JOE KNEW SOMETHING WAS wrong when Marybeth came out of the house to greet him holding her cell phone away from her body as if it were a dead mouse she'd like to dispose of.

Before he could swing fully out of the truck, she said, "I just talked with April. She's at the hospital in Powell. The police are there with her. Someone stabbed Joy right in front of her in their rental house."

Joe's insides clenched. "Say again?"

"Joy answered the door tonight and she was attacked. April got a look at who did it, but the woman ran away."

"A woman? Is April on the phone?"

Marybeth said, "April, it's your dad," and handed Joe the phone.

"April, how is Joy?"

"She was alive when they brought her in," April said. Her voice was distant, as if she were in shock. "There was a lot of blood and she couldn't talk. She's in the ER now. Man, you know how I hate hospitals."

"Tell me what happened."

April recounted the attack, from when she heard the knock

on the door until she called 911 on her phone. Joe winced as she told it. He walked shoulder to shoulder with Marybeth from his pickup to inside the mudroom of their house. Marybeth kept close enough to him so that she could overhear what April was saying.

"You don't know who the attacker was?" Joe asked.

"No. If you're asking me if she was a student or not—I don't think so. I'm pretty sure I've never seen her before. She looked older."

"How old?"

"I don't know," April said, her voice breaking. "Maybe thirties . . ."

Marybeth cautioned Joe to go easy. He softened his tone and asked, "Could you identify her if you saw her again?"

"That's what the cops asked. I said maybe. She was wearing a hoodie, so I couldn't see her face very well. She was taller than me and really skinny. I definitely saw her teeth, and I saw ink on her arm."

"Ink?"

"Tattoos. Like she had full sleeves."

Joe and Marybeth exchanged looks. Wanda at the Stockman's had told Spivak the woman with Dallas Cates that night had worn a hoodie and had full-sleeve tattoos. But it made no sense.

"The cops are out looking for her," April said. "I don't think they've found her yet. I don't know whether she's driving or on foot. They asked me if I heard a car start up outside, but I didn't, I don't think. Joy was bleeding on the floor . . ."

"It's okay, April," Joe said. "You did the right thing. Maybe they'll grab her tonight in Powell. It isn't very big."

"I couldn't get to my gun in time," she said.

Joe said, "You've got a gun?"

"She's got a *gun*?" Marybeth echoed.

"When I found out about Dallas being out, I thought I needed more than pepper spray," April said defiantly. She was good at being defiant, Joe thought.

He felt his own cell phone vibrate in his pocket. He pulled it out. Reed.

"I've got to take another call," Joe said to April. "Here's your mother. You can explain the gun to her."

He handed Marybeth her phone and stepped away.

"IT LOOKS LIKE we got here too late," Reed said with obvious disappointment in his voice. "We didn't miss them by much, though. The lights were on and there are dirty dishes in the sink. The house is a mess. One of my deputies who's been out here before thinks there might be an ATV missing from the shed, but we can't confirm it."

"No idea where they could have gone?" Joe asked.

"Not yet, and it's too dark to pick up any tracks. We'll leave a couple of guys here and come back out first thing tomorrow. If they're in an ATV, they can't have gone too far. But if they're in an ATV, they could have gone *anywhere* in the mountains."

"Gotcha. Could you tell if there were two or three of them there?"

Reed said, "Hold on."

Joe could hear the sheriff cover the mouthpiece and ask his deputies if they'd been able to discern how many people had been occupying the house.

After some muffled back and forth, Reed came back on and sighed. "Bottom line is, we don't know. It looks like three beds have been slept in, but that could mean three or up to six, if they had sleepover partners. And who knows—maybe more. We'll check for prints on the surfaces and DNA in the sheets, but we won't know for a while."

Joe said, "I'm wondering about the woman Wanda told Spivak about. Any sign of a woman there?"

"Unknown at this point," Reed said. "Why do you ask?"

Joe gave him a thumbnail sketch of the attack in Powell.

"April thinks the attacker was going after her, and Joy answered the door in her coat."

"Jesus," Reed said. "Poor Joy. She's a great little girl, you know? Does Dan Bannon know?"

"I don't know," Joe said. "This all just happened."

"Jesus," Reed said again. Then: "Hang tight. I'm going to go ask Dallas if he knows where she is."

TEN MINUTES LATER, while Marybeth was still on her cell with April, Joe's phone lit up. Reed again.

"The son of a bitch says he has no clue about the woman in the bar with him," he said wearily. "Dallas said some gal tagged along with them the other night, but he never got her name. He says women kind of glom on to him all the time and that it's no big deal. Like he's a rock star or something. I think he's lying about knowing her, but I can't prove it yet."

Joe cursed to himself.

"I asked him where his friends went," Reed said. "He claims he has no idea about that, either. He says he's not their boss, and they might just have left of their own free will."

"Did he tell you who they were?"

"He was cagey. He said he met them in prison and they all got released about the same time. He claims he really doesn't know them all that well and he doesn't even know their real names, just their prison handles."

"Which are?"

"Brutus and the Weasel."

Joe took a deep breath and expelled it through his nostrils. Dallas knew that without his friends apprehended, he didn't need to talk.

"I asked him again," Reed said, "and he just shrugged and said maybe they went out trick-or-treating tonight."

"He said that? Those words? *Trick-or-treating?*" Joe said through clenched teeth.

Marybeth overheard and her eyes widened and she lowered her phone.

Joe could hear April's tinny voice say, "What was that about trick-or-treating?"

PART TWO

How easily murder is discovered!

—Shakespeare, *Titus Andronicus*

"THE PROSECUTION CALLS WYOMING GAME WARDEN JOE PICKETT,"
County Attorney Dulcie Schalk said the next day from her small
table in front of Justice of the Peace Tilden Mouton.

Joe sat in between Sheriff Reed and Deputy Spivak in the
first row behind her. They, like Joe, were in full uniform. Instead of benches in an actual courtroom, there were two rows of
dented folding chairs in a small closet-like room in the oldest
wing of the Twelve Sleep County Building.

He rose and shinnied out of the row of chairs and pushed
through the batwing doors toward the witness stand next to
Mouton's bench.

It was the preliminary hearing of Dallas Cates. The night
before, he'd been formally arrested and charged with the first-

degree murder of Dave Farkus. The purpose of the proceeding before the justice of the peace was to establish if there was probable cause to bind Cates over to Judge Hewitt's court for trial.

Mouton still ran the largest feed store in town, although he claimed to be retired from it, and he was still one of the biggest benefactors to the county itself when it came to sponsoring school teams, buying the prize 4-H steer and lamb every year at the county fair, and donating the labor of his employees as well as hundreds of sandbags during the last seasonal flood of the Twelve Sleep River in May. Joe knew from being in the tiny room before that JP Mouton would rubber-stamp whatever the prosecution brought before him. That's what he'd done for nearly twenty years in the part-time job.

Mouton enjoyed being one of the longest-serving justices of the peace in northern Wyoming, and he knew he could hold on to the job for as long as he could sit behind the bench. And it was understood that he could sit behind that bench as long as he didn't buck local law enforcement and stir them against him.

Mouton was short and bald and portly and he looked more and more like a cartoon caricature of a well-fed and slightly daft small businessman—which he was. As his belly grew each year, his belt line rose so that his buckle was just a few inches below his chest. His round face had gotten rounder. He wore glasses as thick as goggles, which he took off only to jab in the air while he made a point.

Joe could feel Dallas's eyes on him as he passed the defense table. Dallas wore an orange jumpsuit with TWELVE SLEEP COUNTY JAIL stenciled across the back. His wrists were bound together with manacles, as were his Croc-clad feet under the table. Next to Dallas was Duane Patterson, the state public defender. Patterson wore an ill-fitting gray suit that looked two sizes too big. He was reading over notes scribbled on a legal pad.

Patterson was a decent man with a very tough job who routinely found himself overmatched in the courtroom. Joe didn't envy him. Patterson had likely met Dallas for the first time that morning and was now charged with representing him in a murder trial. The deck was stacked against him and his client, which is how those in law enforcement preferred it.

In addition to Reed and Spivak, in the courtroom were two observers: Saddlestring *Roundup* editor T. Cletus Glatt, who sat in the first row across the aisle with a reporter's pad on his lap. His reading glasses were perched on the tip of his nose, and he had a disdainful pout on his mouth. In another row, an older woman clicked her knitting needles together while she made a blanket of some kind.

Joe knew that the woman was at every court hearing in the county—it was her hobby. Glatt rarely ventured out from behind his desk at the newspaper, where he spent his time taking potshots at state and local officials, teachers, law enforcement, and "the backwards local culture" of the small community he'd wound up in after being let go from ever-downsizing newspapers across the country. He was a bitter man. Joe had trouble identifying good qualities in him.

"Joe, hold up for a minute before you get sworn in," Mouton said. Joe paused at the swinging gate.

Mouton turned to Cates and spoke directly to him.

"I want to make sure you understand what's going on here today, Mr. Cates. This is a hearing to establish whether there is probable cause to hold you over for a felony trial in district court. The charges have been read by the prosecution and they've presented a copy of the information to Mr. Patterson. Your appointed counsel has indicated you plan to plead not guilty of all the charges. Is that correct?"

"You damned right," Cates said.

"There will be no cursing in my courtroom. So you're pleading not guilty?"

"I'm pleading not guilty."

"Okay then," Mouton said. "So, back to where we were. If probable cause is established here today, bail may or may not be set, or you may be released on your own recognizance until the felony trial. Do you understand all of that?"

Cates shrugged that he did.

"Speak up for the record, Mr. Cates."

"Yes, Your Honor. I understand that I'm being railroaded."

"That'll be enough of that, too," Mouton said. Then: "Joe, come on up now."

DULCIE WAS WEARING a bright red dress and she had her hair pulled back. Joe knew she wore red when she was out for blood. He assumed JP Mouton knew it too.

Dulcie was a relentless and well-organized prosecutor. She was known for not bringing a case to trial unless she was convinced she could win it, and that strategy had become a self-fulfilling prophecy. Her conviction rate was more than ninety-five percent. She was also a straight shooter, Joe knew. He'd learned not to even bring a case to her unless it was bulletproof. She didn't play political games or overreach. The only time she'd overcharged a defendant was when she'd piled on as many charges as ethically possible to send Dallas Cates to prison almost two years before, which had surprised Joe at the time. That's how badly she'd wanted him to go away.

Now here he was again.

Her method in a preliminary hearing was simple and devastating. She'd briskly state the prosecution's case, lay out a timeline of the crime, point out the accused, and ask that the defendant be bound over for trial. She'd call as few witnesses as possible to bolster her case, preferring a bare-bones construction.

Joe had expected that the first witness would be Wanda Stacy—but Wanda wasn't called. He wondered if Dulcie was concerned that the bartender wouldn't come across well or that she was uncooperative. He also knew Dulcie often held back testimony from witnesses she might be saving for the actual trial. Whatever the reason, Dulcie had opted to open the morning with Joe's testimony.

After he was sworn in, she slipped on a pair of fashionably mannish horn-rimmed glasses and looked over them at Joe on the stand. She asked him to state his name and occupation.

"I'm Joe Pickett, the game warden for the Saddlestring district. I'm badge number twenty."

"What does badge number twenty signify?"

"There are fifty game wardens in Wyoming. The warden with the most seniority has badge number one. I'm twentieth in seniority."

"So you've been around a while and you have a good deal of experience in your job," she asked.

"Yes," he said, thinking, *Maybe too much sometimes.*

She guided him through the day he was recruited to assist the Civil Air Patrol and the images he saw on the FLIR, then moved on to the next day and the discovery of Farkus's body. He answered as simply and honestly as he could.

"Thank you," she said, and sat down.

There was a long pause. Joe looked to Patterson, waiting for him to stand up or state that he had no questions.

Patterson, though, still had his head down studying his notes, as if he hadn't heard that Joe's testimony was over. Dallas stared at his attorney with an amused expression on his face, then turned his head and waggled his eyebrows at the JP as if to say, *Look at this guy.*

It was a reckless thing for a defendant charged with murder to do, Joe thought. As if Dallas wasn't taking the proceedings seriously. That was a red flag to Joe. He felt a twinge in his chest.

Then Patterson finally stood up and said good morning to Joe.

"Good morning," Joe responded.

"You weren't always badge number twenty were you?"

Joe sat back. He said, "No. As I stated, the number changes based on how long a game warden is on duty. So the badge number gets smaller the longer I stay on the job."

"That's not exactly what I was getting at," Patterson said, not meeting Joe's eyes. "Didn't you lose your badge number designation a few years ago due to insubordination?"

Joe felt his cheeks flush. "Yes."

"In fact, you were busted down to number forty-eight for a while, weren't you?"

"Yes."

"Objection, Your Honor," Dulcie said as she shot to her feet. "This is a preliminary hearing. This is no place to badger the witness."

"Sustained," Mouton said, taken aback. Then to Patterson, "What's wrong with you, Duane?"

Mouton wasn't the best at proper courtroom rhetoric, Joe thought. Nevertheless, he'd been surprised by Patterson's insinuation—even if it was true.

"Sorry, Your Honor," Patterson said.

"Good. Let's keep things civil."

In reaction, Dallas turned in his chair and looked around the courtroom with exaggerated wide eyes, as if he wanted a good look at everyone who was there to conspire against him.

"Mr. Pickett," Patterson said, "prior to going on the search-and-rescue operation for Dave Farkus, you had dealings with my client, didn't you?"

"Dealings?"

"You had an antagonistic relationship with him. Isn't that true?"

Joe could see where Patterson was headed. He said, "I arrested him for wanton destruction of game animals and he was convicted and sentenced to prison for the offense."

"But beyond that," Patterson said, "didn't you battle with his family?"

"Battle isn't the right word," Joe said.

In his peripheral vision, he saw Dulcie stand up.

"Is there a point to this line of questioning, Your Honor?" she asked Mouton. Joe couldn't recall Dulcie ever making an objection in a preliminary hearing before, much less two of them.

"Well, is there?" Mouton asked Patterson.

"There is, Your Honor. It's important here to establish that the witness was hostile to the defendant prior to the incident."

There it was, Joe thought. He looked over at the justice of the peace.

Mouton had a pained expression on his face, as if what Patterson had said was once again too unpleasant for his hearing room.

"Your Honor," Dulcie said, "this is silly. The witness was asked by the Civil Air Patrol to assist on a search-and-rescue operation. While he was cooperating with them, he saw unidentifiable images on a computer screen and he testified to that. He's helping us establish the premise of the case. He's not making allegations against the accused. How can that be considered hostile?"

"Good point," Mouton readily agreed. To Patterson, he said, "That's enough with that line of questioning, Duane. You're really pushing it with me, mister. Do you have anything else?"

Patterson looked down and his face flushed red. He turned slightly and made eye contact with Dallas, who once again had the half-smile on his face.

It was clear to Joe then that Dallas had put Patterson up to attacking him, and the public defender had reluctantly gone along with his client's wishes.

"Mr. Patterson?" Mouton prompted.

Patterson looked at his pad again. Dallas watched him and rolled his eyes.

To Joe, Patterson asked, "When you were watching the FLIR, could you positively identify the victim as David M. Farkus?"

"No. Not at the time."

"Could you positively identify the accused?"

"No."

"But you assumed both, correct?"

Dulcie stood up again, but before she could object, Joe shook his head and said, "We were searching for a missing hunter named Dave Farkus. We identified an individual on the FLIR in the vicinity of where Farkus was last seen. But no, I could not positively identify the individual as Farkus. And I don't believe the name Dallas Cates even came up that night."

Patterson looked up from his notes at Joe. There was another long beat.

He said, "No further questions."

Dallas shook his head and grinned, as if he couldn't believe what had just happened.

Mouton removed his glasses, pointed them at Dallas, and said, "The defendant shall refrain from acting like this proceeding is one big joke."

"Even if it is?" Dallas asked.

That got a chuckle from T. Cletus Glatt, and Mouton banged his gavel.

"The witness can step down," Mouton said to Joe.

On his way past the defense table, Joe looked hard at Dallas, trying to discern what he was up to. Dallas looked back briefly and smirked.

Dulcie said, "We call Undersheriff Lester Spivak."

DULCIE LED SPIVAK through the events of the day that they discovered Farkus's body, then through the preliminary forensics results.

Reed leaned over to Joe and whispered, "I didn't see *that* coming. Especially not from Patterson."

"It's not Patterson," Joe whispered back.

"Dallas is acting like this is all some kind of joke. Doesn't he know what he's facing?"

"He knows," Joe said. "He's smart. But he has something up his sleeve."

"I wonder what he's going to try and do to Spivak?"

Reed sat back and crossed his arms across his chest and shook his head.

Joe didn't get it. A preliminary hearing in front of Justice of the Peace Mouton wasn't the place to try to attack the prosecution's case unless it was unbelievably egregious, which it wasn't. Going after Joe's credibility on the stand was a waste of time and effort, unless Patterson had a strategy no one had thought of. Patterson wasn't known for his strategic abilities. Besides, he'd spent probably less than an hour with his client before the hearing.

No, Joe thought. Dallas had a strategy of his own.

JOE LEARNED from Spivak that the .223 casings found at the murder scene were manufactured by American Eagle, and that the crime scene techs had discovered a half-empty box of American Eagle fifty-five-grain .223 rounds under the seat of Dallas Cates's vehicle. The blood found on the floor mats, plus a smear of it on the driver's-side interior door handle, was determined to be A-positive, which matched Farkus's blood type.

Spivak explained that the rifle, cartridges, and blood samples had been sent to the state forensics laboratory in Cheyenne for further confirmation. Although several of the bullets had passed through Farkus's body and were therefore not recovered, three intact slugs were found by the coroner and had also been sent to the state lab. The slugs could be matched not only to the American Eagle ammunition but specifically to the rifling inside the barrel of the .223. The coroner said the slugs were found fairly shallow within the body and that, although mushroomed and misshapen, they were in good enough condition to identify.

The coroner also found dozens of pellets in Farkus's body—sizes BB and double-ought—indicating that he'd been hit with shotgun blasts from at least two other assailants.

The prosecution case was impressive, Joe thought. By the time Dallas went to trial, Dulcie should have conclusive DNA test results on the blood found in Dallas's vehicle, as well as forensics matches on the rifle and ammunition.

MOUTON RECESSED the hearing for lunch prior to the cross-examination of Deputy Spivak.

Joe retrieved his cell phone and holster from Stovepipe, an ancient retired rodeo cowboy who manned the metal detector in the lobby.

He was scrolling through his emails—another poaching report had been made in the county to the east, so the ring had struck again—when Dulcie patted him on the shoulder and indicated he should follow her down the hallway.

"Please close the door," she said.

Her office was spare. In addition to framed graduation and

law degree certificates, there were only a couple of personal photos of her parents, as well as a shot of her and Marybeth on horseback. The two of them rode together once a week in the winter and sometimes daily in the summer.

"I don't know what they're up to, but it's pissing me off," she said as she walked around her desk, kicked off her shoes, and sat down. "I'm going to tear Duane a new one for that crap he pulled in there."

Joe shrugged. "It was Dallas."

"But why?" she asked. "Is he just trying to antagonize you?"

"Probably."

"It's a good thing we kept you at arm's length during the investigation and the arrest, then," she said. "Otherwise I could see them trying to spin up some kind of conspiracy. But it won't work with Mouton. I don't even see why they're trying it out now. If I were them, I wouldn't show my hand, and wait until the trial."

He nodded.

She cursed while she pulled a plastic container from a small refrigerator and placed it in front of her. Dulcie ate at her desk nearly every day.

"I was wondering why you didn't call Wanda Stacy first," Joe asked.

Dulcie looked up sharply after she'd removed the lid from her salad. "You didn't know?" she asked.

"Know what?"

"Stacy is in the wind. She didn't show up for work last night and no one knows where she is."

"*What?*"

"Her car is gone and her rental house looks like it was packed up in a hurry. We've got feelers out for her with her parents in Lusk and friends we can find online, but no luck so far. Mike didn't tell you?"

"No."

"He probably thought you knew."

"I've had a lot going on," Joe said.

"That's right! Is April back home now?"

"She got here last night. She didn't like taking time off from school, though."

"I'll bet Marybeth feels relieved having her here after what happened."

"She does."

"No word on who attacked Joy Bannon?"

"Nope."

"How's she doing?"

"Still in intensive care, but the doctors are much more optimistic about a full recovery than they were. Her parents are with her, and they send Marybeth status reports every few hours. Joy's conscious and able to whisper."

"Has she answered any questions about what happened?"

"She didn't know the woman, either," Joe said.

Dulcie nudged the container of salad toward him. "Want some lunch?"

"Thanks. I'll go get a burger."

"That's what I thought you'd say." She smiled. "See you soon." Then: "I'll bet they go after Lester, too."

———

AFTER A DOUBLE CHEESEBURGER at the Burg-O-Pardner on the edge of town, Joe called the game warden in Campbell County as he drove back to the County Building.

Rick Ewig was young and earnest, just two years out of the law enforcement academy in Douglas, and he wasn't in a good mood.

"Another one, eh?" Joe asked.

"Yes, damn it. I got rousted out of bed this morning by the call. A ranch wife south of town said she was on a walk with her dog when she heard a shot and saw a white Suburban about a mile and a half away across their creek. She knew her husband hadn't given permission to anyone to hunt, so she called me direct.

"While she waited for me, she saw two guys throw a dead muley into the back of the Suburban and drive off. I missed them by twenty minutes."

"Buck or doe?" Joe asked.

"Doe, she thinks. She couldn't see any antlers."

It fit the pattern.

"Did she get a good look at the bad guys?"

"Not so she could identify them. Like I said, they were a mile and a half away from her."

"Plates?"

"She couldn't see them, either, but these guys have to be residents," Ewig said. "Either that, or they're rich enough to spend three and a half weeks out here shooting up everything they see and bypassing trophies."

Joe agreed with Ewig. The poachers seemed to be very familiar with the vast landscape of northern central Wyoming and its roads.

"I'm standing over the gut pile now," Ewig said. "No brass on the ground, as usual. But I may have a good partial tire impression up on a two-track where she said she saw them. I've got photos of it and I emailed it to the lab."

"Could you send that to me as well?"

"Sure thing."

"I think we need to get a list of every white Suburban in five counties," Joe said. "We can all work it until we narrow it down."

"I'll make that request. Man," Ewig said, "it's busy enough as it is trying to keep on top of all the openers without these damn outlaws in the mix."

"Yup."

"Oh, hey, I heard about your daughter's roommate . . ."

Joe filled him in until he parked in the lot outside the courtroom entrance and disconnected the call. It was 12:55 p.m. Justice of the Peace Mouton would resume the hearing promptly at 1:00.

JOE WAS MOUNTING THE STEPS when his phone chimed. He paused and opened up the photo of the tire track Ewig had sent. The tread was worn down. So they were looking for a Suburban with nearly bald tires.

He heard a deep burbling motor behind him and a squeal of brakes. Somebody was in a hurry.

He turned as he opened the door to see a gleaming bronze Hummer H2 with County 22 plates that read JUSTIS.

The passenger door opened and a pair of ostrich-skin cowboy boots swung out, followed by the lanky six-foot-four frame of Marcus Hand.

Hand looked just like he did on national cable news from his Jackson Hole in-home-studio residence: a mane of long silver hair, a craggy wide face with piercing blue eyes, huge hands like pie plates poking out from a leather-fringed buckskin jacket. He turned and retrieved his black flat-brimmed cowboy hat from inside the vehicle and fitted it on his head with a flourish that said, *Let's go to war!*

"Hello, Joe, I assume this is where the party is being held," he said. "My client awaits. Please hold the door."

Joe held it because he'd frozen in place, and not just because of the sudden appearance of the most infamous defense attorney in the state of Wyoming.

There was foremost the identity of the woman behind the wheel.

As Hand shouldered by him in the doorway, Joe said, "Tell me that's not—"

"Oh, but it is," Hand said. "And the new Mrs. Hand is an absolute menace behind the wheel. But I'm sure you knew that."

Joe stood there with the door and his mouth open as he glimpsed the delicate profile of the driver as she roared away.

His mother-in-law, Missy, also known as Missy Vankueren Longbrake Alden, and now apparently *Hand* . . . was back in town.

Joe felt like the air had been crushed from his lungs. He scrambled for his phone to call Marybeth at the library.

LATER, AS THE SUN SET AND THE INTENSE DYING LIGHT THROUGH the trees created orange jail bars across the grass, Randall Luthi and Rory Cross stood outside the cabin with a six-inch hunting knife to compete for who would do Wanda Stacy first.

"You sure you want to do this?" Cross asked Luthi in a way that was more challenge than concern. "I grew up playing mumbley-peg."

"We called it 'mumblety-peg,'" Luthi said. "With a *t*. Mumble-*tee* peg. That's the correct way to say it."

"That's a bullshit hillbilly way of saying it."

"Whatever."

"Either way, I'm going to win."

"You've got an advantage," Luthi said sourly to Cross. "Your legs are longer."

"That don't make no difference. It ain't an advantage at all. Now, who wants to throw first?"

"You've got the knife."

"Then I'll start."

They faced each other with their boots spread out as far as each could muster. Cross had shrunk a full two feet of height.

"First guy to chicken out loses," Cross said. "And you lose if you cut the other guy."

He grasped the point of the knife, cocked it over his right shoulder, and threw it down between Luthi's feet. The blade flashed with sunlight and it stuck about thirteen inches from Luthi's left boot.

Luthi sighed and moved his left foot in until it touched the knife and kept his right foot set, thus making the target area more narrow for Cross's next throw. Then he bent over and pulled the knife out of the soil by the handle.

"Don't hit me in the nuts," Cross said. "If you hit me in the nuts, I can't do her properly. Not to mention, I'll have to crush your head like a melon."

"Ha ha," Luthi said. He liked to throw by grasping the butt of the knife handle instead of the point. His hand flashed and the blade stuck in the grass squarely between Cross's boots.

"Damn, that was a good shot," Cross grumbled. He slid his right foot across the grass until it was next to the knife.

"Do we have to use such a heavy knife?" Luthi asked. "I mean, we used to play this with a pocketknife. If I get stuck with this thing, it might take off a couple of toes."

"You can't change blades once the game starts," Cross said. "Those are the rules."

"You're making up the rules as you go along," Luthi complained.

Cross waggled his eyebrows and grinned. He had a cruel grin. Luthi noticed how Cross's eyes lit up when he was hurting someone or doing something dangerous.

Cross flipped the knife and it turned over in the air and stuck six inches from Luthi's right boot.

"You don't have to throw it that hard, you know."

"You throw it your way and I'll throw it mine," Cross said.

Luthi bent over to pull out the blade. His fingers felt stiff and his breathing was getting short.

THE OLD HUNTING CABIN had been exactly where Dallas had told them it would be: through a narrow slot of a vertical striated granite upthrust three-quarters up the face of a mountain. They'd cleared the slot of brush and branches in the dark and there was barely enough space to roll the ATV through it.

Past the slot was a natural bowl surrounded by rock walls. The ancient log hunting cabin was backed into the north wall and built around its variations. In fact, once they got inside, they saw that the back of the cabin literally *was* the rock wall. Someone— Dallas's dad, grandfather, or great-uncle—had custom-cut each log so it fit tight when butted against the granite.

The location was remote and not near any road either of them could see. There was barely a cell phone signal and it faded in and out.

Cross was a decent mechanic and got the old gasoline-powered generator going the morning after they arrived. The machine belched blue smoke and banged away like rocks in a tumble dryer, so they used it sparingly and mainly to charge the phone.

That was one thing Dallas had been adamant about: keep the phone charged and handy for an incoming call with further instructions. And don't use it to call anyone except for the single number programmed into the favorites list.

The Cates clan kept the cabin well-stocked. There was plenty of canned and freeze-dried food, gasoline, lantern fuel, liquor, and ammunition. The old four-wheel-drive Willys Jeep that Dallas had told them about was where it should be: hidden under a tarp within a covered alcove of spruce. The battery was dead, but they charged it up at the cabin and the Jeep started.

To Luthi, the whole setup recalled the methods of backcountry moonshiners from his youth. They also had remote hideouts, caches of supplies, and hidden getaway cars. Big-game poachers like the Cateses and the moonshiners back in Texas had a lot in common, he guessed.

Rural outlaws apparently thought alike.

CROSS DREW THE KNIFE BACK and flipped it down. The blade penetrated half its length into the ground two inches from Luthi's right instep.

"Shit," Cross said. "That was a bad throw."

Luthi nodded. "It was."

He shinnied his right foot over until it touched the hunting knife. There was still about twenty-two inches of space remaining between his boots—a big target. There was only ten inches between Cross's feet.

Luthi knew he had the advantage. But he was concerned about how erratically Cross threw the knife. The big man threw it with force and didn't seem to know where it would land.

Was he doing it on purpose? Luthi wondered. Was the idea to make two bad sticks in a row—which he had—to put enough doubt in Luthi's mind so that he'd quit the game before he got cut?

Luthi bent over and pulled the knife out of the ground. He glanced over his shoulder at the cabin, which was now bathed in shadow.

She was in there. She had no idea what was going on outside: that she was the prize.

"It's been a while since I've been with a woman," Luthi said.

"What do you mean?" Cross asked.

"What in the hell do you *think* I mean?"

Then Cross got it, and a slow smile spread across his face. He said, "When I said we'd play mumbley-peg to see who got to do her, you thought I meant *do* her."

Luthi shook his head, confused. Then *he* got it.

"Shit, really?"

"Those were the instructions."

"Man, that really sucks."

"Yeah," Cross said, but his eyes didn't mean it. "That was the word from on high."

"I thought when you said *do her . . .*"

"Yeah, I know what you thought now. Maybe we could and just not tell anyone."

"I like that idea."

"Me too," Cross said. "So now we're playing for real stakes. The winner gets to nail her first and the loser gets to pull the trigger."

"Deal," Luthi said. He didn't want to lose. He'd never killed a woman before, although he'd come close a couple of times.

Luthi drew back and buried the knife to the hilt squarely between Cross's feet. Once again, he'd halved the target area. Cross sighed and looked skyward, then slid his left boot in until it rested against the knife.

Now it was Cross's turn to get nervous and maybe quit.

He paused and squinted. Luthi looked down. Cross would no doubt want to make his stick in the center of the distance between his feet, if he could, in order to prolong the game.

"Ready?" Cross asked.

Luthi took a deep breath, closed his eyes, and looked away.

EARLY THAT MORNING, they'd waited in the alley behind the Stockman's Bar for Wanda Stacy to finish her shift. Cross had parked the Willys Jeep a half block away behind a souvenir shop, where they could clearly see Wanda's rusty 1999 Toyota Land Cruiser in an EMPLOYEES ONLY—ALL OTHERS WILL BE TOWED space directly behind the building. There was room for her Toyota and Buck Timberman's ancient GMC pickup right next to her car.

They assumed she'd close the place down prior to the official 2:00 a.m. curfew, so they had to stay awake and ready from midnight on. When the back door opened at 12:15, Luthi reached for his door handle, only to realize that the face peering out belonged not to Wanda but to an old drunk with a long silver beard.

The drunk stumbled out the door, threw up on his shoes, and staggered away down the alley.

"False alarm," Cross said. "Just some old guy stepping out on his bar tab." Then he closed his eyes and went to sleep, leaving Luthi to keep watch.

Buck Timberman came out the door fifteen minutes later. He stood in the threshold and stretched his arms straight up, then yawned. It took him a long time to shuffle to his pickup and drive away.

She came out at 1:20, and Luthi almost missed her. She'd shut out all the lights before she opened the door, so he didn't see her profile in the doorway. She was just suddenly outside.

As she turned to lock the door with a key, Luthi nudged Cross awake.

"There she is," he whispered.

The Jeep was so old that it had no interior dome light to come on when they simultaneously opened their doors. Cross unsheathed his hunting knife and held it in his right hand. Luthi had the 9mm Hi-Point pistol he'd found stashed in a drawer in the hunting cabin. It was a cheap semiauto, but it was serviceable.

Their boots thumped across the gravel and Wanda saw them coming just as she turned toward her car after locking the bar's door.

"Stay the fuck away from me," she hissed as her right hand plunged into the side of the heavy purse that hung from her left shoulder.

"Gun," Luthi called out.

They swarmed her and tackled her before she could pull her weapon out of the secret pocket of her concealed-carry purse.

On the ground, she took a deep breath to scream, and Cross hit her hard enough in the jaw to knock her out. Luthi felt her go limp in his arms.

"Stay here," Cross said, untangling himself from her limbs. "I'll go get the Jeep."

They trussed her wrists and ankles with silver duct tape, and Cross did three rotations of the tape over her mouth and around her neck. He did it with glee, and afterward Luthi had to pull the edge of the tape down and tuck it under her nostrils so she could get air.

He found the keys to the Land Cruiser in her purse along with a Taurus .380 pocket pistol that he stuffed in his back pocket.

In Stacy's Land Cruiser, he followed Cross to her apartment building just three blocks away. They left her unconscious on the floor of the Jeep while they mounted the stairs to 2B. Inside, they quietly filled a big duffel bag with clothes from her closet and drawers, plus items from her bathroom like tampons and hair products—things she would likely take with her if she hit the road in a hurry.

En route to the mountains, they stopped long enough near the dam of a reservoir for Luthi to roll the Toyota down the embankment into the water, where it vanished in a hiss of steam and bubbles.

Then he climbed into the Jeep and they went off-road with Cross behind the wheel. Finding the old hunting cabin again was much harder than the first night, and they spent hours lost and cursing before they finally located it at dawn.

They dragged Wanda into the cabin and dumped her on the floor in the corner before collapsing fully clothed into separate iron-framed single beds.

Kidnapping, Luthi thought, was *exhausting*.

IN THE FIRST FEW SECONDS after the knife went through his left foot and pinned it to the ground, Luthi felt nothing but icy cold. But when he opened his eyes and looked down and saw the shaft of the knife sticking out of the top of his boot, there was a lightning strike of searing pain that shot up his leg into his groin.

"*You stuck me right through the top of my foot*," Luthi said through gritted teeth.

"Sorry," Cross said in a faux little-boy voice.

"Jesus, it hurts."

"I'll pull it out," Cross said, stepping forward and starting to bend over.

"No! *Don't fucking touch it!*"

"Okay, okay," Cross said, raising his hands palms out and backing away. "I said I was sorry."

"You did it on purpose," Luthi said. He blinked back tears as he lowered down to his right knee.

"Why would I do that?" Cross asked.

"Because you're an evil fucking bastard *and you wanted to!*" Luthi bellowed.

"Just calm down."

"There's a knife in my foot."

"I can see that," Cross said. Luthi caught something in his tone, and when he looked up, he could see that Cross was fighting back a laugh.

"I'll pull this out and cut your fucking throat with it."

"You'd have to chase me down to do that. Running might be hard at first," Cross said. He ended it with a chuckle.

Luthi gripped the handle of the knife with both hands, looked away, pulled it out, and bellowed. It had hurt worse coming out than going in and had likely cut more of his foot.

His boot was now black with blood, which burbled out of the knife slit on the top of the leather.

"I guess you win, though," Cross said. "There's that."

Luthi raised his face to the sky and yelled again. It helped.

"I saw a first-aid kit in the cabin," Cross said. "Do you want me to help you get in there, or do you want me to go bring it out here?"

"Don't touch me. Don't help me," Luthi hissed as he pointed the bloody knife blade at Cross.

"Fine. Be that way."

Luthi grunted as he got to his feet. The pain now pulsed with every heartbeat.

"Look at it this way," Cross said, "you can do her first."

"I hurt too bad. I can hardly *walk*."

"That wouldn't stop a true stickman," Cross said with a laugh.

Luthi wished he had the 9mm in his waistband so he could pull it and shoot Cross in the face, but he'd left it in the Jeep.

The only way he could walk to the cabin was with an exaggerated limp, because he could put almost no weight on his left foot. Tears still brimmed in his eyes.

He lurched through the front door and saw the shards of silver duct tape on the dirt floor. The window on the other side of the cabin had been pushed out.

"*Goddamn it,*" he cried out to Cross. "She's gone!"

TWENTY-EIGHT MILES AWAY, IN A SMALL HOUSE ON BIGHORN
Road, Dulcie Schalk and Marybeth Pickett recounted the day
and drank wine on the couch in the living room. April and Lucy
sat at the kitchen table and looked on. Two pizza boxes yawned
open on the counter, and Joe removed a slice of pepperoni and
chewed a bite while he poured bourbon over ice in a glass. It was
his second drink in less than an hour.

April looked over. "Can I have one of those?"

"No."

Lucy rolled her eyes and said, "Is this how it works once
you become an adult? You try to solve all your problems with
alcohol?"

"Pretty much, yeah," April said with a shrug.

Joe smiled to himself and poured her a light one.

"My God," Lucy said in mock horror when he placed it in front of her sister.

"I prefer mine with Coke," April said.

"That ruins two good drinks," Joe said, which actually made April grin. He looked over to see Marybeth giving him a *Just that one* look and he nodded back.

"I'd like one, too," Lucy said.

"No way."

Dulcie's voice from the living room began to rise in volume as she described the scene in the courtroom that afternoon to Marybeth.

JOE HAD STILL BEEN STUNNED by the figure behind the wheel of the Hummer as he followed Marcus Hand through the lobby and into the tiny courtroom. So stunned that he'd walked through the metal detector without handing over his cell phone and gun belt and hadn't realized what he'd done until he was through it.

When no alarm sounded, he stopped, turned, and looked quizzically at Stovepipe.

"Crap," Stovepipe said. "I forgot to turn it on again." Then he shooed Joe on. "I'll catch you next time. Just don't shoot nobody."

Joe nodded and went in and reclaimed the folding chair next to Sheriff Reed. Spivak was already on the witness stand. If he were to shoot someone, he thought, he wasn't sure whether it should be Dallas or his mother-in-law.

"You okay?" Reed whispered when he saw Joe's face.

"Nope."

Before he could explain, Hand strode through the doors, placed a fatherly hand on Dallas's shoulder, and faced Justice of the Peace Mouton.

"Your Honor, my name is Marcus Hand."

His voice boomed through the small room.

"I know who you are," Mouton said sourly.

"My client sits shackled before you both literally and figuratively. His hands and feet are shackled to a steel chair, and his freedom has been shackled by inept and disinterested counsel up until now. Your Honor, my client faces the very real and tragic possibility of his liberty being taken away from him, and we've not yet consulted."

Dallas turned his head and beamed up at his lawyer.

So *this* is what he'd had up his sleeve all along, Joe concluded.

To Duane Patterson, whom he'd just insulted, Hand said, "Your services are no longer needed here, sir. Scat. Beat it. *Scram.*"

Joe had never actually heard someone outside a cartoon say the word "scram" out loud. The word seemed to hang there as Patterson dropped his legal pad into his briefcase and rose. As he exited the room shaking his head, he didn't acknowledge either Dallas or Hand.

Mouton said, "Since you're in my courtroom and not on television, I can't change the channel, I guess."

Hand laughed with feigned appreciation at the remark. "Your Honor, given the fact that I've just walked into your"—he hesitated and looked around, as if he'd just found himself in an out-door privy—"*courtroom* after a long and desperate journey from Jackson Hole and this is the first opportunity I've had to enter these august chambers, I would respectfully ask that a delay be granted so I can meet with my client and provide him with the very best possible legal representation that a country lawyer like myself can provide."

At that, Reed leaned over to Joe. "He has two rates, I hear. Fifteen hundred per hour for 'innocent Wyomingites' and two grand per hour for 'out-of-staters,' as he calls them."

Joe nodded. He knew it was true, because Hand had defended Missy several years ago when she was accused of being behind the murder of Bud Longbrake, her fifth husband. Bud's body had been discovered chained to the spinning blade of a wind turbine. She was found innocent of the charges, even though she was guilty. Despite the outcome, she had still complained bitterly about Hand's bill at the time.

Apparently, Joe thought, she'd made up with him. Or, more in keeping with Missy's modus operandi, she'd discarded her most recent man in order to marry the money she'd spent. That, and to have one of the most successful trial lawyers in the nation on the next pillow in case she needed him.

"You want to delay these proceedings?" Mouton asked, red-faced.

"It's only fair, Your Honor," Hand said. "My client deserves—"

"Your client deserves *nothing*," Mouton interrupted. "He and his white-trash family have been a stain on this county since as long as I can remember."

Joe glanced over at Dulcie. She was mortified by Mouton's statement. Joe was, too. He looked over to see Cletus Glatt ferociously scribbling *Your client deserves nothing* into his notebook.

Hand said, "A more prejudicial statement has rarely if ever been uttered in a court of law, and certainly not by a justice of the peace. If that's how you feel, Your Honor, then the only way to proceed is to immediately recuse yourself and we can reschedule this hearing before a judge who has not already decided the outcome."

Joe closed his eyes and sighed.

He didn't open them when Mouton sputtered, "I've had enough with both of you. I'm hereby remanding Mr. Cates to stand trial for first-degree murder before District Court Judge Hewitt. Bail is set at one and a half million dollars."

"That's an outrageous amount," Hand thundered. "Surely you'll reconsider and release my client on his own recognizance— he is extremely well-known in this county as a professional rodeo champion."

"That's the problem," Mouton said.

"I object!" Hand thundered. "This is insane. A million and a half for a young unemployed ex–rodeo champion?"

Mouton looked up. His face was red. "If he can afford you, he can afford that bail amount."

He turned to Dulcie and said, "Surely as an officer of the court, you agree with me."

She slumped over her desk and put her head in her hands.

Mouton pointed directly at Hand and said, "I'd suggest you stop objecting to everything and get ready to earn your outrageous fee. Judge Hewitt doesn't dally. He's the fastest judge in the West when it comes to scheduling murder trials."

"But I'll need sufficient time to present a proper defense," Hand pleaded.

"That's not my problem," Mouton said with finality.

"I JUST PUT MY HEAD in my hands," Dulcie told Marybeth. "I didn't know what to say, because Marcus Hand was right."

Marybeth took a sip and shook her head. "I don't get it. How can Dallas Cates afford to hire Marcus Hand?"

"I was wondering the same thing," Dulcie said as she reached for the bottle wedged into the cushion between them to refill her glass. Joe knew it was their second bottle already, which was out of character for both of them. Lucy was right.

"Joe, how much does a rodeo champion make?" Marybeth asked.

"Not much, really," Joe said. "It isn't like these guys are NBA players or something. Most of them win just enough to keep themselves on the road. They pay for their own travel, entrance fees, medical bills—all of that."

Joe knew quite a few men—and a few women—who had rodeoed. None of them banked enough of their winnings for it to last long. They reminded him of a quote he'd heard years before: *Behind every successful rancher is a wife who works in town.*

Lucy tapped on her phone and said, "Last year, the top cowboy won about three hundred thousand dollars. But number fifty in earnings made seventeen thousand."

"Dallas was a champion for three years in a row," April said. "I know he was making about a quarter of a million a year, because he told that to anybody who would listen to him. Plus, he had endorsements for jeans and shirts, stuff like that."

"That's a lot," Lucy said.

"Not when you spend money like it's going out of style," April responded. "He always had the newest truck, the best trailer. He always popped for the highest-priced rooms to stay in."

She smiled ruefully and said, "Dallas was never generous like the other cowboys. Those guys gave each other the shirts off their backs, and they helped each other out when they could. Not Dallas. He spent money on himself alone. I always hated that, even though I kind of benefitted for a while there when I was with him."

"Three hundred thousand tops, maybe," Dulcie said. "Minus travel, taxes, and all the overhead. So maybe a hundred thousand. And that was two years ago. He didn't make any income in prison. So it's still not enough to retain Marcus Hand."

"Maybe Hand is offering his services pro bono?" Marybeth suggested.

Dulcie barked a laugh and Marybeth joined in.

"Maybe the Cateses had a secret bank account or something?" Marybeth speculated.

Dulcie shrugged. "I don't know, but I doubt it. Either way, that's the least of my worries now. Not only am I up against Hand and his team, but Judge Hewitt will likely schedule the arraignment within a couple of weeks to accommodate his hunting schedule. Hand complained about that, but I have the same problem: not enough time to prepare."

"And I just can't wait until Cletus Glatt writes up the hearing for the paper. I'm up for reelection next year and Glatt needs to sell papers, so I can see him showing me in the worst possible light."

"Glatt was there?" Marybeth asked.

"Yes. And he looked like he was really enjoying himself. Now he'll get to make his points about our backward justice system and the good old boy network that runs the county. What really makes me mad is that he won't be wrong this time."

"What got into Mouton, anyhow?" Marybeth asked.

"I'm not sure, but I think Marcus Hand has a way of bringing that out in people," Dulcie said.

"And then there's the elephant in the room," Lucy added from the table.

AS SHE SAID IT, the grille of the elephant's Hummer H2 burbled up against the outside gate of the front lawn.

"There she is," Marybeth said.

April and Lucy locked eyes. Joe reached again for the bottle of bourbon.

Marybeth addressed April, Lucy, and Joe. "I'm going to listen to what she has to say. I'll be civil and listen and then send her on her way. After all, she's my mother and your grandmother."

"She's the devil," April said.

"I should go," Dulcie said, grasping the arm of the couch to propel herself up. "I've probably had a little too much wine to keep myself contained around the opposing counsel's wife."

"You're going nowhere," Marybeth said with steel in her voice.

Dulcie sat back and looked uncomfortably from Marybeth to Joe.

"After I shoot her, I'll turn myself in to you," he said to Dulcie.

"That's really not funny, Joe," Marybeth said.

THERE WAS A LIGHT RAPPING on the front door, followed by the sound of it opening. Missy never waited for someone to open it for her before inviting herself in.

"Marybeth, honey? It's me."

Marybeth's voice was flat. "We're in here."

And there she was in the doorway, peering out from the dark mudroom into the light. Joe was reminded of a snake coming out of its nest to sun itself.

Although she was now in her late sixties, Missy had maintained her figure, and the designer clothing she wore showed it off. She was tiny and had the body of an actress: compact frame, curves where they should be, and an overlarge head that looked great in photos. Her heart-shaped porcelain face—with high cheekbones and blood-red lipstick—stood out across the room. Despite her age, she didn't have a single gray hair.

"My goodness, look at you all!" Missy said musically behind a hundred-watt smile of perfect white teeth as she took in Marybeth, April, and Lucy. "You all look so beautiful! I'm so glad to see you at last after such a long time."

Her voice dropped an octave when she noticed Dulcie. "You I don't know."

"This is my friend, Dulcie Schalk," Marybeth said. She had yet to get up off the couch.

"Pleased to meet you," Missy said.

"She's the county prosecutor."

Missy's smile still dazzled, but the light dimmed behind her eyes.

The last Twelve Sleep County prosecutor his mother-in-law had encountered had tried to send her to the women's prison in Lusk. Joe had no doubt Marybeth had introduced her friend that way intentionally.

Missy slipped it the way a boxer slips a jab and turned toward Joe in the kitchen.

"Good old Joe," Missy said, dropping another octave as her tone twisted into barbed wire.

"Yup," he said.

Then brightly: "All of you just stay right there where you are. I've got gifts in the car for all of you."

MISSY VANKUEREN HAD SPENT her life trading up through five husbands, each wealthier than the last. The last time Joe had seen his mother-in-law, she'd been seated in a private plane next to a moneyed professional assassin named Wolfgang Templeton, who had headquartered his operation on his ranch in the Black Hills of Wyoming. The airplane had left the federal agents on the ground after they'd swarmed Templeton's ranch.

After he'd fled, an international manhunt had been undertaken, to no avail.

Recently, though, Templeton had resurfaced in Jackson Hole and had turned himself in to the feds. He was facing nearly a dozen first-degree murder charges.

In the time Missy had spent near Saddlestring on the ranch of her fifth husband, Bud Longbrake, she'd made it clear countless times that Marybeth could have done better than Joe and that it wasn't too late for her to trade up as well. The murder trial had revealed her to be more despicable and manipulative than Joe had even imagined her to be.

And now she'd landed husband number six.

HE WATCHED from his place leaning against the kitchen counter as Missy handed out presents. April got a silver-studded bridle for her horse, Lucy a MacBook Air. Although April and Lucy no doubt liked the gifts and thanked their grandmother politely for them, they both set the gifts aside until Missy left. It was their way, Joe thought, of showing their grandmother they weren't as excited about the gifts as they truly were.

"And where's Sheridan?" she asked.

"Working on a ranch," Joe said.

Missy winced and shook her head with disappointment. Joe had no reason to tell her Sheridan's ranch was likely one frequented by acquaintances of Missy herself.

"Can you get this to her?" she asked, placing a wrapped present on the end table. "It's a computer like Lucy's."

"Thank you. I'll make sure she gets it," Joe said.

"And for my brilliant daughter," Missy said. She whirled and handed Marybeth a small box. It was a pair of diamond earrings. Each stone was four times larger than the one on her wedding ring, Joe noted. He assumed the inevitable comparison was meant as a shot at him.

"I can't take these," Marybeth said, attempting to hand them back.

Missy would have none of it. "Please, let me do this one thing for you. You deserve a few nice things in your life."

Another shot.

Marybeth sighed and showed the earrings to Dulcie, who tried to stanch the look of astonishment in her eyes, but couldn't completely pull it off.

"And you," Missy said, as she placed a heavy rectangular object in a brown bag in Joe's hands. He peeked. It was a bottle of Jack Daniel's.

"Oh, thank you," he said.

"It is your brand, isn't it?"

"Not at all. So, did you make a deal with the feds to turn on Templeton before or after he dumped you?"

"Really," she said with the big smile and cold eyes, "this should be a pleasant reunion where I can get reacquainted with my granddaughters—not a time for twenty questions."

"I only asked one."

She ignored him and turned back for the living room. As she did, she held his eyes in a moment-too-long withering glance that told him her opinion of him hadn't changed a bit.

He wondered if the temperature in the house had actually dropped ten degrees since Missy entered it, or if it was his imagination.

TWENTY MINUTES LATER, after Dulcie had feigned an excuse about work and left, Joe washed dinner dishes as Missy caught

Marybeth and the girls up on her life. He'd poured himself another drink and finished what was left in the bottle, but he vowed to himself not to open the Jack Daniel's in her presence.

He half listened to her and kept up a silent revisionist commentary going in his head while he did.

"I got reacquainted with Marcus at a fund-raiser at the National Museum of Wildlife Art in Jackson Hole eight months ago. I was quite blue, because the man in my life at the time had become quite unpredictable and his career took a strange turn . . ."

Joe translated it to say:

She learned she was about to be cut loose by Wolfgang Templeton. Her response to that was to contact Director and Special Agent Chuck Coon of the FBI office in Cheyenne to tell him she knew the location of the famous wanted fugitive she was living with in secret.

"It had been a few years since he'd been my lawyer, but we'd gotten along well, and it turned out he was in the process of recovering from a very contentious divorce. We were like two lonely ships in the night who happened to cross paths with each other at exactly the right moment . . ."

In Joe's version:

While he had seven or eight cocktails at the fund-raiser, she simultaneously worked her charms on him and *convinced him to represent her in making a deal with the feds. She'd turn state's witness and testify against Wolfgang Templeton in exchange for immunity from prosecution, and the federal charges of aiding and abetting a fugitive would be dropped.*

"It was a whirlwind courtship . . ."

She went to bed with him that night and left him begging for more with the tacit understanding that he wouldn't receive the pleasure of her intimate company again until the immunity deal was placed in front of her for her signature.

"He is my soul mate for life . . ."

As have been the previous five (and a half, including Templeton) soul mates for life.

"We needed each other. We live on a beautiful country estate in a special neighborhood—it's called Teton Shadows—outside of Jackson, with views of the Grand Tetons, which I want you all to come and enjoy when you can."

She's bored, restless, and lonely living in a gated enclave with retired millionaires and their trophy wives with firm legs and ridiculously perky breasts who have no idea how long it takes in the bathroom every morning to make Missy look like Missy, and she resents them for it.

"I have my space now, and I've really had the time to settle back and think about my life. I think about being blessed with all the advantages a person could want, but still feeling a hole in my heart. Nothing can fill it but family, and I've been missing you all terribly."

Maybe there was some truth to that, after all. Maybe Missy had finally taken stock and mellowed. Why else would she have come?

Maybe he'd been too hard on her.

Except, Missy was Missy. She hadn't asked Marybeth how she was doing or anything about her job. She hadn't asked the girls what they'd been doing in the years that she'd been gone and out of touch with them, even on birthdays or Christmas.

———

JOE LOOKED over to see how Missy's tale was being received. Marybeth looked like she wasn't really buying it. Her only response to the long story was to murmur "Mmm-hmm" occasionally.

His wife looked relieved when her phone lit up and she looked at the screen.

"It's Sheridan," she said, gathering herself up quickly and leaving Missy on the couch.

Marybeth walked through the living room and kitchen and out the back door with the phone pressed against her ear.

Even though he was sure she'd done it as an excuse to get away from her mother—Marybeth knew the woman better than anyone ever had, and could no longer be taken in by her—Joe followed. He wanted to know if she believed any of what Missy had told them, and he wanted to say hello to Sheridan.

But when he opened the back door it was blocked by Marybeth, who stood still on the back porch. Her body language said something was wrong.

He heard her say, "You need to calm down, honey."

"What is it? What happened?"

Marybeth's eyes were big and her face had drained of color.

She lowered her phone and said, "Sheridan said she was doing her horse chores at the corral this afternoon and saw a woman who didn't belong on the ranch. The woman approached her, but two other wranglers showed up and scared her off and she ran away."

Joe felt his stomach clench.

"She said the woman was wearing a hoodie and she had tat-toos on her neck."

Joe said, "Tell her I'll be down there first thing tomorrow."

"No," Marybeth said, lowering the phone. "I'm going to tell her to come home right now. This can't be happening. Someone is going after our daughters, and we need a plan."

FIVE MINUTES LATER, Marybeth reentered the house with the phone in her hand and walked with determination to where Missy was comparing the food and hotels of Paris and Dubai.

"Joe and I just had a discussion and we've come to an agree-ment," Marybeth said to her mother. "You say your house has a gate?"

"Yes," Missy said, taken aback.

"Does it have alarms?"

"Yes."

"Full-time security?"

"Of course. Marcus needs to be cautious. He's made a lot of people very angry over his career."

Lucy asked, "Mom, what's going on?"

"That was Sheridan who just called. She saw the same woman today who went after April and Joy."

Lucy's eyes got big, and April cursed.

Marybeth said to her mother, "So, when Sheridan gets here tomorrow, we're coming for a visit."

"*Tomorrow?*"

"Yes," Marybeth said, looking over at the surprised faces of April and Lucy. Then to Missy: "I thought you missed us terribly. So we're going to spend some time with you and heal that damned hole in your heart—at least until this woman is caught. Joe will join us as soon as he's done testifying at the trial."

Joe hooked his thumbs in his belt and beheld his wife and swelled with admiration. She was *something*. Especially when it came to protecting their family.

One of the few things Missy had always been right about was Marybeth could have done a whole lot better than *him*.

"Jackson Hole?" April said, then shrugged, which meant "Okay."

"I'll call your principal," Marybeth said to Lucy.

"Just one restriction," Missy said as her eyes glanced off the dog dishes on the floor near the back door of the kitchen. "No animals. We don't have an animal-friendly home. They'll have to stay here."

MISSY LOOKED from Marybeth to Lucy to April as they discussed the arrangements they'd need to make in order to leave the house and Saddlestring as quickly as possible. She looked slightly terrified, Joe thought. He enjoyed that.

Finally, she rose from where she was sitting on the couch and sighed. "Obviously, we're doing this to protect your family, since Joe's not capable of it."

Marybeth started to argue, but Joe held his hand up. He didn't want his wife defending him to her mother.

But it stung, because she was right.

11

WANDA STACY WAS RIMROCKED.

She had done it to herself an hour before, and the enormity of it was just starting to sink in. It had happened as she'd been walking along the edge of a striated ridge looking for a way down the mountain. The full moon had lit her way, bathing the granite in dull light blue. The stars could be seen in such quantity that they appeared almost creamy in the sky, and they provided additional ambient light of their own.

She didn't know where she was or where she was going. All she knew was that somehow she had to go down.

Wanda didn't like the mountains, and she didn't really like being outside by herself, for that matter. She considered herself a people person. It's what she'd told Buck Timberman when she applied for the bartender job at the Stockman's Bar, and the reason he'd given for hiring her. That, and he said she had a nice rack.

Buck hadn't gotten the memo that it wasn't appropriate to say things like that anymore, even if what he said was true. *Especially* if it was true. Wanda liked to be looked at, even though she pretended it meant nothing to her, and it bothered her that as she aged and got heavy, there weren't as many gape-mouthed stares from men as there used to be. She felt guilty when she thought about how much Dave Farkus had lusted for her and how blithely she'd ignored him. She was sorry he was dead, especially since he'd been murdered the day after she'd last seen him in the bar. Farkus was kind of a lovable loser, but he had told some pretty good stories she assumed were at least half true, and he was devoted to her in a way that only a drinker can be to their bartender. She could have been a little nicer to him, she thought, and she would have been if she'd known he was going to go out and get himself killed.

So when she looked out and saw the twinkle of lights that she assumed was a ranch far off in the distance, she was determined to descend and walk in that direction. She vowed to make the trek, knock on the front door of that ranch down there in the valley, and get home in time to sleep in her own bed after the nightmare was over.

She'd never been so miserable. She was hungry, thirsty, and sore from how rough they'd been with her when they took her from town, as well as the walk itself after she'd escaped. She thanked God that her Ariat Fatbaby cowgirl boots had held up and she didn't have blisters on her feet, but it was cold and getting colder. She could see her breath. She wished she'd thrown a coat out the window when she'd pushed it open.

Those lights were a long distance away. She couldn't guess how far the ranch was. Five miles? Ten? She'd never been good at estimating distances.

Unfortunately, the terrain conspired against her. Rather than working her way down the mountain like she wanted to, the ridge stopped her descent and made her circumnavigate the side of the mountain. In fact, walking along the edge of it made her climb a little in elevation.

At some point, she hoped, there would be a natural break in the wall. When she found it, she'd crawl through.

EVERY TIME A RABBIT or marmot scooted out of the scrub and shale in her path, she lost a few years of her life. And when a great horned owl took off from a branch in the timber and flapped away into the night sky a few feet from her face, she'd nearly voided herself.

Wanda had breathed a sigh of relief when she saw a finger of grass extend from the tree line on her left and run through a two-foot crack on the top of the ridge to her right. The dried grass was pale yellow in the moonlight. She cautiously stepped on it to make sure the turf was firm and then followed it to the edge.

The grass covered a steep pathway that snaked down through the rocks and vanished in moon shadow.

She stood there a long time. She wished she had a flashlight—or it was morning—so she could see if the path led all the way to the foot of the mountain.

But when she heard a shout in the timber behind her and a deep bass voice respond to the shout, she knew she had no choice. Those two kidnappers were tracking her. She had a pretty good idea what they'd do if they found her.

So she crossed herself for the first time in her life, said a prayer for the first time in her life, and sat on her butt and eased down the chute.

The grass was slick, so Wanda used the heels of her boots to dig into the turf to keep from sliding out of control. She descended ten feet from where she'd started, then twenty. There were no branches or roots to grab on to if she got into trouble, only smooth rock walls on either side. But she was making progress. She was getting away.

Twenty-five feet down the chute, it simply ended on a narrow shelf of rock. When she reached the shelf, she stopped her momentum and stood up on it with shaky legs. She kept one hand back on the grass to steady herself and bent forward, hoping that the pathway resumed beyond the precipice. Instead, there was darkness. Far below, a band of moonlight illuminated slabs of shale the size of her car. There was a terrifying drop between where she was and the shale.

She couldn't go any farther down, and there was no way she could climb back up the pathway she'd come down. It was too steep and there were no handholds.

"Rimrock" was a term she'd heard hunters use before. It was a situation unique to the mountains that resulted in either rescue or death.

She closed her eyes and said, "*Shit.*"

This, she thought, was no place for a former Miss Saddlestring Rodeo to die.

WANDA HAD NOT always hated the mountains. Up until she was twelve years old, she'd been ambivalent about hiking and camping and other outdoor activities. She was a tomboy then, with an eye for horses; boys held no interest for her. When her stoic and tight-lipped father asked her if she wanted to go fishing with him and her uncle Les that August, she'd agreed, because she was having a fight with her mother about some now-forgotten incident and she wanted to punish her with her absence.

They'd taken Uncle Les's pickup into the Bighorns. Wanda sat in the middle. The winding gravel road they used afforded spectacular views of the Twelve Sleep River Valley. It was cooler up in the trees than it had been in town, and she liked that, and she enjoyed being with her dad. He, like Uncle Les, drank can after can of beer on the trip up. Uncle Les would stop in the middle of the road so her dad could get out to pee or retrieve two more cans from the cooler in back. She smiled to herself to see her dad loosen up and joke in a way that was completely unfamiliar to her. At first, she liked it.

Uncle Les worked in the oil fields around Midwest and Casper. He'd been married once previously and he married again to a woman with two kids. Wanda had met her stepcousins at the wedding. They were weird, and Wanda didn't like them. Jay, a year older than Wanda, was into sci-fi and fantasy, and he spent all his time reading creepy novels and playing complicated first-person-shooter video games. Tina, a year younger, was spoiled and demanding and would fall to the ground and wail if she didn't get her way. Wanda was glad Uncle Les had left them at home.

When they'd arrived at a shaded campsite, her dad and Uncle Les set up the tent and unfolded lawn chairs around a fire ring. She was fascinated to watch her dad assemble his fly rod, string it with line, and pull on a fly-fishing vest and creel. He seemed excited to get going and almost boyish about it. It was a side—a happy side—of him she wasn't familiar with at home. She remained in camp when they went fishing on a stream near the campsite and regretted her decision within an hour. There was absolutely nothing to do.

If she sat out in the sun, it burned her skin red. If she retreated to the shade of the trees, she was bitten by mosquitoes and deerflies. If she went in the tent, she baked. There was nothing to read, nothing to watch, and nothing to listen to except the low hum of bees and other insects in the wildflowers.

As she sprayed herself from head to toe with greasy insect repellent, she wondered why people went camping when they had perfectly fine houses to live in.

Her dad and uncle returned before dusk, and each had a stringer of small brook trout. She watched and cringed as they fried a pound of bacon in an iron skillet and then laid the fish—*with their heads and tails still on*—into the sizzling hot fat. While they did it, they laughed and told jokes and drank more and more beer.

She made herself eat a couple of the small fish and tried not to look at their cooked white eyes. Uncle Les urged her to eat the crispy tails and fins, and claimed that, when salted, they were just like crunchy potato chips. He was approaching her with a palmful of curly black tails when he stumbled and his leg caught the pan handle and he knocked the skillet into the fire. There was a *whoosh* of flame and black smoke, and the last of the fish tumbled into the fire pit. Her dad and uncle laughed as if it were the funniest thing they had ever seen. It was the first time she'd ever seen her dad dead drunk.

Wanda crawled into her sleeping bag early just to get away from them. She was gritty with dirt and sticky from the insect repellent, and she hadn't brushed her teeth or washed up. It was horrible.

Her dad and uncle drank around the fire and told stories late into the night. Her dad told one long story about a coworker he didn't like, and he used the word *fuck* so many times, she was shocked. She'd never heard him curse so much or so easily. Uncle Les said his stepson Jay was "a little pussy" and that Tina was "a high-maintenance future welfare queen."

Wanda wanted to go home.

SHE AWOKE a couple of hours later clasped in a bear hug, with Uncle Les's tongue in her mouth. It tasted of stale beer and tobacco.

He held her tighter as she struggled, but she was able to turn her head and scream. A few moments later, there were heavy footfalls outside the tent and the flap was thrown open.

"Les—what in the *fuck* are you doing?" Her father's voice was thick and slurry.

"Nothing."

"Nothing? *Get away from her now.*"

Uncle Les released his grip on her. She didn't realize he had thrust one of his hands into her sleeping bag, and it was hot against her thigh. He sighed as he withdrew it.

"Wanda, honey, are you all right? I'm sorry—I must have passed out in my chair."

She couldn't get a word out. Her mouth tasted terrible, and she turned her head and spit onto the floor of the tent.

Uncle Les clumsily got to his knees and crawled out of the tent.

"Sorry, Wanda," he said over his shoulder.

Until then she hadn't known that his pants were loose and his belt unbuckled. But when he stood up unsteadily, his jeans fell and pooled around his ankles. His fat legs were colored orange by the firelight.

There was a heavy blow of flesh on flesh, and Uncle Les said "*Oof*" and toppled backward, causing the tent to collapse. Wanda felt his weight on her again through the fabric, and heard several more thumps and "*Oofs*" until her dad quit hitting and kicking his brother.

"You can sleep in the truck," her dad said to Les. "I've got your keys, so you can't take off without us."

"I don't know what I was thinkin'."

"If you hurt her . . ."

"I didn't!"

"Wanda, did he do . . . anything?" Dad asked.

"No," she said. "But he was getting ready to, I think."

She felt more blows rain down on Uncle Les through his body on top of her.

Finally, Dad said to Les, "Now get up."

"If you'll stop pounding on me, I will, big brother."

SHE SPENT THE REST of the night staring at the stars in her sleeping bag next to her father. They lay side by side in the grass, using the fabric of the broken tent as a ground tarp. Luckily, it didn't rain on them. When the stars got too bright and piercing, she closed her eyes, but she could see them through her eyelids. Her dad eventually fell to sleep and snored. She could hear Uncle Les snoring the same way inside the truck.

The next day, they didn't talk about what had happened and it never came up again. Uncle Les got divorced again and moved to Texas.

And since then, Wanda Stacy had stayed away from the mountains.

Until now.

DIRECTLY ABOVE HER IN THE DARK, the big one named Rory Cross said, "Luthi, get over here."

She'd heard them use each other's names when they drove her out of Saddlestring.

In the distance: "What?"

"Come over, I'll show you."

"I'm coming."

Luthi's voice sounded pained, she thought, like he was injured. Cross said, "Look at this."

An orb of light rose above the rocks from the top of the rim.

She guessed that one of them had turned on a flashlight. She flattened herself against the grass of the chute, just in case they turned the beam that far down and saw her.

"See where that dirt is churned up?" Cross said. "I think she tried to take that all the way to the bottom."

"Think she made it?"

"A big girl like that? Hell no. I think she slid down there and flew into the rocks."

After a long pause, Luthi said, "I think you're probably right. Where else could she go?"

"She's a big ol' splatter mark somewhere down there."

"I wish we knew for sure."

"We can come back tomorrow in the light. Find the body and whatnot."

"*You* can come back. But I'm all for getting back to the cabin. My foot is *killing* me."

She thought for a second about calling out. Maybe, just maybe, they'd drop a rope through the chute to her and pull her up. Maybe she was more valuable to them alive than dead? She still couldn't figure out why they'd even targeted her in the first place, but she assumed it was a case of mistaken identity. No one she knew had any money for a ransom payment, except maybe Buck Timberman, but he was so tight she could see him refusing to pay up. And all of her friends were as broke as she was.

Then Cross said, "You won the game, but didn't get the prize." And then, faux dramatically: "I think our work here is done."

"I wish we knew for sure," Luthi said. "We don't want her telling anyone about us."

Cross chuckled and the flashlight was turned off. Apparently, the conversation was over.

She didn't cry out. For whatever reason, they wanted her dead and gone. So even the idea of ransom was out. She tried to think of who she could have offended to make them so angry with her they'd do something like this. She could think of no one.

Sure, she'd seen them with that handsome cowboy Dallas Cates and the tattooed woman in the Stockman's that night. But they'd barely exchanged words.

Maybe it had something to do with that?

It made no sense.

SHE DIDN'T HEAR THEM LEAVE, but a few minutes later Luthi cried out, "Rory, slow down. I can't keep up." Then: "Damn you! Slow down."

WANDA SAT on the outcropping with her back to the chute and looked out into the night. The ranch house was still out there, but a few of the lights had gone out.

Above her, those relentless stars were back, and just like twenty-six years before, she could still see them when she closed her eyes.

HER HEAD JERKED UP when a pebble bounced off her shoulder. It was freezing out, but not cold enough to see her breath. Despite that, she hugged her knees and tried to keep warm until the sun came up. She was surprised that she'd fallen asleep at all.

She wondered how long she'd slept. Five minutes? An hour? They'd taken her phone away, so she didn't know what time it was. All she knew was that it was still dark. The lights were off at the distant ranch house except for a single blue pole light that looked like a tiny lone star on the black sagebrush prairie below her.

Another pebble fell and lodged in her hair. She reached up and plucked it out, and when she did the back of her arm brushed against something she hadn't noticed before.

A rope. And the end of it was twitching as if it were alive.

There was a grunt from above and she sat up and scuttled to her left or she would have been stepped on by a pair of massive boots that thumped on the shelf.

Cross looked at her, grinned, and said, "There you are. I would have gotten here sooner, but I had to go back to the cabin for a rope."

She trembled and asked, "Are you here to hurt me or to rescue me?"

He shrugged. "I guess we'll try and figure that out together, Wanda."

HE STOOD THERE bathed in moonlight while catching his breath from the descent. She noticed the dull glint of the moon on the grip of a pistol that poked out from his back pocket.

She said, "If you wanted me dead, you could have just left me here to die of exposure. So I'm guessing that I'm worth more to you alive."

"That's a good guess."

"I'm thinking you've done this," she said with a sweep of her hand to indicate everything around them, "for money. I can't think of any other reason."

"Maybe so."

His tone was slightly mocking, almost jaunty. She tried to ignore it.

"Well, I don't have much money, but what I've got, you can have. Tie that rope around me and pull me up, and you can drive me into town to an ATM. My mom and dad are retired, but they've got some money in the bank. I've got the keys to the Stockman's, and I know where Buck's safe is hidden. I don't know the combination, but I'd think you could get it out of him. We'll get plenty of money, and I'll give it all to you and your friend."

"He's my associate. Not my friend," Rory said. "I've got plenty of money coming in, but I guess I can always use a little more."

She felt her shoulders relax a little. He seemed to like the idea, even though he claimed he had *plenty of money coming in*, which was curious. He turned and plucked the rope from where it hung against the chute and inspected it as if trying to figure out how he'd tie it to her.

"And I won't prosecute, either," she said. "I'll pretend this all never happened."

"Tell me," he said without looking over at her, "how much did you hear the other night in the bar?"

"What?"

"When we were discussing some plans. How much did you overhear?"

She shook her head. "Nothing. I honestly can't remember anything besides we talked about eating wild game. I was kinda flirting with that cowboy. That's what I remember."

"So you didn't hear a thing besides that?"

"Honestly, no."

"But you know we were all together."

"So what? You have a right to sit with your friends in a bar."

"Associates," he corrected.

"Associates."

He paused a long time and nodded his head. "You know what, you're right about getting you out of here. Especially if you didn't hear anything. But you have to fuckin' promise me you won't try to get loose and run again. We spent half the night chasing you, and now you know there's no place to run, right?"

"Right. I promise," she said. "I don't like being alone outside."

He took a deep breath and expelled it slowly. His eyes were wide and they shone in the starlight. It made him look a little crazy, she thought.

"Let's tie this rope under your arms," he said. "First I'll tie a strong loop in the end of it. I'll climb up ahead and pull you up when I get back to the top, but you've got to help. No offense, but I can't pull you up all by myself."

"I'll climb the rope," she said. "I'll make it easy on you."

"That's a good girl, Wanda," he whispered.

She pushed herself up and walked to him on stiff legs.

"Turn around and raise your arms so I can tie this on."

She did. She looked down to see if he'd loop the rope under her breasts or over the top of them. Instead, before she could react to what was happening, the rope flopped over her head and he pulled the slipknot tight around her neck. She gagged and reached up to try to loosen the rope.

Rory leaned back, raised his right foot, and placed the sole of it on her wide buttocks. She tried to turn away from it, but he shoved hard and she dropped over the lip like a full bag of flour and without a sound.

He sidestepped quickly so that when the rope became taut from her weight below, it wouldn't slip under his jaw and take his head off.

A second later, the rope moaned as it pulled tight. He reached out and placed his hand on it and he could feel it quivering as she swung and kicked below.

It took a full minute before the rope went still and he could feel nothing through it. He found it fascinating and oddly arousing that he could actually feel her life leave her through the rope itself. When she stopped kicking, it was like the rope itself had lost its soul.

Rory dug a folding knife out of his front pocket, opened it, and cut the rope near his feet. It popped and coiled back around his legs. He listened until he heard a crunching sound below like a bag of cubed ice dropped on concrete.

He said, "Sorry, Wanda. I wouldn't even have come back, but my associate is a pussy and he wanted to make sure. So blame him, not me."

Then he grasped the rope with both hands and started climbing.

TWO WEEKS LATER, JOE SAT IN THE LAST ROW OF THE TWELVE
Sleep County courthouse next to Deputy Spivak for the pretrial
motion hearing before the first-degree murder trial of Dallas
Cates was to begin. As was his custom, Judge Hewitt had already blown through the bail review, preliminary hearing, and
formal arraignment stages in the past ten days, as if his hair—or
the court building itself—was on fire.

The motion hearing was the last step before a trial date was
to be set, a jury empaneled, and opening statements were made.
In Hewitt's courtroom, motion hearings were usually perfunctory occasions, and Joe rarely attended them as his cases pro-
ceeded through the system. But Dulcie had asked Joe and Spivak
to be present in case Marcus Hand tricked her with a substan-

tive motion to dismiss or delay the trial and she had to call on their testimony to bolster her argument to proceed. Although she'd been quoted in the Saddlestring *Roundup* as saying that the case was airtight, she obviously didn't put anything past Marcus Hand.

She'd told Joe that she'd been shocked that Hand hadn't filed a motion for more time, because she said she would have concurred with it. That Hand seemed agreeable to the fast track of Hewitt's trial scheduling made her more nervous than usual about the case.

She'd been extremely pleased at the results of the forensics analysis from the state crime lab. They'd matched the blood found in Cates's vehicle to Farkus's blood, and they'd concluded that the casings located at the crime scene and the slugs removed from Farkus's body were from the same .223 rifle found in Cates's car.

A call to the prison in Rawlins confirmed that, despite Dallas's claim that he knew his two associates only as "Brutus" and "Weasel," their given names were Randall Luthi and Rory Cross. Corrections officers said the three had been well-acquainted inside and had all been released at approximately the same time. Despite an all-points bulletin issued by the sheriff's department, neither Luthi nor Cross had been picked up.

Airtight. Slam dunk.

Judge Hewitt had a way of glowering and moving that made him seem tightly coiled and ready at any time to explode. He entered the courtroom from his chambers wearing both his robes and the perpetual look of agitation he projected in order to browbeat attorneys into moving things along. He'd been a judge for twenty-one years, and Joe had gotten used to the fast, no-nonsense pace in his courtroom. Under his robes, Hewitt wore a shoulder holster with a .45 in it, and he'd whipped it out on more than one occasion.

The courtroom had high ceilings, with poor acoustics, and it hadn't changed much since it was constructed in the 1890s. The walls were still covered by old paintings depicting 1940s versions of local Western history: cavalry charges, grizzly bear hunts, pow-wows, covered wagons loaded with cherubic children. Only the politically incorrect images of blood-soaked massacres of pioneers by Indians had been replaced recently with renderings of nearby Yellowstone Park.

Other than Deputy Spivak and Joe, the only other observers in the room were T. Cletus Glatt and a private investigator named Bruce White, who was employed by Marcus Hand. White was an ex-military policeman with a buzz cut gone gray, wide shoulders, and sad, seen-it-all eyes. He sat directly behind the defense table. White wore a blazer over a crisp, white, open-necked shirt. He exuded physical strength and professionalism.

Joe was struck with how comfortable Dallas Cates appeared to be. He slouched back in his chair and tipped up his chin from time to time to stare at the ceiling while Hand and Dulcie argued minor procedural points. He acted as if the hearing were a waste of his time.

He didn't sit up until Hand said, "Your Honor, in our final motion we urge the court to immediately drop all of the charges against our client and let him walk out of here this afternoon a free man. We'll be doing a community service, Your Honor. The quicker we get this case dismissed the quicker the authorities can pursue an actual investigation for the real killer of Dave Farkus. As you know, Your Honor, most homicide cases are solved within the first forty-eight hours, or not at all. Two weeks have already been wasted in the prosecution of the wrong man."

Hewitt squinted at Hand, whom he'd faced before. Bored, he asked, "Of course you have to ask. But on what basis?"

Hand rose to his feet. "On the basis that we can prove to you and the prosecution that Mr. Cates was set up by local law enforcement. On the basis that we can prove that *all* of the evidence in this prosecution was planted by the authorities in this county to make it appear that my client is guilty.

"I'll be blunt, Your Honor. Never in my thirty years practicing law have I seen a more egregious case of police misconduct."

Dulcie leaped to her feet. Her face was red.

"Your Honor, that's an irresponsible argument. He's accusing the police of the worst kind of behavior with absolutely nothing to back it up."

Joe perked up. As Judge Hewitt had stated, nearly every defense attorney made a motion for dismissal of the charges prior to the trial. But Hand's strong statement and Dulcie's reaction to it signaled something serious was in the works.

Dulcie glanced over at Glatt, who was manically writing down quotes, then back to Judge Hewitt. "The defense is attempting to poison the jury pool in advance with specious charges that will make their way into the community. He's also attempting to destroy the reputation of honest law enforcement officers."

"Honest officers?" Hand said with a contemptuous chuckle. "Really? The defense is set to prove to you that the only thing honest about one particular witness in this proceeding is his honest goal to frame my client."

Joe nervously shifted his weight from his right butt cheek to his left. He'd been confident that Hand would attack him and every piece of evidence—that's what Marcus Hand did. But—

"We will prove to the court," Hand said as he rotated a hundred and eighty degrees and slowly raised his hand to point, "that Twelve Sleep Sheriff's Department undersheriff Lester Spivak deliberately and systematically used his power and authority to manufacture a murder charge against my client."

Joe turned to Spivak. The deputy's face was white and his eyes were wide open. He worked his jaw so vigorously that Joe could hear his teeth grind together.

"Your Honor," Dulcie said, "may I approach the bench to discuss this?"

"Both of you," Hewitt said, jabbing his index finger at Hand and Dulcie, "get up here *now.*"

JOE HAD VISITED his family twice at the Hand compound north of Jackson Hole since they'd cleared out of Saddlestring. Although he talked with Marybeth every night and they texted each other during the day, he certainly missed seeing them. In all honesty, though, he'd been so busy he scarcely would have seen them if they'd stayed home. It was early November and four different big-game hunting seasons were open and roaring in various areas within his district—deer, elk, moose, and bear. He'd been in the field from an hour before dawn to two or three hours after dusk.

He'd enjoyed his surprise bachelorhood for exactly two nights when his dinner consisted of thick grilled steaks and beer. He ate without worrying about vegetables or side dishes. After that, the house seemed to get emptier every night he came home. He felt guilty for not being able to protect his far-flung family, because that was truly the most important thing to him and the reason for his existence. And he felt resentful that Marybeth and the girls had fled to Missy's, of all places, for safety. That was a twist of the knife.

Even Daisy seemed out of sorts, although she had the run of the house. She seemed to miss her family and Tube, the half Lab, half Corgi, seemed depressed as well.

The juxtaposition between his district during hunting season and with the elite gated community Missy and Marcus Hand lived in was striking. He'd go from dust, blood, carcasses hanging in trees, and hunters with a five-day growth of beard offering him a gulp of whiskey to an elegant and mostly silent enclave where gardeners and landscapers had been instructed to step behind trees while members drove by.

Joe had to sit idle at the entrance gate until a uniformed guard called Missy to allow him entrance. Each time, Missy stalled just long enough in giving her approval to make sure her point was made.

When the gate swung up, he drove his muddy four-wheel-drive on pitch-black asphalt and through manicured grounds where the only other vehicles were Range Rovers, Mercedeses, and BMW SUVs—or golf carts. The Grand Tetons walled off the western horizon like tiger teeth. To the east was the Gros Ventre Range, to the south the Hoback Mountains, and to the north Grand Teton National Park and Yellowstone.

The Hands lived on Snake River Drive in a sprawling, low-slung seven-bedroom, six-bath home constructed of natural river rock. It was sleek and elegant and decorated in typical Jacksonian New West nouveau riche style: cathedral ceilings in the great room, elk antler chandeliers, bronzes of writhing trout, fly-fishing originals on the walls, Navajo rugs on the flagstone floors.

For the first time in their lives, each of his daughters had her own bedroom, bathroom, and walk-out patio. Even April, who was determined not to like either Jackson Hole or their temporary headquarters, had succumbed to the easy luxury of it . . . for the first week.

By the second week, Marybeth said they were all getting bored and restless, not to say increasingly suspicious of Missy's full-time and uncharacteristic charm offensive. According to Marybeth, Missy behaved as if she'd finally attained her life's goal of being surrounded by her daughter and granddaughters in one place. This was the woman, she reminded Joe, who had more than once said she was too young to ever "feel" like a grandmother, and who had instructed them all when the girls were young never to use that hated word.

As a result of the tension and boredom, as well as the fact that Jackson's tourism season roared on into the fall, April had taken a job as a wrangler and part-time cook for a hunting camp. Sheridan was employed as a hostess in a chic Thai restaurant. Marybeth had arranged with Lucy's teachers to send their assignments to Jackson via email and text message so Lucy wouldn't get too far behind. They'd all made several excursions to Powell to visit Joy Bannon in the hospital, who, according to Marybeth, was recovering well.

But this new arrangement was getting old for all of them.

And the woman who'd attacked Joy and stalked Sheridan had been neither seen nor caught.

THERE HAD BEEN ONLY seven people at the funeral service for Dave Farkus, which had taken place outdoors at the cemetery on the hill that overlooked Saddlestring. In addition to Joe, the Presbyterian minister, and the funeral director himself, Cotton Anderson was there with his ex-wife, Buck Timberman was in attendance to pay his respects to one of his best customers, and Farkus's sister, Bloomie, hid behind dark glasses and chain-smoked throughout the event. Until then, Joe hadn't known Farkus had a sister.

The minister had never met Farkus, so the short eulogy he gave was generic. In the end, he rushed it because the wind kicked up and ruffled the pages in his book and he had trouble keeping track of the text.

Joe wore a jacket and tie and his $2,500 silver-belly Stetson Rancher. The hat fit tight enough that the sudden wind didn't lift it off his head. Inside the sweat brim was the inscription *To My Range Rider Joe Pickett From Wyoming Governor Spencer Rulon*. It had been a parting gift from the previous officeholder.

The funeral—and the lack of attendance—made Joe melancholy. Less than half a dozen there? Farkus *must* have touched more people in his fifty-plus years on earth and in the valley. He wished he'd known Farkus better, and he regretted the many times he'd cursed the man over the years.

When the minister closed his book and turned on his heel for his pickup, Bloomie approached Joe. In a smoke-hoarse voice, she said, "Dave would have liked it that you were here. He really admired you."

"He did?"

She nodded, and ash blew off the tip of her cigarette onto the shoulder of her black dress. "Whenever I saw him, he told me about the adventures the two of you had together. He said you saved his life when you floated him through the rapids on a river, and he said he was there when you recovered the ashes of your father from your truck."

"Both of those things are true," Joe said. In his recollection of those events, he'd never really thought of doing them with Farkus—like they were some kind of team. In Joe's memory, Farkus had simply been present. And he'd been peripheral and annoying. That Farkus remembered them the way he did made Joe feel guilty and small.

"He said you were a good man."

Joe didn't know how to reply.

"Too bad he was such an asshole at times, though," she said. "Maybe more people would have showed up at his funeral."

With that, she shook her head and walked across the dry grass toward her car.

JOE ATTRIBUTED the increase in hunters in the mountains to the fact that the poaching ring seemed to have paused their operations. There had been no new reports, tips, or leads.

Rick Ewig had come through with a list of white Suburbans in Twelve Sleep County, and there were twelve of them scattered over five thousand square miles. Joe had been too busy with his day-to-day duties to check on them all, but he'd cleared three of the vehicles when either their tire tread didn't match up to the evidence at the scene or the owners of the vehicles could be ruled out.

In regard to Dallas Cates's case, Joe had heard from Sheriff Reed that the forensics and DNA results had come back positive, and Dulcie was champing at the bit to go to trial.

And the day before, while Joe was out of cell phone range checking on an elk camp near Hazelton Road, he'd received a message from new Wyoming governor Colter Allen's office asking that he return the call. It was the first time Joe had been contacted by the man who'd replaced Governor Spencer Rulon, and he had no idea what the call was in reference to. Like his predecessor, apparently, Allen was inclined to bypass the protocol of talking first to Joe's supervisors and preferred to go direct.

When Joe had called back, it was after six p.m. and the governor's office was closed for the day. He'd left a message that he'd be in court in the morning, but free in the afternoon.

But that was before Marcus Hand had made the motion that the case should be immediately dismissed.

———

THE BENCH CONFERENCE WITH HAND, Dulcie, and Judge Hewitt was long and intense. Joe observed with growing alarm as Dulcie waved her arms as she made a point, and as Marcus Hand stepped back from her as if afraid she might strike him. His arguments to Judge Hewitt seemed calm but serious. More than once, Hand turned his head and looked at Deputy Spivak sitting next to Joe.

"What is going on?" Joe asked him. "Did you do something you shouldn't have?"

Rather than reply, Spivak shook his head quickly, as if he didn't want to deal with the answer.

Joe felt something cold start to build in the pit of his stomach.

When the conference broke up, Dulcie charged back to her table with her heels clicking like castanets and her murderous eyes fixed on Spivak the whole time, and Joe knew trouble was on the way.

"THE DEFENSE WOULD LIKE TO CALL BRUCE WHITE TO THE STAND, Your Honor," Hand said after he'd resumed his place behind the defense table.

Joe noted that Hand performed differently when the trial was before a judge and not a jury. He was calmer, and he stayed in one place so he could glance down at his notes. But in front of a jury, the attorney who'd perfected the "eight percent theory"— of being so persuasive despite the evidence to convince at least one juror of his client's innocence—he was a mesmerizing presence.

White snapped to attention and strode through the swinging doors to the witness stand. As he was sworn in, Dulcie turned slowly in her chair and glared at Spivak once again.

"Lester . . . ?" Joe asked.

"Not now," he snapped.

After White was sworn in and had gone through his credentials and his employment by Marcus Hand, the attorney asked White to recount his actions since he'd arrived in Saddlestring, in particular his first visit to the Twelve Sleep County Sheriff's Department six days before.

White withdrew a Field Notes pad from his breast pocket and opened it. "On November tenth, I entered the sheriff's office on North Main at ten-thirty a.m. The sheriff was out, but I showed my private investigator's license to the officer in charge and asked if I could inspect the evidence locker. I offered to let an officer come with me the whole time, but the deputy said that wasn't allowed."

As if anticipating the first line of inquiry Dulcie would pursue when she got a chance to cross-examine White, Hand said, "Why did you zero in so quickly on the sheriff's department and why did you request to check out the evidence room?"

"Our office—*your office*, I mean," White said with a slight smile, "received an anonymous tip. Someone told our receptionist that our client was being framed. This person said to find what was missing from the evidence room, and all the rest would be self-evident."

Hand stroked his chin. "So the anonymous caller appeared to have inside knowledge of the murder investigation?"

"That was my conclusion."

"Was the caller a man or a woman?"

"The receptionist said it sounded like a young woman . . ."

"Objection," Dulcie said. "This is hearsay evidence. Mr. White didn't speak to the anonymous caller himself."

Judge Hewitt waved her off. "Because this is a motion hearing, I'll allow it."

Dulcie sighed and sat back down.

"Thank you, Your Honor," Hand said. Then to White: "So what did you do next after you entered the sheriff's department?"

"Since they wouldn't let me into the evidence room, I asked if it was okay to take a look at the log. The log is where law enforcement personnel and officers of the court sign in and out when they want to look up or retrieve items tagged into evidence for court proceedings. It's a public record."

White was good on the stand, Joe thought. He was serious, articulate, and gave precise answers.

Hand asked, "Did you find anything of particular interest to this case on the log-in records?"

"Yes, sir."

"What did you find?"

"I found that on midnight of October thirty-first—Halloween night—Undersheriff Lester Spivak signed into the evidence room during the last few minutes of the shift for the officer assigned there that evening."

"Did the log state what Undersheriff Spivak was after?"

"It did not."

Joe let out a sigh of relief.

Hand asked, "Isn't that unusual in your experience?"

"Yes, sir."

Dulcie objected while still seated. "Your Honor, Mr. White

cannot have any intimate knowledge of the internal procedures of our sheriff's department. He was just a visitor there."

Hand produced images of the log from a file and gave copies to Judge Hewitt, Bruce White, and Dulcie. She studied her copy and audibly sighed.

"What do you see there, Mr. White?"

"I see page after page of entries where an authorized person logged into the evidence room to look at or retrieve a certain piece of evidence. The item they are seeking is referenced by the evidence tag number as well as a description of the item."

"And on the entry log-in made by Undersheriff Spivak on October thirty-first, what is the item number he is seeking?" Hand asked.

"There's no entry in that box. Nor is there a description."

Joe squinted. He wasn't sure where Hand was going, although Dulcie, the judge, and a nonchalant Dallas Cates certainly did. And so, it seemed, did Spivak.

"And when did Undersheriff Spivak come out of the evidence room?"

"That's not specified," White said. "It was after the officer in charge went off shift and Deputy Spivak obviously didn't sign out."

"That's also unusual, isn't it?"

"Your Honor," Dulcie said, but her voice had lost its passion, "again, there is no way—"

"Looking at the pages in front of you, Mr. White," Hand cut in, "do you see a single instance where someone signed into the evidence room and failed to sign out?"

"No, sir."

"Objection overruled," Hewitt snapped at Dulcie.

Joe studied Hewitt's face. He looked angry and his eyes were getting more and more hooded. But he wasn't angry at the defense.

"When you noticed the discrepancy in the logbook that day, what did you do?"

"I asked the officer in charge if he would do an inventory of the items in the evidence room to see if he could find out what was missing. He didn't want to do it, but when I said I'd come to this court for an official request order, he set about doing it."

"Was the sheriff aware of your request?"

"I don't know. If he was, he didn't stop it."

"Was Undersheriff Spivak aware of your request?"

"I don't know that, either."

"So," Hand asked, "how long did it take for the officer in charge to complete the inventory?"

"I just received it this morning," White said.

"So, six days. Six long days," Hand said, shaking his head in disappointment.

"Is that a question?" Hewitt hissed.

"No, Your Honor, just an observation."

"There's no jury to perform for, Mr. Hand. Make your observations someplace other than my courtroom."

Hand bowed in apology, then asked White, "How many items did the officer in charge report were missing from the evidence room?"

"Two, sir."

"Only two," Hand said. "So unlike some evidence rooms you've observed in your career, that's pretty impressive that only two items of evidence were unaccounted for?"

"Yes, sir."

"And what, pray tell, were the two missing items?"

White again referred to his notes, although Joe suspected he was doing it more for effect than to refresh his recollection.

"The first item missing was evidence tag number 0707190015-A. The number is a reference to it being entered into evidence at seven p.m. on July 7, 2015. There are other items with the same prefix but they're designated 0707190015-B, 0707190015-C, and so on."

"What was missing item 07190015-A, according to the inventory report?"

Joe held his breath.

"Item 07190015-A was a Smith & Wesson M&P15 rifle chambered in .223."

Joe let it out. It was the same rifle found in Dallas Cates's vehicle the night he was arrested. He felt like he'd been headbutted in the chest.

"Does it have a serial number?" Hand asked.

"The report indicates the serial number was filed off. The item was seized from the trunk of a car in a drug case but apparently not used in the trial."

"And who was the arresting officer in that particular drug case?"

White chinned toward the back of the room. "The record says it was Undersheriff Spivak."

"Was there anything else you discovered by looking over the logs as it pertains to Undersheriff Spivak and this particular rifle?"

"Yes, sir. As you'll see in the copy of the log everyone has in front of them, Undersheriff Spivak checked out the .223 the first week of October as well. The log indicates he had it for three days and returned it to be logged back in."

Hand paused, letting what White had said sink in.

Joe was flummoxed at first about what it meant, and then it came to him. Spivak had borrowed the rifle and no doubt fired it, probably at the police range. It wasn't all that unusual for officers to test and train with different weapons. If Spivak had fired the .223, he'd also expended shell casings he could have collected and saved to scatter around the murder scene.

"You said there were two unaccounted-for items. What was the second missing item, Mr. White?"

Again, an unnecessary look at his notebook. "The second item was a blood sample taken after a subject was arrested for a DUI in August."

"A blood sample?" Hand asked theatrically. "Like a vial of blood?"

Joe knew Dulcie should have objected, because White couldn't testify as to a container he'd not seen. But she didn't.

"I assume so," White said.

"And who did the sample belong to, according to the record?"

"David M. Farkus."

Dulcie slumped in her chair and her head nearly hit the table. Joe's breath came in shallow gulps.

Hand pressed on.

"Mr. White, you have brought some interesting artifacts into the courtroom today, haven't you?"

"At least I think they're interesting," White said reasonably.

"What are they?" Hand asked White. Then, to Judge Hewitt before Dulcie could render an objection: "These objects have not been entered into evidence yet, Your Honor. They were just found. We will of course enter them if necessary, but I doubt it will be necessary."

"*Artifacts*?" Hewitt said with sarcasm.

"Show us," Hand said to White.

Bruce White leaned back in his chair and dug his hand into his front pocket and pulled out a crumpled white envelope. He waited for Hand to ask him to open it, then he did.

Three small metallic objects tumbled out of the envelope into White's left palm.

"What are those?" Hand asked White theatrically.

"Bullets."

"From what kind of weapon?"

"My expert opinion is that they come from a .223 rifle."

"And where did you find them?"

"I dug them out of a sandbag at the Twelve Sleep County Sheriff's Department shooting range. They were found in a specific area of the range reserved for the sheriff and undersheriff. Although I haven't had the time to send them in for analysis, I would speculate that they came from the Smith & Wesson M&P15 in question."

"How interesting," Hand said. "How *convenient*."

Joe turned his head and stared at the side of Lester Spivak's face, but the deputy wouldn't look over.

———

JOE HEARD HAND'S ARGUMENT for dismissal of all charges against Dallas Cates through a fog. He looked up when Judge Hewitt asked Dulcie if she wanted to cross-examine Bruce White.

With a sigh of resignation, Dulcie said, "Your Honor, I have no questions for the witness."

Hewitt turned to Hand and told him to proceed.

"Your Honor," he said to Judge Hewitt, "the prosecution's entire case—unless they've got some trick up their sleeve they haven't shared with the defense—has just gone *poof.* Their entire case was built on a three-legged stool that has collapsed.

"The first leg was to positively place my client in a bar with other unknown associates the night before the murder of Dave Farkus to provide a motive for killing him. Unfortunately, the bartender who would make that identification has vanished and no longer appears on the witness list the prosecution has provided us.

"The second leg of the stool was the weapon—a .223 Smith and Wesson assault rifle—that left casings at the murder scene and slugs within the body of Mr. Farkus, and which was later miraculously discovered in my client's vehicle as he drove home from the grocery store. Who found the weapon? Undersheriff Spivak—the same man who had 'borrowed' the so-called murder weapon earlier, fired it at the department shooting range, and who had the opportunity to toss shell casings around at the murder scene like candy at a Fourth of July parade and press slugs from the rifle into wounds on Mr. Farkus's dead body. This is the same Undersheriff Spivak who used his knowledge of the staffing change at the sheriff's department to slip into the evidence room and slip out without logging in the items he borrowed.

"The third leg of the stool was the blood evidence. Dave Farkus's blood was found on the interior and exterior of my client's vehicle. Now we know that a vial of Mr. Farkus's blood was taken from the evidence room the night before Undersheriff Spivak and his team went to the murder scene. No doubt that blood came in handy when my client was apprehended under false pretenses and arrested for murder.

"Your Honor," Hand said in his deepest bass as he bent over his table and shook his woolly head from side to side, "there is no stool. There is no case against my client. After what we've learned today, surely you won't ask the fine taxpayers of Twelve Sleep County to pay for the bogus prosecution of my client."

Joe twitched when Hewitt banged his gavel so hard the handle broke.

"I'm pissed off," the judge shouted. "Motion granted to dismiss."

He stood up and pointed to Dulcie, Spivak, and Joe.

"Miss Schalk, Mr. Pickett, and Undersheriff Spivak, I would like to see the three of you in my chambers in five minutes."

To Dallas: "You're free to go, young man. But I'd suggest that when it comes to leaving my county, you don't let the door hit you in the ass on the way out."

Dallas nodded at the judge and gave himself a double thumbs-up.

Then he slowly turned around in his chair and winked at Joe.

Hand said, "Your Honor, shouldn't I be invited to your

chambers as well? Isn't this an improper ex parte communication with just the prosecution team?"

Judge Hewitt turned his head to glare at him, his eyes narrowed into snakelike slits.

"I think maybe I'll just go home," Hand said.

"Fine idea," Hewitt hissed.

AT THE SAME TIME ON THE EASTERN FACE OF THE BIGHORN MOUN-
tains, Nate Romanowski yelled, *"Rope!"* as he tossed a thick coil
of it into the air in front of him. The rope fell out of sight. He'd
shouted the warning even though he knew there wasn't a living
soul in sight this far from the road, but his training from special
ops died hard.

He double-checked the carabiners on the anchor he'd fash-
ioned around the trunks of two ancient spruce trees, then looped
the rope through the braking belay device on his climbing belt,
grasped the line with his right hand near his hip, and backed
over the edge of the cliff.

Nate was not only an outlaw falconer with a covert operations background whose life had been intertwined with the

Pickett family for more than a decade, he was also half-owner of Yarak, Inc., a falconry services firm that desperately needed more birds to keep up with demand. He needed to feed the pipeline of falcons-in-training for when they'd be deployed.

That was why he was rappelling down a sheer granite cliff with a falconry bag slung over his shoulder. Inside the bag were five Dho-Gazza-style falcon traps of his own design, anchors and climbing bolts to hold the traps in place, and live pigeons immobilized by a wrap of athletic tape to keep them still to serve as bait.

The traps were rolled-up three-foot squares of thirty-pound Dacron fishing line knotted into airy loops. When unfurled and stretched out tight between anchor rods or bolts—with a live flapping pigeon hung by a string in front of it—the trap would entice peregrine falcons to enter it and become entangled in the line.

He knew there was a good population of native peregrines in the area, and he'd seen the whitewash of their excrement on the surface of the cliff face. He'd trapped several of them there before to hunt with. He needed at least three young birds to round out what he referred to as his "air force."

Weighting down the bag was his holstered .454 Casull five-shot revolver from Freedom Arms.

Just in case.

SINCE ALL FEDERAL CHARGES had been dropped against him as a result of a mission he'd undertaken in the Red Desert of Wyoming on behalf of a shadowy federal agency the year before,

Nate and his lover and co-owner Liv Brannon had launched Yarak, Inc. in full. They'd both been surprised how fast the enterprise had taken off.

Yarak was all about nuisance-bird abatement, meaning Nate and his birds were hired to scare away pests. Nothing put the fear of God into starlings, pigeons, seagulls, or other problem birds like a falcon screaming through the sky.

Prey species—whether problem birds, game birds, snakes, or rodents of various sizes—were born knowing that the distant silhouette of a falcon against the sky meant lethal trouble for them. The threat was imprinted into their DNA.

Often, the victim wouldn't know they'd been targeted until they were hit. A peregrine falcon on the wing could descend from the clouds at more than two hundred miles per hour, and it was the fastest creature in nature. So when Yarak, Inc. arrived and put their birds in the sky, problem species wisely cleared out.

They'd been hired by farmers and winegrowers as far away as Oregon and California to keep nuisance birds from eating their crops prior to harvest. Golf courses hired them to scare off wild geese. Refineries and owners of transfer stations paid Yarak to chase away birds that nested in sensitive equipment. A large amusement park in Denver had hired them to prevent pigeons from pooping on their customers.

Nate's air force consisted of two Harris's hawks, four prairie falcons, and seven peregrines—along with three contract part-time falconers.

Liv handled accounting, back-office administration, and marketing while Nate oversaw all the work in the field. Unfortunately, he realized, Liv was such a good marketer and their services were in such demand that he was being run ragged. Thus, he needed more birds.

GOING STRAIGHT and working hard had its rewards, he'd found. For the first time in years, he could make phone calls on unsecured lines, fly on airplanes, and not worry about being viewed by closed-circuit cameras mounted on every building. And he was doing professionally what he'd always done personally: partnering with the greatest creatures alive to train, fly, and hunt.

But the transition had its downside. Nate traveled constantly and his cell phone was always turned on and within reach. Instead of living in outdoor mews, the falcons were transported from place to place in a retrofitted panel van that reeked of high-nitrogen bird excrement. He didn't like sleeping in strange beds. He hadn't talked to his friend Joe Pickett in months, or mentored Joe's daughter Sheridan, his apprentice in falconry. He barely talked to Liv about anything but business and the next job.

He wanted to be with her, wanted to listen to that smoked-honey Louisiana accent and let it wash over him. Instead, she was always on the other end of a cell phone call.

Most of all, he'd lost solitude and a vital, unhurried connection with the natural world around him. He could feel it slipping away from him as he spent day after day at work. Where he'd once been in tune with the sun and stars, the winds, the wildlife, and the rivers—he was now back in the world and back on the grid.

He missed sitting naked on a tree branch watching the river

flow beneath his feet. He missed sitting quietly by a spring waiting for pronghorns and other big-game animals to come to him and audition for his next meal.

And most of all, Nate missed the freedom of killing people who were better off dead.

He'd gone from human abatement to bird abatement. But at least he was no longer destined for federal prison.

FIFTEEN FEET from the lip of the cliff, and before he unwound his first trap, Nate did a lazy free spin around to take in the valley below him.

It was a cool, cloudless day and he could see for miles. Buckbrush in the folds of the foothills was already turning bright crimson. Pockets of aspen in the midst of the dark pine forest were lighting up yellow. Distant mountain peaks were already snowcapped on the horizon.

It was magnificent country, as vast as it was heartless. And so different from the manicured golf courses and wine country he so often worked now.

Satiated, he spun around lazily and used his boot toe against the granite to stop the revolution. He got to the work at hand. Nate assembled the frame, stretched the fishing-line trap tight, and anchored it to the rock wall at an angle. He reached down and retrieved a bound pigeon and tied one end of a leather jess to its foot and the other end to the frame of the trap. Then he stripped the tape from the bait bird with his teeth and let it go. The pigeon flapped madly but couldn't fly away. Its movement and activity would attract raptors miles away in the sky.

When he was done, he thanked the pigeon for giving up its life, and he moved on to the next trap location thirty feet down and fifteen feet to the right on the cliff face.

Dho-Gazza traps were highly effective and held the trapped falcons tight. They were so effective, in fact, that he'd made a commitment to check them every six hours. He didn't want a trapped falcon to become injured when trying to free itself from the fishing line snares, or starve to death waiting for the falconer to come back.

If he ever let that happen, Nate knew, he'd have let down not only the falcon but himself. And he'd have to think long and hard about whether keeping Yarak, Inc. going at such a blistering pace was even worth it.

AFTER THE THIRD TRAP was set and he'd ranged as far to the left on the sheer rock wall as his ropes would allow, Nate sensed movement far below him and he looked over his shoulder.

Wildlife in general, he'd learned, seemed to react the same way to a man hanging on ropes above them as they did to a drift boat on the river: oblivious. While they were keenly aware of any potential threat on the ground, their wiring short-circuited when it came to looking up. While he was rappelling down a cliff face, he was practically a raptor himself.

More than once, he'd descended into the middle of a herd of elk sleeping in the timber or once practically on the back of a somnambulant bull moose.

This time, though, it was a half-dozen large ravens. They were strutting around on the rocks below him, crowding one

another, pecking at each other as if annoyed, and all keenly interested in something lodged below them between two car-sized
boulders.

Nate had an irrational hatred of ravens. He hated them as
much as he loved falcons. He'd tried to explain his vehemence
toward them to Liv once and she'd concluded that he must have
had a terrifying experience with them in his youth or in a past
life. He wasn't sure what it was, but he did know that ravens
gathered where there was carrion to feed on.

He rappelled closer to them. He got so close that he could
clearly see their blue-black feathers, their pointed matte-black
beaks, and their tiny demon eyes.

"Get out of here," he growled.

Not until his boots hit the top of the boulder did the ravens
take off. They didn't go far. They rose as a single entity and lit
on another big rock about fifteen feet away.

He glared at them and thought about reaching into his falconry bag for his revolver. Nate was fast and accurate with the
weapon. He knew he could probably take out three of them in
explosions of blood and black feathers before the others could
fly away.

That's when he noticed that one of the birds had a long strip
of bloody cloth in its beak. Another had a red strip of flesh.

He shrugged out of his climbing harness and let it drop to
the top of the boulder with a jangle from the loose carabiners.
Then he sank to his knees and peered down into the shadow
between the adjacent boulders.

The body of a woman.

She was broken—her arms and legs at unnatural angles. The

soft flesh of her arms, thighs, and face had been stripped away. There was a musky stench. The body had obviously been there for a number of days.

As his eyes adjusted, he could see the noose that had eaten into the skin of her neck, and the clean-cut end of the rope that had fallen and coiled around her.

This was no climbing accident.

He sat back on his haunches and, unlike the ravens or other wildlife, he looked up. There was a shelf of rock three-quarters of the way up the rock face, and what looked like a grassy slide to it from the top. He'd considered putting his last trap there, but he didn't have enough spare rope to get over that far.

Then he heard snatches of conversation in the wind from far above. From his position, he couldn't see up and over the edge of the rock face to see who it was. Not unless one of them bent forward and peered down over the edge of the cliff.

Nate reached into his bag and his fingers closed around the grip of his weapon.

"She's down there in them rocks," a deep male voice said.

"Where?" Higher, twangier, Southern.

"Down in them rocks. There's no way she walked away from—" and the breeze took the rest of the sentence away.

"I'm just sayin' I woulda liked to've had a go at her first. That's all I'm sayin'."

A laugh.

"Come on, look over the edge," Nate whispered as he thumbed back the hammer and pointed his gun straight up. If one of them exposed himself, well, that would be that.

As he waited, Nate felt like the old Nate. He didn't second-guess himself. He was sure from what he'd seen below him and what he'd heard above him that these two had been responsible for murdering her.

Then . . . nothing. They just stopped talking and went away.

He waited a full five minutes before he lowered his weapon. By then, his arms were trembling.

Nate sat back on the boulder and shook his head. Why couldn't one of them have just looked down?

HE GATHERED UP HIS GEAR and eyed the ravens. They were just waiting for him to leave so they could go back to stripping the carcass. He wished he had something he could cover the body with, but he didn't.

Nate noted the location. He didn't need a GPS to know exactly where he was.

The sun was elongating into an oblong shape before it dropped behind the western mountains. It was a two-hour hike to where he'd parked his Jeep, and another hour until he could get a cell phone signal and call his friend Joe Pickett.

This time, he thought, trouble had found *him*.

That poor woman. He wondered why they'd done it to her. But whatever it was, it didn't matter. They'd need to pay for it, whoever they were.

He was back in the world and back on the grid. But it was almost as if he'd never left.

15

JOE DROVE HOME CAUTIOUSLY THAT NIGHT, MORE INEBRIATED
than he wanted to be—or should have been. He kept a close eye
on the road ahead and in his mirrors for town cops or deputies.
Given what had happened in Judge Hewitt's courtroom that
day, he wasn't sure what kind of mood the locals would be in or
if he'd be able to talk his way out of a traffic violation or DUI
charge, which could be a career killer.

At least Dulcie, whom he'd left still cursing in the Stockman's Bar, was close enough to her house to get home quickly.
But at the rate she'd been drinking—round after round of scotch
on the rocks while challenging Joe to keep up with her—she'd
likely have to walk, although *stagger* was more like it. He'd

ordered only club soda after his second bourbon and water on an empty stomach, but he could feel the effects.

Joe was angry at himself for staying so long at the bar with her. Part of the reason was his own anger and frustration, and another part was she seemed too unstable for him to leave her there by herself.

He'd finally excused himself after she promised to go home. He offered to walk her there, but she got offended and said she could take care of herself and showed him the 9mm in her handbag. He relented.

On his way out of town, he stopped at the Burg-O-Pardner for a double cheeseburger to go for dinner. Daisy stared at the greasy bag on the truck seat as if to bore holes into it with her eyes. Twin strings of drool hung from her mouth to the floorboards. He'd neglected to feed her earlier.

"Oh, go ahead," he said. "I'll open a can of soup at home."

Daisy devoured the meal in three quick bites and shed the bag to the floorboards with a shake of her head.

Joe saw a pattern of green stars in the dark to the left side of the road and instinctively hit the brakes to let a herd of five mule deer—their eyes reflecting green in his headlights—cross the road in front of him. The sudden stop nearly threw Daisy off the seat.

"Sorry," he said to her.

Be more careful, he said to himself.

In his bourbon-fueled state, he noted that the herd consisted of a buck, a doe, two yearlings, and a fawn. Just like his own family.

And just as vulnerable.

DULCIE HAD BEEN beside herself in the Stockman's. He'd never seen her like that and he didn't ever want to see her that way again. Her fury had built in Judge Hewitt's chambers as she was dressed down for bringing such a sloppy and questionable case, and it grew when Undersheriff Spivak tried to defend himself.

"He did it," Spivak cried. "We all know he did it. All I did was try to make it a stronger case."

Joe believed him, although he, like Dulcie and the judge, wanted to strangle him. He recalled how adamant Spivak had been on their way up to the crime scene about finally nailing Dallas. He'd all but telegraphed his intentions, if Joe had been sharp enough at the time to pick up on it.

He'd obviously ridden into the mountains with casings from the .223 in one pocket and spent rounds from the same gun in the other—just in case. When Spivak said he'd "take care of the body," and sent both Steck and Joe away, he had the opportunity to plant the slugs. No wonder, Joe thought, the coroner had observed they were "shallow."

But Spivak surprised Joe with his lack of remorse, even when a stricken Sheriff Reed arrived and asked for his badge and gun and told him he was suspended, pending charges against him. Spivak really believed he'd done the right thing, that he "risked his own neck to help put away a douche bag who threatened the entire community."

It was a look into Spivak's soul Joe wished he'd never seen. The lack of accountability was staggering. Joe had noted similar traits in criminals and violators he'd encountered, but rarely, if ever, in a fellow law enforcement officer. He suspected that the absence of virtue was a growing trend in the nation as a whole, and one he didn't understand or embrace.

"You of all people have to understand," Spivak had pled to Joe. "You of all people know what kind of person we're dealing with. *He did it*. He's guilty as hell. We know he killed Farkus. And if I'd let him stay out on the street, other people would have gotten hurt."

"And now they will," Joe said.

Spivak looked back gape-mouthed, not comprehending what Joe had said.

"I JUST FUCKING WONDER how many other cases he 'helped' with," Dulcie had said to Joe at the bar. She was talking so loudly and gesticulating with her hands as to scare other customers away. When she'd used the word "helped," she made air quotes.

Joe noticed that Buck Timberman was eyeing them both closely. It was the look he got before he called the cops to intervene.

"Do you realize how many convictions he's been a part of? How many times he's testified in criminal trials?" she asked Joe. "Now all of those criminals I've put away will be racing each other to file appeals. He's tainted everything we've done for the last few years—every case. He's dragged me and all of us into the mud with him."

Joe nodded and sipped his drink.

"Two more," Dulcie said to Timberman, who slowly shuffled

for the bottles of bourbon and scotch behind him. Joe waved him off the bourbon and gestured for another club soda.

"Judge Hewitt thinks I knew something about it," she said. "He all but accused me of working with the sheriff's department to falsify evidence. And he probably thinks you knew about it, too."

"Maybe," Joe said. It didn't sit well with him.

"Did you see this coming in any way?" she asked him.

"Nope. But now that I think back, I should have been more suspicious."

"I thought for a second that maybe . . . *maybe* Spivak had something to do with the killing. But I don't think so. He just wanted to make sure we nailed Dallas."

Joe agreed.

"This is the kind of thing I absolutely hate with every fiber in my being," she said loudly. "I *love* the law. I love justice. I love putting dirtbags away. Lester Spivak has just made it so every defense lawyer I go up against can play this card against me. And every voter in the county will wonder if they're voting for a corrupt prosecutor from now on—if they even vote for me at all.

"I can't run again," she said solemnly, as if the thought had just hit her. "I'm going to have to move far away from here and go into private practice. But I'll never be far enough away that people won't know. T. Cletus Glatt and the Internet will make sure of that."

She wheeled on her stool and waved at Timberman. "Two more!"

Joe had barely started on the last one. "Dulcie, I—"

"Damn it," she hissed as she rotated back around. "Now that son of a bitch is going to be bulletproof."

Joe was confused and shook his head.

"Dallas Cates," she said. "He's just gotten a Get Out of Jail Free card courtesy of Lester Spivak. There's no way Judge Hewitt would let him be tried again in his courtroom."

"Would it be considered double jeopardy?" Joe asked.

"No, not technically. The charges were dismissed, so Dallas didn't go through a trial. But we can't try him again for the murder, because all the defense would have to do is call Spivak as a witness to show corruption and malice against Dallas Cates on behalf of law enforcement. Even if Judge Hewitt allowed a retrial it would result in an acquittal.

"So now Dallas is out on the street and more dangerous than ever, because he knows we all have to tiptoe our way around him or he'll scream harassment and file a civil suit that bankrupts the county."

She bent toward Joe and waved her finger in his face. Her eyes glistened with anger and alcohol.

"The only thing Lester said today that made any sense was that Dallas murdered Farkus. In my heart, I believe he did. And now that son of a bitch is free as a bird and on our streets where he'll strut around rubbing our noses in it."

He knew she was right.

She said, "Did you see the way Marcus Hand looked at me? With pity? Do you know how much that hurt?

"I'm calling Marybeth," Dulcie declared. "She is absolutely *not* going to believe this."

He winced in anticipation.

AFTER DULCIE HAD GIVEN the news to an incredulous Marybeth in Jackson Hole, she handed her phone to Joe.

"She wants to talk to you." Then, to Timberman: "Two more!"

"She didn't just order two more, did she?" Marybeth asked.

"She did."

"I don't think she needs another one. You, either."

"I agree."

"I've been wondering what happened all afternoon. Don't you answer your phone anymore?"

"What? Oh, I had to leave it in my truck when I was at the courthouse," he said, removing it from his pocket and unlocking it. "I guess I forgot to check it."

The screen showed five missed calls. Two from Marybeth, one from the governor's office, one from game warden Rick Ewig, and one from an unknown number.

Marybeth sighed. "I can't believe what happened in court today. What do we do now?"

Joe had no answer.

She said, "Now sounds like it might be the worst time possible to come back, but I don't see any other choice. My board has been very gracious, but it's been two weeks and I've used up all my vacation time. I can't run a library from here, and things are starting to fall apart. They're starting to get anxious, and I don't blame them."

"What are you saying?" Joe asked. In his peripheral vision, he watched Dulcie slam a drink and reach for another.

"Sheridan went back to her job at the dude ranch today," she said. "I couldn't convince her to stay. She was bored, and she's as stubborn as her father once she makes her mind up.

"April is more than ready to get back to school. She wants to be there when Joy recovers and comes back, and she wants to get back on the rodeo team before they think about pulling her scholarship—and she has a point. Lucy can only do so much from here and maintain her grades."

Joe nodded to himself.

"Joe, are you there?"

"Yes."

"You can't nod. I can't hear you when you nod."

He sat up and said, "Yup."

"I wish I could say that my mother is driving me out, but I can't. She's been a saint. I don't even know who she is anymore, but she does everything she can to make us all comfortable and give us space. She's so . . . *nice*. All I can think of is, she's up to something."

"She has to be," Joe agreed. "Maybe—"

"No," Marybeth said firmly. "I won't ask her for money. I don't want to be obligated to her any more than I am. There are always strings attached, and I'm beyond that."

"Yup," he said, chastened.

"We don't have a choice," she said. "We need to come back. We can't run from a crazy tattooed woman for the rest of our lives." After a beat, she said, "Or anyone else."

He knew she meant Dallas.

He said, "See if you can get another week. Just a week. Talk to your board and the girls."

Marybeth didn't say anything for a long time. Next to him, Dulcie was telling Timberman that maybe she could move to Cheyenne, Casper, or Cody and set up a private practice.

"A week," Marybeth said. "Do you think things will be better by then?"

"I do," Joe said, even though it felt like a lie.

AS THE DEER PASSED through his headlights, Joe found himself staring at their afterimage long after they were gone. Stopping his truck had given him a moment to think.

His life was a dangerous mess and he couldn't sort it all out.

His family was gone, but making plans to come back when danger might be at its peak.

He was exhausted, out of sorts, and hadn't eaten a solid meal in two weeks.

He asked himself:

What had happened to Dallas's accomplices from that night? Who were they? What motivated them? Would he ever learn what that was all about now that the trial had been dismissed?

How in the hell did Dallas afford Marcus Hand?

When would Wanda Stacy ever show up again?

Why hadn't the tattooed woman ever been caught?

Would the poaching ring ever be identified and arrested?

Did any of these things even connect?

And most of all, what would Dallas Cates do now that he was back on the street? Would he follow up on his vague and specific threats to avenge what he claimed Joe had done to him and his family?

―――――

WITH A KIND OF MENTAL THUNDERCLAP, he knew the partial answer to the last question might soon reveal itself.

As his headlights swept across his lonely house, there was Dallas. He half sat, half slouched against the white picket fence with his arms crossed over his chest.

The brim of his cowboy hat rose as he looked up. There was a wide smile on his face. His big championship rodeo buckle glinted in the headlights like a flare.

Joe was suddenly very sober.

DAISY SAW DALLAS CATES AND GROWLED. THE HAIR ON THE BACK of her neck bristled into a ridge.

With an unsteady hand, Joe plucked the microphone from its cradle on the dashboard to connect with the dispatcher in Cheyenne. He knew he had just a few seconds to decide whether to pull in, park, and face Dallas—or drive on.

He decided. Driving on was an act of cowardice, even though he could hear Marybeth and all three of his daughters in the back of his mind imploring him to keep going.

"This is GF-20 arriving at my home to find Dallas Cates standing here waiting for me in the dark."

"Come again, GF-20?" the distant voice asked.

"Please note what I just told you in case something happens," he said, and keyed off. He knew the exchange was recorded for posterity. He just hoped that no one ever had a reason to call it up.

Joe turned into his usual place in the driveway of the detached garage. Dallas's head swiveled slightly to follow him, but he didn't move from his place on the fence.

Joe took a quick look around. He still wasn't used to arriving at his house to find it dark, vacant, and lonely looking. In normal circumstances, the arrival of Dallas would have cued barking dogs and porch lights going on. But these weren't normal circumstances.

Joe didn't want to hesitate too long inside the vehicle and convey fear or trepidation. Dallas fed on that.

He noticed Eldon Cates's old Dodge pickup parked fifty feet up the road. There was no sign of Dallas's compatriots, but Joe knew there were plenty of places for them to hide in the dark—including inside his own house. Like everyone else in Twelve Sleep County, Joe never locked the door.

He turned off the engine but kept the headlights on to provide at least some light. Enough bounce-back illumination from the closed garage door light reached over to Dallas that Joe could see a condensation-cloud halo around his cowboy hat.

Fishing his small digital recorder out of a seat pocket, he turned it on and slipped it into his right breast pocket. His twelve-gauge Remington Wingmaster shotgun was loaded with buckshot, but as usual, it was behind the seat. He wished it was in easy reach.

"Stay, Daisy," he said. He took a deep breath, opened his door, and swung out.

If Dallas was armed, Joe couldn't see the weapon on his person. He hoped not. Dallas was much more likely to hit what he aimed at with a handgun than Joe had ever been.

Not that Dallas necessarily needed a weapon, Joe thought. Dallas was wider, stronger, and younger than Joe. The man's neck was as thick as Joe's thigh. And he had a well-deserved reputation for his volcanic temper and quick fists when he got into a fight growing up—which was often.

Joe did a mental inventory of his gear belt: .40 Glock in its holster, two extra magazines, handcuffs, bear spray. He thought he'd likely reach for the bear spray before anything else if it came to a sudden physical confrontation.

He walked within fifteen feet of Dallas and stopped. His own shadow covered Dallas and he couldn't see him well.

"What are you doing here?" he asked, stepping a foot to the side so he could see the man better.

Dallas held his grin. "Your house is paid for by taxpayers, right? Well, I'm a taxpayer. I have as much right to come here as anyone."

Joe waited for more.

Dallas chinned toward a wooden hand-painted sign on the fence next to him that read GAME WARDEN STATION. "April told me you have hunters and fishermen showing up here at all hours, and you have a duty to talk to them, right? It ain't like it's your own private home."

"Okay, so what can I help you with?"

Dallas's smile twitched. "I've got so many things to say, I don't hardly know where to start."

"Start by stating your business. Then you can get in your truck and drive away."

Dallas chuckled and shook his head. "You're nervous, aren't you? I can't remember seeing you so keyed up before. What is it—a guilty conscience? You look like you're ready to snap."

Joe *was* ready to snap. He feared a kill-or-be-killed moment and he glanced toward the dark house to see if there was any movement of the curtains or blinds. Nothing.

"It's just me," Dallas assured him.

"Hey," Dallas said, snapping his fingers, as if a thought had just come to him, "are you recording our conversation right now? I know that's one of your game warden tricks—you can legally record a conversation in Wyoming if at least one of the parties is aware of it."

Joe didn't answer.

Dallas said, "But if one of the parties asks about a recording, you're required to fess up. You can't lie about it."

"I don't lie."

The grin got larger and more boxlike. "*Right.*

"See," Dallas said with an *Aw, shucks* grin, "I learned a few things from the jailhouse lawyers down in Rawlins. Not that it was a good use of my time overall, of course. I wasted a fucking year and a half of the most productive time of my life sitting on my ass in a place you never should have sent me to."

"I'm recording our conversation."

"Then I guess I refuse to participate. Nothing I say from here on out can be considered truthful. Did you get that on your tape recorder?"

Joe nodded. Dallas had used a tactic that would exempt whatever was said from being used later in court—if it ever came to that.

"Now that that's on the table, I'll start. First," Dallas said, "I knew it was a total frame-up the second I saw your Deputy Bonehead slinking around in the parking lot of the grocery store. I looked out and seen him standing there with his back to my dad's truck.

"He kind of looked the other way and did this"—Dallas raised a knee and kicked back with his boot—"and broke my taillight out. I knew then what was going on."

It was an old cop trick—a way to justify pulling someone over. Joe didn't doubt that it had happened the way Dallas told it. Spivak must not have realized the license tags were expired until later.

Joe darted his eyes toward the corner of his house and around the barn to see if the forms of Dallas's thugs could be seen in the dark. He was pleased to see the side-by-side heads of Marybeth's three horses—Rojo, Toby, and her new gelding, Petey—silhouetted against a low-hanging cloud in the sky. If the horses were calmly waiting to be fed that meant there were no strangers lurking in the corral.

"Then, of course," Dallas continued, "when Bonehead claimed that he found that rifle . . . I knew he was messing with me. I'm not gonna violate my parole by driving around with a gun in my car. Not when I know every cop in the county wants to bust me. I knew he was hoping I'd blow a gasket so he could pop me in self-defense. Luckily I kept my cool."

Joe nodded in agreement.

"So what did that idiot do?" Dallas asked. "Did he actually shove them slugs into the bullet wounds on Farkus's body? Did he do it with his finger or use a screwdriver or something like that?"

"I don't know."

"Oh yeah, I'm sure you don't."

"Finding out he took Farkus's blood sample was a surprise."

"What a *dick*," Dallas said with a menacing laugh.

"Why did you hunt Farkus down?" Joe asked.

"*What?*"

"You heard me."

"I didn't kill Dave Farkus. Why would I? He was just another old drunk in the bar."

Realizing he'd brought up the Stockman's without prompting, Dallas said, "Sure, I seen him that night in the bar. But that was no reason to go after him. I didn't hate him like I do you. If anything—and I'm not admitting a goddamn thing—I could see a situation where Dave Farkus just got himself in the way. It wasn't personal, I'm sure.

"And even if I did him in, it don't matter now, does it? I've already been on trial and it got dismissed. There's no way you can arrest me again for the same crime, and we both know it."

"That's true," Joe said. "I'll wait until you do something stupid. Judging by your track record, I don't figure I'll be waiting all that long."

"Ha!" Dallas barked facetiously. "Good one, Joe."

"Where are your three pals?" Joe asked.

"My three pals?"

"The two men and the woman with tattoos. Randall Luthi, Rory Cross, and the woman."

Dallas shook his head slowly, as if perplexed by the question.

"Start with the woman in the bar with you that night. Where is she? Who is she?"

Dallas shrugged. "I didn't get her name. She was just a random buckle bunny who was hopin' I'd notice her. Believe it or not, that happens with me all the time. Think about your daughter, Joe."

"Her *name*."

"I already told you—I don't know who she is or what her name was."

He was good at playing innocent, but there was a tell, Joe observed. Even though his facial expression didn't change, Dallas blinked much more rapidly while he was lying. And he was blinking now.

"Who were the two male thugs you were with? Luthi and Cross," Joe asked. "The ones who got out of your house just before the cops showed up."

"'Thugs' is kind of a shitty word."

"And right on the money," Joe said.

"They were friends of mine. I met them in Rawlins. I have no idea where they took off to."

More blinking.

"Why didn't you tell us their names?"

"Why? So you guys could frame them, too? I don't do that to my friends."

"Do you know anything about the disappearance of Wanda Stacy?"

"Who?"

"The bartender that night. The one who might have overheard your plans."

Dallas feigned trying to recall her. Finally, he said, "She might have wanted me to pay a little more attention to her, is all.

I think she was way past her sell-by date, if you want to know the truth."

"Here's the thing I can't figure out," Joe said. "What are you offering these pals of yours? Don't tell me they do anything you tell them to just because you're such a charming guy. Where did you get the money to pay for Marcus Hand to represent you and three thugs to risk their lives for you?"

Dallas chuckled and patted his massive belt buckle. "Maybe they just want to be close to a champion? Did you ever think of that?"

"Is there anything you won't lie to me about?" Joe asked.

Dallas nodded sincerely and said, "There are a few things. I think you know what they are."

Joe didn't follow up. There was no need to.

"You know what you did to me, don't you?" Dallas asked. "You and that county prosecutor got together and sent me to prison on charges that would have gotten anybody else a ticket and a fine—if he wasn't named Cates. It either eats at you inside or you're one cold son of a bitch."

Joe didn't argue. There was nothing to argue about.

"You killed my brother Bull. Shot him right in the face."

"In self-defense," Joe said.

"That's your story. Deputy Bonehead's got his story, too."

"Don't link us together."

"Of course not," Dallas said with a jeer. "You're Mr. Pure as the Driven Snow and Bonehead is corrupt. Like I really believe that. At least Bonehead wasn't responsible for my dad's death and crippling my mother for life. That was all *you*.

"And what about my brother Timber? He gets out of prison

and goes all the way up to Billings and decides to throw himself off a building? Am I supposed to buy that?"

Joe said, "The building was a hospital where my daughter was recovering from what happened to her when you kicked her out of your truck. A hospital."

Dallas waved off the distinction. "Here's what I know. One week I'm on top of the world and on top of the rodeo standings. I've got a mom and a dad and two brothers and property that'll someday be mine. The next week, I'm so busted up I'll never rodeo again, and only my mother is still alive—barely. She'll never walk again and she'll die in prison."

He jabbed his finger at Joe. "*That's* what I fucking know."

For a moment, Joe found it hard to breathe or swallow. He knew he could counter everything Dallas had said, but there was no doubt Dallas believed his own version. And what hit Joe the hardest was how much of what he'd said was . . . true enough.

Gesturing toward the front of the house, Dallas said, "Speaking of: Where the *hell* is your family?"

"Not here."

"Well, I got *that*. Did they all run off? Are they scared like you?"

Joe had no way to answer the question without putting himself on the defensive.

"They're on a trip," he said.

"What about April? I spent many a lonely night thinking about that girl. Actually, more than thinking about her, if you know what I mean."

Joe felt the hairs prick up on the back of his neck and on his forearms.

"She's a goddamned *tiger* in the sack, you know," Dallas said. "I always wondered where she learned all the things she knows. Was it in that house over my shoulder, or somewhere else?" His eyes were locked on Joe's face to note his reaction.

"That's enough of that," Joe said through clenched teeth.

"Or what?"

Joe heard Dulcie's voice in his head say, *He's fucking bullet-proof right now.*

"I'm guessing they'll be back soon," Dallas said. "Tell them they don't need to be in no hurry. You and me have some issues to work out before they get involved."

Joe cocked his head. He had no idea what that meant.

Dallas raised his hand and gestured to his eyes with two outstretched fingers, then pointed them at Joe's face.

"You and me," he repeated.

Joe got it even though Dallas was being deliberately obtuse. He'd misread Dallas's intentions. Joe himself would be first. In a way, it was a relief, because it spared his family.

Then he realized what Dallas was actually saying, and it was worse than anything Joe could have imagined. Joe would go first, leaving his family alone and unprotected. Then, one by one, they'd be next.

It was the cruelest thing Joe could conceive of. And Dallas knew it.

"You know what you did to me, don't you?" Dallas asked.

"I do."

"You knew I'd come back."

"It doesn't have to be this way," Joe said. "You could stop it. It doesn't have to be a vicious circle."

Dallas seemed to think about it. At least he was quiet for a long time.

Then he looked up and said, "I'm not carrying. You have that gun on your hip. You could do a Bonehead move and take me out like you did Bull. Maybe plant a gun to make it look good. *You* could end it now."

"I'm not built that way."

"I knew you'd say that," Dallas said with a smirk. "April told me enough about you."

"Don't come near my family," Joe said.

"Oh, don't worry," Dallas said. "You won't be around to worry about that."

DALLAS WALKED deliberately close to Joe as he headed toward his truck. Close enough that Joe could smell his animal scent as he passed by.

Joe turned and focused on Dallas's wide back. At ten feet, even Joe could hit that target.

He couldn't shoot a man in the back, though. Not even Dallas.

Instead, he closed his eyes and listened to the sound of his own blood roaring in his ears.

JOE WALKED through every room of his house with his shotgun to make sure no one was hiding out. He checked the closets and under the beds.

He took his shotgun with him to the barn to feed the horses, and was spooked when a great horned owl sailed from its perch in the rafters and out through a stall opening into the night. He watched it vanish down the barrel of his weapon and breathed a sigh of relief that he hadn't blasted it out of the sky.

Inside, he placed the weapon on his dining room table within easy reach as he thawed a package of elk steaks in the microwave. More than once, he glanced out through the living room window for approaching headlights.

What Dallas had said seemed to hover over him and press down on his head and shoulders.

You could end it now.

You won't be around to worry about that.

Joe listened to it again on his recorder. He'd need to download the conversation to his home computer so there was a record of it, for posterity. A record for the investigators in case Dallas got to him.

He checked his phone again. There was no reason to return the call to the governor's office until the next morning. He ignored the missed call labeled CALLER UNKNOWN.

Under Rick Ewig's message, he thumbed CALL BACK.

"Joe!" Ewig said when he answered. "I heard what happened today. Sorry, man."

"Thanks."

Joe could hear a television in the background and the yelp of an infant. Ewig had two small children.

"Hey, I got a lead on our poaching ring," Ewig said.

Joe was grateful for the distraction.

"You know there are a bunch of industrial buildings to the

west of town, right? Places where the energy companies have just up and left?"

"Yes."

Joe had seen road after road of abandoned oil and gas company shops outside of Gillette that just a year earlier had been occupied.

"Well, somebody called and said they'd seen activity in the middle of the night at one of them. The cops checked it out and called me and I found a wild-game processing facility. Stainless-steel tables, wrapping paper, coolers, the whole nine yards. I also found plenty of trace evidence: hide, hairs, blood they didn't get cleaned up. And out back in an old dumpster were nine or ten carcasses. Mostly does and cow elk, like our ring goes after."

"Well done," Joe said.

Ewig had photographed the facility and sent both the digital photos and evidence samples to the state lab in Laramie. The Gillette PD was checking it for fingerprints and trace fibers.

"It's under surveillance," Ewig said. "Maybe we'll catch our boys in the act of butchering a deer."

"I hope so," Joe said. "Keep me posted."

AS HE TALKED, he paid no notice to Daisy gathering herself up from where she'd curled at his feet and padding toward the front door. Tube was already there wiggling her backside.

He didn't notice Daisy's tail flitting back and forth like an errant windshield wiper—the way she greeted familiar guests.

But when he disconnected the call with Ewig and looked up,

the threshold of the mudroom door filled with the person of Nate Romanowski.

"Don't you return calls anymore?" Nate asked.

"You must be the unknown number."

"Sounds just like me."

Nate looked trim and tan. His blond ponytail had been bleached by the sun. He wore a long-sleeved shirt with *Yarak, Inc.* embroidered over the breast pocket.

"It's good to see you, Nate," Joe said. "Welcome back."

Nate looked around at the empty house, and his eyes lingered on the shotgun on the kitchen table.

"Something's up," he said.

"Yup, it is," Joe sighed.

PART THREE

No one fights dirtier or more brutally than blood; only family
knows its own weakness, the exact placement of the heart.

—Whitney Otto, *How to Make an American Quilt*

AS THE SENIOR NIGHT-SHIFT SECURITY GUARD OF TETON SHAD-
ows, Gary Bulla had long ago learned not to be surprised by
who stopped outside the gate wanting to be let in. He'd seen
movie and television stars, politicians, singers, and other celeb-
rity faces in expensive cars who were vaguely familiar and whom
he'd later have to look up on the Internet after he either cleared
them with residents or turned them away.

He'd tried not to stare inside the car when a U.S. senator he'd
seen giving a speech at the Democratic National Convention
drove up with his trousers bunched around his ankles and the
back of a woman's head bobbing up and down in his lap. He'd
tried not to gape when a slim, blond ex–country singer and current pop star last seen on the Grammy Awards appeared at the

wheel of a Lexus SUV with mascara running down her face from tears and her chin trembling.

Professionalism and discretion were important if he wanted to keep his job. So was keeping the riffraff out.

Bulla wore a handheld radio and a Sig Sauer 1911 Scorpion .45 on his belt. When someone he didn't know arrived at the gate and said they were there to see one of the thirty-five owners within Teton Shadows, but they weren't on the official visitation list, he'd ask the driver to wait until he received verbal confirmation that it was okay. He made no exceptions.

One wall of the office was filled with monitors linked to the bevy of closed-circuit security cameras stationed throughout the gated community. During the daytime, the views were filled with lush green lawns and perfectly trimmed pine trees. At night the grounds looked somewhat garish under the overhead lamps. A portable heater hummed against the late-fall cold.

Security guard at the exclusive subdivision had been the best job he'd landed since he arrived in Jackson Hole to be an outdoor gear inventor and entrepreneur three years before, only to discover that the combination sleeping pad/sleeping bag/one-man shelter he'd designed in his garage in Milwaukee had already been patented and manufactured and was selling poorly. He'd tried to interest the outdoor-gear manufacturer that had turned him down with another idea—a multi-tool that was both a hatchet and a marijuana pipe—but they'd shot that down as well.

On his desk inside the small security shack outside the gate was a drawing for a one-man float tube that could double as a shelter for two in the wilderness. He was careful to cover it each time a visitor pulled up so they couldn't steal his idea.

When they didn't arrive in luxury cars or massive vehicles like Missy Vankueren Hand's Hummer H2, residents as well as visitors showed up on mountain bikes, ATVs, golf carts, and even horses. It wasn't what they used for transportation that could get them in, it was who they were or who they were there to see.

What he'd never seen, though, was a bedraggled woman on foot approach the gate pulling a child's red wagon behind her.

Bulla squinted his eyes as she got closer, and he could see her better under the entrance lights. She was thin and her clothes were dirty and oversized. Straw-colored hair spilled out of the opening of her pulled-up hoodie and looked greasy in the harsh light. One of the wheels of the wagon squeaked as it rolled.

He stood up and placed a manila file folder over his drawing so she couldn't see it. Then he opened the door and stepped out onto the flagstone porch with his right hand, as always, near his .45.

"You look like you might be lost," he said.

The woman with the wagon kept coming until she was just below him on the asphalt entry. When she finally stopped, the squeak stopped as well. He noticed that whatever was in the child's wagon was covered by a blanket.

"Is this the place where the Picketts are staying?" she asked. "I'm a friend of the family."

She had hollow eye sockets and thin lips. The skin of her face was pitted with the scars of long-ago acne. What he thought at first were gloves turned out to be swirling tattoos on the backs of her hands. A line of ink tears dropped down her cheek from her right eye.

Bulla was used to seeing hipsters all over Jackson Hole, and they sometimes came to the gate. Baggy clothes, hoodies, strategically unkempt hair, no makeup. But there was always *something*—designer frames, an Apple Watch, a wristband in support of some fashionable cause or other—that said the hipster was a hipster and not a bum.

This woman looked more like a tweaker than a hipster.

"Are they expecting you?" he asked.

"They should be." He caught a glimpse of bad teeth. Yes, he thought, a tweaker.

Bulla knew that Mrs. Pickett was out with Mrs. Hand. They'd gone through the gate toward Jackson twenty minutes earlier in the H2. He hadn't seen the Pickett girls, but he assumed they were at the Hand residence.

"I'll need to see some ID," he said. "I'll give them a call."

"ID?"

"ID."

"It's in my wagon," she said vacantly. "Just a sec and I'll get it."

Bulla sidled closer, curious to see what was under the blanket.

She reached under the material and groped around. Her fingers appeared to close around something.

Bulla leaned toward her.

She slipped the ax out from under the blanket and gripped the handle with two hands and swung it.

The blade sliced a thin oval of flesh out of the top of his shoulder and made a *thunk* sound as it buried in his neck.

"MARCUS WILL BE COMING HOME TOMORROW," Missy said to Marybeth as she commandeered the H2 on the highway from town.

Marybeth nodded as she studied her mother behind the wheel. As always, she was speeding, driving nearly seventy in a forty-five-mile-per-hour zone and whipping around tourists who obeyed the law. That hadn't changed even though everything else about her seemed to have. The take-out Thai food they'd picked up for dinner smelled pungent and filled the interior of the car.

Marybeth said, "Yes, I heard from Joe and the prosecutor what happened at the trial."

"Of course you did." Then: "Marcus doesn't lose, you know."

Marybeth wanted to say that her mother knew more about that than anyone, but she held her tongue.

"The only problem with a trial that short is the paltry billable hours," Missy lamented. "I hope they negotiated a flat rate for an acquittal. It would be a shame if Marcus's firm could only charge for his few days on the case."

"And the fact that a monster who wants to get revenge on my husband is back out on the street," Marybeth said.

"Well, there's that, I suppose," Missy said breezily.

"How did Dallas Cates afford to hire Marcus? Where did he get the money?"

Missy shrugged. "I don't get involved in those kinds of details. All I care about is that *someone* is paying the legal bill."

"Right."

"Let's not talk shop and have a disagreement. I'll suggest to Marcus that he not discuss his client around the house."

"That's probably a good idea," Marybeth said.

"I'll also suggest that he not walk around naked while you and the girls are here. He has a tendency to do that. He used to walk outside to get the newspaper naked, but the neighbors complained."

Marybeth winced at the visual in her mind.

"He'll get used to it," Missy declared.

"Get used to what?" Marybeth asked.

"Oh, nothing. You can still stay as long as you want. As you know, we've got plenty of room."

"Have you talked to him about it? Is Marcus okay with us being here?"

"He will be," Missy said with steel in her voice.

"So he isn't now."

"He'll come around."

"Joe wants us to stay another week," Marybeth said. It felt strange to talk to her mother as if she were a real and normal person. Marybeth wasn't accustomed to it.

"You can stay longer."

"Really?" Marybeth asked. Missy actually wanted them around.

"We're all ready to go back," Marybeth told her mother.

"*I see.*" Missy sounded hurt.

"It's not that we don't appreciate your hospitality. We just have to return to our lives. The girls have school, I have my job. I miss Joe."

Missy blew out a puff of breath. "You'd actually leave this and go back to . . . *that*?"

Marybeth gritted her teeth and said nothing.

Missy said, "I've learned over the years that it's possible to overlook serious flaws in a man if you're safe and secure. What I don't understand is choosing to settle. You're beautiful, smart, and well-educated, but you choose to stay in that grubby existence with a man who can barely provide for you and my grand-daughters."

"There's a library here, you know," Missy said with exasperation in her voice. "It's actually modern and well-funded. And there are plenty of wealthy patrons who have second or third homes in the valley."

"There she is," Marybeth said, eyes flashing. "The mask just slipped. This is the mother I know. You've been hiding behind that other person the whole time."

"I have no idea what you're talking about," Missy said.

"I get it now. I should have seen it earlier, but I actually thought that in your old age you'd become sentimental."

Missy flinched at the words *old age*, as Marybeth knew she would.

"The idea was to get us all here in the lap of luxury so we'd get used to it and want it for ourselves," Marybeth continued. "Then we'd collectively come to the conclusion that this is what we *really* wanted. You assume everybody thinks like you do. You can't even imagine the possibility that someone could live a full, rich life with a husband she loved in what you consider a grubby existence."

Missy's expression hardened, but she didn't look over. She almost missed the turnoff to Teton Shadows and had to slam on the brakes to make it. The Thai food tumbled off the backseat to the floorboards, and several cartons opened and spilled out.

"Now look what you've done," Missy said. "I hope some of it is salvageable."

Marybeth tried to ignore the comment, but being blamed for her mother's own actions was a flashback to her youth. Missy was quick to assign blame for her mistakes not to herself but to whoever caused her to lose control.

"You don't like Joe because he knows you for what you are."

"That's ridiculous," Missy said with an eye roll. "I don't like Joe because you deserve better, and so do my granddaughters. Every mother wants the best for her child."

"You are the least motherly mother I've ever come across. You don't get it. You should want me to be happy—which I am."

"I want you to not embarrass yourself or embarrass me," Missy spat as she neared the gate and slowed down to a full stop.

Marybeth was stunned and furious. "We're leaving tonight."

"Don't be foolish. It isn't safe back there, which is why you're here," Missy said. "Hmmm, I don't see Gary."

Marybeth couldn't stand to be in the car with her mother another moment. "I'll open the gate," she said as she jumped out.

As she entered the guard station, she saw two things at once: Gary Bulla on the floor in a pool of blood and, on a closed-circuit television monitor, a woman with an ax approaching

Missy's house. A child's wagon had been pulled up into the front yard.

Missy tapped on her horn to urge her to hurry up and open the gate.

Instead, Marybeth swiped her cell phone to unlock it and punched 911.

A female dispatcher picked up within seconds. Marybeth tried to remain cool.

"My name is Marybeth Pickett and I'm at the entrance gate to Teton Shadows. The guard here has been attacked and injured and he's on the floor and bleeding out. I can see on the video monitor that a woman is approaching my mother's house with an ax. You need to send law enforcement out here as soon as possible. My daughters are in the house."

There was a long pause on the other end. "Please calm down, Mrs. Pickett. What can you see on the screen?"

Marybeth felt a flash of rage. *Please calm down.*

"Look, I'm as calm as I can be. Now send the cops before more people get hurt."

"I'll see who's available, but stay on the line," the dispatcher said.

Marybeth could see Missy in the H2. She was obviously steaming over the delay. Missy shoved the transmission into park, shut it off, and climbed out of the vehicle.

"I've got to call my daughters and warn them," Marybeth said to the dispatcher.

"Ma'am, you need to stay on the line . . ."

Missy crossed in front of her headlights and approached the door to the guardhouse. Marybeth covered the mike on her phone and raised her voice: "Mom, don't come in here."

Missy waved the warning away and pushed through the door. She gasped when she saw Gary Bulla on the floor.

Marybeth had to ignore her and concentrate on the situation. With a trembling hand, she found the hold prompt on the screen of her phone and speed-dialed Lucy's cell. Lucy was better at answering her phone than April, who usually let it go to voicemail.

Lucy picked up. "Hi, Mom. What's up?"

Marybeth closed her eyes. "Lucy, right now there's a woman coming to the front door with an ax. I think she's the same one who attacked Joy and April. The same one Sheridan saw. Run and make sure the front door is bolted."

"Who is she?"

"Never mind," Marybeth snapped. "Bolt the door *now*."

On the screen, the woman paused on the front porch for a moment as she lifted something to her mouth. By her hunched-over posture, it looked like she was making a call on a cell phone. Marybeth didn't know what the woman was doing or who she was calling, but she was grateful for it. After a few seconds, the woman returned the phone to her hoodie pocket and raised a closed fist and pounded on the heavy walnut door.

Behind her, Missy asked, "Who is that crazy woman you're looking at? Did she do this to Gary?" She gasped again and said, "Hey—*that's my house!*"

"Please, Mom," Marybeth pleaded. "Not now.

"Where are you?" she asked Lucy.

"Doing what you told me to do," Lucy said, slightly out of breath. Marybeth could hear the knocking on the door through the phone.

Lucy said, "There. It's bolted. Where are you?"

Marybeth felt a tremendous weight lift off her shoulders.

"I'm watching you on video from the guardhouse."

As she said it to Lucy, the woman on the porch reached out and tried to work the handle on the door that had just been locked. It didn't open, and Marybeth was flooded with relief.

"She's trying to get in," Lucy said. She was frightened now and her tone was shrill.

"Where's April?" Marybeth asked.

"In her room, I guess."

On the monitor the woman on the porch leaned back and grasped the ax handle with both hands and swung it toward the door. Lucy screamed and Marybeth could hear the *thunk* through her speaker.

"What is she doing?" Missy cried out behind Marybeth. "Does she have any idea how expensive that door is?"

"Shut up!" Marybeth hissed at Missy.

She recalled that the dispatcher was on hold. She said, "Lucy, stay on your phone. I've got to talk to the police and I'll be back in a second."

"Mom—"

Marybeth switched to the initial line halfway through a sentence.

"—Mrs. Pickett? Are you still there?"

"I'm back," Marybeth said. "Is someone on the way?"

"We've dispatched two units."

"How long will it take?"

On the screen, the woman swung again, and the ax blade sent splinters flying.

"They'll get there as soon as possible, ma'am. Now please stay on the—"

"How fucking long will it take?"

"One unit is less than five minutes away," the dispatcher said.

"Tell him to hurry. The woman is hitting the front door with the ax now. There are two young women—my daughters—inside."

"What is the address, ma'am?"

Marybeth turned to Missy, who was covering her mouth with her hand and watching the monitor.

"What's your physical address?"

Missy was speechless. Marybeth didn't know if it was because of Gary's injuries, her granddaughters in immediate danger, the damage to an expensive walnut door, or all three.

Marybeth said to the dispatcher, "Marcus and Missy Hand's house on Snake River Drive. Two-oh-four, I think."

"Got it." Marybeth heard the dispatcher repeat the address over the air. As she did, the woman on the porch hit the door again. She was aiming at the wood near the lock. Marybeth knew if the blade struck it just right . . .

To Missy: "Where are your keys?"

"My keys?"

"The keys to your car! You shut it off, and I'm going to knock down the gate and stop that woman."

Missy frantically patted herself down but came up empty. "Maybe I left them in my purse . . ." she said, nodding toward her H2.

"Forget it," Marybeth said. To the dispatcher: "I can jump in the officer's car when he gets here and guide him there."

"Ma'am, we have a policy about civilians riding in patrol vehicles—"

Marybeth cut her off and switched to Lucy. "I'm back."

There was a loud crunch, and Lucy said, "She's about to get in." There was panic in her voice.

"Go get April and run to Marcus's office," Marybeth said. She'd noticed that Hand's door had a stout bolt lock on the inside, because he apparently wanted complete privacy from Missy from time to time. "Close the door and lock it. Keep your phone on."

"Okay," Lucy said.

Marybeth heard gurgling and looked down. Bulla was covering a terrible wound in his neck with his right hand and trying to pull himself up with his left. Until that moment, she'd thought he was already gone.

"Help him," she said to Missy.

Missy looked back with horror in her eyes.

"*Get down there and help him.* Try to stop the bleeding."

Then she heard an approaching siren.

She looked up at the monitor. It was surreal. The woman was still hitting the front door, and now light from inside streamed out. But it wasn't yet open. The attacker wasn't hitting at the door with the fury she'd had when she started. Maybe, Marybeth hoped, she was getting tired.

As the siren got louder, Marybeth shook her head from side to side. She could only hope that the officer could get to Missy's house before the woman could summon up a second wind and break inside.

Blue and yellow wigwag lights lit up the tree-lined entrance to Teton Shadows and the siren wailed.

Marybeth found the button to raise the gate on a console and punched it. The mechanism hummed and the gate rose. She pushed her mother aside and ran out onto the road, waving her arms.

The baby-faced Teton County deputy cut the siren and his window slid down. He leaned over into the passenger seat and looked up at her.

"Let's hurry," she said to him, and climbed in beside him. He looked terrified.

Lucy's voice sounded tinny through the speaker on the phone in her hand.

"Mom—I think she's in the house."

18

IN THE PREVIOUS HOUR, JOE AND NATE HAD CAUGHT UP WITH each other so quickly, it seemed like they'd never really left off. When Nate described the body he'd found in the rocks that afternoon, Joe said, "Sounds a lot like Wanda Stacy."

"Wanda who?"

"The bartender I told you about."

"Ah, right," Nate said. He sipped at a glass of bourbon. Joe had already had enough for the night and he'd brewed a pot of coffee.

"I'll call Sheriff Reed and tell him," Joe said. "Can you take his guys to the location?"

Nate nodded darkly. He avoided working with law enforcement types as much as possible, with Joe being the lone exception.

As Joe raised his phone, it lit up with a call and he looked at the screen.

"Unknown caller," Joe said.

"It isn't me this time," Nate said.

Joe hesitated for a moment, then punched it up. Too many hunters, fishermen, and landowners seemed to have his private cell number these days. He couldn't risk not answering a random call if it turned out to be a tip or an emergency.

"Joe Pickett."

"Hey, bad news," a male voice said. The voice was distant and sounded muffled, as if the connection were poor or the caller had covered his microphone with a cloth.

"Excuse me?"

"I'm calling with some really bad news, man. There's been a bloodbath in Jackson Hole. A fucking bloodbath at some resort place. You know Teton Shadows?"

Joe went cold. He'd told no one where Marybeth and his daughters were. Perhaps Marcus Hand had mentioned it to someone, but—

"Yeah, it's ugly," the caller said with what sounded like false empathy. "Really fucking ugly. I guess some crazy lady with an ax killed your wife and daughter Lucy. An ax! Imagine that. Chopped them right up! April got it, too, but I guess she's still alive. They took her to the hospital, which is good. We'd like to finish that one up close and personal, if you catch my drift."

He was stunned. He knew what he'd heard, but he couldn't process it. The living room seemed to rotate on its axis around him and he felt an otherworldly floating sensation.

"Yeah, some meth-head tweaker, is what I heard. She broke

down the door with an ax and started hacking away. The cops caught her, but not before she did a hell of a lot of damage."

"Who are you?" Joe asked. "Is this Dallas?"

"Dallas who?" the man asked in a high-pitched voice that sounded a lot like Cates.

"If what you're telling me is true, you're a dead man," Joe said.

That got Nate's attention, and he jumped to his feet as if prepared to charge out the front door and pull someone apart with his bare hands.

The caller chuckled and said, "You missed your chance."

The call was disconnected.

Joe was frozen in place.

"Who was that?" Nate asked.

He couldn't speak. For a moment, he didn't realize the phone was buzzing in his hand again.

When he looked down at the screen he saw it was from the Teton County Sheriff's Department. It was the call he'd feared all of his life as a husband and father.

"My God," he whispered to Nate. "It might be true."

Nate looked back with narrowed eyes, trying to read the situation. Joe could barely move because he felt like all of his blood had drained out of him, leaving only a chilled husk.

"Aren't you going to answer that?" Nate asked.

Joe couldn't move.

"Joe, answer it," Nate said softly.

He pressed ANSWER and raised the cell to his ear.

"Joe, I'm calling you on this phone because mine ran out of battery . . ."

It was Marybeth. Joe closed his eyes and sat back in the chair. He pressed the phone so hard to his face that it hurt.

"I thought I'd lost you," he said. "I just got this call . . . He said you and the girls were attacked and killed."

"Well, half of that is right," she said. "I'm okay. I'm okay and the girls are fine. They're shaken up, but not hurt." Then: "What about this call?"

He explained what the caller had told him and ended it with "I think it was Dallas Cates."

Marybeth was silent for a moment. "I saw that woman call somebody. Now we know who it was."

Joe glanced up to see Nate pacing the floor aggressively. "It's Marybeth," Joe said. "They're all okay."

His friend's face changed from concern mode back to revenge mode in a split second. Joe nodded his agreement, then turned back to Marybeth as she explained what had happened.

The tweaker was trying to crawl through the hole she'd chopped in the door as Marybeth and the Teton County deputy got to the house. The woman was half in and half out with the ax apparently on the inside threshold when the deputy turned his spotlight on her.

The deputy told the tweaker to freeze in place, but the woman continued to struggle to get into the house. She pulled so hard that her hoodie tore loose on the splintered wood and she tumbled inside wearing only a dirty bra, but she caught her right foot in the hole.

The deputy acted fast and ran to where she was. He held the tweaker by the foot so she couldn't proceed any farther inside while they waited for backup. Marybeth ran around the house and entered it through the unlocked back door. She found April and Lucy in Marcus Hand's office and ushered them outside. When they got to the front, a second sheriff's department unit had arrived and more were on the way.

Marybeth led the second deputy around back and through the house to the living room. The woman was on her belly on the tile floor, trying to pull her foot out of the grasp of the first deputy. She grunted like an animal and cursed the "fucking cops" and tried to reach for the ax handle that was just beyond her grasp.

"She was out of her mind on meth or something," Marybeth said. "She was literally foaming at the mouth when they cuffed her and took her away."

"Who is she?" Joe asked.

"I don't know. They said she has no ID, and she's not talking yet. All they found on her—besides the ax—was a burner cell phone and a wad of cash. Something like five grand."

"Is she the one who attacked Joy and April?" Joe asked.

"April says yes. It's her."

Joe finally allowed himself to breathe. He waved away the offer of a bourbon and water from Nate.

"You did everything right," he told Marybeth. "You're like a mother bear protecting her cubs."

"You're damned right," Marybeth said. "And *my* mother was completely useless the whole time."

Marybeth said the guard, Gary Bulla, was in critical condition, but his chances to survive were better than she would have thought.

"I'm so glad you're okay," he said. He recalled his moment of absolute horror after the first call. For a minute, his life had gone empty, and all he could think was that he wished he were dead, too. The sensation he'd had of being untethered—of floating up and out of his body—still lingered. It would take a while to get over it, and he never wanted to revisit that experience.

"I'm tough, you know," she said.

"Tougher than me," he said.

"With the tweaker in jail, we can come home now," she said. "I've got to give a formal statement of some kind to the deputies. So do the girls. But then I think they'll let us leave. It's over, Joe. We can come home."

He said, "Dallas is still out there."

"I can't stay another minute in my mother's house."

"That I can understand," he said.

He listened for a while longer, and she recounted the ticktock of the entire night in more detail. He knew she needed to verbalize it, to get it all out, even though she'd already told him the basics of the story. It was how she processed what she'd gone through. Joe had learned many years before to simply listen and not interrupt.

AFTER THEY ENDED the long call, he said to Nate, "I'll call Reed if you're okay with leading him to the body tomorrow."

Nate agreed. "I need to get back up there anyway and check my traps. He can come along. Aren't you coming?"

"No," Joe said. "I'm going to Jackson tonight. I want to see my family, and I want to talk to that tweaker. I want to find out who she's working for and why she was there."

Nate stared at Joe with his hawklike blue eyes for what seemed like five minutes before he said, "What's going on?"

Joe sat back. Nate, like Marybeth, knew him too well for Joe to try to mislead him.

He said, "For the past couple of weeks, and especially tonight, I had mixed feelings when it came to Dallas Cates. Even though I knew he was a bad dude, my heart wasn't into sending him back to prison. I knew how he got there in the first place, and it *was* sloppy. He'd lost his livelihood and he'd lost his family. There was no way I couldn't take those things into consideration and see my role in it."

Nate said with a sympathetic roll of his eyes: "Go on, Dudley Do-Right."

Joe ignored him. "There's some truth to the fact that this whole valley has always treated the Cates family like white trash, and much of that was well deserved. There's a kind of mob mentality I don't like. The Cateses had such a bad reputation that some people would justify anything to keep them down. Spivak, for instance. He screwed everything up because he thought the ends justified the means when it came to locking up Dallas Cates.

"But it can't go any further than this," Joe said. "Not with that phone call he made to me. I really thought for a few minutes that I'd lost *everything*. I can't get over it, and I just want to put him away for the rest of his life. Or kill him and end this."

"There's my boy," Nate said. "So how do we do it?"

"First," Joe said, "remember that I'm a sworn officer of the law. I can't just go after him, and I won't do that. I'm not judge, jury, and executioner."

"Leave that to me," Nate said with a cruel smile.

"No. I can't do that, either. But what I can do is work to connect all the dots so that we have a legitimate case against him. I think it starts with that tweaker."

Nate said, "I'm not sure where you're going here."

"That's okay. But in the meanwhile, can I ask you a favor for tomorrow?"

"Ask away."

"When you take Reed's guys up to find that body, could you not mention the two thugs you overheard? At least not yet?"

Nate's eyes narrowed and the smile got bigger. "That would be my pleasure," he said.

JACKSON HOLE APPEARED IN THE DARK NIGHT LIKE A TANGLE OF Christmas tree lights wedged between nearly vertical mountains. The moon exposed pale blue ski runs on Snow King Mountain.

It was two-thirty in the morning when Joe parked his pickup in front of the Teton County Sheriff's Department office on South King Street. Although only 207 miles as the crow flies from Saddlestring, it had taken six hours and 350 vehicle miles to get there through the sleeping communities of Dubois, Thermopolis, and Worland. Driving east to west across a state knuckled with north-to-south mountain ranges and rivers slowed things down. He'd crossed the Bighorn Mountains, paralleled the Bighorn River through Wind River Canyon, avoided the towering Wind River Range, and skirted the Gros Ventre Range to get there. Twice, he had to slow down for elk to cross the highway in his headlights and he'd almost hit a black bear loping across the road on Togwotee Pass.

His back ached from the long drive and his legs felt stiff as he climbed out of the truck. He'd had plenty of coffee to keep him awake, and his first stop inside the vestibule of the sheriff's department was the men's bathroom.

Cop shops always had a particular odor and sound—especially if there were people in custody in the jail cells. The glazed cinder-block hallway that led to a lighted receiving desk smelled of body odor badly masked by disinfectant. Inebriated snores and shouted sleeping sounds from the prisoners emanated from the air vents and echoed down the hallways.

He approached the Plexiglas window at the end of the hall and startled a heavyset woman who was reading a thick novel by Diana Gabaldon.

"My name is Joe Pickett," he said through the round chrome grille mounted in the center of the glass. He rotated his upper body so she could see the badge and name tag over his uniform pockets. "I'm here to see my family."

"I can see you're a game warden," she said, "but I'll still need to look at your ID."

As he fished his wallet out of his back Wrangler pocket, he said, "My wife reads those."

"Nothing gets my motor running like a man in a kilt," the receptionist said as she looked over his state ID as well as his driver's license.

"So I hear," he said.

He'd left his weapon and gear belt in his pickup so he wouldn't have to lock them up while he was inside.

"They're all back there in the waiting room," she said, handing back his cards. "All four of them. That was a hell of a thing that happened tonight. We see a lot of odd things in Jackson, as you can imagine, but a female nut with an ax? We don't see that very often."

"I'm glad to hear that," he said.

The steel door next to the counter unlocked with an electronic *clunk.*

ON THE WAY to a door marked LOUNGE, he passed through a squad room filled with high-walled cubicles. The overhead lights were muted, and it was quiet and empty inside except for two deputies who tapped at keyboards. Their faces were lit up by the glow from their computer screens.

They both looked up as he walked through the room. Joe approached the one nearest to him, a boyish deputy with a high-sidewall haircut.

"I'm Joe Pickett from Saddlestring. Are you one of the guys who helped my family tonight?" he asked.

The deputy, whose name badge read MCNAMEE, said, "I was the first on the scene with your wife. I'm working on the incident report now."

"I heard what you did," Joe said, extending his hand. "I want to thank you for keeping your cool."

McNamee blushed. "If you woulda known how fast my heart

was beating at the time, you wouldn't say that. I thought that woman would pull her foot out of her boot and get away."

"But she didn't," Joe said. "You held on."

The second deputy was much older and had a thick white mustache and a belly that hung over his belt.

"And you made the arrest," Joe said. "Good work."

"Doin' my job," the man said. He introduced himself as Ed Estrella. "Hey, it was more exciting than working a car wreck or arresting drunk skiers, that's for sure." He smiled and turned back to his screen.

"You're heroes," Joe said. "Thank you."

McNamee blushed some more.

"Do you have a name or a motive for the woman you arrested tonight?" Joe asked.

"Neither," McNamee said. "We do know she walked past four houses on her way to the Hand place, so she had a target in mind. And your wife and daughter told us about her stalking them and injuring your daughter's roommate. Right now we're guessing she was trying to finish the job in one fell swoop."

Estrella said, "She won't tell us her name. All we know at this point is she's covered with crappy jailhouse-quality tattoos. We're hoping she'll start singing when the drugs wear off. We won't get the blood sample we took from her officially analyzed until later this morning, when the lab tech comes in, but she has the look of a meth head. We see a lot of them around here."

"How would I go about talking to her before she lawyers up?" Joe asked.

Deputy Estrella assessed Joe as if for the first time. Joe was used to being on the other end of a cop-eye.

"Permission for that would have to come from the sheriff himself."

"Sheriff Tassell?" Joe said.

"Yes."

"I know him. We worked together on a case a few years back, after the local game warden here took his own life. In fact, I was assigned to this district for a while. Could you please call him and tell him I'm here and I want to interview the suspect?"

The deputy shot out his arm and looked at his wristwatch. "It's nearly three in the morning."

"I understand," Joe said. "I also know that Marcus Hand is coming back here from Saddlestring right behind me."

Both men flinched at the name, and Estrella whispered, "*That cocksucker.*" Then, realizing who was in front of him, he said to Joe, "I'm sorry I called him that name. It just slipped out, because he's not exactly a popular guy around here. Are you related to him?"

"Nope," Joe said. "I don't claim him at all."

Estrella was visibly relieved. To McNamee, he said, "Go ahead and call the sheriff."

"Why me?" McNamee asked.

"Because I've got seniority and you don't." To Joe: "We'll see what we can do."

"Thank you again," Joe said. He nodded the brim of his hat toward the door. "I'll be in there."

Joe felt slightly guilty for intimating that Hand represented the tweaker, and he knew the deputies would likely figure that out once they thought about it. Why would Marcus Hand represent a woman who tried to break into his own house? Regardless, the simple mention of his name had resulted in a visceral reaction.

He just hoped they didn't think about that until Tassell had given Joe permission to talk to the suspect.

MARYBETH RAISED HER EYES from an old issue of *Wyoming Wildlife* magazine from a stack of them on a side table as Joe entered the room. She looked both relieved and exhausted, with dark rings around her eyes from stress and lack of sleep.

"Hi, honey," he said.

Tossing the magazine aside, she stood up so he could embrace her. She melted into his arms and he could hear her sigh deeply.

The room was institutional light yellow with several old photos of the Tetons on the cinder-block walls and was filled with mismatched steel-frame furniture, a coffeemaker, and a watercooler. It was likely used as a pre-interview room and for a place for the families of victims to gather together away from the squad room.

Lucy threw off a light blanket from where she was resting on a couch and joined them in a hug. She was beaming. April watched from a hardback chair with one skeptical eye open for a moment before deciding to get up and do the same.

Joe couldn't recall a Pickett family group hug happening before and he wasn't sure he loved the idea of it. Nevertheless, he wished Sheridan was there as well.

Missy sat by herself in the far corner, resting an elbow on the top of her crossed legs and staring blankly into the middle distance. She stayed where she was, and Joe was grateful for that.

"You need to get us out of here," April said to Joe. Lucy agreed.

"Yes," Missy said bitterly. "Get them out of here, by all means."

"You look surprisingly at home detained in a police department," Joe said. "Why is that?"

She rolled her eyes and dismissed him with an angry wave of her hand.

Deputy McNamee poked his head inside the lounge and cleared his throat to get their attention.

"I talked to Sheriff Tassell," he said to Joe. "He gave you permission to talk to the suspect, but on two conditions."

Joe waited for the terms.

"One, I have to be in the room with you, and Deputy Estrella will be observing on the monitor. We'll be videotaping the conversation, and we're to intervene if anything improper happens."

"Two . . ." McNamee lowered his voice and looked down as if to spare Joe's family from what he was about to say next. "He says after you've had your interview, you need to get out of Teton County as soon as you can."

"Did he say why?" Joe asked.

"He said trouble follows you wherever you go."

"True enough," Joe said.

"Follow me to the interview room."

"I'm just the messenger," McNamee said to Joe over his shoulder as they walked down the hall.

"I understand."

———

MCNAMEE FLASHED his key card in front of a reader and twisted the handle of a dented metal door. He opened it and stepped aside for Joe to enter first.

The room was small and spare: a heavy wood table with a gouged top, three metal folding chairs, and a video camera with its red light glowing mounted in the top corner of the room.

The woman who'd been arrested sat behind the table with her cuffed hands in her lap. Her head was bent forward with her chin resting on her chest. Long dirty-blond hair hung in front of her face like a peekaboo curtain.

"There's someone here to see you," McNamee said to her.

She raised her face and glared at Joe with glassy eyes.

He said with surprise, "Hello, Cora Lee."

McNamee glanced at the camera and then at Joe. "You know her?"

"Yup. But I'm not sure she knows me right now."

Cora Lee Cates had been Bull Cates's wife. Joe had arrested them both for possession of an elk killed out of season and in the wrong area while Bull worked as a hunting guide. They'd been estranged when Joe killed Bull in self-defense, and he hadn't seen or heard of her since that night.

Cora Lee was a sturdy, foul-mouthed blonde who'd gotten married to Bull and immediately packed on fifty pounds. Joe knew that from seeing their wedding photo at the Cates's compound. In the shot, they both wore camo-themed formal wear. She wasn't that bad looking at the time.

But she was now a shadow of the Cora Lee he remembered. The

bone structure was the same, as well as the down-turned mouth that was spring-loaded to snarl and spew curses. But she'd obviously gone down a destructive path since leaving Bull that included crystal meth addiction. She'd lost a lot of weight, her face was cadaverous, her teeth were yellow-brown with several missing, and she'd covered her arms, legs, and neck with multicolored tattoos. The tattoos were of serpents, dragons, and hard-faced women with fangs that dripped blood. They were crudely drawn and sloppy, as if the tattoo artist she'd gone to was using Cora Lee for practice.

The realization that Cora Lee herself was in this room hit Joe hard. So the woman seen by Wanda Stacy hadn't been a wannabe buckle bunny who had horned in on Dallas's meeting, as Dallas had claimed. The woman was his sister-in-law.

Joe pulled a chair out and sat across from her with his hands on the tabletop.

A glint of recognition registered in her eyes.

"Why is he here?" she asked McNamee in a raspy voice. "He's the murdering asshole that killed my Bull."

"She knows me," Joe deadpanned.

"What does she mean you killed her bull?" McNamee asked.

Joe held up his hand to request to the deputy that he hold his questions for now. "I'll explain later."

"Cora Lee," Joe said, "why have you been stalking my family across half the state?"

"Why do you think?"

"Maybe you can tell me."

Cora Lee's mouth curled down. "An eye for an eye, a tooth for a tooth."

"Ah, got it," Joe said. "You're out for revenge. Just like Dallas."

Joe could feel McNamee's eyes on the side of his head. But the deputy didn't interrupt.

Joe said, "So far, you've knifed a college student because you mistook her for my daughter, and you nearly cut the head off a security guard who was just doing his job. I'd say you are pretty bad at this eye-for-an-eye business."

"*Fuck you.*"

Joe steepled his fingers. "But you've still got your gift for a witty comeback."

Cora Lee raised her manacled hands and extended a finger to her cheek. "See these tears? These tears came from what you did."

"I see."

Under the table, one of Cora Lee's legs began to shake. Joe could feel the vibration through the tabletop. He didn't know if it was due to fear, anger, or meth withdrawal. He guessed a combination of the latter two. He hoped she didn't have a seizure right in front of him.

"All you had with you when the good deputies here made the arrest was a kid's wagon, an ax, a cell phone, and a wad of cash. I want to know about the cash. Who gave it to you?"

"I'm not talking to you," she said.

"You just did. Now who gave you five thousand dollars in cash? I can't imagine you earned it legitimately."

"I said I'm not talking to you."

"Was it Dallas? Did Dallas get you all riled up and send you out with the addresses of two of my daughters? How much more money did he promise you if you got to them?"

"You murdered my Bull."

"It wasn't murder, and I was cleared for it. You forget the part where he ambushed me and shot up my truck without warning. He got it when he got too close to look in the cab to make sure I was dead. I had no choice, but that was a dumb move on his part. Bull was always kind of dumb—but not dumb enough to risk it all by agreeing to kill innocent people for five thousand dollars."

She glared at him, but she had trouble focusing. He found it hard to glare back because he was distracted by her missing teeth.

"The only way to play this out is to cooperate with law enforcement," he said. "I'm sure the judge will take it into account that you decided to help uncover what this is all about. There's no need to protect Dallas anymore. If the situation was reversed, you can bet he wouldn't protect you. I can hear him now. He'd say, 'Cora Lee? She was the skank that run off on my brother when he needed her the most.'"

Joe thought he picked up in Cora Lee's face that somewhere deep in her reptile brain he'd hit a nerve.

"What did he promise you if you hurt members of my family?" Joe asked. "How much more cash to keep you knee-deep in meth?"

"He didn't promise me nothing," she said. "I did it for Bull."

"The man you left? That's really hard to believe, Cora Lee."

"I didn't do nothin' for Dallas," she half croaked, half cried.

The tremor that had been isolated in her leg seemed to spread through the rest of her body. Her hands shook violently and her teeth chattered in spasms.

Joe sat back, unsure what to do or say next.

McNamee said, "Maybe we better stop before she has a seizure right here. I'll call the EMTs."

Cora Lee was sweating now, and Joe could smell her metallic, chemical odor.

He looked up at the camera and said to Estrella, "You heard it. Her name is Cora Lee Cates, and it was a clean interview until she ended it. And she never asked for a lawyer."

Joe slid his chair back and stood up. McNamee was in contact with the hospital on his shoulder mike. They were sending a team to the jail as soon as possible.

The deputy ushered Joe out of the room and shut the door.

"I'll stay here and keep an eye on her until the EMTs get here and take her away," he said. "You can go back with your family."

"Are you done transcribing their statements?" Joe asked.

"I think so."

"Thanks again," Joe said, shaking McNamee's hand. "I had no idea how that would go."

"She scares me," McNamee said.

"Me too," Joe agreed.

"Bad things happen when you take the meth away."

"Yup."

"So what's the deal about you killing her bull?"

Joe told the story, and McNamee's eyes widened. When he was done, the deputy said, "Now that you tell me, I think I heard something about that."

They traded cards and contact details, and Joe turned to reunite with his family.

Halfway down the hall, Joe paused in his step.

I didn't do nothin' for Dallas, she'd said.

20

AT THE ENTRANCE GATE FOR TETON SHADOWS, JOE, MARYBETH, and the girls found it blocked by a sleek Wyoming Highway Patrol cruiser that was parked across both lanes. Missy's H2 had been rolled into the grass in the borrow pit.

As Joe slowed to a stop, a uniformed trooper stepped out from the brush on the side of the building, zipping up his fly. He strode into their headlights, gesturing for them to stay back.

He was a big man with a flat-brimmed Highway Patrol hat, and he was wearing aviator sunglasses in the dark. The sole purpose of the glasses, Joe saw, was the effect it gave when he reached up to theatrically whip them off his face and glare angrily through the windshield at who was inside. Then he put his right hand on the grip of his weapon and walked slowly around the front of Joe's pickup.

Joe sighed.

"I'm sorry, I can't let you through," the trooper said. He was red-faced and beefy and his name tag read TILLER. "We've got a crime scene inside."

"I know," Joe said. "My family came from there. Now they've been cleared by the sheriff to leave and we're going back to get their stuff."

"Not on my watch," Tiller said.

Joe wondered how many times Trooper Tiller had aggressively whipped off his glasses and said things like "Not on my watch" in his law enforcement career. He was that kind of cop— the kind who was spoiling for a fight or a confrontation.

Joe was determined not to do or say anything that would complicate the morning any further. He said, "I'm slowly reaching for my ID" as he leaned forward and removed his wallet from his back pocket. He made sure to let his left elbow slip over the open rim of the driver's-side window so that Tiller could see the Wyoming Game and Fish patch on his uniform shoulder in the beam of the flashlight.

Tiller took Joe's driver's license and looked it over. Then he shined the light on Joe's face to match it up with the photo, then he did the procedure a second time. Joe knew he was being messed with, but he didn't know why.

"I know you," Tiller said without warmth. "You're that game warden."

"Yup."

"Joe Pickett," Tiller said as he handed the license back. "You know, some of us in law enforcement try to keep our names out of the paper."

"So do I," Joe said. "I just have a knack for being in the wrong place at the wrong time."

As he said it, he heard April and Lucy titter in the backseat. They didn't yet realize there was sometimes a conflict between state agencies that did law enforcement, and that some cops like Tiller resented the freedom and autonomy game wardens had as part of their job. Joe had heard troopers over the radio complaining that all game wardens did was drive around in their state pickups with their dogs and do little other than fish or hunt. It wasn't true in Joe's case, but he didn't want to broach the subject with Tiller. He just wanted to get past the gate.

"When can I get through?" Joe asked.

"When I get authorization," Tiller said. Meaning: *Sometime tomorrow when I go off shift.*

For the second time that night, Joe was responsible for a call that woke up Sheriff Tassell. In person this time, he briefed him on the situation. "If you want me to leave your county, you'll need to talk to this trooper," Joe said.

Tassell sighed and said, "Hand him the phone."

After a brief talk, the trooper gave the phone back. "He said he's getting tired of special requests to contaminate the crime scene, but you're free to go."

"Who else is he talking about?" Joe asked.

"The man of the house. Marcus Hand." He said the name with obvious distaste. "You heard of him?"

"Sure have," Joe said. He thanked the patrolman and put the transmission into drive.

As they rolled past the guardhouse, Marybeth cautioned the girls not to look inside, but they did anyway.

"There's a lot of blood in there," April said.

"I hope I don't get sick," Lucy whispered.

MARCUS HAND WAS SPLAYED out in a huge leather recliner in his living room with a full tumbler of dark-hued bourbon and the bottle on the floor next to him within easy reach. His feet were up and he wore shearling slippers, but he hadn't undressed from the suit and string tie Joe had seen him wear the day before in Judge Hewitt's courtroom.

Hand watched Marybeth, April, and Lucy troop through his home to pack their clothes and belongings from their respective rooms without saying a word.

Behind Hand, Joe saw the splintered opening in the front door and a bloody single-blade ax on the tile with an evidence marker next to it. The central heating was humming in the background, trying in vain to ward off the cold fall air pouring through the hole.

Hand gestured to Joe to come into the living room and have a seat on the couch next to him.

"This is Jefferson's Ocean," Hand said as he took a sip. "It's some of the finest bourbon I know. They put the bourbon barrels on sea vessels and sail around the world, and the whole time the liquor is subject to temperature swings and the gentle rocking of the ship that brings out the smoky and vanilla taste of the charred wood. Supposedly, every barrel crosses the equator four times."

Joe sat on the edge of the couch, but didn't respond.

"I usually save it for when I win a big case or a huge judgment, but I have to say I might be cheating this time, given how quickly and easily it went. Would you like a taste?"

"No, thank you," Joe said. "I'm driving."

"A gentleman would offer that you all stay the night, but as you know this isn't a house as much as it is an official *crime scene*."

Joe said, "They're ready to leave anyway."

"And I'm ready to get my house back," Hand said quietly. "I hope you don't think I'm rude, but my home is my sanctuary. I can't imagine living in a house filled with estrogen."

"I've lived in a house filled with estrogen all my adult life," Joe said. He wondered how much bourbon Hand had consumed before they got there.

Hand shuddered at the thought and changed the subject.

He said, "Herself is staying at the Four Seasons in town tonight. She doesn't want to revisit the scene of the crime quite yet."

Joe nodded. He thought that Missy not coming right back also had to do with the fact that her daughter and granddaughters were clearing out. For a second, he almost felt sorry for her.

He came right out with it. "How did Dallas Cates afford your fee?"

Hand flinched theatrically, as if Joe's question had startled him. But Joe knew nothing really startled the man.

"I don't know the answer to your question. All I know is that a cashier's check from the Bank of Winchester cleared my bank. That's all I was concerned about."

Winchester was a small ranching community twenty miles

west of Saddlestring in the foothills of the Bighorn Mountains. Joe was very familiar with it.

"Now he's back on the street," Joe said. "He's been out long enough to threaten my family and me. And I think he was in contact with Cora Lee Cates, his sister-in-law. She's the crazy woman who tried to break down your door with an ax."

"Yes?" Hand said. "And what? Are you intimating that I should be wallowing in shame for facilitating his release?"

"Yup. At least a little."

Hand chuckled and took a sip. It was apparently so good he had to close his eyes for a moment.

When they reopened, Hand said, "The money, manpower, and resources of the almighty state were all lined up to put my client in prison for the rest of his life. This was after they—*with your willing approval*—overcharged him the first time, just so none of you would have to look at him."

Joe felt his cheeks flush.

Hand continued. "Even with all those advantages, they still felt the need to cheat. We exposed the cheating, is all. The prosecution should be feeling guilt and shame—not me. Unfortunately, though, the politicians, bureaucrats, and their beady-eyed minions are incapable of those emotions. Being a bureaucrat means never having to say you're sorry. And the system won't hold them accountable. Thank God I've got Bruce White on my payroll to do that.

"Joe, too many cops on your side of the law look down on defense attorneys, and I know it. I know in particular they look down on *me*. But it's your side that has every advantage. The cops and the prosecution use taxpayer money to bankroll their actions, while on my side an honest defense has to be paid for by a private individual. The deck is always stacked against us, so there is some satisfaction in drawing three cards and winding up with a straight flush—if you know what I mean."

Joe grunted that he'd heard and understood what Hand was saying.

"Unlike the prosecution," Hand said, "I don't hold everybody on the other side in contempt. I appreciate good cops and good prosecutors, even if I'll fight like hell for my client and try to beat them. I appreciate you, Joe, because I know you're a good man and you take your oath seriously. But people like Spivak . . ." Hand faux spit onto the tile next to his lounger. "People like Spivak hurt men like you more than you'll ever know."

"Yup," Joe said.

"Dallas Cates is free, and that's too bad, because I think we're both pretty sure he's guilty as sin," Hand said.

"You admit it," Joe said with surprise.

"It was obvious. But that's no justification for perverting the judicial system any further. There are already too many innocents in jail and too many guilty people walking free."

Joe said, "But he can't be tried again for murdering Dave Farkus. It's not right that a murderer gets away with it."

"That's correct, but it isn't my fault," Hand said. "Our founders built in protections to guard against people like Deputy Spivak. The mighty power and money of the state shouldn't be used to try a defendant over and over again until they get a jury to agree with them."

Hand paused a long time before he leaned forward in his chair and placed his big hand on Joe's knee. "Dallas Cates is a danger to society, and most of all he's a danger to all of you."

Joe felt a chill go through him. He said, "Don't I know it."

"You'll have to deal with him in other ways."

Joe nodded and looked away.

"I hope you're successful," Hand said. "As for Herself . . . well, she might come down a little differently. At least as far as you go."

"Believe me, I know," Joe said.

"THAT'S WHAT CORA LEE SAID," Joe told Marybeth. "'I didn't do nothin' for Dallas.' She said it twice, and it got me thinking."

Joe drove his pickup with Marybeth in the passenger seat as they climbed Togwotee Pass toward Saddlestring two hours before dawn. The bed of the pickup was filled with bags and suitcases. It was a two-vehicle caravan with April at the wheel of Marybeth's van. April had called twice to complain that Lucy was loudly singing show tunes to keep them both awake.

Through the speaker in his wife's phone, Joe could hear Lucy singing from *Hamilton:*

"I'm young, scrappy, and hungry
And I'm not throwing away my shot!"

Lucy had a good singing voice.

After Marybeth told April that it was better to be awake and annoyed than exhausted and at the wheel of her car, she disconnected the call and picked up her discussion with Joe.

"So where are you going with this?" she asked.

He said, "As you can imagine, one of the most important factors in figuring out a crime or a scheme to commit a crime is the motivation of the criminals. Sometimes it's obvious: they want money to buy drugs or they want to poach an elk to hang the head on a wall. But when bad things happen almost at random, it gets confusing. It's hard to keep your guard up when you don't know what's coming next, or most of all *why*.

"I understand why Dallas wants retribution, as much as I hate to say that," he continued. "But what doesn't make sense is how his two thugs and Cora Lee fit into the picture. Dallas has a way of conning people into doing what he wants them to do, but is he really so convincing that he can get a couple of low-life convicts and his sister-in-law to go along with him? What do they get out of it? Dallas used to be a big-shot rodeo star with cash to burn. Now he's a busted-up ex-con."

"How does Cora Lee fit into this?" Joe asked rhetorically. "She walked out on Bull—and the whole Cates family—days before he bought the farm. Even when they were together, they had a rough relationship. They used to get into drunken fistfights at the Whistle Pig Saloon. Once, Cora Lee chased Bull out into the parking lot with a pool cue and split his head open with it. I know they threatened divorce against each other a half dozen times. I just can't see that Bull buying it somehow made Cora Lee so distraught that she devoted her life to coming after us."

Marybeth said, "No one knows what really goes on within a

family or a marriage. Sometimes you learn that the couple that looks the happiest together really hate each other. And the unhappy couple can't live without the other one, despite appearances."

"That's kind of wise," he said with admiration.

"But in Cora Lee's case, I have to agree with you," she said. "I can't see why she did what she did unless she's just crazy with drugs. But where did she get the money to travel around and stalk our girls? Somebody financed that. Plus, there are too many people involved. We're missing something."

They drove in silence for a while, each with their own thoughts.

Finally, Joe said, "Marcus Hand said he got a cashier's check from the Bank of Winchester for his fee. Doesn't it seem kind of odd that Dallas would bank forty-five minutes from his compound when there's five or six banks closer in Saddlestring?"

"Not really," Marybeth said. "He got that from his mom. She made a point of not doing any business in town if she could do it somewhere else. They used to drive all the way up to Billings to shop for groceries, even though it took the entire day. Brenda was at war with us even if we didn't know it or appreciate it, which probably made her even more angry. It was her way of showing what she thought of the business owners and everybody else in Saddlestring—including me."

Joe shook his head and whistled.

Marybeth said, "She once showed me a library card from the Natrona County Library in Casper just to spite me. She wanted me to know that she didn't use my library."

"I think I'll wander over to Winchester tomorrow and talk to a banker," Joe said.

"And I'll get online and try to find out what I can," Marybeth said. "Cora Lee did something between the time she left Bull and when she showed up here. She may have left a trail in cyberspace I can find. I wish we'd known she was involved before now."

AS THEY DROVE UP Bighorn Road in the predawn, the eastern sky was a bright rose color: almost cartoonishly vibrant and electric with morning sun.

Marybeth sat back and said, "Look at the sunrise, Joe. It looks like it did last summer when we had those forest fires."

They exchanged a quick look as they came to the same realization, and Joe stomped on the accelerator and left April in a spoor of dust.

The pickup's rear wheels fishtailed on the last turn up the mountain toward their home, but Joe kept the truck on the road.

"Oh my God . . ." Marybeth gasped as she covered her mouth with her hands.

Their house was engulfed by fire. Flames rolled angrily out from the open door and window frames of their home, and thick coils of black and tan smoke rose into the sky. Behind the house, the barn had burned to the ground. The roof had collapsed and all that was left was eight blackened support poles sticking up through the ashes.

Joe said, "Stay here" as he slammed to a stop fifteen feet from the front picket fence, which was also aflame. Marybeth paid no attention to him and threw herself out of the truck as well.

They stood in silence as the heat from the fire stung their

flesh and they breathed in smoke and scorched air. Tears on Marybeth's cheeks reflected orange from the fused sunlight and the fire itself.

Rojo and Toby grazed on the hillside a quarter mile away, and Daisy came bounding down the road from a copse of trees as April pulled in. They'd escaped the fires somehow.

Marybeth's new gelding, Petey, and their dog Tube were missing.

Joe seethed and recounted Marcus Hand's words.

"You'll have to deal with him in other ways."

RANDALL LUTHI CRIED OUT AND AWOKE SUDDENLY WHEN SOME-
body kicked the sole of his wounded foot through the blankets
of his bed. The pain was sharp, and when he opened his eyes, all
he saw at first were stars.

He fumbled under his bed until his hand found the grip of
the 9mm and he brought it out and pointed it toward the source
of his pain.

"Goddamn you, Cross," he hissed. "Why'd you do that?"

"Do what?" Rory Cross said, half asleep from the other side
of the room.

Before Luthi could level the weapon, it was wrenched out of
his hand.

Dallas chuckled drily and said, "A little slow on the draw there, I'd say."

The stars in Luthi's eyes dissipated and the unmistakable wide-shouldered build came into focus. Dallas spun the gun on his index finger through the trigger guard and handed it back upside down.

"Good thing nobody with evil intent wanted to sneak up on you this morning," Dallas said, "or you'd both be dead. I thought we talked about rotating sleep schedules so someone could keep a lookout. Didn't we talk about that?"

Luthi chinned toward Cross in the other single bed. "It was him. I took the first four hours last night."

Cross's dull morning face twisted into a grimace as he glared at Luthi from across the room. His silence was an admission of guilt.

"So what are you doing here, Dallas?" Cross asked.

"He's trying to change the subject," Luthi accused.

Dallas ignored him. He turned and sat down heavily at the foot of Luthi's bed. Luthi quickly moved his injured foot so Dallas wouldn't injure it further by sitting on it.

"I told you boys," Dallas said. "I wouldn't be long in custody. I told you I'd be out. I'm free as a damned bird, thanks to Marcus Hand and a fuckup of massive proportions by Lester Spivak."

"He's the one who planted the rifle in your truck?" Cross asked.

"He was the one." Dallas smiled.

Luthi sat up and sniffed. "Why do you smell like smoke?" he asked Dallas.

———————

LUTHI SCRAMBLED the last of their eggs in a half-inch of bacon grease while Dallas and Cross drank strong coffee at the crude table near the woodstove. Dallas had filled them in on the events since he'd been arrested, saying it had all gone better and smoother than he'd even hoped.

"We were ten steps ahead of them the whole time," he said. "Still are."

Dallas looked over the rim of his coffee cup and asked, "Did you guys take care of our problem?"

Meaning Wanda Stacy.

"Luthi wanted to bone her first," Cross said. "I saved her from that horrible experience."

Dallas snorted a laugh and Luthi felt his ears get hot. Two weeks in a remote hunting cabin with Cross had been a miserable experience. Rather than getting along or simply staying out of each other's way, they'd each come to hate the other guy. Luthi had thought several times of sneaking up behind Cross and putting a bullet in his brain. He assumed Cross had thought about doing the same thing to him, although it was hard to read the man. The only thing that had kept them there together was the imminent return of Dallas. That, and waiting for the phone to ring again.

Now that Dallas had shown up, Luthi felt palpable relief.

"So where's the body?" Dallas asked. "Did you bury her deep like I told you?"

"Just as good," Cross said eagerly. Too eagerly, Luthi thought.

Dallas got still. "What does that mean exactly?"

"He threw her off a cliff," Luthi said from where he stood with his back to them at the stove. "She landed in some big rocks we can't even get to."

"I told you to bury her deep, Rory," Dallas said.

His voice was preternaturally calm, the way it got before he went off on someone. Luthi had seen that happen in Rawlins. A Mexican inmate said modern-day rodeo cowboys were pussies for wearing protective vests when they rode bulls. Dallas had calmly asked the Mexican to repeat what he'd just said. When the Mexican did, Dallas pummeled the man in a flurry of blows until he went down. Then he'd stomped the man's head until blood came out of his nose and ears.

The remarkable accomplishment afterward was when Dallas, who hadn't even broken a sweat during the beat-down, convinced the CO that the Brothers on Block A had been responsible for the attack. He knew that the Mexican wouldn't talk and the Brothers would deny it to no avail. That was the reality of incarceration.

Now, Luthi turned slightly so he could see over his shoulder what would happen next.

Rory Cross was six inches taller than Dallas and outweighed him by fifty pounds. Not that it mattered.

Dallas jumped to his feet with the grace of a cat and his fists worked like pistons—*one-two, one-two*—so fast in Cross's face that he didn't have a chance to raise his arms to ward off the blows. The man went limp and his head rolled to the side and he fell off his chair and crashed to the floor.

Luthi turned with the cast-iron skillet in his hand. Dallas

stood over Cross and said, "If somebody finds that body, I'll make sure to bury *you* deep."

But Dallas didn't hit Cross again and he didn't stomp him while he was down like he had the Mexican. Cross moaned and rolled over to his belly. Blood from his mouth and nose patterned the dirty floor beneath his chin.

"Ready for some eggs, Rory?" Luthi asked, as if nothing had happened.

Dallas looked up. His face, which had been a taut mask of rage as he stood over Cross, transformed into something softer, as if he were coming out of a trance. For a moment, Luthi imagined seeing that mask on Dallas as he lowered himself into the chute to mount a bareback bronc or a Brahma bull.

Dallas said, "*I'm* hungry. In fact, I'm starved half to death."

He stepped over Cates and reclaimed his seat at the table. He squinted suspiciously at Luthi. "You've been chomping at the bit to tell me that about the girl, haven't you?"

"Since it happened," Luthi said as he placed the skillet in the middle of the table.

"You're just as much at fault," Dallas said. "I told you both to bury her so deep she'd never get found. Didn't I tell you that?"

Luthi held his ground and chinned toward Cross on the floor. "He did it on his own. Ask him. Hell, I couldn't even keep up with him. Have you seen my foot?"

"What happened?"

"Mumblety-peg," Luthi said as he scooped gray-looking eggs onto Dallas's plate. "He lost."

"Looks like you lost," Dallas said between voracious bites.

"And it's mumbley-peg, not mumblety-peg. Is that some kind of Texas horseshit?"

Then: "Get up, Rory. You aren't hurt so bad."

Cross grunted and reached up to steady himself on the chair as he pulled himself to his feet. Luthi enjoyed seeing the fat lip and rapidly closing right eye on Cross's face.

"Eat," Dallas said. "We all need to keep up our strength, because we ain't going to be here all that long. Not since Cora Lee got herself caught in Jackson."

Luthi was surprised. "The cops have her?"

"That's what I just said." Dallas sighed, obviously annoyed. "Why is it that neither one of you seems to hear a goddamned word I say?"

"Do they know about us?" Luthi asked.

"Naw," Dallas said. "They just got her last night. I knew she'd get herself into trouble. I was against having her be a part of this from the beginning. That's why I never clued her in to the whole thing. Luckily, she just knew her part. Even if she talks, she won't have much to say about us that could stick. The judge dismissed the charges, and I can't be tried again for it."

Luthi was partly relieved, and he said so. Then: "What about us?"

"Don't worry about it," Dallas said breezily. "There's not one iota of evidence they can use anymore on any of us, and Cora Lee isn't exactly a credible witness. You're okay."

"The cops—do they know our names?" he asked Dallas.

"Sort of. Not your real names, though. I told them I knew you guys only as Brutus and the Weasel."

"Shit," Luthi whined. "I told you I hate that name."

Cross settled into his chair across the table and managed a bloody smile.

"The Weasel," he said as twin streams of blood ran from the edges of his mouth to his chin. "The Squealing Weasel."

"How would you like a fry pan hitting you in that mouth of yours?" Luthi asked Cross.

"Boys, boys," Dallas said. "You're starting to make me think that cooping you two up together for so long was a mistake."

"You think?" Luthi asked heatedly.

Cross dabbed at the blood on his lip. "He's kind of high-strung, that's for sure. Must be his feminine side coming out."

Luthi started to reach for the handle of the skillet, but Dallas shot his hand out and stopped him.

"*Boys,*" he warned.

"ANY CALLS?" Dallas asked after Luthi had cleared away the breakfast dishes.

Cross shook his head no.

Apparently, Luthi thought, his mouth hurt so much he didn't want to talk anymore. It was the best thing to have happened in days, maybe *ever.*

"We may have to go rogue," Dallas said, as much to himself, Luthi thought, as to the two of them. "I ain't sitting around here with my thumb up my ass waiting for that phone to ring. Events are accelerating and we might have to end this thing on our own."

"Do you have a plan?" Luthi asked.

Dallas smiled and said, "I've had a plan since the minute they sent me to Rawlins. In fact, I got it going just last night."

There was a high-pitched *skree-skree* sound outside the hunting cabin and Luthi and Cross both froze.

"What the hell was *that*?" Luthi asked quietly. Cross's eyes were raised to the ceiling.

Dallas wasn't concerned. He shook his head and said, "Haven't either one of you heard a red-tailed hawk before?"

LATER, AFTER DALLAS HAD GONE outside to "get rid of some coffee," Cross said, "Randall?"

Luthi looked over. Cross was sitting heavily on his bed with his big hands resting on his knees.

Cross said, "Just so you know, I don't blame Dallas for pounding the shit out of me. I blame you."

"You should blame yourself," Luthi said quietly.

"When this is all over, you and me are going to have a reckoning."

"I look forward to it," Luthi lied.

"I'll just bet you do."

WHILE HE WAITED IN THE SMALL LOBBY OF THE BANK OF WIN-
chester, Joe contemplated the large bronze out on the front lawn
that could be seen through the windows. The artwork was of a
full-sized grizzly bear with its rear left foot caught in a massive
steel-jawed trap. The bear strained at the end of a taut rusty
chain in a desperate attempt to pull free, and it looked over its
humped shoulder with panic on its face.

Joe ruefully empathized with the grizzly.

The bronze had been out on the front lawn of the bank for as
long as Joe had been in Twelve Sleep County, and it had always
struck him as a violent, discordant, and totally symbolic image
of the tiny mountain town twenty miles from Saddlestring. The
main street of Winchester contained three bars, two restaurants,

the bank, a tiny insurance agency, a farm and ranch implement dealership, a general store, and six empty storefronts that had long been boarded up.

Winchester, like its residents—who were timber cutters, ranch hands, unemployed energy workers, and subsistence trappers—was raw and rough-hewn. It was a place where people who had no place to go ended up. They considered the residents of Saddlestring haughty.

Joe got several suspicious looks from bank customers as they entered and did their business with one of the two tellers. A game warden in uniform was unwelcome in a town where elk poaching and above-the-legal-limit fishermen were common. He sat with his hat in his hands and nodded at locals he recognized from encountering them in the mountains. Most nodded back.

"Sorry, Mr. Pickett, I understand you want to see me?" the president of the bank said to him as she opened the door to her office. "I was on the phone and it went much longer than necessary, as these things tend to do."

She extended her hand. "Ashlyn Raymer. I'm the president of the bank."

"Thank you. You can call me Joe," he said.

"And you can call me Ashlyn," she said as she led him toward her office door.

"Are you related to Kelsea Raymer?" he asked. "She's the chief forensics analyst of the U.S. Fish and Wildlife Forensics Center near Denver. I worked with her on a case a couple of years ago."

"I think she was related to my ex-husband," Raymer said curtly as she skirted around her desk. "I never met her, and I really don't talk to those people very much."

"Gotcha," Joe said.

Ashlyn Raymer was heavy and short with a carefully made-up attractive face and perfectly coiffed red hair. She'd been involved in a minor scandal when she'd been vice president of a savings and loan in Saddlestring involving accusations of embezzlement, but had avoided charges by claiming the missing sums were the fault of poorly trained employees and sloppy bookkeeping. She'd agreed to leave, and the S&L had agreed to sweep it under the rug if she made reparations and signed a confidentiality agreement. Winchester was the natural landing pad for her, Joe thought. Winchester welcomed people who'd had trouble in Saddlestring, because they fit right in.

"I'M SORRY to hear about your house," she said as she sat down and put on a pair of fashionably large-framed glasses. "Was it a total loss?"

"Yup."

Although he'd managed his district for more than a decade, Joe was still amazed how fast word traveled throughout the county.

"How is your family holding up?"

"They're staying with Dulcie Schalk until we can get things figured out," he said. He noticed that Raymer flinched at the name of the county prosecutor. "We lost a horse and a family pet, so it's a traumatic experience for everyone."

"I don't know what I'd do if I lost any of my cats," she said as she pointed toward framed photos of felines on the credenza behind her. "They're *my* family."

Joe didn't want to hear about her cats. He wasn't in the mood. As he'd left that morning, Lucy was still crying about the loss of Tube, and April was glaring at him as if it were his fault their house had burned down with her few remaining possessions inside it.

He still hadn't wrapped his mind around the situation, and the only way he knew how to deal with it was to go to work the next morning. He needed forward momentum amid the loss of his house and the sick realization that his family was suddenly homeless. The phone message that he'd left for his agency director before she got to the office that morning was curt and perfunctory: "My house got torched last night."

He could only imagine her reaction, since the structure was owned by the department.

Joe hoped his forward momentum wouldn't be stopped short like the grizzly outside at the end of the chain.

Although it was obvious to Joe what had happened the night before when he saw blackened fuel containers from his garage scattered throughout the ashes, Sheriff Reed had requested an arson investigator from the Division of Criminal Investigation in Cheyenne to investigate the wreckage and make a determination of its cause.

"I'm here to find out what I can about one of your customers," Joe said.

Ashlyn Raymer raised her eyebrows and looked at him over the top of her glasses. "Do you have a court order? We aren't in the habit of revealing private banking information about our depositors unless compelled or by auditor request."

"I can get a court order if I need to," he said. "I was hoping we could move a little faster and avoid it. But if it's going to be difficult, I can have an order on your desk from Judge Hewitt this afternoon."

Hewitt was leaving any day to fly to Texas to hunt wild hogs on a private ranch and Joe hoped Raymer wasn't aware of that.

"I'm not trying to be difficult, Joe," she said defensively. "I just need you to know that we take great pride in maintaining the confidentiality of our customer's financial transactions. Think of us as a kind of Swiss bank placed way out here in the boonies. We have plenty of customers from around the state, and even Saddlestring, who bank here because we maintain a level of confidentiality not found in larger towns. I can't promise you I can help until I know who you're asking about."

"Dallas Cates," he said.

She paused for a moment and smiled with relief. "I *can* help you after all, because Dallas isn't a customer here."

Joe cocked his head. "It's my understanding that he obtained a large cashier's check from here a week or so ago to pay for his defense in court."

"Then your understanding is wrong," she said. "He's never been a customer, even when he was on the circuit making money and before you people sent him to Rawlins."

Joe was puzzled. Was Marcus Hand mistaken? It didn't make sense. Where his money came from was something Hand would be sure about.

"Is it possible that he had an account under another name?" Joe asked.

She shook her head no.

"Is it possible that he accessed a family corporate account of some kind?"

Raymer paused for a moment and said, "No" with finality.

"Can you help me out here a little?" Joe asked. "Someone drew a fairly large cashier's check from this bank and I was led to believe it was Dallas."

"You were led to believe wrong," she said. Her tone became professorial. "A cashier's check is a particular instrument that is guaranteed by the bank itself and drawn from the bank's own funds. We would never issue one for someone without a balance to cover it, and Mr. Cates is not an account holder here."

"Huh," Joe said. He sat a moment in silence and thought about what she'd said and how she'd said it.

He asked, "So was the check drawn on behalf of someone else who has an account here?"

"I'm sorry, but I can't help you with that," she said.

"I know I'm missing something here," Joe mused.

"That's not my problem," she said. "Now, if you'll excuse me, I have work to do."

"Then I thank you for your time," Joe said and stood up.

She remained seated at her desk, but she reluctantly shook his hand when he extended it to her.

JOE CLAMPED on his hat halfway across the lobby as he walked toward the glass double doors and then a thought hit him and he turned on his heel. Ashlyn Raymer had shut her door behind him and she was on the phone again. She'd swiveled around in her chair, so her back was to him.

He approached the bank teller who looked the oldest and, he hoped, had been there the longest.

"I was just talking with Ms. Raymer about a court order to access an account," he said to the matronly woman, who wore steel-framed glasses and a lime-green pantsuit. "I forgot to ask her about the last time there was activity in Eldon and Brenda Cates's account. Would you mind looking that up for me?"

It wasn't technically a lie. They had talked about a court order. But he was misleading her in the hope that she'd go with it.

She did.

"You mean for C&C Sewer? They closed that when Eldon . . . died."

Joe nodded. "Did they have personal accounts aside from the business account?"

"Brenda did," the teller said. "Eldon wasn't on that account."

"Interesting."

"She wore the pants in that family and handled all the financials," she said. "Most of what they did was on a cash basis. I think they did that to avoid taxes."

Joe tried not to betray the building excitement he felt.

She continued. "Up until Brenda went to prison, she did the same thing every month—deposit twenty-one hundred dollars and then disburse just about the whole balance a couple of weeks later. She barely maintained a balance worth mentioning."

The teller rolled her eyes and said, "This went on for at least eighteen *years*. Believe me, that's how long I've been here."

"I see," Joe said. He removed a small Field Notes pad from his pocket and jotted down the figures as much for her benefit as his. He'd learned long ago that when he opened his notebook, some people felt compelled to help fill it. It made them feel useful and important.

"Can you confirm the exact amounts?" he asked, as if he had an idea already what they were.

"I can do it out of memory," she said with a sly smile. "Every month, a deposit of twenty-one hundred dollars, then a disbursement of two thousand eighty-two dollars and ninety-six cents. Leaving a monthly balance of a whopping seventeen dollars and four cents."

"For eighteen years?" Joe asked.

"Until she went to prison," the teller said. "Then the transactions stopped."

"When did she deposit the large sum?" Joe asked. It was pure speculation.

"A month or so ago," the teller answered. She looked around and then lowered her voice and leaned toward him. "Out of the blue."

"And it was for how much again?" he asked quietly.

"Millions," she whispered back. "You'd have to get the exact amount from Ms. Raymer. She's been acting as a personal banker on that account and she deals directly with the account holder."

This time, he knew he didn't contain his surprise. "Like more than one million?" he asked.

She nodded her head up and down. "Much more, I think. But again, you'd have to get that exact amount from Ms. Raymer."

"Where did she . . ." he started to ask. He thought better of it. The sum was wholly unexpected and incomprehensible to him. He knew that even if Brenda sold their company, the equipment, their compound—and the acreage it sat on—there was no way it would generate close to a million dollars.

Scrambling to think and keep up the ruse, he said, "And the monthly two thousand dollar–some disbursements she used to make—did she take it out in cash?"

The teller shook her head. "Automatic transfer."

"And that went to who again?" he asked.

"You don't know or you can't remember?" the teller asked, leaning back. She was on to him, and he felt guilty for leading her down the path they'd taken, although he valued the lead.

He thought: monthly deposits made for years, automatic monthly disbursements made for years, then huge return.

He said, "They went to the Winchester Independent Insurance, correct?"

Her suspicions vanished and she said, "Correct."

Just then, Raymer threw open her door and marched up to Joe and the teller.

"Unless you're opening an account, I need to ask you to leave," she said to him. To the teller: "You're not to answer any more of his questions."

"Yes, ma'am," the teller said. "He said he was talking with you . . ."

"The personal banker for Brenda Cates," Joe added.

"I think we're done here," Raymer said to them both. He mouthed *Thank you* to the confused teller before he turned and marched toward the door.

When he paused in front next to the grizzly, he looked over

his shoulder to see Ashlyn Raymer with her hands on her hips making sure he was leaving for good this time.

Under her watch, he climbed into his pickup next to Daisy and said, "Act like we're going home."

His dog looked at him with the same puzzled but empathetic expression she always displayed when he talked to her.

Joe turned out of the parking lot to the main street and watched Ashlyn Raymer and the bank get smaller in his wide mirror as he drove in the direction of the highway.

When they were gone, he slowed and performed a U-turn.

There were two cars—a new Chevy Tahoe outfitted with a winch and gun racks and a beat-up Dodge Neon with a high school graduation tassel hanging from the rearview mirror—parked on the side of the small Winchester Independent Insurance building. The structure was a single-wide trailer fronted with siding to make it look less like a single-wide trailer. The name DAVID GILBERTSON, AGENT was painted on the door.

Joe pulled his pickup in next to the Neon and told Daisy to stay. He made sure when he got out that he was no longer in the line of sight from the bank building up the street, which he wasn't.

He mounted the unpainted two-by-six steps and opened the front door and stuck his head inside.

A young female receptionist—no doubt the driver of the Neon—looked up expectantly from a desk eighteen inches from the doorframe. She wore a tight summer dress even though it was fall, and her hands were poised over her keyboard like a praying mantis to avoid scarring her painted inch-long fingernails.

"Is David Gilbertson in?" Joe asked.

"Who may I ask is . . ." She hesitated as she caught herself repeating her standard telephone greeting, and finished with, "At the door?"

"Game warden Joe Pickett." He grinned as he showed himself in and closed the door behind him.

She rotated in her chair to shout down the narrow hallway in back of her, thought better of it, and swung back around to poke the intercom button using a pencil instead of a nail tip. "David, there's a game warden here to see you."

After a pause, a male voice said, "Damn it, I'm sure I bought a conservation stamp this year. Maybe I didn't."

"It's not about that," Joe said, so Gilbertson could hear. "It's about an insurance policy."

"Okay," he said with a sigh. "Come on back."

DAVID GILBERTSON WAS in his late fifties and he wore an open-collar shirt under a corduroy sports jacket with a shooting patch on its breast. He had unruly hair but a precise silver mustache, and the wall behind him was covered with mounted mule deer, elk, bear, and pronghorn antelope heads. The seven-point royal elk head and antlers in velvet were particularly impressive, and almost too large for the room itself. A dusty twenty-two-inch rainbow trout replica was missing an eye.

Gilbertson was one of those men who lived to hunt and would do just about anything to support his habit. He didn't hunt to feed himself, but to put trophies on the wall. Joe often had trouble with men like him, but there were many more of them around than there were Joes.

Gilbertson, like Ashlyn Raymer, had once been prominent in Saddlestring with his own agency on Main Street and the corporate logo of a major insurance carrier over his name on the sign. Joe wasn't privy to the details, but something had happened between the carrier and Gilbertson at about the time Gilbertson bought eighty acres of prime elk-hunting ground in the mountains and had built an elaborate cabin for himself. Whatever had happened, the carrier cut Gilbertson loose and the man moved up the highway and opened an independent agency in Winchester.

"Mind if I have a seat?" Joe asked, nodding toward a single steel-framed chair across from Gilberston's desk. The chair was piled high with newspapers and hunting magazines.

"Just move all that stuff to the side," he said. "I don't get that many walk-in clients."

"I understand," Joe said, although he didn't.

As he sat down, Gilbertson's handset lit up and the receptionist announced that "Ms. Raymer from the bank is on the line."

Gilberston leaned forward and reached for the phone when Joe said quickly, "This will only take a minute."

Gilbertson paused. Joe knew why she was calling. He hoped Gilbertson didn't.

The man punched the intercom and said to his receptionist, "Tell her I'll call her right back."

Joe breathed a sigh of relief, but tried not to show it.

"So," Gilbertson said, "what can I do for the game warden today? Are you interested in life, auto, or health? But I warn you—health insurance premiums are through the damned roof, now that we got Obamacare."

"I've got health insurance through the state and I drive a game and fish truck," Joe said.

"So, life insurance," Gilbertson concluded. "Good for you. Not enough people think about what will happen to their family when they're gone. Are we talking about term or whole life? There are dozens of options, and I'm sure we can find a plan that meets your budget and provides for your wife and family."

"Actually," Joe said, "I'm interested in the policy Brenda Cates took out on her husband, Eldon."

Gilbertson's eyes narrowed slightly at the mention of the names, and they darted back toward his phone. Now *he* knew why Raymer was calling as well.

"I'm also interested in that trophy elk of yours up there," Joe said. "I was wondering how it came to be that you shot it while it was still in velvet, because we both know that's usually long before the season opens. Where on earth did you find that creature on the mountain in season?"

Gilbertson eyed Joe and his mustache twitched. He ignored the intercom, looked over Joe's shoulders, and shouted down the hall.

"Dawn, go ahead and take your lunch break."

"It's only ten?" she protested in the form of a question.

"Dawn . . ."

"Okay, okay. But don't expect me back until one, since you're making me leave early."

"Fine," he said with a man-to-man *Damn women* signal to Joe. Joe didn't respond.

When the outside door closed, Gilbertson said, "She's fine to look at, but I'm not sure she's going to work out. I haven't had much luck with recent graduates of Winchester High."

"Have you thought about maybe hiring someone older with experience?" Joe asked wryly.

"I've thought about that, but it didn't take."

"Anyway," Joe said, "do you want to talk about Brenda's insurance policy or tell me a hunting story about that trophy in velvet over your shoulder?"

"I'd rather talk about Brenda's policy. It's not privileged information after there's been a payout."

Joe nodded.

Gilbertson sat up and shot out his arms to clear his shirt cuffs from his jacket sleeves, then rested his elbows on a stack of papers and steepled his fingers, as if getting down to business.

"I inherited that policy in my book of business when I bought the agency six years ago," Gilbertson said. "I always thought it was a stupid policy, if you want to know the truth, but why make an issue of it when it paid me a good commission? See, term life used to be a lot more expensive than it is these days, due to medical advancements that have prolonged everyone's life.

"When Brenda took out that policy on her husband nineteen years ago, it was a little over two grand a month. Today, for a twenty-year fixed term, it would be around seventeen hundred. She was paying four hundred more a month than she needed to, but I guess I never really told her that."

"I see," Joe said. He scratched notes in his pad. Joe felt his phone vibrate in his breast pocket with an incoming call, but he ignored it and let it go to message. He didn't want to interrupt David Gilbertson.

"The policy would have termed out at twenty years—which would have been this year if Eldon hadn't . . . *died.*" He said *died* as if it were the wrong word, which technically it was. "The premium would have increased substantially next year for the same benefit. I guess Brenda got lucky that way. Eldon lasted nineteen of twenty years."

"What was the payout?" Joe asked.

"Seven-point-five million."

Joe was speechless for a moment. He almost didn't notice his phone vibrate again, this time with an incoming text message.

After a beat, he said, "Brenda Cates took out a seven-point-five-million-dollar life insurance policy on her husband nineteen years ago?"

"And I don't think he ever even knew it," Gilbertson said, nodding. "From what I understand, she put just enough in the bank up the street every month—she called it her 'egg money'— to have them pay me the premium. I think she had the bank make the deposits instead of making them herself so Eldon wouldn't get wise to it. He probably thought she was adding to a savings account every month. She was kind of keeping the transaction at arm's length, so to speak."

Joe said, "*Seven-point-five million.*"

"Yes, sir. It was the largest payout I've been involved in since I bought the agency."

"Good Lord."

"I met Eldon a couple of times," Gilbertson said. "I had him pump out my septic tank. He was a crabby old son of a bitch. He wasn't worth any seven-point-five million dollars in my opinion, that's for sure."

"But he was to Brenda," Joe said.

"I guess so," Gilbertson said with a shrug. "Either that, or she knew Eldon and Eldon's ways well enough that she was pretty sure he'd buy it early. I'd actually bet on *that* scenario."

Joe nodded his head. *There it was*, he thought. *Motivation for all concerned.*

Joe said, "So the payout was deposited in one lump sum at the bank up the street."

"That's what I understand."

"And the good Ms. Raymer is the trustee of the account."

"Yes, but you should probably confirm that with her. I'm talking out of school here."

"I think I did confirm it with her, although I didn't realize it at the time," Joe said as much to himself as to Gilbertson. "Now things are starting to make more sense to me."

"Then are we okay here?" Gilbertson asked. He didn't even need to look over his shoulder at the out-of-season elk mount to emphasize what he was getting at.

"Yup," Joe said, closing his notebook and standing up. "But I might come back one of these days and give that trophy head a closer look. And I might want to see some of the mounts you've got up there in that hunting cabin of yours."

Gilbertson got the scared look in his eyes again.

Joe continued. "Now, is there anything about this particular situation you might not be telling me? Now is the chance to clear the air. Anything that might be relevant that you're aware of?"

"Not really," he said. "Except that I have lunch with Ashlyn about once a week. We're friends, kind of. You have to be friends with the banker in a town this small."

"Yes?" Joe said to prompt him.

"Since she was named trustee to that account, she always has a second cell phone with her. It's one of those cheap ones—the prepaid kind. I've never seen her make a call on it, but she always has it with her. I guess that's so she'll be available at a moment's notice."

Joe nodded.

"Don't think too badly of Ashlyn, though," Gilbertson said. "Seven-point-five million is a lot of capital for a small-town bank these days. Especially when the feds are trying to drive them all out of business."

JOE DESCENDED the wooden stairs and closed the door behind him, his head swirling with new revelations and scenarios.

He didn't recall receiving the two phone calls until he was on the highway back to Saddlestring. He removed his phone and checked his screen.

The call was from a 777 prefix that meant state government, followed by a low-digit series that indicated the governor's office.

The message was from Marybeth and it read:

Call me. I found out where Cora Lee's been hiding.

Joe made a decision based on priority . . . and called his wife first.

23

THE MIDMORNING MIST WAS BURNING OFF THE HAYFIELDS AND the hundreds of symmetrical round bales from the last cutting of the year as Joe sizzled by on the highway toward Saddlestring. As the mist lifted, the dark mountains to the west asserted themselves and took their place on the horizon.

For Joe, everything was becoming very clear.

MARYBETH ANSWERED on the first ring.

"Twelve Sleep County Library, this is Marybeth."

"Of course it is," Joe said. "I called your cell."

"I'm out of practice," she said with a laugh. "You wouldn't

believe the mountain of work I've got in front of me after being gone so long."

"I believe it," Joe said. "That place can't function without you."

"Sometimes I wish it could."

"So what did you find?"

"Cora Lee was easy to find," she said. "Just a simple Google search and some follow-up with our databases."

For years, Marybeth had been Joe's unpaid researcher while he was in the field. Through friends in law enforcement, she'd obtained the passwords and procedures to official crime database programs including NIBRS (National Incident Based Reporting System), NCIC (National Crime Information Center), ViCAP (Violent Criminal Apprehension Program), and RMIN—the Rocky Mountain Information Network, which included Arizona, Colorado, Idaho, Montana, Nevada, New Mexico, Utah, and Wyoming.

"I'm listening," Joe said.

He could hear her tapping on keys. She said, "Cora Lee Cates was arrested and convicted of possession and intent to sell methamphetamine and soliciting in Rock Springs a year ago. She was sentenced to fifteen months in prison, but she only served nine. She was released September twentieth of this year, so she's been out a little more than a month."

"Good work, but I guess I'm not surprised," Joe said. "Cora Lee went bad fast after she left Bull."

"And it looks like she went right back on the pipe as soon as she got out," Marybeth said. "But why go after our daughters?"

"I may have an answer to that," Joe said. He recounted what he'd learned that morning in Winchester.

"*Seven-point-five million?*" Marybeth said incredulously. "That's a pile of money."

"It's a war chest," he said. "Remember when we talked about motivation? Dallas doesn't need it—he's out for revenge. But this might explain how he's able to hang around and terrorize us with no visible means of support. And it might explain how he keeps his thugs loyal and working for him—or why Cora Lee was so relentless. This kind of scheme doesn't work in a vacuum—it has to be financed."

Marybeth was silent for half a minute. She said, "I heard something this morning, but I don't want it to be true. I heard some of my patrons talking about it after their book club."

"What's that?"

"They were saying how surprised they were that Lester Spivak drove his twelve-year-old to some kind of elite gymnastics camp in Colorado Springs yesterday. They were saying how odd it was that a man under investigation and suspended without pay could afford something like that."

Joe gripped the wheel so tightly his fingers turned white.

"Tell me I'm wrong to be suspicious all of a sudden," Marybeth asked with sincerity.

"I don't think you're wrong," Joe said. "But it means this thing goes a lot deeper than I thought possible. I wouldn't be at all surprised to find out there had been a disbursement from the Bank of Winchester to Spivak in the last day or two. I'd like to know the names of all the people getting paid off from that account."

She said, "I'll talk to Dulcie about getting a warrant for that information. After all, she should be easy to find because we're all in the same house together." She laughed a sad laugh that wrenched at Joe's heart and made him even angrier about the situation they were in.

Then it hit him. He asked, "Cora Lee—was she sent to the Sweetwater County Jail or the Wyoming Women's Center?"

"Let's see . . ." Marybeth said as she clicked on her keyboard. "Okay—it was the WWC."

The state had only one women's prison and it was located in Lusk in the eastern part of the state.

"We know who else is there, don't we?" he asked.

"Brenda Cates. But . . ."

"I know," Joe said. "She's a quadriplegic and supposedly held in isolation. But if there's anybody mean enough and smart enough to orchestrate all that's happened to us, it's Brenda. Plus, she has access to a war chest to make it happen."

"My God," Marybeth said.

"I'm dropping Daisy off at Dulcie's," Joe said. "Then I'm taking a trip to Lusk. I should get there by three this afternoon."

"What if she won't talk to you?" Marybeth asked. "Don't you have to be on a list of some kind?"

"She'll talk to me," Joe said. "She won't have a choice. Inmates are compelled to talk to law enforcement whether they want to or not."

AFTER COAXING HIS RELUCTANT LABRADOR to leave his truck and go into Dulcie's backyard for the rest of the day, Joe took I-25 south toward Casper. The journey to Lusk would give him time to work through what he now knew and to think about his next steps. He looked forward to both, although he was exhausted from lack of sleep. There would be a mandatory stop at Lou Taubert Ranch Outfitters in Casper to buy a set of new clothes. Every stitch Joe owned had burned up in his closet and he'd been wearing the same uniform shirt and Wranglers for more than thirty hours.

The Bighorns continued to fill his passenger-side window as he neared Buffalo. Strings of aspen in their fall colors looked like yellow veins through the dark pine forests.

Joe made a mental list of the people he needed to talk to as he drove. He started with the governor's office.

Colter Allen had served as the new governor of Wyoming since January, replacing Spencer Rulon, who had completed his second term. Allen, unlike Rulon, was a Republican. He'd run on a traditional platform of gun rights, revitalizing the energy sectors, suing the federal government on every imaginable front—his campaign slogan was "Stick It to the Feds"—and vowing to take over federal lands, which comprised more than fifty percent of the landmass of the state. He won with seventy-six percent of the vote over a bespectacled University of Wyoming political science professor who ran on renewable green energy and workforce training to turn out-of-work coal miners into baristas and software programmers.

Prior to becoming governor, Allen had been a Big Piney–area lawyer, rancher, and land speculator. In addition to being a high school rodeo champion and U.S. Marine, he'd attended Yale Law School—although he said very little about that during the campaign.

Joe had met Colter Allen once when the man campaigned in Saddlestring and he didn't know yet what he thought about him.

The Big Piney game warden had told him Allen was arrogant and hard to deal with, but Joe kept an open mind. Thus far, the shake-ups in state government Allen had promised hadn't taken place, and the state hadn't reclaimed an inch of federal land.

Joe missed Rulon, who'd been mercurial and charismatic at the same time, and he'd always be grateful to the ex-governor for making some of his financial problems go away and for facilitating the release of Nate Romanowski from a slew of federal charges. As far as Joe knew, Rulon had established a law practice in Cheyenne. He'd been very quiet since Allen replaced him.

Colter Allen was a tall man with wide shoulders, longish silver hair, a movie star jawline, and bushy eyebrows. In what Joe saw as a further attempt to make people forget about that Yale Law School stain on his record, he wore jeans and scuffed boots, a string tie, and a Western-style yoked sports jacket. His dog was a blue heeler he referred to as "the first dog," and it went everywhere with him. First Lady Tatie was a skeleton-thin outdoor-clothing heiress, and she'd had enough face-tightening medical procedures to appear perpetually astonished.

"GOVERNOR ALLEN'S OFFICE," the receptionist said in a stern tone.

"This is game warden Joe Pickett returning the governor's call."

"Please hold."

Joe slowed as he passed through the town of Buffalo. The highway patrolman who was based there was known to be zealous about giving out speeding tickets.

A twangy deep voice said, "Joe Pickett. You're a hard man to get a hold of. One would think it would be easier for a governor to speak to one of his employees."

"I'm sorry, sir," Joe said. "I did call back, but I missed you."

Allen ignored the apology and said, "I was just talking to Linda this morning," meaning Linda Greene-Dempsey, the director of the Wyoming Game and Fish Department. "She seems quite concerned about you."

"Sir?"

Allen chuckled. "She says you are tops on the list for destruction of state property—and this was before your house burned down."

Joe sighed and said, "Yup."

"That's quite a record. I also heard you once arrested Governor Budd for fishing without a license. You wouldn't do that to me, would you?"

"Actually, I would," Joe said.

Allen didn't laugh. He said, "That's not what I wanted to talk to you about. The reason I'm calling is that my chief of staff was cleaning out some of Rulon's records and he came upon a couple of files with your name on them."

Joe felt a twinge in his stomach. He could guess where this was going.

"He referred to you as his 'range rider,'" Allen said. "My understanding is that he gave you a couple of off-the-books assignments over the years and you did well on them."

"Well enough, I guess," Joe said.

The truth was more complicated. No investigation Joe completed had been without serious flaws. If anything, he'd managed to be on-site at the right time and he'd angered the right people, which caused them to overreact in incriminating fashion.

Allen continued. "Rulon played his cards close to the vest most of the time. He didn't seem to have a lot of faith in the personnel in his administration, and even though he could bluster with the best of them—as we know—he rarely told even his friends what he was really thinking. So I find it really interesting that he seemed to trust you."

Joe recalled that Rulon had once said to him, "You possess special skills. Your talent for bumbling around until the situation explodes into a bloodbath or a debacle is uncanny. I don't know how you manage to do it."

"Well," Allen said, "now that I've been here nearly ten months I can see how it might be helpful from time to time to have a range rider myself. Someone who is duty-bound, loyal to me, and capable of keeping his mouth shut."

Joe didn't know how to respond.

"Did you hear what I just said?" Allen asked, obviously peeved.

"I did, sir."

"Is there a reason why you wouldn't want to work with Governor Allen like you did for Governor Rulon?"

"Not at all, sir."

"Good," Allen said. "That's good. That's what I wanted to hear."

He seemed like the kind of man, Joe thought, who liked to refer to himself in the third person and who demanded acquiescence.

"I can see what Rulon was doing," Allen said. "He'd send you out there into situations where it wasn't unusual for a game warden to be around. No one would think much of it because you guys are usually out there on the fringe of things anyway, right? So you'd insinuate yourself into a situation like the one up in the Black Hills or last year in the Red Desert. But rather than looking for outlaws who didn't have a fishing license or a conservation stamp, you were actually working as the eyes and ears of the governor of Wyoming."

"That's about right, sir."

"I know it is," Allen said. Joe heard the familiar click of the speakerphone being disconnected. When Allen came back, his voice was more clear and lower in volume, as if the governor didn't want anyone passing in the hallway to overhear him.

He said, "I've gotten a couple of calls from some donors up in Campbell County. They say there's a movement starting among the out-of-work coal miners. These guys are mad at government in general for shutting down their jobs. There's talk about groups of men meeting at night to curse every politician in the country—including *me*."

Allen sounded defensive when he said it. "Don't these rubes know it was the greenies that created the war on coal? Greenies in Washington, to be precise. Not state government. Not me. Don't they know the difference?"

Joe didn't answer, because it was a rhetorical question.

"No, they don't," Allen said, answering it. "According to the people I talked to, these guys expect me to reverse the war on coal, as if I could just sign an executive order and make natural gas more expensive. They seem to think I can repeal all the renewable energy mandates from communist cities like Boulder and San Francisco!" He was outraged.

Joe didn't remind Governor Allen that he'd promised to do just that if elected. After all, Joe thought, what politicians ran on and what they did once they got into office were often two completely different things.

Allen continued. "The word is, these guys plan to protest and stir everyone up. They want to disrupt public meetings, and they plan to show up at a ribbon-cutting event I've got on my calendar in Moorcroft. You know the type: blue-collar rednecks with jacked-up four-wheel-drives, plenty of guns, and beards like those *Duck Dynasty* hillbillies.

"So I want you to go up into coal country in the next few days and poke around. Go hang around Gillette and Wright. Find out who these guys are and who the ringleaders appear to be. Dig up some dirt on them we can use if we have to. I'll bet there are outstanding warrants on some of them, failure to pay child support—that kind of thing. Maybe we can round them up and nip this in the bud."

Joe paused a long time before he said, "That's not what I do. I don't do political."

"What do you mean?" Allen said with heat. "*Everything* is political."

"Not in my world."

"Then what good are you?" Allen asked. "What good are you to me?"

"Maybe not a good fit," Joe said. He couldn't believe he'd said it to the new governor, although he meant every word of it.

To Rulon's credit, Joe thought, he had never asked him to

serve as a political hack to go after real or perceived enemies. The cases Rulon had asked him to investigate were those that fell outside the lines of local law enforcement or the state's Division of Criminal Investigation.

"I'm a busy man," Allen said in a fit of pique. "I don't have time for personal ethics. I was hoping you'd show me the same loyalty you showed Rulon."

"I will, sir," Joe said, not knowing if he really meant it. He was astonished how childish Allen came across. Joe was used to the smoother—if deliberately obtuse—stylings of the former governor.

"Maybe down the road I'll come up with an assignment that meets your high standards," Allen said. "If so, I may give you a call. That is, unless I find another range rider who is easier to work with."

"Whatever you think, sir," Joe said.

"I was thinking about you in regard to this British problem they've been trying to meet with me about. Did you know there was a British consulate in Denver with real diplomats?"

The abrupt change of direction *did* remind Joe of Rulon.

"No, I didn't."

"Well, there is. And some snooty Brit official wants to meet with me in private."

"What's it about, sir?"

"According to him, rich English executive women have come to Wyoming and turned up missing. It sounds bogus to me."

"Are there more details?"

"I haven't met with him, so I don't know. And when I have more information, you can bet I'm going to ask someone other than you to look into it."

With that, Governor Colter Allen terminated the call without another word.

AFTER THE DISCONCERTING CONVERSATION with the governor, Joe listened to a message on his phone from Sheriff Reed.

"It's her," he said. He was out of breath and Joe could hear the wind whistling in the background. "Your buddy led us to the body of Wanda Stacy. It's hard to tell the exact cause of death at this point because the animals have been at her, but it looks like she was hanged and then dropped from the cliff above us. There's a rope around her neck."

The sheriff's voice was hard to hear after that because there was a lot of cross talk. His deputies were asking him how he wanted the body transported back, whether or not they should try to climb the rock face, and several other questions.

Joe waited, and Reed finally came back on his phone.

"If you run into your buddy Nate, please give me a call right away. We need an official statement from him for the murder investigation. He led us up here, and when I turned around, he was gone. He just vanished. No one saw him go."

Sounds like Nate, Joe thought to himself.

AS HE PASSED the small town of Kaycee on the way to Casper and then Lusk, Joe raised an imaginary glass to the memory of rodeo star and country singer Chris LeDoux, who had ranched in the area. Joe never missed an opportunity to do that.

It was important.

He found LeDoux's "Western Skies" on a playlist on his phone and blasted it through the cab.

I gotta be where I can see those Rocky Mountains
Ride my horse and watch an eagle fly

The last line was about being buried beneath "these western skies," and Joe smiled grimly to himself. He agreed with the sentiment—Chris LeDoux was buried under those skies, after all—but Joe didn't want Dallas Cates to be responsible for it.

He scrolled through the CALLS RECEIVED list on his cell phone and found the UNKNOWN CALLER one from two nights before. Then he waited for the spotty cell signal to improve.

Now that he knew more about the size and scope of the forces lined up against him and how they were financed, it was time to go on the offense. Turn it right back around at them before they made their next move.

This time, he knew, he had to put a stop to the cycle of revenge and recrimination. His family had to be safe to lead their lives without the fear that Dallas or one of his minions would knock on their door—or try to chop it down with an ax.

He felt a slow roll of fear course through his body. He didn't know if he was fast enough, mean enough, or smart enough to end the vicious circle once and for all.

But he knew who might be.

24

NATE ROMANOWSKI HAD SPENT THREE HOURS MOVING FROM TREE
to tree and rock to rock to get into a position to see into the
natural mountain alcove where the hunting cabin was located.
He'd gone about it like a big-game hunter or a hunter of men:
slowly, stealthily, with all of his senses opened wide.

As he circumnavigated it, he'd take a few steps, then stop,
listen, and sniff the air. He was careful not to step on any
dry twigs and always to keep cover between himself and the
cabin site.

An hour before, he'd come upon a small group of elk—three
cows, two calves—bedding down in a pool of deep shadow
within the timber. He'd smelled them before he saw them, and
he'd approached so slowly with the wind in his face that they

hadn't known he was there. One of the mother cows licked the face of her young one and he could hear her rough tongue on the surface of the calf's forehead. Rather than spook the animals so they'd run away and risk the chance of being seen in flight, he'd backtracked and climbed a long half-circle around them through the trees.

Not until he was a quarter of a mile away and upwind of the elk had he heard stirring—the sound of light footfalls and huffs of exhalation. They were moving, but doing so quietly—looking for another place to bed down.

THE HUNTING CABIN was hidden away in a strategic location: one way in through a natural break in a granite wall. Because of the high ridge on three sides and a thick copse of mature spruce on the fourth, there was no way to see inside the cirque unless he could get lined up with the opening or somehow from above. He noted that the opening was filled with fresh-cut brush and pine tree limbs to hide and block the entrance.

Nate found an ancient cedar with gnarled and twisted branches that stood alone among much younger trees. It was an anomaly in the pine forest and it skied over the tops of their crowns. He used the weathered knobs along its trunk as hand-holds and he jammed his boot tips into the deep long creases to get leverage until he was able to reach up and get a firm hold on the lowest branch. Then it was a matter of pulling himself up branch by branch until he reached the top of the surrounding lodgepole pine trees. Although the branches were at times too far apart to climb easily, the palms of his hands had picked up enough sap from the sweating bark that his grip was tacky.

Spiderlike, he was able to stick tight to the rough bark and to keep climbing. He pressed himself tight to the trunk and kept it between him and the cirque as he climbed farther, so his outline wouldn't be seen against the sky.

After climbing as far up as he could before he reached small and brittle branches that couldn't support his weight, he wedged himself into the tight V of the trunk. He paused to rest and to get his breath back. When his breathing returned to normal, he hugged the tree with both arms and leaned off to the side to see around the trunk.

Inside the cirque was a small log cabin with smoke hovering around its chimney, two beat-up vehicles parked on the side of it, and a flat mountain meadow that stretched from the structure to the wall of spruce. A high-banked spring creek cut through the meadow and he could hear the tinkle of live water.

Then there was the sound of men's voices and three of them came out of the cabin one after the other. They all had long guns, and the man in the lead had a heavy canvas bag thrown over his shoulder.

NATE WATCHED in total silence as Dallas Cates—he recognized him from before—lined up empty cans and bottles on a collection of cut stumps near the wall of spruce. The two others he was with, a big man who moved stiffly as if injured and a smaller wiry man who walked with a pronounced limp, stayed back and loaded the guns. The canvas bag was filled with boxes of ammunition. They also had handguns, which they placed side by side on an uneven picnic table.

He could tell by the way the men appeared to chide one another that a shooting competition was about to begin.

Nate was pleased they had their backs to him and were shooting the other way. Otherwise . . .

He settled into his V and touched the grip of his .454 Casull. He didn't like how it felt in his hand because his palm was covered with sap. But at this distance he knew he could steady the weapon against the trunk and make an accurate shot, and maybe two more if his targets got confused and didn't know which way to run for cover.

He'd start with Dallas.

But there was no way he could shoot three men in the back. Especially not without knowing for sure that they'd been responsible for the death of the woman he'd found in the rocks or that they were absolutely guilty of taking out Dave Farkus and going after Joe Pickett and his family. Even in his wildest days doing special ops, and later when he was unmoored, he was never a back shooter or cold-blooded killer. And he wasn't going to start now.

Nate located his cell phone in his falconry bag and powered it up. He was surprised to see that he had two of four bars in signal strength, and attributed his good fortune to being at the highest place on the mountain at the moment. He'd always hated cell phones, but he saw how necessary they were to his business. In fact, he'd received three missed calls from Liv in the last eight hours when he'd had his phone off. He'd call her back . . . later.

He scrolled through the numbers listed as favorites to find the one he'd labeled DUDLEY DO-RIGHT. Before he could punch up the number, the phone vibrated with an incoming call. DUDLEY DO-RIGHT was calling *him*.

Nate waited until Dallas and his two companions started shooting before pressing ANSWER.

"I can't talk long," Nate said, raising his voice above the *pop-pop-pop*.

"Where are you? Is that shooting I hear in the background?"

"In a tree. Yes, it's shooting."

"Who is shooting?"

"Dallas Cates and his two thugs. Target practice."

"You've got eyes on them?"

"Affirmative."

"Are they at Eldon's old hunting cabin?"

"Affirmative."

"That's where I thought they might be. That's where Bull and I had it out."

"I can't talk long," Nate repeated. He glanced around the trunk. When they stopped to reload, there was the possibility he could be heard.

"And you're actually in a tree?"

"Yes. A cool old cedar."

"Why am I not surprised?"

"I can't talk long," Nate said again, this time with a hiss in his voice.

The shooting stopped and Nate muted the phone so he could barely hear Joe, and for sure he wouldn't be overheard by anyone in the cirque.

"Does the sheriff or anyone else know where you are?" Joe asked.

"No," Nate whispered back.

"Good. Can you keep your eyes on them for a while?"

"*Yes.*"

"I'll call when I can."

"Don't call," Nate said. "Come."

"I'll do that." Then: "If you see one of them take a cell phone call, let me know right away. Send a text if you can. I need to know if anyone makes contact with them."

"Affirmative."

"And Nate—thank you."

Nate disconnected the call and powered the phone down as the shooting resumed.

He thought, *Why target practice?*

Pop-pop-pop, followed by the boom of a heavy rifle.

Then he heard a shout directly below him.

"I see you up there, douche bag. Do not even *think* of reaching for that gun of yours."

Nate leaned back in the V and peered down through the branches. The first thing he saw was the black O of a shotgun muzzle pointed directly at him. Farther down the barrel, the cheek of Deputy Sheriff Spivak was pressed against the butt of the weapon. He had both eyes wide open and he was wearing civilian clothes.

Pop-pop-pop. Boom.

"Grab the grip of that revolver with your index finger and thumb," the man said. "Draw it out gently and so I can see it the whole time. Then drop it, and don't let it hit the ground anywhere near me."

Nate calculated his odds. Spivak had a clean shot and Nate had no place to hide. He was literally up a tree. And as fast as he was at drawing his weapon, cocking it, and firing, he wasn't faster than a shotgun blast.

He did as he'd been told. He dropped his revolver through an opening in the branches and heard it thump into the soft ground. He was angry that Spivak happened to arrive while Dallas Cates and his thugs were shooting. The sound of his vehicle coming up the two-track had been drowned out by gunfire.

Pop-pop. Boom.

"Climb down, tough guy," Spivak said. "If I even think you're trying anything hinky, I'll cut you in half." Then: "Dallas is going to be interested to hear what you have to say. So will I. Who were you chatting with a minute ago, anyway?"

Pop-boom.

25

AS JOE DROVE THROUGH DOWNTOWN LUSK—POPULATION 1,567, elevation 5,015—he noted that the inscription carved into the stone archway of the Niobrara County courthouse stated: A PUBLIC OFFICE IS A PUBLIC TRUST. He said aloud, "Governor Allen needs to make a trip up here."

He slowly drove by Rawhide Drug and Silver Dollar Bar ("Welcome Hunters!") and glanced up the hill at the elegant brick Victorian structure that overlooked the town like a weary matriarch. The building was crumbling and boarded up now, but it had once been a house of prostitution that served many of the local ranchers and ranch hands as well as passersby. It had been owned by a prominent woman who spent vast amounts of her hard-earned money on local philanthropy. The story Joe had heard was that the house had been such a focal point of the community that at one time the small town that had built up around it was called Lust—but the name was changed to Lusk by an offended post office employee in Washington, D.C.

There were banners on restaurants, bars, and hotels announcing to visitors that they were ENTERING TIGER TERRITORY, and painted cats' paws in the streets led to the high school football stadium. Homecoming week, Joe guessed.

He turned left on Griffith Street and wound past the Niobrara County Weed and Pest Control building. He crossed over a set of railroad tracks that paralleled the road near the old train depot. Eventually, he saw a hand-painted and hand-lettered sign that read:

STATE OF WYOMING
WOMEN'S CENTER
DEPARTMENT OF CORRECTIONS

THE PRISON ITSELF was a low-slung and sprawling red-brick building set into a grassy hillside. It was surrounded by a twelve-foot chain-link fence mounted on poles that bent inward toward the building grounds and was topped with rolls of razor wire.

There were four rows of parking within the circular lot, with one row designated for visitors. Joe pulled in. Nearly all of the other vehicles had state plates as well.

He heeded the notice mounted on a light pole that said

ATTENTION: PLEASE SECURE FIREARMS IN YOUR VEHICLE by securing his shotgun behind the seat and leaving his holster in a coil on the driver's-side floor.

Flagpoles bearing Wyoming and U.S. flags flanked the walkway to the entrance. There were banks of solar panels on the top of the building and no signs of life on the grassy yard inside the fence. The grass was still green on the lawn, unlike at the higher elevation he had just come from. He noted a puzzling whiff of dank sea air and saw that it came from a large building to the west marked AQUACULTURE. It seemed very odd, he thought, to smell the sea in an arid small town surrounded by vast ranches and located within an ocean of grass and short scrub and chalky bluffs.

At a reception desk inside, he handed over his credentials and badge and asked a florid man wearing a DEPARTMENT OF CORRECTIONS patch on his sleeve if he could see the warden.

"We don't get many game wardens," the man said with an appraising eye. "I don't think any of our petticoat prisoners are in here for game violations."

"Petticoat prisoners?"

"That's what they used to call 'em back in the old days," the man explained.

Joe wandered away from the desk as the check-in officer placed a call to the warden. Although Joe was not yet inside, he was struck by how different the facility already felt from the men's prison in Rawlins. At the men's prison, he could smell testosterone in the air, and he'd been on high alert for sudden acts of violence. The women's prison felt almost gentle and relaxed. He doubted the high fence and razor wire had ever been tested.

On a bulletin board mounted to the cinder-block wall, he

looked at the schedule of classes held to help inmates obtain their GED. Also, workshops for quilting, needlepoint, welding, and woodworking. A faded notice said, SIGN UP HERE FOR THE FAMILY DAYCARE FACILITY. He wondered what that was in reference to.

Behind him, the check-in officer hung up his phone and swiveled to a computer monitor to process a visitor badge.

"A CO is on the way to escort you to the warden's office," the man said. Then, in the tone of a mantra repeated thousands of times over the years, he said, "No cell phones in the facility, no knives in the facility, no tools including Leatherman tools in the facility, no guns in the facility, and you'll need to sign this form to agree to a search or pat-down at any time."

"Gotcha," Joe said. "But I'm law enforcement and I'm here to interview a prisoner."

"Oh." The man assessed him over the counter and squinted. "I guess I don't think about game wardens as, you know, regular cops. But I guess you are."

"We are," Joe said.

"Normally, no blue jeans. Black jeans are okay. But since you're a game warden and it's practically part of your uniform, I'll allow it."

"Thanks," Joe said, relieved. He'd purchased the new Wranglers in Casper, after all.

While he waited, he turned his back to the counter and speed-dialed Marybeth. When she answered, he said, "Just listen, okay?"

"Okay," she whispered back.

He slid his phone into his breast pocket.

———

A MOMENT LATER, a shadow darkened the opaque glass portal on the other side of a steel door next to the front desk. The check-in officer punched a button that unlocked the door and a corrections officer pushed it open. He wore a similar uniform to the man at the desk, but was equipped with a shoulder-mounted radio and handcuffs clipped onto his belt.

"You're here to see the warden?" he asked. He was short, with a beer-barrel chest, a round boyish face, and a red Vandyke beard. His name tag read DOOLEY.

Joe followed CO Dooley down a narrow hallway painted institutional beige.

"First time here?" Dooley asked over his shoulder.

"Yup."

"It's nothing like Rawlins," Dooley said. "I was there for three years. This is a whole different ball game."

"What do I need to know?"

Dooley paused and smiled. He apparently wanted to tell Joe the difference before they reached the warden's office. Dooley spoke in a low, man-to-man tone, and Joe leaned in toward him to hear.

"Each place has its challenges, as you can guess, but the challenges here have to do with personalities and obvious temptations, especially for a male CO. Some of these women know the only card they can play is, you know . . ."

Joe nodded.

Dooley said, "In Rawlins, you always had to have your head

on a swivel in case some inmate wanted to shank you or stomp the hell out of another inmate. Those guys, a lot of them, are in Rawlins because they did something violent and hateful. Here, it's all about bad relationships and bad families. Nearly every one of these ladies got tangled up with bad men somewhere along the line. In Rawlins, you've got predators. Here, for the most part, you've got victims.

"In Rawlins, you always had to be ready to respond to a real fight where somebody could get killed. When we get the emergency call here it's more likely a shouting match or a scratch fest. It's the difference between a real fight and a catfight, if you know what I mean."

"I see."

He said, "The only truly vicious fight I've ever had to respond to where blood was shed was between two women who had children by the same low-rent gangbanger. Apparently, the guy didn't tell either one of them about the other baby mama. Those two couldn't even be in the cafeteria at the same time or they'd start trying to gouge the other's eyes out or throw a tray at each other's heads. But the fight wasn't about status or power, like you see in the men's prison. It was over a man and it involved kids."

Dooley flushed red. "I'm a happily married man," he said, showing Joe his wedding ring. "I go to church every Sunday. They know it, all of them. But that doesn't stop some of them from trying to get my attention and offering to do things, if you catch my drift. When you're here day after day, you get to know them and they get to know you. They sense your weak spots, you know? And some of them can be as manipulative as hell. Here, you have to worry about the subtle and suggestive things. So just be on your guard."

"I will," Joe said, although he wasn't sure exactly what Dooley was saying. The man seemed to be battling through some demons of his own.

"Some of 'em remind you of your mom or your grandma," Dooley said. "Nicest people in the world. Some of the sweetest ladies I've ever met are in here. Sometimes, it's hard to remember that they *did* something bad to wind up here. But there's plenty of hard cases, too. It's easy to see why they're here. Are you married?"

"Yup."

"Daughters?"

"Yup."

"Some of them will remind you of your daughters," Dooley said. "It'll break your heart."

OUTSIDE THE WARDEN'S CLOSED office door, Dooley said, "I'll wait for you here and escort you to the interview room." For whatever reason, he didn't want to go with Joe to talk to the warden.

Joe nodded and knocked on the door.

"Come in," a voice replied. It was female, confident, and strong. "I'm Martha Gray. I'm the warden of this fine institution."

"Joe Pickett."

Warden Martha Gray had a wide-open face, piercing eyes, and snow-white hair. She wore a dark business suit and pearls.

She looked him over with discerning eyes and then gestured for him to have a chair.

He sat. She waited for the door to close behind him.

"I hope CO Dooley wasn't telling you tales out of school," she said. "He's a talker, and some of the girls have figured out they can shake him up. It's the reason we've reassigned him to administration from the general population."

"He was perfectly pleasant," Joe said.

"Good. I demand that my COs act professional in every aspect of their jobs."

He instantly liked Warden Gray. She came across as competent and no-nonsense. That wasn't always the case with bureaucrats, as Joe had come to learn. Too many spent their careers keeping their heads down and counting the hours until retirement. The first impression Joe had of Warden Gray was that she seemed to take her job seriously and she wanted to do it well. She was also smart and demanding. That was probably the reason, Joe thought, that CO Dooley had chosen to remain outside in the hall. He wondered if Marybeth—whom he thought of as in his pocket at the moment—had gotten the same impression of her. She was better at reading people than Joe was.

"My understanding is that you're here to interview one of my girls," she said.

Joe nodded. "Brenda Cates."

Gray took a deep breath and slowly let it out. "Brenda," she said with a wry smile. "Brenda is a special case, isn't she?"

He wasn't sure how to respond.

She said, "I house two hundred and seventy-three women

here and they run the gamut. We're a full-service institution and we have minimum- to maximum-security facilities throughout our three wings. The vast majority of my girls live in mimimum-security pods. We have our complications, but for the most part the atmosphere and behavior are calm and rational as long as everyone follows the rules and regulations. We reward good behavior and we punish bad behavior. If we've got a girl who's really trying hard, we make it clear to her that if she keeps it up she might land one of the good jobs, like in the Aquaculture building."

"I meant to ask you about that," Joe said.

"We raise tilapia here," she said with obvious pride. "Most of the tilapia served in the best restaurants in Denver come from here. It's also a calm and enjoyable place to work. The smart girls aspire to that."

She sighed and said, "I like an awful lot of these women, but you can never completely trust them. It just works out better for everyone that way."

"Then there's the East Wing," Gray said. "That's the maximum-security unit. We have eighteen women there right now, and half of them don't belong."

"I don't understand," Joe said.

"It can get intense when women live with each other without their kids or partners," Gray said. "Cliques form and there are partnerships and alliances that harden. A percentage of them go what we call 'gay for the stay.' So there are lovers' quarrels and nasty breakups. If you've got three women in a cell, you can pretty much count on two of them teaming up against the third. Sometimes my girls act out just so they can spend some time in the East Wing for peace and quiet. There's no interaction with other inmates and they get their meals delivered. It's a no-drama wing. If you've got daughters . . ."

"*Now* I understand," Joe said with a grin.

"So you get the gist. But we have six girls in the East Wing who absolutely need to be there for the safety of the rest of the population, as well as my COs'."

"And Brenda is one of them," Joe said.

She nodded solemnly. "Brenda is the queen bee of the East Wing, I'm afraid."

"Doesn't really surprise me," Joe said.

"You wouldn't know it to look at her, would you?" Gray said. "I like to think of myself as a student of psychology. You have to be good at this job. I try to anticipate problems and head them off before they happen.

"I'll admit that at first I read her completely wrong. I remember meeting Brenda the first day in the intake unit. I thought: matronly old thing, quadriplegic, confined to a specialized wheelchair. She hasn't changed her hairstyle since 1966, I'd guess. If you didn't know her, you'd think she was your grandmother or your frumpy old aunt. She'd lost her husband and two of her sons and she didn't have anyone left—or so we thought."

Gray said, "Despite the nature of her convictions, we placed her at first into the general population. We don't automatically assign murderers to the East Wing—only those who are potentially violent to themselves or others. We thought: What harm could an elderly woman do who'd never been incarcerated before and who couldn't use her limbs? Then we realized that beneath that Ma Kettle exterior is Ma Barker."

She laughed and said, "You're probably too young to get that analogy."

"Not at all," Joe said. "I've got some history with her family."

"I know about it," Gray said. "I've heard your name spoken in vain by both Brenda and Cora Lee Cates."

He nodded.

"They don't like you."

"I know. Tell me about what Brenda did to get assigned to the East Wing."

"Right," Gray said. "She has a chip on her shoulder, as you probably know. She thinks everyone in authority is out to get her, that we all look down on her and her family. As I've mentioned, running this place is a delicate balance at times. We try to find a happy medium and stay there.

"But she's a pot stirrer—an instigator. Brenda has a way of turning girls against each of the COs and each other and making the weak ones loyal to her. Brenda isn't violent, because she can't be. But she has a way of manipulating her followers into doing what she wants. She demands loyalty and punishes those who won't give it to her. We had no choice but to remove her from the general population into isolation on the East Wing. After that, the problems stopped."

"Because that's where she wanted to be, after all," Joe said.

"Yes, I believe that to be true." Gray sighed. "But knowing her feelings toward you, should I be concerned about your visit?"

"I'm not here to push her wheelchair down a flight of stairs, if that's what you're wondering," he said.

"Too bad," Gray said. Then, flashing a smile: "I'm kidding, of course."

"Of course. Can I ask you a few questions about her before the interview?"

Warden Gray glanced at her wristwatch. It was nearing five.

She said, "My husband is planning to take me out to dinner for our thirty-fifth anniversary tonight."

"Congratulations," Joe said. "I don't want to keep you."

"Don't worry about it," she said, waving him off. "I had to remind him about it this morning. And he can't take me out until I get home, right? So ask what you want to ask. But be warned that I might watch the interview on the monitor. I'm *very* interested to observe that exchange."

"Will you videotape it?" Joe asked.

"Of course."

"Good."

At that, she arched her eyebrows. "You're up to something, aren't you?" she asked.

"Yup."

HE BRIEFED Warden Gray on his encounters with Dallas, Cora Lee, and both the banker and the insurance agent in Winchester.

When he was done, she mused, "So that might explain how she came up with the money for her tongue-controlled wheelchair."

"Tongue-controlled wheelchair?"

"Brenda arrived in a four-thousand-dollar electric wheelchair, courtesy of your tax dollars and the Department of Corrections," Gray said. "It was equipped with a sip-and-puff system that allowed her to manipulate the chair through a plastic tube near her mouth. She could make the chair go forward or back and make left- and right-hand turns. But she didn't like it because the tube had to be cleaned frequently, and she hated that it was always in front of her face.

"This new chair is an experimental prototype designed by Georgia Tech that cost something like fifteen thousand dollars, if I remember correctly. It operates through a tongue stud that transmits to a headset. The headset is connected to some kind of computer in the chair itself. Rather than four functions, she can go anywhere she wants at whatever speed she thinks about, because the nerves in the tongue are connected directly to her central nervous system. It gives her much more mobility. All she has to do is think about where she wants to go and that chair goes there. All we have to do at night after we get her into her bed is plug in the chair to recharge the batteries inside the equipment. Every two weeks, a local certified nurse makes a house call on Brenda and makes sure the old girl is healthy and that her chair is working properly. That chair is really quite amazing, I must say. And now I know how she was able to afford it."

"Interesting," Joe said.

He explained that, in his theory, Brenda had figured out a way to communicate with Dallas, Cora Lee, and others from inside the prison.

"No way," Gray said, shaking her head. "That's impossible."

She explained that there were no cell phones allowed within the general population and none had ever been discovered. Security in the East Wing was even tighter. She said that "phone withdrawal" was the most painful ordeal for younger prisoners when they entered the prison.

"What about email?" Joe asked.

"Not a chance," she said. "Computers, iPads, any kind of electronic communication device, is prohibited. We don't even allow Kindles or Nooks. If an inmate has to send an email, we allow them to send it via a DOC tablet, and the message is read by staff and archived before it is even sent. I'd have to approve it if Brenda made a request to send an email, and I can promise you she never has. I'm not sure she even used email or phone messaging in her real life."

Joe agreed. Then: "Phone calls?"

Again, Gray shook her head. "There are designated hard-wired phones available by appointment only. Every call they make is recorded and digitized. Any call made by an East Wing inmate is listened to as it happens. I'd be surprised if Brenda Cates made a single call the entire time she's been here."

"Isn't that unusual?" Joe asked.

"Not in her case," Gray said. "Who would she call?"

"Her insurance agent and banker," Joe said.

"She's made no calls."

"Does she get visitors? Maybe someone is acting as a messenger to the outside world?"

"She hasn't had a visitor. Not even one."

Joe was flummoxed.

Then Gray had a recollection. "I take back what I just said. Cora Lee visited her about two months ago."

Joe filed that away in his mind and said, "Go on."

"As you know, Cora Lee was here for nine months. For the first ninety days, she was a total pain in the ass. She spent all her time getting tatted up, and she didn't play well with others *at all*.

After she got in a screaming match with a few of the sisters, we had to put her in the East Wing for a while. After that experience, she was a model prisoner. Her improvement apparently convinced the parole board that she'd cleaned up her act, but I had trouble actually believing that."

"When Cora Lee was in the East Wing," Joe asked, "did she have access to Brenda?"

"Inmates are denied interaction with each other. But I'm not naive. If something happens on one end of the building, they know about it immediately on the other. News travels so fast through whispers and rumors that it would astound you. We call it Inmate-Dot-Com, and it exists in every prison and it always has. So I have no doubt that if Brenda and Cora Lee wanted to communicate, they probably figured out a way to do it."

Joe nodded. "I wonder if Brenda had a few words with Cora Lee on what she wanted her to do after she got out on parole. I wonder if that's why Cora Lee straightened out after she left the East Wing."

"I can see that happening," Gray agreed with a nod. "Brenda has a way of pressing others into service. And if she had all that money to spread around . . ."

Joe said, "Yup. But we still don't know how she issued orders."

"I'm hoping you'll ask her that question."

"Oh, I'll ask," Joe assured her.

"Wait here," Gray said as she pushed her chair back. "I'll go talk to my East Wing supervisor to get the interview room ready. And I'll make sure the video system is working."

"Thank you," Joe said.

———————

AFTER SHE'D GONE, Joe removed his phone and asked Marybeth, "Did you get all that?"

"I did. I think that Dooley guy is kind of creepy, but I really like the warden. I almost feel sorry I eavesdropped."

"I need your brain on this. So what do you think?"

"I'm not sure, but hang up and give me a minute. I have a thought I need to check out."

"Regarding what?" he asked.

"Tongue-operated wheelchairs," she said, and disconnected.

JOE SAT BACK in the chair and closed his eyes. His stomach was in turmoil and he breathed deeply to try and settle it down.

He recalled Brenda not from her trial, but from that moment when, on her back and helpless, she'd locked eyes with him and held her gaze until he'd finally broken it by looking away.

She'd been a venal and twisted woman before that moment. Joe could only imagine what she was like now.

He was about to find out.

"MALE ON UNIT!" DOOLEY CALLED OUT AS HE LED JOE DOWN THE
hallway toward the interview room in the East Wing. The pas-
sage went from the administration wing through the heart of
the prison. When Dooley called out the notice, women in their
cells stopped what they were doing and looked out to catch a
glimpse of him. The inmates were housed eight to a cell with
their names and photos attached to the cinder-block wall around
their doorframe.

Joe had never been stared at like that before, and he hoped
his face didn't turn red.

"Keep your eyes straight ahead and don't look back at them,"
Dooley advised, sotto voce. "You might not like what you see."

But of course Joe did. What he saw was an amalgamation of

curious wide expressions, dead-eye stares, smirks, and in one instance a pair of large bulbous white breasts when an inmate hiked up her orange smock top to flash him. She laughed maniacally after he passed.

"Rhonda likes to do that," Dooley said with a tired sigh.

Joe grunted.

"That was nothing," Dooley continued in the same tone. "For a while we couldn't figure out why the commissary was selling out of lollipops all of a sudden. We couldn't keep them in stock. Then one of the inmates fessed up to say that some of the lovers who were assigned to different cells had invented a game: one of them would take the lollipop and put it up in her . . . you know . . . and pass it along to her girlfriend to taste. Then the girlfriend would do the same and pass it back. Pretty sick, you know? Suffice it to say you can't buy lollipops in the commissary anymore."

"Gotcha," Joe said. He was glad Marybeth hadn't heard *that*.

HE FELT THE VIBRATION of an incoming text message as they passed from the West Wing through the Central Wing. Joe noticed the curious stares and knowing nods from COs, and at least twice heard the words "Brenda Cates" whispered behind the cell doors. It was Inmate-Dot-Com in action—the word of his pending interview spreading throughout the prison faster than he could walk to get there.

Two COs manned the steel-barred entrance door to the East Wing, and one of them triggered a switch to open it. Joe followed Dooley through and heard the heavy door hum and lock behind him.

The East Wing was smaller than the others, just a short hall-way with closed doors on both sides of the walls. Single photos were on the right side of each doorframe.

Dooley stopped at an unmarked door and rapped on it with his knuckles. While he did, Joe glanced at his phone. The message was from Marybeth and the subject line read: Tongue-control.

The unmarked door opened just wide enough for a bespec-tacled hipster in civilian clothes to look out. He had a three-day growth of beard and his unkempt appearance said "IT guy."

"Come in," he said to Joe.

"And with that, I exit the stage," Dooley said.

Joe thanked his escort and stepped inside the room. It was dimly lit. A bank of video and audio equipment was stacked on a counter that was fixed to the wall. Warden Gray sat at another counter in a folding chair with a pair of earphones wrapped around her neck. The monitor in front of her showed the view from the inside top corner of an empty room painted white. In-side the white room was a stainless-steel desk with a microphone stand mounted to it and three spare metal chairs.

"They're bringing her in," Gray said.

"Does she know why?" Joe asked.

"No."

"So she doesn't know I'm here?"

"No."

The hipster tech made a few clicks on a keyboard to activate the microphone inside the room and to begin the recording.

"Ready," he said.

While they waited, Joe pulled out his phone and opened the

message. There was a link to a scholarly treatise on the tongue-controlled wheelchair written by an engineer at Georgia Tech. Marybeth had typed, *Check out the illustration!!!!*

Photos and graphics loaded slowly as he read the text, and then he saw what Marybeth had found.

"We've got her," he said.

Martha Gray looked up and Joe handed her his phone. As she scrolled down through the article, she gasped, then said, "Well, damn it. I can't believe we missed that. I'm going to have someone's ass for this."

"Who would have thought?" Joe said, taking the phone back.

"*Damn it,*" Gray repeated emphatically.

There was a metallic click through a speaker from inside the interview room. Joe looked up to see Brenda Cates whir inside and stop just short of the desk. A CO followed, frustrated that she'd suddenly powered her chair out of his hands.

Brenda was a large woman. Her gray hair had turned snow white, but her look was familiar: tight curls and metal-framed cat's-eye glasses. She wore a thin high-tech headset with a suspended transceiver poised near the outside of her mouth to track the movement of her tongue to send commands to the chair.

Joe noted that her arms and legs—which had always been thick but toned from hard physical labor around her compound—now sagged like tubes of heavy goo. Her hands lay lifeless on her lap, and her fingers were slightly curved and looked like talons.

She tilted her chin up and stared straight at the camera. Joe felt a tremor inside him as if she were looking through the lens and video cable into his eyes.

"Why am I here?" she asked.

The CO who had ushered her in backed out of the door and closed it. Now she was alone.

Joe said to Gray, "I'm going to say some things to her I'm not proud of, but you'll need to trust me."

"Don't cross the line," Gray said. They both knew that it was legal to mislead a suspect during an interview as long as it was designed to elicit information that could be legitimately used at trial. The trick was to not threaten the subject and to not be too egregious with the line of questioning.

He placed his cell phone, keys, pocketknife, and change on the console counter and patted himself down to make sure he hadn't forgotten anything that could be used as a weapon. The only thing he kept was his notebook, which he'd need.

"Here we go," he said.

JOE PAUSED OUTSIDE the door to the interview room to collect himself. The CO who'd brought Brenda into the room from her cell across the hall said, "Good luck."

"Thank you, I'll need it," he replied. Then he pushed the door open quickly and strode inside.

At the sound, Brenda instantly backed up her chair a few feet and whipped it around to face him, since she couldn't turn her head to see.

"Hello, Brenda," he said.

Her eyes flashed behind her glasses and her breath began to puff out of her nose in a staccato. For a second, Joe was afraid she might hyperventilate and have a seizure.

Once, Brenda's reaction to him might have included turning away, kicking at the dirt, fidgeting, or crossing her arms over her breasts in defiance. It was as if all of her being and emotion had been forced from her body into her neck and face and she was barely able to control either.

He walked around her to the other side of the desk, and she rotated slowly, almost unconsciously, to track him.

He said, "Boy, that's quite a chair you've got there."

Joe sat on one of the chairs and slid his notebook out of his breast pocket. "I bet you're surprised to see *me*," he said. "You probably figured I wouldn't be around by now, huh?"

"I'm not talking to you," she said as she turned her chair slightly and looked at the corner behind Joe instead of at him. Then she said to the camera, "Get me out of here *now*."

"Sorry, but you don't have that choice," he said. "You're compelled to participate in an investigation. Either that, or Warden Gray has to impose punishment on you. For example, she could put you right back in that sip-and-puff chair you didn't like. Or maybe put you in one of those old-fashioned ones that needs to be pushed around by a CO."

"I paid for this myself," she said defensively. He knew he'd hit a nerve. He noted the faint Ozarks accent in her cadence.

"We'll talk about where you got your money in a minute," he said. "Let's start with something else. I'm guessing you haven't talked to Dallas since the charges were dropped against him. It's just been a couple of days, but a lot has happened since then that you might not be aware of."

She clamped her thin lips together and glared at the corner. But he knew she was curious about what he had to say.

"Cora Lee went off the rails," Joe said. "She tried to chop a hole in the door of a house where my family was staying. Got caught, though, and now she's in custody and singing like a bird. Didn't you think that she'd get right back on the pipe as soon as she got some money in her hands? She might have promised you she'd keep clean, but meth addicts are meth addicts and they'll say just about anything. Even to the mother-in-law who's sending her money and pulling her strings."

"I don't believe you," Brenda said. "You're a liar and a murderer."

"I'm neither," Joe said. Even though her allegations weren't true, it still stung to hear them.

"You shot Bull point-blank and you were there when Eldon broke his neck falling in that hole. You had something to do with Timber's death, because he never would have jumped off no balcony on his own. He was scared of heights. Then you crippled Dallas by running him over. Don't say otherwise, because I was there."

Joe let it go. There was enough truth in what she said that it was pointless to argue.

"Why don't you turn around and look at me?" he asked softly.

"I never want to see your face again except on your obituary in the Saddlestring *Roundup*," she spat.

Joe glanced up at the closed-circuit camera and shrugged.

Then: "Brenda, I'm here for one thing and one thing only. I want this to end. It's in your power to make that choice and end it right here and now. It's time to call off the dogs. That way no one has to get hurt—especially my family. You've got to know by now that when it comes to protecting my family, I'll do anything it takes. *Anything*, Brenda. That's why I'm here.

"I know you've always had a special place in your heart for your last remaining son. Dallas was always your favorite, and not just because he was a rodeo champion. He deserves better than this. You're the only one who can cut him loose and let him go free. But he won't do it unless you give him permission."

Joe let that sit.

After nearly a full minute, Brenda said, "Go to hell. I've got ghosts to answer to."

"I'd say the only thing you answer to is your evil instincts," Joe said. "I know you're from Jasper County, Missouri, and there's nothing down there they love more than a good family feud. I know you had a really tough life before you met Eldon. You have a well-deserved chip on your shoulder. But I'm asking you to let it go. You can change, Brenda."

"And you can go straight to hell, Joe Pickett," she whispered. "I'm thinking Eldon, Bull, and Timber will be waiting for you there."

Joe again glanced up at the camera as if to say, *I tried.*

"You remember my friend Nate?" he asked. "The one you tried to ambush? The guy you nearly killed? Well, at this minute he's watching Dallas and those two thugs of his you're paying off. They don't know he's there. All it will take is a call from me and . . . things might just get Western. If they do, you'll be completely alone in the world. Is that what you want?"

She didn't reply or look over, but Joe could see he had her full attention.

He said, "Do you understand how many innocent people have been hurt or killed since you set your revenge in motion?"

She didn't flinch.

"You orchestrated it all from in here, but I'm not sure you know how it all played out," he said. "People who had absolutely nothing to do with me got caught up once you started plotting and throwing money around. A college student named Joy Bannon—you might know her family—got hacked up by Cora Lee just because your daughter-in-law was too strung out to tell the difference between Joy and April.

"Dave Farkus got gunned down because Dallas and his thugs *thought* he might have heard something. Same with a bartender named Wanda Stacy. They hung her and threw her off a mountain so she wouldn't testify in court. All of them were innocent, Brenda. You're all self-righteous about getting even with me, but you've got innocent blood all over your hands."

"Bullshit," she said. "It's not my fault. I can't control everything that happens."

"Of course you'd say that." He thought, *She's engaged. Whether she knows it or not, she's admitting her role.*

"I talked to your insurance guy in Winchester," Joe said. "He told me about the life insurance policy you took out on poor old Eldon all those years ago. Did Eldon ever know about that?"

"He didn't need to know," she said. "I could see what kind of man he was despite everything I tried to do for him. I *earned* that money fair and square for sticking with that man all those years. I could see he'd never change and that he'd end up dead before his time."

"And you cashed in on it," Joe said. "Seven and a half million dollars. You were just looking ahead, right?"

"I knew I'd need it," she said with a sniff. "I had a family to take care of. I didn't know at the time you'd kill most of them."

He ignored that shot.

"You knew Ashlyn Raymer would make payments to whomever you designated as long as she got a commission on every check, right?"

Brenda narrowed her eyes. "That woman promised to keep her mouth shut. I shoulda known a banker would turn out to be crooked. That's why I never trusted them."

"Right," Joe said. He opened his notebook and pretended to read through the pages. "How did you find out about Deputy Spivak? When did you know he'd help you out to botch the case against Dallas if you could finance his daughter going to that gymnastics school?"

She shook her head and said, "Dumb luck."

"What's that mean?" Joe asked.

"Your Deputy Spivak wasn't exactly true to his wife," Brenda said. "He had a fling with a little slut when he went to the Law Enforcement Academy in Douglas for some kind of training. He told her all about his wife who wouldn't sleep with him and his daughter who had a special gift. He told her he'd do anything to advance his daughter's sports career."

Joe wasn't sure where this was going, but he didn't stop it.

"The slut was a meth head like Cora Lee. She got caught with too much of it on her and was sent here for a while, and she shared a cell with my useless daughter-in-law. She told Cora Lee all about your deputy, so we were able to reach out to him. He likes money. It ain't all about his daughter."

"Why go after Dave Farkus?" Joe asked.

"I had nothing to do with that," she said.

"Why go after Wanda Stacy?"

She shook her head as if she'd never heard of her until a few moments before. Joe was surprised that he believed her. But he was convinced he'd drawn out enough from her to bolster his case.

"This ends now, Brenda," he said. "It's over and we can all walk away. Even Dallas."

For the first time, she rotated her chair a half turn so she could meet his eyes. She said, "Not until every member of your family is gone—like mine are gone. I know Dallas. He'll defend my honor and the honor of our family name to his last dying breath."

Joe stood and shook his head from side to side. He said, "Not if he isn't around anymore. Like I said earlier, you're the only one who can stop this."

Brenda's eyes hardened, a small smile carved into her face. "I'm not getting out. I'm going to die in here either way. Dallas knows how to make sure my last days are happy ones."

"You never quit, do you?" he said with a sigh.

"Never have. Never will."

He snapped his notebook closed and slid it into his pocket and started for the door to get the CO.

He heard the electric motor in the chair rev to a high whine and he barely got turned around in time before she slammed it into him. The steel footrests banged hard into his shins, and pain shot up his spine.

Joe reached out for the wall to steady himself as Brenda reversed the chair a few feet, set her mouth, bent her head forward as if the crown of it were a battering ram as well, and made the chair shoot forward. It was remarkably fast. He managed to make another half turn before it slammed into his left knee and knocked him off his feet. Before he could grab her, she reversed the chair out of his reach.

Orange bangles floated across his eyes. He found himself on his hands and knees. When he looked over, the footrests were positioned at head height.

She prepared for another run. He knew if the footrest hit him square in the temple or smashed the bridge of his nose up into his brain, he'd be done for.

Joe grunted and threw himself at her chair before she could build up a head of speed. The footrests raked his shoulder, but he reached below them and grasped the front of each. He scrambled to his feet and lifted the front end of the chair off the floor so the chair tipped back. Her head flopped to the side and her eyes flashed white as he continued to lift. The back wheels of the chair spun and smoked and scored the tile on the floor. The forward momentum of her wheels helped him lift the front of the chair.

He flipped her over backward and she spilled out of the chair onto her side and lay still. The wheels of the chair were still under her power, though, and they continued to whine as if the chair were trying to escape on its own.

As the CO burst through the door, Joe leaped on the chair and used his weight to hold it in place. He thumbed open the latch of the plastic console on the right armrest.

An iPhone 6 was nestled inside the console and he unplugged the eight-pin cable from the bottom of it and lifted it out. The motor of the chair went still and the wheels slowly stopped turning.

On the floor, Brenda craned her neck to see what he'd done. When he showed her the phone, she said, "Put that back!"

"Nope," he said. It hurt to stand up straight, but he did it anyway. He turned toward the camera in the room and displayed the phone to it.

Marybeth had been the key. Her quick research had shown that, rather than building a dedicated microcomputer to power the tongue-controlled chair, the engineers at Georgia Tech had programmed an application for a smartphone that would serve the same purpose. When the new high-tech chair had arrived at the Wyoming Women's Center, no one, including Warden Gray, had thought to research the technology of how the chair operated.

Brenda had received a chair that responded to her thoughts and commands, as well as one that contained the means to communicate to the outside world. The only reason she didn't stay more in touch with her son and the others, he guessed, was that Brenda had convinced someone—or paid him or her off—to remove the phone, dial it for her, and hold it up to her face so she could issue orders. That someone wasn't on the floor of the East Wing every day.

He said to the camera, "You said a local certified nurse visits Brenda every two weeks or so. I wouldn't be surprised if those visits corresponded with all of the outbound calls made on this phone."

Behind him, Brenda cursed as she thrashed her head back and forth.

"Yup," Joe said.

To the CO, Joe said, "If you can find a normal wheelchair,

I'll help you get her into it." He gestured toward the tongue-controlled chair. "This one will be out of commission for a while, which is good, because it nearly killed me."

WHILE THE CO RETRIEVED a wheelchair from the infirmary Joe squatted down next to Brenda.

Her eyes raked over his face like razors. There was spittle on the corners of her mouth and a string of mucus from her nose to the floor.

"You won't be needing this," he said as he gently removed her headset. She arched her neck to make its removal as difficult as possible.

Then he fished a bandanna out of his jeans pocket and wiped her mouth and nose clean. She tried to turn her head away from him, but she couldn't wrench away far enough that he couldn't reach her. Her skin was soft and it was covered with a thin layer of downy hair.

"I'm sorry," he said.

He felt no sense of triumph or satisfaction. What he felt was sadness as deep as he'd ever experienced before.

"DID YOU GET ALL THAT?" Joe asked Warden Gray wearily when he entered the video room.

"We got it *all*," the IT guy said.

"My God," Gray said, "that was . . . incredible. Are you okay?"

Joe winced and said, "Bruises is all, I think."

"It happened so fast," Gray said with wonder. "She could have killed you before the CO had time to respond."

"And she would have tried."

Gray stood up and put her hands on Joe's shoulders. "You were magnificent," she said.

Joe smiled bitterly. "I beat up a seventy-three-year-old quadriplegic and took her phone. I've had better days."

AFTER INSTRUCTING THE IT GUY to download the call records from the iPhone and email them to Dulcie Schalk's office, Joe said, "I need to keep this phone a while longer. You've got all the data off it."

Gray started to object, but she thought better of it.

"I suppose we can look the other way," she said. "I need to meet a man for dinner."

"Happy anniversary."

"Thank you. I hope this brings you some peace."

"We're getting closer," he said.

HE NEARLY CRIED OUT from the pain and abrasions on his legs and shoulder when he climbed into his pickup. First stop before leaving Lusk, he decided, was to buy a jumbo container of ibuprofen for the ride back to the Bighorns.

He'd glanced at the iPhone call records as they were being sent digitally to Dulcie's office. Most of the numbers were unfamiliar, but they were similar to one another with the same 862 area code from where the phones had been imported. He assumed the calls had been made to prepaid burners purchased at the same time and distributed to Dallas, his thugs, and Cora Lee. The calls with a Winchester prefix would likely correspond to the burners purchased by Ashlyn Raymer and David Gilbertson.

The lone number not associated with the burners had an area code of 272: eastern Pennsylvania. Joe knew the number belonged to Deputy Lester Spivak, because he had it stored in his own phone. Spivak had never had it changed when he took the job in Twelve Sleep County.

With the outgoing call record from Brenda's phone and the financial records obtained from the Bank of Winchester by subpoena, there would no doubt be a pattern of calls to Raymer, followed by withdrawals from Brenda's account, Joe thought. Other calls from Brenda would connect to a timeline that included the attacks on Joy Bannon and April, Sheridan's sighting of Cora Lee, Dallas's meet-up with Weasel and Brutus, and Spivak's deliberate botching of the arrest of Dallas on the highway.

Dulcie would have new evidence to charge Dallas, his thugs, and even Brenda if she chose. Spivak's botching of the original case would be an afterthought. Dulcie could redeem her reputation in front of Judge Hewitt and a jury.

The open circle would close. But that would come later.

His first call was to Nate.

There was no answer.

27

RATHER THAN DRIVE HIS PICKUP THE LAST TWO MILES UP THE mountain to the Cateses' hunting lodge and risk being heard or seen, Joe pulled off the two-track and nosed his vehicle into a stand of willows. He shut off the headlights and turned the motor off. The adrenaline that had surged through him from his fight with Brenda and the discoveries they'd made had finally worn off and he was beyond bone-tired. Only the pain of his wounds kept him awake.

That, and finding Nate.

He loaded his shotgun with seven rounds of double-ought buckshot and filled a daypack with gear: satellite phone, radio, spotting scope, zip-tie cuffs, a camera with a zoom lens, water, rope, flashlight, a first-aid kit, and other gear. He winced as he shouldered the pack on his back. That blow to his shoulder hurt the most of all.

After putting his keys under the driver's-side floor mat, he gently shut the door and walked away. The night sky was clear and the stars creamy. The temperature had dropped to the mid-forties and the wind was still.

HE PARALLELED the two-track up the incline, but stayed in the massive aspen grove that stretched from the foothills, where he'd parked, to the tree line on the summit itself. Most of the yellow leaves had dropped from the branches but were not yet crispy to walk on. His boots upturned mulch on the forest floor and it smelled dank and musky. The dead carpet of yellow leaves seemed to soak up the starlight and he could see his boots.

Joe tried not to spend too much time inside his own head as he climbed. Instead of contemplating how he'd feel if Nate had been hurt or killed fulfilling Joe's request to keep Dallas and his thugs under surveillance, he tried to focus on what he saw, what he heard, and what he smelled.

He had a pretty good idea that he recalled seeing the "cool old cedar" tree Nate had referenced earlier in their phone call. It was not only the highest tree on that area of the mountain, but it afforded the best view inside the rock enclosure where the cabin was located.

On his return across the state, he'd filled in Marybeth and told her what he needed to do. She urged him to wait, although she was just as worried about Nate. Then he called Sheriff Reed and told him where Dallas and his two men were located.

Reed had just returned to Saddlestring with the body of Wanda Stacy, and he cursed Joe for keeping him in the dark so long about where Dallas was holed up.

"We can't charge him again for Farkus," Reed said.

"With this new evidence, you can," Joe said. "And you can add Wanda Stacy. I'm thinking that if we grab those two thugs Brutus and Weasel alive, they'll turn on Dallas in a heartbeat to save themselves. You and Dulcie will have plenty of charges to add to the list—including arson and causing the death of my poor horse and dog."

Reed said he'd call up his deputies and meet Joe on the two-track that led to the cabin. He told Joe to wait for them to arrive before proceeding to the hunting camp.

Joe said, "I'll meet you there," and disconnected the call while Reed yelled at him to stick tight.

HE FELT MORE THAN SAW that the hunting cabin was less than a quarter mile in front of him. Maybe it was the whiff of wood smoke from the cookstove, or the general hush in the air because the birds and animals had established a perimeter—he wasn't sure.

But he slowed down and thumbed the safety off his shotgun. He made deliberate steps forward on the forest floor—heel first, then a slow rock forward to the ball of his foot—to avoid snapping a dry twig.

He found the massive cedar by noting the absence of stars directly above him where the top of the tree reached into the sky.

"Nate?" he whispered.

No response. But he smelled something metallic in the air.

Joe slid out of his pack and dug inside it to locate his head-lamp. The lens could be choked down from bright to dim, and he dimmed it to the minimum before turning it on.

He held it up close to the trunk of the cedar and saw the blood.

There was a thin spray of it from the gnarled root up across the bark. It looked as if a housepainter had flicked his brush at a wall. It looked arterial, and Joe felt his toes curl.

"Nate?"

No response.

He twisted the lens of the lamp for more light and saw distinctive drag marks on the ground from the tree that went to his right. The twin grooves looked like they'd been made by the heels of boots.

Joe left the pack on the ground and, as silently as he could, followed the tracks. He had to push through a dense caragana bush as well as hundreds of knee-high aspen shooters pushing up from the earth.

After ten minutes, he heard what he thought was a moan.

"Nate?"

There was a distinctive grunt, then another moan. It was the moan of a man.

He shouldered the shotgun and moved from tree to tree. The sound got louder.

Via the starlight that filtered down through the skeletal aspen branches, he saw the dark form of a body in the leaves ahead.

"Uhnnn. Help me." The voice was pained and unrecognizable.

"Nate," Joe said as he rushed forward and bent over the form.

He reached up and turned the headlamp to full to find Lester Spivak's bloody face. Spivak clamped his eyes shut against the beam and grimaced.

The man was on his back with his hands tightly clamped on the sides of his head in a *Hear no evil* gesture. Next to him on the leaves were a pair of disembodied human ears. They had *not* been surgically removed.

Joe hissed, "*Nate.*"

The brush rustled and Nate Romanowski pushed through. He looked unhurt, but his hands were covered with dried blood.

"He's dirty," Nate said.

"I know, but did you have to rip his ears off?"

"That was his choice," Nate said.

Joe looked down at Spivak, who once again cringed from the full beam of light in his face. The blood on his skin was crusty.

"I don't think he'll bleed out," Joe said.

"No great loss if he does."

"I need my first-aid kit to bandage him up. I left it with my pack by the cedar tree."

"Really?" Nate asked, incredulous.

"Really."

He shrugged and went to retrieve it.

"You're lucky to be alive," Joe said to Spivak.

Spivak moaned.

When Nate returned, he handed Joe the kit and said, "He was going to march me into the hunting camp and show me off like his bitch," Nate said. "We couldn't have that, could we?"

"I'm glad you're okay," Joe said to Nate. "I got worried when you wouldn't answer your phone."

"Couldn't risk it," Nate said. "I knew you'd show up eventually."

Joe found a couple of thick pads and a roll of gauze and said to Spivak, "Take your hands away."

While Joe wound the gauze around Spivak's head, Nate said, "He was dirtier than you thought. It was Spivak who convinced Dallas and his monkeys to go after Dave Farkus and Wanda Stacy. Seems he was worried they might have overheard his name spoken that night in the bar and he was afraid they'd tell someone and blow his cover."

Joe paused and glared at Spivak. "Is that true?"

Spivak moaned again.

"Why would he tell me that if it wasn't true?" Nate asked. "That was just after ear number two came off and I told him I'd stick my fingers up his nose and rip it off next. So it was a two-ear confession. Those are the best kind, you know. The most reliable."

"What did he tell you after you took off the first?" Joe asked.

"He told me to go to hell."

Joe finished the wrap. He wasn't as gentle as he could have been.

He said, "I'll cuff him and we can deal with him later. Are Dallas and his pals still at the cabin?"

"Last I looked, they were sitting outside playing cards by lantern light."

Joe stood and said, "Thanks for keeping your eye on them. I appreciate it. But I wish you wouldn't do that with the ears."

"It's been a long time," Nate said. "I kinda missed it."

"I've got a plan for what comes next," Joe said.

"Does it involve blowing Dallas's head clean off his body?"

"I hope not."

"Tell it to me anyway, I guess."

JOE WAITED at the base of the cedar tree for Nate to climb as high as he could. After Nate was in position with his .454 Casull aimed at the three men in the hunting camp, Joe tapped the tree to indicate he was leaving.

He could smell both wood smoke and cigar smoke in the air as he neared the clogged opening of the enclave. Joe didn't know if Nate could see him in the starlight, but he guessed he could. His heart raced as he got close enough that he could hear someone—not Dallas—shout, "I got you this time, you son of a bitch" with finality as he apparently slapped his cards down and laughed.

Joe hugged the granite wall and sidestepped along it to the left. The wall was between him and the men inside the opening and the rock was still warm from the sun that day but cooling fast. It had the texture of sandpaper and it hurt his bare hands and knees when he found a fold in it and crawled up. He did so slowly and only after double-checking each grip and foothold. He knew if he made a sound, he'd be in trouble.

THERE THEY WERE, just as Nate had described them. Dallas, Brutus, and Weasel sat at an old picnic table playing cards under the cold blue light of a lantern. A half-full whiskey bottle reflected the orange of the lantern mantle. Dallas had a cigar clamped in his teeth and the cherry glowed red.

From his angle on top of the ridge, Joe could see only their upper bodies. Two of the men had their backs to him. Dallas faced him.

He was seventy-five yards from the picnic table. It was too far for an effective shotgun blast, but not so far that he couldn't pepper them all if necessary. Nate wouldn't have that problem.

Joe raised his binoculars and focused them in. There was a cell phone next to the whiskey bottle. Dallas and his thugs were using stick matches as poker chips, and Dallas looked like he was winning.

He held Brenda's iPhone next to his body to shield the lit screen and tried to guess which number from her call list would correspond with the burner on the picnic table. He scrolled down the list to the very first call made more than a month and a half before. He guessed that Brenda would have called her son first to launch her scheme. So he tapped that number.

It took longer than he thought it would, but the burner phone lit up on the picnic table and all three men froze. One of them— Joe assumed it was Weasel, based on his profile—said, "*It's her.*"

Dallas lowered his hand of cards and opened the phone and said, "Mother."

"Not quite," Joe responded.

He watched as Dallas jerked the phone away from his face and double-checked the number on the screen. Then: "Who is this?"

"This is Joe Pickett, and I need you to listen to me. Right

now there's a bullet the size of a nickel aimed right between your eyes. If you stand up or make any sudden movement, that'll be the last thing you'll ever do.

"You burned down my house and killed my dog and my wife's new horse. So just give me an excuse to pull the trigger, Dallas, and I'll happily oblige."

Dallas was still for a moment. Then he combed the darkness, trying to pinpoint Joe's location. His eyes narrowed as he homed in on the cedar tree that towered over the hunting camp.

"That's right," Joe said.

"What's going on?" Weasel asked with mild panic.

"Shut up," Brutus warned him.

Joe said, "Tell your stooges to stay put."

He watched through the binoculars as Dallas murmured something to them. Both men turned and started scanning the darkness as Dallas had done.

"This is Brenda's phone," Joe said. "I got it from her chair. Spivak's been arrested, Cora Lee is in jail, and Brenda is back in isolation without her chair or her phone. We know about Wanda Stacy and Dave Farkus. We know *everything*. Sheriff Reed is on his way. It's your choice how you want this to end."

"It ain't ever going to end," Dallas said. But he didn't reach for a weapon and he didn't stand up.

Joe said, "Tell Brutus and Weasel to put their hands on top of their heads where I can see them."

Dallas waited a long ten seconds, then relayed the order.

At first, both men simply stared at him.

Dallas said, "Do it, goddamn it," loud enough that Joe could hear him through the phone as well as through the air.

Reluctantly, both men complied.

"Tell them to stand up slowly and walk over to the campfire and get on their bellies."

Dallas repeated it. Weasel stood, followed by Brutus. They stepped over the picnic bench stools and limped toward the dying fire.

Then Weasel stopped and turned. "It was Rory who killed that girl," he shouted. "I didn't have a damned thing to do with it."

"Shut the fuck up, Luthi," Cross hissed.

"Rory Cross—he's your killer," Luthi yelled as he dropped his right hand to point his finger at Cross.

"I said shut up!" Cross barked as he dropped *his* hands and reached behind his back.

Joe had no time to react before Cross drew out a pistol and aimed it at Luthi two feet away from him.

The gunshots—*bang-BOOM*—happened so close together they almost sounded like one. Luthi grabbed at his chest and teetered back from the impact of Cross's bullet as half of Cross's head exploded into red mist. The bodies of both men hit the ground at the same time.

"And then there was one," Joe said into the phone as he fought through the shock of what had just happened.

He heard the *snick-snick* sound of Nate's revolver being cocked again.

Joe said to Dallas, "They would have turned on you anyway. They were motivated by cash from Brenda, and that's dried up."

"Yeah," Dallas said, suddenly weary.

"It wasn't her idea at first, but Brenda has set you free."

"Is she okay?" Dallas asked. "I haven't seen her in a while."

"She's still mean," Joe said.

Dallas chuckled.

"Put the phone down on the picnic table and put your hands on top of your head," Joe said. "I'll be there in a minute."

"Can I finish my cigar?" Dallas asked.

"Sure. You do that."

"This ain't over."

Joe said, "How about we pick it back up when you get out of Rawlins in fifty years? How's that work for you?"

"That works just fine."

Dallas tilted his chin up and blew out a thick cloud of smoke. He was grinning.

THE PREDAWN SUN WAS IGNITING STRINGY CIRRUS CLOUDS OVER
the top of the eastern mountains in his rearview mirror as Joe
headed back toward the Twelve Sleep River Valley. Far below,
mist clung to the serpentine contours of the river itself, waiting
for the sunlight to disperse it. The first heavy frost of the fall
bunched in the shadows and folds of the foothills like a scout
waiting for the real army to arrive.

He was so exhausted that his head swam with hallucinations
that were part recollection, part imagination: an owl flying
through the pines with eyes on each side of its head, Dallas puff-
ing on his cigar while his associates twitched with death rattles
at his feet, a phantom elk sporting reindeer antlers hung with
Christmas tree bulbs that darted out of the roadside brush but

really wasn't there after he hit his brakes, and Brenda Cates pitching ass over teakettle in her wheelchair.

An hour before at the hunting camp, Sheriff Reed had said, "Too bad Lester had that terrible accident. He must have fallen from a tree just right to get those injuries to his head. It couldn't have happened to a nicer guy." Then, to Joe: "We've got this under control, although I have no idea where we're going to put so many bodies. You look like hell. Go home, Joe."

And he did. Nate hadn't stuck around for the sheriff and his team to arrive, and he'd long since vanished into the timber. He'd said something about checking his falcon traps.

JOE WAS SO OUT OF IT that he instinctively drove to the pile of ashes that had once been his house. He'd forgotten it was no longer standing. As he neared it, he saw his own truck was parked where he always put it, but that didn't make sense. After all, Joe was *driving* his pickup.

Another hallucination caused by sleep deprivation, he thought.

Then Rick Ewig climbed out of the green Ford pickup and waved at him.

Joe pulled alongside. It hurt so much to climb out that he grunted like a very old man getting out of a lounge chair.

"Man, are you okay?" Ewig asked, genuinely alarmed.

"Nope."

"Want me to drive you somewhere?"

"I'll be fine," Joe lied.

Ewig gestured at the blackened pile that was once Joe's

house. "How long do you suppose it'll take the agency to build a new one?"

"No idea."

"If it's like everything else, it'll take a long time. I wonder where you'll be living in the meanwhile?"

Joe shrugged. He hadn't had time even to think about it.

"You can always move your family in with me," Ewig said. "They might not like that, but I've got two extra rooms since Viv and the kids moved out."

"Thank you for the offer. I'll need to talk to the boss about that."

"Good luck." Ewig laughed. None of the game wardens in the field wanted to have the conversation with Joe's director that Joe was about to have.

"I identified our poachers," Ewig said. "At this minute they're cutting up two white-tailed deer in that warehouse I told you about. I got a call and followed them. They didn't know I was behind them."

Joe looked up quizzically. "They're there now?"

"Yes. They're packaging deer steaks."

"But you're here."

"Yeah," Ewig said, leaning over the top of his pickup hood on his elbows. "There's something I wanted to run by you in person. I didn't want to call, and I sure as hell didn't want to talk to you about it over the radio."

"What's that?"

"Well, it turns out I know these guys," Ewig said. "They're good men. Friends, even. The three of them worked at the coal mines until they were shut down a few months ago."

Joe nodded for him to go on.

"I heard through the grapevine about what's been going on," Ewig said. "These three guys have been delivering packaged meat to other unemployed coal miners and their families. They haven't sold the meat or wasted it. They're trying to keep people fed and in the area in case the mines ever reopen. That's why they only killed non-trophy animals. They wanted the meat."

"It's still poaching," Joe said.

"It is. But you know what'll happen if we arrest them and file all the charges we can throw at them. These guys will have to forfeit their guns, trucks, and all that equipment they bought to package the meat. They'll lose hunting privileges for life, probably, and they'll have to pay fines that none of them can afford. We'll be kicking them when they're down. It isn't their fault their jobs got jerked out from under them. Governor Allen made all kinds of promises about helping them out, but so far he hasn't done a damn thing."

Joe thought for a minute. "Then tell them to stop."

Ewig eyed Joe. "Are you serious?"

"Yup."

"This is between you and me, right?" Ewig asked.

"Yup."

"I'll give them a really stern lecture," Ewig said. "I'll put the fear of God into them, so they'll never poach another deer again."

"Sounds like a plan," Joe said.

"It'll be a hell of a stern lecture," Ewig said with obvious relief.

AFTER EWIG DROVE AWAY, Joe climbed back into his truck and aimed it toward Saddlestring.

He keyed his cell phone and woke Marybeth.

"I'm on my way home," he said.

"I wish we had one," she said.

ACKNOWLEDGMENTS

The author would like to thank the people who provided help, expertise, and information for this novel, including Col. H. Kenneth Johnson, Al LaPointe, and Alex Heil of the Wyoming Wing Civil Air Patrol; Betty Abbott, John Martin, and Joe Wilson at the Wyoming Department of Corrections; attorneys Terry Mackey and Becky Reif; and Don Budd.

Special thanks to my first readers Laurie Box, Molly Donnell, Becky Reif, and Roxanne Woods.

Kudos to Molly Donnell and Prairie Sage Creative for cjbox .net and Jennifer Fonnesbeck for social media expertise and merchandise sales.

It's a sincere pleasure to work with professionals at Putnam, including the legendary Neil Nyren, Ivan Held, Alexis Welby, Christine Ball, and Katie Grinch.

And thanks, of course, to my agent and friend Ann Rittenberg.

Beyond roads, beyond streetlights, beyond backup...
Welcome to Joe Pickett's beat

'Exhilarating' *Sunday Times*

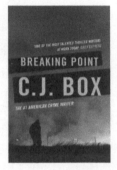

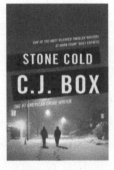

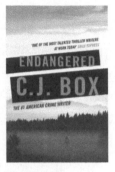

Joe Pickett – 13

Joe Pickett – 14

Joe Pickett – 15

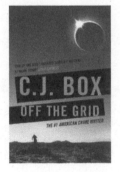

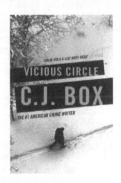

Joe Pickett – 16

Joe Pickett – 17

Cassie Dewell – 1   Cassie Dewell – 2   Cassie Dewell – 3

Cassie Dewell tracks a killer

'Heart Stoppingly Good' *Daily Mail*

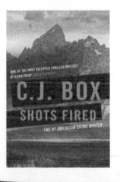

Short stories from Joe Pickett country

'Solid-gold A-list must-read' LEE CHILD